About the Author

Alexander was born in Ukraine and raised in a small town in Russian Siberia. Growing up between two countries, he absorbed both languages and cultures. In 2013, he was spiritually guided to relocate to Vancouver, Canada. He graduated with an MFA in film production and creative writing from the University of British Columbia. During his education, Alexander worked on self-financed art films he wrote and directed. A unique and profound connection with his new home grew day by day, and soon, he felt a sense of destiny and divine purpose in Vancouver. With the help of the Sechelt spirits, he continued studying shamanism and spiritual healing practices. Alexander practices communication with the souls, spirits, angels, and Heavens through drumming, meditations, and dreaming practices. In addition, through past-life explorations, he reclaimed his soul's purpose of an embodied spiritual guide. He works directly with souls, assisting them on their spiritual paths, resolving their past traumatizing deaths and rediscover their purpose in life.

Eurydice in Love
A Poetic Fairy Tale

Alexander Formos

Eurydice in Love
A Poetic Fairy Tale

Vanguard Press

VANGUARD PAPERBACK

© Copyright 2023
Alexander Formos

The right of Alexander Formos to be identified as author of
this work has been asserted by him in accordance with the
Copyright, Designs and Patents Act 1988.

All Rights Reserved

No reproduction, copy or transmission of this publication
may be made without written permission.
No paragraph of this publication may be reproduced,
copied or transmitted save with the written permission of the publisher, or in accordance
with the provisions
of the Copyright Act 1956 (as amended).

Any person who commits any unauthorized act in relation to
this publication may be liable to criminal
prosecution and civil claims for damages.

A CIP catalogue record for this title is
available from the British Library.

ISBN 978 1 83794 191 9

Vanguard Press is an imprint of
Pegasus Elliot Mackenzie Publishers Ltd.
www.pegasuspublishers.com

This is a work of fiction. Names, characters, businesses, places, events and incidents are either the
product of the author's imagination or used in a fictitious manner. Any resemblance to actual persons,
living or dead, or actual events is purely coincidental.

First Published in 2023

Vanguard Press
Sheraton House Castle Park
Cambridge England

Printed & Bound in Great Britain

Acknowledgements

I would like to start by acknowledging the contributions of Heaves and beings of the firmament. Without divine, spiritual guidance, this book would never be written. I particularly like to thank Mary Magdalene for the gifts she brought into my life. Dear Mary, thank you for entering into the relationship with me. You guided me to write this work, even though I was unaware of your presence half of my journey. Yet once you fully manifested and I accepted to be a channel of your wisdom, my life transformed in the most beautiful ways. I can't thank you enough for your magical light full of grace, devotion, and compassion. I thank you for supporting me when I doubted my path, my faith, and my purpose. Only with your help I surrendered to challenging, spiritual missions bestowed upon me. You tenderly nudged me to embrace the truth of my heart, and I'm forever grateful that you were there for me when I needed you the most. I bow in reverence to the magic of your essence and the beauty of your heart.

The Soul Family

Eurydice Eloise Wayles. My dear soulmate of eight lives, thank you for being a muse of this book. I honor everything that you are. Your light brings inspirational beauty into this world, and I thank you for enveloping me in it. When we met, we struggled to understand why our love story was only occurring in the spiritual world. When we studied our story, it became evident that we met to heal the shared traumas of our past lives on a soul level. Our souls met to write a true tale of our eternal love song. Through adventures into our past, you learned how to follow the path of your heart, and requested to record your healing journey. As your humble servant, I channeled this book from you, to share your story with the world. I would never be able to do this without your mischievous presence and your immense Magdalene's heart full of love. This work is our divine child, and I couldn't be more grateful that Nature designing our relationship in this way.

Veronica Formos. My dear soulmate of many lives. I thank you for always being there for me during the writing process. Your insights and edits became an important part of this work. Many ideas and beliefs expressed here we discussed in heated battles, and that's how we arrived at the ultimate truth. Writing this work turned out to be our war against darkness, and you are the best spiritual brother to go to war with. I thank you for allowing me be your husband for ten years. We've been through so much together, but we never surrendered to the madness of this world. Thank you for holding the space for my tears when I was in desperation, defeated, and demoralized. Thank you for accepting and seeing Eurydice for who she is. Without your support of our love story, this work would never be completed.

Suzanne Adams. Dear friend, I would like to thank you for tumultuousness and uncertainty you've brought into my life. Your darkness enveloped my apartment on many occasions, forcing me to halt my writing completely. Yet our fight turned out to be a blessing in disguise. I searched for ways to heal your traumas, and results of our explorations elevated this work in a beautiful way. I honor our commitment to present your side of our story in the way you asked. Eurydice and I thank you for sharing this transformative journey with us. All four of us created this work with a hope to release our shared traumas.

Damian of Stockholm. My dear nemesis, here we are! It's still hard to believe that I actually completed this work while fighting your darkness. You've brought extreme chaos and destruction into my life, but today I can only thank you for these gifts. I promised to tell your story to the world, if Eurydice would win in this life. I'm grateful for the opportunity to share your story of an immortal spirit, who serves darkness. Even though you are living only in the spiritual world, I will never question your existence, and I believe that your soul's journey is equally beautiful as anyone else's. I thank you for pushing us to face our fears. Without the nightmares you gifted us, this work would never be possible.

Emilia Aurelia May. My dearest beloved soulmate, thank you for appearing on my path when I searched for my next divine intervention. You are my original twin flame and I'm glad we recognized each other. We haven't met for centuries and I missed you. You've propelled me to the next level of my spiritual education and I would never complete it without you. Your magic opened up new talents in me and resolved my ancient grief. Your passion for books lives in your soul and I feel blessed for your help with this manuscript. Your revisions and contributions are indispensable. I would never figure out the ending without conversations with you. I'm grateful to witness your magic in everything that you do. Your Magdalene light enriches our world and heals stranded souls.

Sergey Formos. Dear Father, I would like to thank you for everything you've done for me. You lived the life of a martyr so that I would have a future. Your soul chose death when I needed spiritual empowerment the most. Since then, you've guided me on my path from the other side. Without your death, I would never move to your promised land of Vancouver and, therefore, never wrote this work. You chose such a life to ask for my forgiveness for the pain you caused in our past life. And you chose such life to absolve your sins of an SS officer. By helping me to become a healer, I'm helping you to pay the debt you owe to humanity. Thank you for the love you are sending me from between lives.

Wilhelm Keitel. Dear friend, I wish to thank you for the spiritual guidance from the other side. You always arrive with much-needed advice, and I wouldn't finish this work without your assistance. I also thank you for helping me to die on my terms in the past life. Without trust between us, I would never meet Eurydice. You've been my spiritual father, giving me the strength to embrace my innate powers. And I also thank you for the sacrifices you've made. You always tried to live by your heart and listened to advice from above. Your soul is a spiritual guide of death and I'm grateful to have such a teacher on my path of mastering the essence of this transformation. I'm becoming a better guide just by knowing you.

Nataly Stevenson. Dear soulmate, thank you for joining me on the extreme adventures into death planes. I would have never understood my essence, without your help. I will always remember our journey with Isis and Osiris. I'm sorry that I died on you three times, but I hope you can see now a higher design of our story. You've became yourself, through these experiences and I'm grateful we figured out why we met again.

Sepideh Merchant. My dear friend, I thank you for the light and compassion you bring into this world. I thank you for everything you've done for me on my journey. Without your help, I wouldn't a safe space to write this work. You were there for me when I needed help, and I will always be thankful for your support.

Healers and Guides

Elizabeth Woolridge Grant. Dear Elizabeth, I don't have enough words to thank you for helping us to complete this book. Your music and poetry literally saved Euryidce and me, healing the emotions of our broken hearts. You've become the guardian Angel of our love story. Your light elevates and uplifts lost and stranded souls. It always enriches and inspires Eurydice and me in unique ways. You are a wonderful energy healer and a spiritual guide. I feel truly grateful to live in a world where your art exists.

Kemila Zsange. My dear friend and spiritual guide, thank you for helping us to create this work. I came to you to face the darkness that's been haunting me for centuries, and we ended up exploring every one of my past lives. You helped me to process every scar of my soul, that prevented me from living my best life. And, of course, you taught me how to face the highest grief of losing the love of one's life. This work would not be accomplished without you.

Alanna Allan. My dear friend, thank you for everything you've done for me. I would have never completed this manuscript without your magical, energy-healing powers. You are a true magician who uplifts wounded souls. I'm grateful for the opportunity to express my loving admiration of your talents. Thank you for holding sacred space for my tears of a broken heart. You've helped me to resolve some of my deepest grief and eliminate the emotional scars caused by my mother and the monsters of Russia. I'm thankful to behold how the light of your soul enriches this world in many ways.

Selena Jones. Thank you for being a wise and patient teacher to me. I planted seeds for this work in my sacred garden of the spiritual realm at our first new moon meditation in January 2021. You've taught Eurydice and me how to dream big and follow our hearts. You've connected us with ancient souls of these lands and their stories enriched this manuscript. You uplift souls in many unique ways, and I'm grateful to know you.

Friends

I would like to thank Sharon McGowan, Rachel Talalay, Peggy Thompson, C.C. Humphreys, Nakita Clemens, Danielle Butlin, Suzanne Malinowski-Plaquin, Isabelle Shivangeli Rum, Tegan Tarot, Susan Lyons, Vincent Tremblay, Janet Gaynor for helping me on my writing journey.

I would also like to thank every soul that came to seek my guidance while I was writing this book. Each of you was my teacher as much as I was yours, and I honor your truths. I'm thankful to share this journey with every one of you. Your questions helped me to understand myself and this world better, so this book would not be possible without your support. We live and breeze the collective energies of Vancouver. Some of you lived centuries ago, and some of you live now, but we came together to heal through sharing the traumatic stories of our lives. Through this process, we eliminated the pains of our souls and of these lands. Please continue to follow your heart, and never forget to shine your light, as that is the reason you came to this Earth.

It's also important to mention the writings of Tom Kenyon, Judi Sion, Mercedes Kirkel, Amber Dawn, T.S. Eliot, Mikhail Bulgakov and Boris Pasternak for inspiring me on my writing journey.

I also express my appreciation and gratitude to everyone at Pegasus publishers who helped me to share this work with the world.

Land acknowledgements

I would like to thank the spirits of Burrard Inlet, Coal Harbor, Stanley Park, Lost Lagoon Lake, Lighthouse Park, Buntzen Lake, Pemberton Mountains, Sechelt Inlet, and Hidden Grove Forest for their active participation in the creation of this work. I humbly welcomed the access to the accumulated knowledge of triumphs and tragedies of these lands and their transient residents. Stories and rhymes of the spirits were channeled and woven into the fabric of this fairy tale. Every advice was embraced with reverence to create a story that honors the perceptions and values of these Lands. I consider Spirits of British Columbia the co-creators of this book.

I would also like to thank spirits of Monticello, Boston and Washington, D.C., spirits of Paris, France and Seine River, spirits of Kyiv, Poltava and Chernivtsi regions of Ukraine, spirit of Flaten Lake in Sweden, and spirits of Baikal Lake in Siberia for their insightful guidance, and inspirational encouragements.

Dedicated

To my soulmate of eight lives, Eurydice,
Who blissfully dances in Vancouver sky
Illuminating our troubled world
With her majestic beauty and grace.

Dear princess of Sechelt waters and lands
Your divine femininity shines celestial light
While inspiring my artistic nature
As I reclaim my soul's highest purpose.

You've questioned my love for you
In three lives that we shared
Creating tragic dramas and wounds
That haunt us to this day.

To heal us, my heart and my soul
Crafted this manuscript as testament
That love between our souls was always
Honest, eternal, and unconditional.

PROLOGUE

Once upon a time, a divine intervention occurred in the kingdom of British Columbia, a land of breathtaking beauty, ancient magic, and supernatural essence. On November 14, 2020, an angelic providence sent knight Benjamin on a blind date with princess Holly, his destined woman of supreme female excellence, grace, and beauty. Once Holly looked at Benjamin for the first time, unconditional love enveloped their souls, descending in waves from Heavens. It was love at first sight, as Benjamin instantly recognized the feelings he carried for this woman through centuries. They never spent a single life without each other, as fate and eternal love bonded our soulmates. Benjamin knew right away that only this woman would elevate him to his highest glory, realizing he had been searching for her his entire life. On that night, Holly, as Benjamin's heavenly muse, unleashed the full force of his creative talents and magical powers.

Only Holly did not fall in love with Benjamin, as the evil spirit of the Underworld, Damian, had already entrapped her. He was taking control over Holly, and it was the last day for her soul, whom angels named Eurydice, to contact Benjamin. Eurydice used the powers of her land to summon Benjamin. Once their souls remembered their ancient bond, Eurydice requested Benjamin's help, as she was in imminent danger.

Recognizing his enemy, Damian swiftly prevented our soulmates from discovering the healing truth that arises from the first blooms of love. Using the most potent demonic spells of dark magic, he could easily manipulate Holly. Damian cursed our princess five centuries ago. Life after life, Eurydice fell victim to the brutal game Damian played with her, and our times were no different. Soon the Dark Prince captured and imprisoned Holly in his lavish castle in downtown Vancouver. Damian persuaded Holly with intimidating lies, so she built another heart wall, and rejected Benjamin's love. Damian convinced our princess that Benjamin was not a real magician and he only wanted to possess her for his sexual pleasures.

Once Holly followed Damian's whispers, he forced her soul out of the body and chained Eurydice in his demonic dungeon.

Benjamin cried endlessly from missing his soulmate, desperately longing to share his affections with his divine woman. Experiencing beautiful but conflicting feelings of love became his ultimate suffering and his emotional prison. Yet, after many sleepless nights, he learned to tolerate his pain. Once Benjamin discovered Damian's sinister plan to murder Holly before her twenty-seventh birthday, he decided to act. Even though Holly didn't want to see Benjamin again, our knight believed he could still save his woman from her tragic destiny. Empowered by love, faith, magic, poetry, confidence, and perseverance, Benjamin embarked on the ultimate quest of his life to liberate his princess from the ancient curse.

As Damian hunted Holly's soul through centuries, Benjamin relentlessly constructed new paths to defeat him. Both adversaries knew Eurydice's uniquely divine talents and her highest destiny of a soul with Magdalene's heart, so neither was ready to surrender. Using dark magic, Damian became an immortal spirit five centuries ago. Now he could enter any person who had a corrupted heart. In other lives he used different people to terrify Eurydice and intimidate Benjamin. But this time Damian decided to become Holly, so he could experience life as her.

Damian was not an ordinary evil spirit. He was a powerful creature with a glorious past. Once, Damian manipulated the King of Sweden, setting him at odds with other European monarchs. Another time, he fought against spirit of freedom in French Empire. And in his most celebrated life, Damian empowered the King of New York to wage war against other American Founding Kings, instigating conflicts between patriots, and spreading ideals of slavery. Eurydice had to sacrifice her life for her nation, and empower Benjamin from the other side to defend American Independence from Damian's evil plan.

Benjamin and Damian represented the balancing energies, as they were created equally powerful spiritual guides, working directly with the souls. Only one worked for the forces of Light and the other for Darkness. Benjamin desired to help souls grow, while Damian wanted to destroy them. The adversaries always treated each other with mutual respect and conceded without hesitation upon losing a battle. Our rivals honored the laws of our world. Neither could break the eternal principles established by

Nature and Heavens. Following the law of free will, Damian could only use coercion to envelop Holly's heart in fear and block her true feminine magic. Benjamin couldn't save Holly from Damian's traps once she consented to follow his illusions. He couldn't use force to liberate Holly, even though her life was in danger.

Yet another rule of Nature constrained Damian. Upon inception, a woman was created superior to a man, with unmatched abilities like intuition, clairvoyance, grace, and wisdom. A woman had only one ultimate flaw to balance her magical powers. Female soul was more susceptible to the attacks of dark energies and creatures of negative vibrations, who lived in the dark spiritual realm and prayed on vulnerable humans. By higher design, only a destined man could guard his woman's soul against darkness with the magic of unconditional love. Only a pure, loving masculine heart could shield Holly against manifestations of sinister energies. If Damian could destroy Benjamin's magical protection and will to fight, he could own Eurydice for eternity. She carried the healing powers of divine femininity, and by owning her, Damian could reach new levels of power and amplify his demonic abilities.

Damian desperately needed Eurydice. After hunting her for so long, our time was his last chance, as Eurydice was finally ready to claim her divine feminine powers and illuminate the world with Mary Magdalene's celestial light. Damian always dreamed to capturte this beautiful soul in his hellish abyss. Eurydice narrowly escaped his traps in the past, but she always achieved that with Benjamin's help, as that was how they were designed. Eurydice required the highest unconditional love to shine in her true glory. And, she also needed complex, mystical teachings to grasp the scale of her innate, magical abilities. Only Benjamin's soul could provide both, as he believed in her and saw true essence of her feminine heart, even when she couldn't. Only he could teach her how to confront inner darkness with faith, passion, and love.

In this life, angels blessed Benjamin with supernatural powers of white magic, telepathy, clairvoyance, and time travel so he could reverse Damian's curse. With miraculous abilities, our knight could see the spiritual realm, the higher destiny of souls and communicated with the spirits of the lands. He could heal wounds of souls by reliving their traumatic deaths with them, remove dark energies from the bodies with his hands and fight demonic creatures with his drum.

Damian's curse was activated three times in the past when Eurydice betrayed her feminine essence and questioned Benjamin's love. Each time, Damian was allowed to murder Eurydice before her twenty-seventh birthday. He significantly diminished her self-confidence, rebelliousness, fearlessness, and resilience through these traumatic deaths. Damian sabotaged her ability to properly evaluate the events of her life, as she always died terrified and confused, entrapped in the darkness of his lies. Each time, Damian crafted a state of terror and pain, causing Eurydice to lose herself in the darkness of death. Benjamin always prevented Damian from capturing Eurydice for eternity, but each time Damian secured a chance to try again. The Dark Prince also preyed upon Benjamin's grief as his nemesis buried the tortured body of his woman, engulfed in feelings of tormenting grief and sorrow. Tragic funerals and sudden parting devastated Benjamin, as life without his soulmate felt lonely, sad and empty.

Today, my dear reader, we are witnessing the final chapter of this ancient battle. Benjamin's previous defeats wore him down, but now he had only four years to prevent another tragic death of his beloved. Benjamin would use his magic to kill Eurydice's demons and dispel the origins of Damian's curse. Exploring their past, Benjamin would fearlessly heal their traumas and discover a unique connection of their souls through poetry. Our knight crafted poetic incantations of love and turned them into a perfect weapon against Damian's evil sorcery.

Benjamin knew how small was his chance of saving Holly, but he was determined to try against all odds. If Holly would not believe that Benjamin truly loves her, Damian could kill her again. But in grand scheme of things, it doesn't really matter how our story would end. The journey is more important than the destination. I wish to share with you a story of how Eurydice and Benjamin healed each other with unconditional love. I also wish to tell you everything I know about these two fascinating love birds and their infinite, epic love story of rhyming lives.

Magical Tale of Eternal Love

While she's alone, and waiting for his triumph
While he's alone, exposing wild deceits
Their souls through nights, together flying,
Explore past stories of the love they lived.
Adoring poems, they're creating fiercely
Enriching life with words of love and tears;
They wrote a tale about one holy princess
And now, invite the world to witness it with cheers.

They welcome you to see their story,
Of two in love who never rest
With a tragic stance but never worried,
They will endure their highest test.
You'll hear their songs and their wild prayers
You'll witness their connection of true love;
They live above all sinister naysayers
Through torments, lovely poetry they'll craft.

A noble journey destiny's revealing
Requires arduous intents,
True courage to accept deep feelings
And inspirations from their old regrets.
I must prepare you for the trials
Of dreams that will be crashed by fears
I will explain their wildest cryings
While grief and death, their love distills.

CHAPTER I

Benjamin moved to the kingdom of British Columbia, following divine guidance, as he passionately searched for his true destiny. For seven years, he worked tirelessly to adjust to his life in Vancouver. He knew that the spirits of these lands summoned him, although he wasn't sure why. In his new home, Benjamin was tempered by many challenging and traumatizing experiences, eventually loosing himself after a series of crashing failures. Then, one day, as he planned his escape from Vancouver back to the kingdom of Ukraine, the land spoke to him. Our knight was finally ready to embrace his ultimate purpose and become a noble white magician. And for him it was only possible through the radical transformation of divine love. His soulmate Holly moved to Vancouver in October 2020, searching for unconditional love, and her soul requested Benjamin's guidance on her path.

Benjamin had many demanding obligations at this time, so his life was extremely chaotic. He struggled at his day job, fought to obtain legal permanent status, tried to promote his art, and attempted to embrace the path of a magician's apprentice. On top of that, Benjamin's dearest brother and soulmate, Phillip, required his immediate spiritual help. Like twins, Benjamin and Phillip were inseparable, always facing their triumphs and disasters in unity. They belonged to one soul family, empowered by the same sky spirit. Brothers came to Vancouver together to study as magicians at the famous Academy of Rival Snakes. Learning art, philosophy, death, and magic, they passionately embraced their supernatural powers.

In October 2019, Phillip fell crazily in love with his soulmate, Becky, the duchess of Pemberton. Even though Becky expressed her affections to Phillip, they had a tumultuous love-hate romance during their first year together. Our duchess was a vainglorious and obstinate lady. Her stance was quite understandable, as she was born a very charming woman, and her spirit family ruled over the Pemberton mountains and lands.

Benjamin introduced Phillip to Becky. Becky came to Benjamin, desperately seeking spiritual guidance. Hunted by demonic entities, Becky searched for a way out. These creatures deceived Becky to abandon her true feminine mission, and her soul got stranded in between the worlds. Benjamin quickly discovered that Phillip was her assigned spiritual guide, and only he could help her. Disoriented by evil persecutions while carrying the trauma of the past tragic death, Becky was afraid to open up to a real commitment and believe in unconditional love. Phillip could see Becky's highest spiritual essence, so he was determined to shield her aura from sinister attacks with his pure love. Seeing how troubled Becky was, Benjamin had to assist his younger brother through this challenging romance. Together they spent countless hours planning the best approaches to heal Becky's soul, Suzanne.

Yet another noble battle waited for our knight. The same month he received a conscription notice to fight in the Great American Spiritual War, and he passionately embraced this noble calling. Dark forces descended upon the American Empire, desiring to enslave this nation and establish tyranny. Benjamin was an indispensable warrior of significant importance for American spirits, as his soul possessed sacred, magical knowledge about American inception. His unique connection to the history of these lands provided important insights for American patriots.

As you can see, my dear reader, Benjamin had no time for romantic adventures. Our knight was exhausted every minute of every day, barely finding time to sleep between battles. But then, on November 04, 2020, his spiritual guide Wilhelm arrived with a message: "You must meet one woman. Your special woman."

Unexpected news shocked Benjamin and he struggled to embrace a possibility of such new reality. He couldn't offer much to any woman, so he didn't even consider courtship at this time. He was a promising young knight with magical talents, but his achievements still lived in the future. As a struggling immigrant, Benjamin didn't have any savings or property, so he believed he shouldn't waste the time of any Earth goddess if he couldn't offer her a sense of security along with his honest heart. Even though Benjamin trusted his guide, he debated Wilhelm, begging to postpone this rendezvous until his pressing entanglements are resolved. But

Wilhelm insisted that the meeting must happen now, as time was of the essence.

When Benjamin finally surrendered to go on this blind date, Wilhelm presented a condition. Benjamin had to pay one ounce of gold to Wilhelm to organize the meeting. An ounce of gold could cover two months of his rent and it was too much for Benjamin. Yet Wilhelm only followed the laws of Nature. This payment was a fee for Benjamin's spiritual education. Having free will, Benjamin had to willingly choose to suffer, sincerely giving something away without expecting anything in return, honestly exercising the idea of a sacrifice. He argued with Wilhelm again, but his guide explained that this meeting would open the doorway of self-discovery for Benjamin. He always followed his heart and now he was rewarded for his hard work with this divine opportunity. Benjamin prayed for a chance to become an authentic magician and it was finally here. He had to meet this enigmatic woman.

To prove the importance of this date, Wilhelm handed Benjamin a photo of Holly's hands, and once our knight saw her fingers, he realized that Holly was his soulmate. Certainly, being soulmates doesn't imply romantic love by default. Souls can be lovers in one lifetime but choose to be friends or relatives in the next one, embracing any relationship for their growth, while exploring all types of connections, entanglements, teachings, and variations of love. Anyone can recognize a soulmate through the eyes, as they never change from life to life. But our lovers had such a special connection that Benjamin recognized Holly's soul through her fingers, and he fell in love.

On the eve of the meeting, Benjamin confessed his emotions to Phillip, asking for his blessing. Phillip was concerned about sacrificial payment, as they shared finances, often struggling to survive. But he knew Benjamin would only embrace a spiritual mission if it truly resonated in his heart. Phillip trusted intuition of his brother, but soon he witnessed a premonition and shared a wise prophecy with him. "Tomorrow, you will see Holly's eyes, and you will fall in love. But this woman would be scared to embrace you, since her heart is traumatized. She will reject you and break your heart. I beg you, don't go."

"You know, I feel the same way about tomorrow," Benjamin replied, "but at the same time, I know I must bravely take this road. Our hearts are designed to be broken. That's how the light of divine, shining glory gets in. I must allow her to break my heart. I hope this pain will become my triumph. This journey is not about a woman for me. This is a test of my faith. I believe in my spiritual guidance and I feel this date will help me discover my divine purpose in life." Our brothers shared the eerie sensation of inevitable sadness and grief, but both embraced the spiritual gifts life has prepared for them.

The following evening, Phillip's prediction came true. On November 14, 2020, Benjamin arrived at the Botanist Restaurant on the shores of the majestically beautiful Burrard Inlet. Once Holly looked into Benjamin's eyes for the first time at precisely 8:12 p.m., the divine love enveloped our soulmates, leaving them both speechless. Benjamin had never seen such beautiful eyes, yet he had seen these eyes so many times before. Recognizing Holly's soul, Benjamin could not stop looking at this remarkable woman, mesmerized, bewildered, bemused, but incredibly inspired. His worries disappeared, and nostalgic sensations enveloped him. Once Holly started talking, another overwhelming wave of love consumed his heart. Benjamin had never heard a more mellifluent and euphonious voice. She spoke like the most beautiful bird of her land, and Benjamin could joyfully spend eternity listening to her whispers.

At 8:21 p.m., Benjamin saw a wonderful vision of their future wedding, and now his heart dreamed of a chance to propose to Holly. If someone gave Benjamin a choice at that moment – either marry Holly right now or never see her again – Benjamin would embrace his woman without hesitation. He had never felt so strongly about anyone, hoping to share his life with Holly if she would allow him to love her. She was his most beloved soul in the whole wide world, and as long as he could spend precious minutes in her presence, his soul was in joyful harmony, shining love and peace into the world.

Benjamin was unaware that such divine love between souls even existed. This was one of the most beautiful and traumatizing feelings a human could ever experience. A corrupt heart could never sustain such love. Only a strong man with nobility, integrity, and honest self-love could receive such a blessing. This love was a gift from angels. By falling in love with this woman, Benjamin fell in love with his true essence. He praised voices from the skies for guiding him to find Holly, finally realizing why he had to move to Vancouver in first place.

Of course, dear reader, you may say it's insanity to desire a marriage after spending only eight minutes with someone. But when you uncover the vicissitudes of this long and never-ending romance, you will realize that such love was inevitable for these souls. Their connection, full of peripeteia, spanned eight centuries, and today it was shining with renewed strength. The angels guarding our mortal plane designed this story, carefully crafting the rhymes of destiny, as these lovers were entangled beyond any reasonable imagination.

Holly was not an ordinary princess, and Benjamin was not a typical knight. Both of them had supernatural powers and unique soul missions of magicians. Once they fell in love, they transformed each other, exposing the innate truths of their radiating hearts, opening secret doors of their souls, and manifesting their highest potentials.

Our lovers felt completely comfortable next to each other, and nothing could take them apart. Two and a half hours flew by in an instant as they engaged in the most natural and easy-going conversation of their lives. Nothing they've experienced before felt so liberating. They talked about the spiritual realm, magic, past lives, cinema, art, and the beauties of Paris. They shared their opinions about politics, psychotherapy, conspiracies, and the meaning of life while admiring how masculine and feminine essences are uniquely designed to complement one another, creating alchemy that enriches the world. Benjamin told Holly of the movies he crafted about lost souls and the essence of death. Holly told Benjamin about her passion for drawing, fascination with Monet paintings, and shared cute stories about her beloved cat, Mr. Dance. They exchanged genuine opinions about the most complex topics with no judgments or reservations. Our lovers freely and passionately spoke their minds; their hearts prevented them from lying to one another.

They lost track of time, exploring their sparks until the restaurant suddenly closed. Holly and Benjamin stepped onto the street, but neither wanted to say goodbye. It was dark and cold outside, so Holly invited Benjamin to her place. Our knight never agreed to such offers on a first date, preferring to engage in a slow dance of love without rushing with inevitable intimate desires. Only he couldn't say no to Holly, dreaming of spending as many minutes in her presence as she would allow him to.

They exchanged unambiguous looks as they entered her apartment. Right in the hallway, Holly suddenly jumped at Benjamin and kissed him intensely on the lips. Our knight never experienced such asserted and passionate compulsion from a woman. He perceived it as an attack, yet he quickly surrendered, as he felt Holly was honestly expressing the truth of her heart. She had dreamed of kissing her knight for eight decades, and he was finally here. Benjamin forgot the rules of a virtuous gentleman and embraced the present moment. Benjamin kissed Holly back and allowed himself to enjoy it. When Holly stepped away from her ambush, she assessed Benjamin's sensations with the cutest smile. Looking directly into his eyes, she whispered, "Benjamin, your eyes are changing colors. They are sparkling with different hues. I've never seen eyes like yours." She softly continued with genuine excitement, "I know you. I feel like I know you."

At that moment, Benjamin ecstatically said what he's been dreaming to say for the entire evening, "I know you too, dear Holly! I know your eyes."

They stopped short of saying the three magical words of lovers. After all, it was only their first date, but 'I know you' sounded like a beautiful and spectacular rhyme. In reality, Holly didn't say those words. It was a distress signal from Eurydice, the last thing she could do, before Damian would take over. Eurydice's words have initiated Benjamin's journey to retrieve her from Underworld, even though he didn't realize it at this moment.

As the clock struck midnight, our lovers had to say goodbye. While Benjamin was putting on his jacket and shoes, Holly opened a gift bag from her knight. Next to a bottle of champagne and bath salt, Holly found a book. A profound shock ran through her body as she saw the cover of *Violet Bent Backward over the Grass* by Lana Del Ray. She couldn't believe that a man, who knew nothing about her, had brought her a book she had dreamed about.

"Benjamin, how did you know? Oh wow! Thank you! Seriously, how did you know I really wanted this book? She's so wonderfully great, but people misunderstand her so much. She is my favorite poet."

"Mine too! Yes, she shares her deepest truths, and I don't know why people criticize her so much. She captures the essence and complexities of a female experience so eloquently," Benjamin replied.

"Exactly! What a coincidence. I can't believe my eyes." Holly twirled the book in her hands, now even more reluctant to let her man go. "Please tell me, how did you know that I dreamed to get this book?"

"Well, I've mentioned to you that I'm learning to become a magician. I'm still only an apprentice, but this is what I do," Benjamin replied, staring down at the floor. He was still shy to claim his powers. Holly slowly crawled to Benjamin on her toes. She reached to zip his leather jacket while carefully and lovingly adjusting his collar.

"Here, I don't want you to get cold out there." Holly gazed at Benjamin through her eyelashes. They both dissolved in the profound beauty of this romantic moment and smiled. Then, she gifted him a goodbye kiss.

The famous Vancouver rain started as Benjamin left Holly's building, but our knight couldn't stop smiling. Now Benjamin has uncovered the mystery of famous Vancouver rains. Eurydice was crying without her man. This was Holly's kingdom, so when her heart was crying from the endless pains of life, her Nature cried in unison. New waves of love descended upon our knight as he discovered a new appreciation for this city – the princess of this land was as gorgeous as her dominion. Benjamin's heart and soul expressed their wish to fight for this woman. Soon, like in his favorite childhood musical, *Dancing in The Rain*, he swirled through intersections while whistling the tune of a man who fell in love with his muse. With no umbrella, Benjamin danced through empty streets, soaking wet, yet shining with happiness.

At home, our ecstatic knight contemplated his experience on a balcony, overlooking Vancouver, while listening to Lana Del Ray's *"NFR"* record on vinyl. Benjamin smiled proudly and victoriously as he bought Lana's book, only relying on his intuition. He didn't use any spells or occult incantations. He only listened to his heart. Our knight masterfully constructed a beautiful metaphysical bridge to reach Holly's soul through poetry. As if Holly's fingers, through the photo, told him what kind of book, they dreamed of holding.

"This world is holy. There are no coincidences in life," Benjamin said before falling asleep, "Thank you, my dear Holly, for this day. I love you. Have a good night."

Suddenly, a voice from above immediately replied, "Goodnight, Benjamin."

Benjamin was overwhelmed by the whirlwind of emotions, so he thought he had imagined this voice, and he fell asleep. Yet through seeing Holly's eyes, he established contact with Eurydice, and now she spoke to him, desperately reaching for Benjamin's protection and guidance. She asked spirits to summon Benjamin from distant lands, and her plan worked. Only she was in danger, as Damian was much closer than she thought.

CHAPTER II

One day spirits of the Burrard Inlet and its shores realized how many dark snakes, dragons, spiders, and demons had arrived in their land. The army of evil creatures destroyed this kingdom in the most sinister way. Corrupt politicians, money laundering, real-estate scams, stock exchange frauds, drug epidemics, and other evils eviscerated communities of hard-working citizens. These destructions were of a magnitude no one could have ever predicted. It was clear that empowering the ancestral tribes and creeds who historically lived on these lands would not be enough to confront what spirits witnessed. The widespread pandemic of corrupted hearts led to the loss of many souls. Consumerism, narcissism, arrogance, condescending judgements, pursuits of external validation, worship of false idols, and rejection of divine laws of Nature destroyed people's connections with their hearts.

Only spirits of waters and lands decide who would live in their kingdom. It was their domain and every human was merely their guest. As humans could not own anything, coming from nothing and turning into ashes upon death, spirits were often confused by the actions of sinister humans who tried to claim the ownership of their lands. The spirits knew that humans could only rent their domains. No other options were available to humans; that was their essence – arriving and leaving with nothing tangible. Souls came to Earth in human bodies to love, grow, acquire a deeper understanding of their essence, complete their destined missions, eventually moving towards becoming one divine, blissful light. People were only allowed to take their experiences and feelings upon death, nothing more. Unfortunately, stubborn mortals could not simply accept these facts of life. They obsessively demanded control over life itself, fought to surrender to reality, and continued to build their Babylonian tower so they could scream at angels for not giving them enough gold. Sympathy for broken men and women was common among spirits, and they never judged when people failed to acknowledge their mortality.

Only observing widespread corruption, spirits needed to act. The spirits never looked at skin color or nationality when empowering a particular soul for a mission. They knew that souls chose their race, gender, and land upon birth for higher reasons. Spirits empowered souls based on their ability to act in the best interests of all involved and never harm others. So, spirits summoned healers, teachers, and magicians to enrich their kingdom. They gathered a new army of noble warriors to fight against dark deities.

That's how our spiritual brothers Benjamin and Phillip received an invitation to come to this land. They arrived in Vancouver in December 2013, on the day of Holly's birthday. Both were unaware of their unique missions, thinking their guides presented them with a path to advance in their spiritual education. They were excited to study in the prestigious Academy of Rival Snakes, famous among magicians worldwide for its unique guarding spirits and their never-ending dance battle that made this place so powerful. Dreaming of mastering magic, our brothers were not interested in romance, yet fate brought them here to experience true love.

Upon arrival, Benjamin and Phillip went to thank their spiritual hosts. Standing on the shores of Burrard Inlet, next to the Stanley Park, and observing the mountains of Sechelt in the distance, as the sun was setting over the vast waters, they felt this city was their true home. They never felt so at peace anywhere else, so they thanked their innate intuitions and every higher being for helping them discover this place. Serendipity brought them this chance, and they experienced magnificent transformation upon arrival. They never visited Vancouver, but spent their entire inheritance from their late father, Sergemir, to move here. They took a tremendous risk with this decision, as these were their only savings. But now, talking to the spirits of Burrard Inlet, excitement radiated from our knights. They were in love with these lands, but little did they know they were already in love with their women.

Soon the soul of their late great-grandfather Michael spoke the words of encouragement. Like our brothers, he moved to Vancouver from the kingdom of Ukraine, and now his spirit was guiding them. After death, his soul remained in Vancouver to guard the lands and assist our knights from the other side.

Benjamin and Phillip's paternal line always embodied the energy of spiritual warriors of Light. Every man in their family was a knight. Their family name, Frumos, was well-known in Bukovina in the kingdoms of Ukraine and Romania. Many villages had their noble warriors with that name, and people looked at them with the utmost respect. Generations of ancestors fought to shield Bukovina from its enemies. One of the ancestors was Făt-Frumos, who saved his princess, Ileana, from the devils of the Underworld and became famous for his trials. People wrote fairy tales and even made a movie about his incredible adventures. Like our knights, Făt-Frumos had magic powers and could travel between realms of existence to fight demonic monsters and vicious beings. And as in our story, Făt-Frumos always faced unpleasant and painful choices. When arriving at life's crossroads, he would hear his guide's words: "If you turn right, you will be in sorrow; if you turn left, you will be in sorrow." This was the destiny of any knight with magical powers. He would inevitably suffer, but he could choose what to suffer for. It is the only way to temper the true character of a peaceful warrior. Their ancestors also fought the army of Duke Dracula, as Bukovina bordered the kingdom of Transylvania. They successfully protected their land from the occupation of this dark deity. And, of course, they fought relentlessly in the Second World War, protecting their land from Soviet and German armies.

Benjamin carried profound gratitude to the spirits of Bukovina for their teachings, but this wasn't the land of his powers. His father, Sergemir, was always listening to his heart, and he encouraged brothers to move to Vancouver. Sergemir did everything he could to help Benjamin and Phillip. He eventually sacrificed his life so that brothers could use the inheritance to move to Vancouver. Once, sitting in their village of Sloboda in Bukovina, Sergemir addressed his son. "Benjamin, I dream you find your path one day. I'm struggling to comprehend the scale of your talents. I'm not a magician as you are, but I must tell you one thing. I feel you should move to Vancouver. My grandfather Michael lived there, and I always sensed we are connected to that land. I don't think I will be granted a chance to step onto that blessed land, but I am convinced you ought to. I know you love our motherland, but your destiny awaits you there. You are a wandering warrior, so carry your truth with dignity. I can't force you against your free will, but I urge you to consider it. One day you will have to move, and when you do, please remember my words."

By 2020 Benjamin turned thirty-seven years old and completed everything required of a knight who stepped into full adulthood. He prostituted his talents always asking for less than he deserved in the youthful passion of self-rejection. He fervently tried to be someone society told him to be, fighting his heart in order to conform. He fell to the lowest points following the directions of modern broken society and its false systems of beliefs. But one day he finally rejected all indoctrinations imposed upon him throughout his life. He resorted to his heart and prayed for a divine mission. He was seeking a higher cause, confronted by his dispensable masculine nature. Benjamin dreamed of sacrificing his life for the unity of mankind and his kingdom's future. He was ready to give his life for a righteous cause without hesitation. Benjamin never stopped when challenges appeared on his path. He always swiftly restored himself after each defeat and continued his pursuit as a renewed person. Once he finished his apprentice studies in many aspects of life, death and spirituality he finally became a man of conviction and shined with integrity, ready to face any challenge.

Benjamin was on a journey to master his warrior skills. He received the knowledge of ancestral magicians and learned how to destroy sinister energies, feeding upon human auras, sucking their energies, and corrupting their souls. Each day, Benjamin lived between the worlds, fighting in different planes of existence. Our knight could easily visit Underworld, Purgatory, and the Death dimensions while safely returning with indispensable knowledge. As a magician, Benjamin mastered the art of death and resurrection. He trained other souls in this craft, including his closest soulmates. Benjamin learned to travel to the darkest places of our world to spread the seeds of forgiveness, kindness, love, and light. He intentionally exposed himself to the world's evils to decimate them with his noble heart. He could absorb and process the darkness of others, healing them through shadow energy work. The souls of magicians can access the world of Light and Darkness equally to heal our reality and witness another perspective of life upon death. Some wounds of our world could only be resolved in between states of existence, as they were created in that reality.

The white magicians of Light maintained the universal balance of these energies, executing the laws of Nature.

Our knight fought for his truth for centuries, believing in righteousness of raising his weapons against the dark ideology of Tyranny. For Benjamin, people were born with unalienable rights endowed by the divine Mother Nature and Father Skies upon the creation of this world. Nothing was more important for Benjamin than fighting for freedom and liberty. Humans are never born free, imprisoned in bodies and circumstances. The birth in the animal body is a death for the soul, as souls intentionally become limited beings, embracing the physical sufferings for their growth, to live the path of inner liberation. Benjamin could not tolerate how tyrants all over the planet persuaded and coerced humans to believe that people were bonded to live as obedient slaves. Nothing was more important for Benjamin than freedom, not even his life. On this path, he vigorously pursued restoring the real magic of Nature which tyrants took away from humans.

Benjamin was a man, ready to do anything for his beliefs, but then a woman appeared on his way, a woman he didn't expect or desire. She was forced upon him by divinity. Holly was unlike any other woman for Benjamin. Once he met her, he forgot about tyranny, oppression, war, and slavery. Now he could only think about her.

Benjamin was not aware that many knights, princes, and kings of Holly's lands dreamed of being her suitors. They swirled and danced around her, gifting her expensive jewelry, luxury bags, dresses and designer shoes, only for a chance to have another date with her. Holly was spoiled with attention all her life, as the seductive grace and tender beauty she wore so elegantly made men act irrationally. Her feminine energy hypnotized them in an instant, and there was no escape. Her lush lips and doe eyes made men fall to their knees when they pass her by.

However, her spiritual mother, Ariadne – the spirit queen governing the Sechelt forests and mountains – had stringent demands for the possible suitors of her soul. Eurydice was her most beloved daughter, as Ariadne knew about her spiritual mission. Eurydice was destined to progress as a divine feminine being, to embrace and fully embody the archetypical energy of supreme Goddess Mary Magdalene and radiate her energy into the world. Eurydice carried the grand essence of Magdalene's energy in every life and slowly learned to fully embody it.

Even though Eurydice was born with such a destiny, no soul could carry a goddess' energy upon creation. Such status must be earned through intense and traumatizing experiences, as eventually, such a soul would be tasked to heal others. Each soul has unique challenges and is tempered in their own way. Still, not every soul is designed to endure the tortures, mutilations, rape, intense suffering, and brutal, traumatizing deaths required to achieve the status of a spiritual empress. Eurydice could only endure such experiences because Benjamin was always beside her, shielding her with love and guiding her through death. He was always the last person who held her hand. He always buried her body while healing the wounds with his prayers and taking her darkness upon himself. Eurydice was required to live a life of transformation in Holly's body. To shine her truth, Holly must experience different tribulations as Mary did before becoming a healer and a faithful companion to her divine husband. Only with Benjamin's guidance, Eurydice could learn how to harness and embody her supreme powers.

Ariadne knew that the evil spirits of the Underworld and black magicians would attempt to entrap her daughter. Fear consumed the spirit queen of Sechelt when she learned about Damian because there was another stipulation in Eurydice's Book of Life. A man, who could shield her from demonic entities, must carry the purest unconditional love possible. Ariadne held the hope that several suitors could potentially protect her daughter, but she was desperately grasping for straws. Unconditional love slowly disappeared from our world, and surely not many men could compete with the love that has existed for centuries. Ariadne didn't know that only Benjamin could confront Damian's sinister spells, but she prayed to the spirits of her domains to assist her troubled daughter. And that's how the first rendezvous of our lovers was created by the spirits governing Holly's kingdom.

Our world is full of natural and honest magic, despite the attempts of demonic deities to prove otherwise. Pure miracles are hard to recognize, especially when illusions of evil are so shiny, bright, appealing, and instantly available. Natural magic always takes time, effort, and hard work, so no wonder humans who seek quick and immediate pleasures abandoned it. Our noble knight was set to prove the divine nature of our world with the help of his gorgeous princess. Our lovers believed in magic, so their lives were full of everyday miracles.

Holly and Benjamin desired salvation, begging the world to show them a path out of their insecurities, misery, and self-loathing. They wanted to find their essence, to see the glory of their never dying souls. Yet they didn't know it was only possible through love. Benjamin appeared on Holly's path when she unraveled herself and magnetized a man with unconditional love. She invoked the attraction of pure love in the dream world, and now her soul searched for her man in the physical reality. Holly appeared on Benjamin's path when he discovered himself, and magnetized his adventure of the highest masculine nobility. He asked for a challenge that would test his faith and show him the depth of his righteous heart.

If a man carries the energies of strength, intellect, and the desire to act in this world, then a woman carries the energies of meaning and significance; she fills that action with purpose and guides that masculine perseverance in the right direction. Even when a woman loses her path, she is still a bit wiser, more subtle, tolerant, and graceful than a man, and that's where her ultimate strength lies. These qualities, not the raw power, help her prevail over the complexities of her destiny. A man is just a tool for a woman to shape reality. A man can't initiate the path of love because if he strives to be honest, righteous, and virtuous, the love becomes his reward. He receives highest love when his work and missions are completed. For a man, the love is always a validation of his achievements. And only a woman has the power to illuminate a higher path of destiny for her man because she creates life with her feminine magic. A woman gives birth to a new life both in spiritual and physical realms. But before a woman can bring a new life into the world, she has to 'murder' her imperfect man so he can be re-born into a higher version of himself. That's what our Secheltian princess did to Benjamin, as she dreamed to build her best life.

As a man and a woman, Holly and Benjamin carried opposite energies into the world, but they were always equal co-creators of their fairy tale. Benjamin was a hero who stepped on an unusual journey, but his woman initiated his path. This story is an adventure of a woman as she uses her man's energy to create the world of her dreams. Holly desired to be saved through love. If she didn't call for help, Benjamin would continue fighting his wars. As a man, Benjamin dreamed to discover the deepest treasures of his essence and he asked spirits to show him the entry point into another realm, where he could uncover his unique masculine strength and spiritual talents. He embraced the most complex test of his life, when he agreed to meet Holly. He desired to walk a path of trials, and challenges. Through temperance he dreamed to find the purpose that would make his soul shine.

Benjamin tried many things to find a path to become a true magician, but it turned out that he needed to fall in love with this complex lady named Holly, to experience the pains of grief and to cry from a broken heart. That is how Benjamin woke up in an entirely new reality, fully committing his energies to fulfill the requests of his princess. Angels created a new world for Benjamin and timed everything so perfectly that he almost slipped into this new, supernatural life through cracks in time and space. One moment our knight was editing a political art film, and the next moment he was writing a love poem to a woman he had known for just a few days.

On November 14, 2020, Benjamin woke up feeling like a new human. He sensed the immense strength in his heart, finally ready to claim his spiritual sword. He was genuinely happy that morning. He accepted the lessons from positive or negative experiences equally, absolving previous resentments, failures and disappointments. Each of his trials was important for his growth. Benjamin always knew he could heal and enlighten the world with his spiritual guidance. He strongly believed that humans could only be who they were created to be. Still, the pressures of pure survival turned him into a hermit in exile. He was frustrated that he still had not received his righteous sword. He thought he completed every required task but remained an apprentice for years, battling through contradictions and rejections. Hiding from the world, while full of disillusionment, one day Benjamin finally found unconditional love for himself. As he tried and failed, as he descended into the sins of the world and returned back, our knight discovered his divine path. He fully embraced his destiny from a place of honesty and courage. He completely surrendered to his heart and intuitively opened a portal of direct communication with the spiritual realm, finally accepting their higher guidance.

Benjamin felt somewhat perplexed during his morning routine, looking towards the unknown abyss. He was exhausted, processing many things at once, but he finally felt whole in his heart, empowered to move beyond his self-imposed limitations. Subtle confidence enveloped him when he remembered he had spent last night with Holly's soul in the dream world without ever seeing her eyes in person. Benjamin's conversation with Phillip drew Eurydice's attention, and she arrived to listen in secret. Once she attested that Benjamin was falling for her, she presented herself in the dream state since it is the most comfortable realm for interactions between souls. In his dream, Benjamin appeared in an unknown mysterious forest, which he had never visited. The silhouette of Holly, her soft hand, and the walk through the pitch-black forest presented a tale of his possible future. At the end of the dream, he briefly saw the eyes of his princess. The vision convinced Benjamin to face Holly and suffer for love. Benjamin haven't even seen the face of this woman, but he knew he would fall in love tonight.

With joyful, yet conflicting anticipation, Benjamin went to buy Holly a gift. He knew nothing about this woman except how her hands looked, so he resorted to his usual choices – a bottle of French champagne and an exquisite box of bath salt. But Benjamin wanted to be remembered, so he searched for a personal gift to make him stand out among her other suitors. He entered a bookstore with that simple wish. Benjamin mindlessly browsed through the endless shelves, trying to trust his inner feelings while reminiscing about his dream. Suddenly he stumbled on Lana Del Rey's poetry book she published just a few weeks ago. Without second-guessing, Benjamin grabbed two copies of the book – one for Holly and one for himself. Benjamin felt his woman would enjoy these rhymes, and they could connect through them.

Once Benjamin returned home, Wilhelm arrived with a visit. He sympathized that Benjamin was exhausted and worn off from his former spiritual battles, but he explained that a new, grander one was about to commence. It would be a battle for love and emotional bliss to fill Benjamin's heart's chalice to the brim and share this healing energy with the world. It seemed like a beautiful battle to fight for – Benjamin dreamed that his heart could overflow with love and forgiveness. But Wilhelm also said that this journey would be arduous and require years of work. Yet our knight was ready to embrace his new reality outlined by Nature and the inevitable sacrifices.

Benjamin understood the value of this unique divine opportunity which life presented to him. After Wilhelm left, Benjamin intuitively opened an empty notebook, took a pen, and wrote down the story of his dream. Before seeing his enigmatic Holly in person, he wanted to capture his initial perception of her. Benjamin was unaware that his muse had already sent her inspirational magic in his direction. She created this dream, which compelled Benjamin to write. Through poetry, he entered into a place that Holly whispered in the dream, - the town of Sechelt. He knew such a place existed not far from Vancouver but had never been there. Yet he was confident he spent last night in Sechelt with the soul of his beloved woman.

Benjamin closed his eyes, trembling with unknown sensations. Suddenly Holly took complete control over his thoughts, feelings, and dreams. He had never seen this woman's face; he only briefly saw her eyes in the dream, he knew about her existence only for eight days, but now he felt as if he always knew this woman. Somehow, he felt she was a part of him and this love for her felt incredibly familiar. Benjamin realized that free will was about embracing what your soul have prepared for you. It was an uncomfortable realization, but our knight felt how love was already spreading through his body. He felt he must follow this woman. In the pursuit of happiness, Benjamin jumped into the abyss of the unknown, of pain and hardships, with a hope to emerge renewed. He saw Holly as his ultimate life teacher. He was ready to face love, face a girl, but ultimately face himself.

Sechelt forest, Sechelt land

I woke up in the woods in the middle of the night. It's
    pitch dark.
I don't know how I got here, and I can barely see a thing through a
    mist;
As I have never been here physically, I'm puzzled. What is this place?
This forest is foreign to me, yet it feels like home.

And then I hear a voice in front of me
A most graceful and mellifluous voice,
Most gentle, carrying, and sweet
The melody of my woman, whom I've never met:

"Shishalh, Shishalh, Shishalh
Sechelt, Sechelt, Sechelt
Please take my hand; my poet, take my hand
My soulmate, my teacher, my friend
My traitor, my husband, my lad
Defend this hand, you held through times
Each time we lied
Each time we cried
Each time I died
I'm reaching out to confide
Amazing reminiscences
Of the many mysteries we shared
Through my spellbinding fingers.

I'm a white girl of Scandinavian descent
But I was born on this enchanted land
Like warrior sisters who fought till the end
Like shamans, empowered by the slain in Sechelt.

They come to me in dreams and visions,
We meet under the shining moon

*Next to the sparkling waters of forgiveness
To drum together healing tunes...
Without them, I'm nothing
Without us, they're dead forever
So we're together here to speak
As no one ever dies to perish.*

*They are grand, but who am I?
And why do we share poetic rhymes?
We live as one, but we don't look alike,
Their lake reflections are not like mine –
My skin is pale and strangely bright
Their skin is of the other kind –
Yet, we're forever intertwined,
Transmitting the same angelic light.*

*I've scattered blessings left and right
But spirits chose me for my might
So please, my dearest weirdest knight,
Envelop me in your romantic light.*

*Sechelt, Sechelt, Sechelt
Shishalh, Shishalh, between the waters shines my land*

*My soulmate, please look after me
Your Russian language is so alien in here
But next to me, you will be free
Once we will mend our hearts.*

*So take my hand, my poet, take my hand,
My prophet, my lover, my friend
Allow me to show you the dreams we can share,
With dreamers who lived in Sechelt."*

*I'm so bewildered as I follow her,
What is this place she calls Sechelt?*

I never walked upon that land
But what she says feels so correct
And now her shadow silhouette
Uplifts me with her passionate intent
I know this lady, but we've never met
As I forgot old dramas of our tragical duet
But she'll escort me through this land
Through the dreamy forest of her mystical Sechelt.

As we have reached the shores
She wanted to retreat
But I adored her with my gaze
And now she can't compete
With feelings from past lives
Arising to the surface
And so she stays with me
To cuddle on my shoulder.

The morning sun appears to shatter our convictions,
As we're amazed and chained to view
Intensely lucid, bright predictions
Of the tragic love that we'll pursue.

She led me to the light through her night forest
She has explained why we are here
She's guiding me to find my purpose
And I will take away her sins and fears.

Our love is shining through surrender
Through hands, we cherish with a grace
Through eyes, we know; that live forever
Through touches, we may once embrace.

CHAPTER III

When Benjamin returned from the first date with his princess, he quickly fell asleep. The feeling of the highest love brought a state of complete peace upon Benjamin. Only this night turned into something unprecedented as seeing Holly's eyes opened up his supernatural and mystic powers. Throughout the night, Benjamin saw a stream of intense, torturing memory flashes from another lifetime. The dream was lucid and realistic but also very dark. Neither Benjamin nor Eurydice died peacefully in that life, but that was the reality for many souls who lived through the ugliness of the Second World War. The souls of our lovers carried severe trauma after their brutal deaths, which Damian used to create new traps.

Benjamin woke up the following morning with a severe panic attack. He gasped for air, and tears poured from his eyes. "Holly is dead! Holly is dead. I can feel this. She was killed last night!" Benjamin screamed aloud. He realized that he was not a Benjamin but his past self. He looked at the mirror and saw the body of a woman named Camilla. He scanned the room, but this was not his apartment. He stepped on the balcony, and instead of Vancouver's West End, he saw the third arrondissement of Paris in the summer of 1938.

At thirty-three years old, Camilla was a high-ranking Wehrmacht spy fighting against Soviet Empire. Camilla led a French cell of five incredibly talented spies. The Wehrmacht hired her in 1930 as a translator, but her innate talents were acknowledged immediately. At the same time, she worked for American intelligence services, convincing them she was a double agent when in reality, she exploited their recourses in a way she felt noble, to fight Russians.

Eurydice embodied Camilla's most intelligent and trustworthy asset, known as Eloise. On the day of this brutal nightmare, where a maniac tortured Eloise to death, during her last mission, the Second World War has begun for Camilla, even though the Sudetenland annexation and the

Molotov-Ribbentrop pact were only the prospects of the future. Seeing the harrowing images, in her sleep, Camilla felt they were real. She knew Eloise was dead, even though she hadn't received any sound confirmation. As she shared a deep soul connection with Eloise, Camilla inconsolably cried on the balcony, trying to reason with her heart. She hoped she was mistaken, but the reality slowly creped in and Camilla was faced with accepting that the love of her life was gone.

The highest ideals, morals, and beliefs evaporate at any war once it becomes personal. Eloise died at the hands of the Soviets, so for Camilla, each person, who identified themselves with diabolical Soviet ideology, was her sworn enemy. She no longer cared about the future of her kingdom of Germany; now, it became about vengeance for her. In any way the God would allow, how she often liked to say. She only wanted to avenge her soulmate with the full force of her status. She had no other motifs to continue being a spy, as the world was rapidly crumbling.

Camilla and Eloise worked together for years to prevent the next world war. They firmly believed in protecting Europe from the ideology of Tyranny. For almost two decades, the leaders of the Soviet Empire tried to impose Tyranny on many kingdoms through coercion, propaganda, widespread terrorist attacks, and wars. And by 1938, the new face of Tyranny had also emerged in the kingdom of Germany, Camilla's homeland. She was a true patriot of her nation, believing the new war would never be in the best interest of her people. She believed in a free and prosperous kingdom of Germany, while Eloise felt the same about her homeland, the French Empire. The love between these two women was so strong that it protected the French Empire, as it never endured the Soviet occupation, unlike most European kingdoms. For Camilla, safeguarding Eloise's homeland and preserving the spirit of freedom was imperative. Our soulmates bravely assisted in stopping the Soviet Empire from building a worldwide slave system.

Initially, Camilla and Eloise only gathered intelligence, but by 1937 the reality constructed by the vile military actions of the Soviet Empire, bringing creeping occupation upon its neighbors, dramatically changed the minds of Europeans. Soon our soulmates would be tasked to murder Soviet agents by the Wehrmacht orders. Even though many German generals hoped to lead the country out of the inevitable madness, Camilla never blindly followed their orders. She had the same strategy working for Americans and exercised caution with every operation she created. Camilla and Eloise always trusted their feminine intuition, and did what resonated in their hearts. They always felt a sense of purpose after every successful operation, the one they believed in. Yet by 1938, they were already murdering the traitors of Germany as the civil war between the Wehrmacht and the SS escalated.

As a head of operations, Camilla always carefully considered the decision to eliminate the target. She needed irrefutable proof of the real crime or truly malicious intent before proceeding with such mission. She believed in a level playing field and followed her integrity. When they were required to eliminate an asset, Camilla ensured it was undoubtedly necessary. She avoided murdering another human, but Soviet agents became more violent, so the power dynamics of the conflict changed. Camilla and Eloise understood professional risks but were ready to die for their beliefs. Our ladies used poison as their weapon of choice, like their Soviet enemies. They handled guns and knives, but poison felt closer to their female hearts. Like a gentle touch, it took lives away more peacefully. And if you, my dear reader, can picture Eloise's incredible beauty and radiating allure, you would say that corrupt men were lucky to die at the hands of this stunningly gorgeous, tall French blonde. Most men embraced dying in her arms, as her seductive and playful nature made their last minutes unforgettably special.

On the night of Eloise's death, Camilla guided her soulmate again through the plan of their operation, and both cried from laughter, discussing how every man turns weak in Eloise's presence. Lustfully craving her, they would completely forget their ideology and affiliations. In her presence they only wanted to touch Eloise's naked body, so she played her targets gracefully and exquisitely.

Yet something went wrong during Eloise's last mission. When Camilla replayed the details of her nightmarish dream where she oversaw Eloise's murder from the soul level, she spotted an otherworldly presence. She couldn't explain her sensations with her rational mind. Camilla always trusted her reason, but today the sobering sensation of supernatural presence enveloped her heart. Her female intuition overpowered her mind, and she trusted her highest inner voice. Something terrifying happened in that room, and only demonic and mystical explanations made sense to Camilla.

The dream memories from last night appeared before Camilla's eyes again. Her soul was next to Eloise, and she witnessed her murder in vivid detail. Once Eloise arrived at her victim's apartment, expecting him to be alone, another man showed up. Damian possessed a friend of her target. This man stabbed Eloise from behind driven by the demonic being inside of him. The knife entered Eloise's body under her left shoulder blade and pierced through her heart. Camilla witnessed how Damian continued his ritualistic dance around Eloise's motionless body, peeling her skin from her left shoulder down to her breast and then to her waist. He enjoyed every one of his multiple strikes as blood quickly filled the room. The face of this man was ecstatically demonic. He didn't know that Eloise worked for the Wehrmacht. He killed her for pure enjoyment.

Eloise's death set Camilla on a mission to uncover the truth about Damian. Dark Prince forced Eurydice to run in terror from her body so she would be entangled in demonic nightmares of death, convinced that Camilla betrayed Eloise. Damian deprived Eurydice of one of the most significant gifts of life – the ability to observe the unfolding events triggered by death and properly analyze the entirety of life from higher perspective. Souls retrospectively look at their past to accept life's lessons, observe the actions of their soulmates, grasp their impact on the world, embrace the consequences of their actions, and, most importantly, understand who truly loved them.

As Camilla tried to process her visions, paralyzed by this drama, she understood how powerful her connection with Eloise was. She didn't know what exactly happened to Eloise or whether she was alive. Yet she knew that her dream was as real as anything she had experienced in her waking life. She was next to her beloved in some magical way, and she was convinced she witnessed what truly happened that night. While Camilla cried over Eloise, she realized she also cried for Paris. She observed the streets of her beloved city, and a new sensation struck her heart. The air in Paris felt differently as demonic spirits descended upon this magical city. Camilla struggled to breathe from her tears, realizing what was coming.

Benjamin jumped from his bed once the dream abruptly ended. He was hysterically crying in his Vancouver apartment, finally awakened.

Emotions overwhelmed him, and he felt like he was going insane from the perplexity of his predicament. He couldn't stop crying for hours, as if grieving Holly's death, although his rational mind knew she was alive. Camilla's tears became Benjamin's, and her emotions turned into his physical pains, but slowly, he returned to his present reality, reminiscing about last night's magic. The memory of Holly's eyes brought joy to Benjamin's heart, which was scared by night visions. Soon our knight cried happy tears too. Eloise was not dead, as she was alive as Holly. She transcended death because Benjamin could remember her.

Illuminating love and peaceful bliss enveloped Benjamin as he danced through the room to his favorite songs. "She is here! I have found her; my sufferings finally paid off," Benjamin proclaimed ecstatically. He thanked spiritual beings for helping him to find Holly, but most importantly, he was grateful that his heart could love like that. But when Lana Del Rey's *Tomorrow Never Came* suddenly started playing, another wave of dark memories descended on Benjamin. The song was about two lovers who drifted apart, but the lyrics reminded Benjamin of another story from the day of Eloise's death.

Camilla came to the Luxembourg garden, where she was supposed to meet Eloise for a debrief. She spent hours waiting on their designated bench, hoping she was wrong about her premonitions, but Eloise never showed up. It was getting darker, and the pouring rain descended on Paris as Nature cried in unison over Eloise's tragic death. Soaking wet, Camilla realized her visions had to be true, and her tears merged with the rain. Benjamin experienced every part of that memory, as the song had transported him into that space and time, immersing him in Camilla's emotions. Like in the song, Camilla waited for Eloise on a park bench, in the pouring rain, yet she never came. Through his tears, Benjamin sang lyrics, addressing them to Holly.

Tomorrow never came for Eloise, and Camilla's life was never the same after that day. After seeing this memory, Benjamin realized it was also true for him. Benjamin saw in Holly's eyes the genuine truth of her heart. He was convinced it was impossible to say 'I know you' to another person on the first date without feeling a sense of a divine connection. But Benjamin knew he was not of Holly's status and couldn't offer official courtship to his princess due to his financial insolvency. Still, his elevating love blinded his rational mind. He wanted to run to Holly, bring her coffee in bed and cook breakfast for her. He wished she would join him on a walk around the seawall or maybe watch a movie under a cozy blanket. His mind was racing between dreams and fantasies, so he called Wilhelm for guidance.

"I feel that I won't see Holly for some time. Is it true?" Benjamin was scared to ask.

"Yes, you won't speak with Holly, text her, or see her until your next scheduled encounter." Wilhelm patiently and supportively explained the future to Benjamin.

"So, what do I do? I can't just sit here with my love for her. I want to embrace, praise, and protect her. I wish to dance with her. Can I at least send her flowers?"

"You can't send her flowers. You must wait, cherish every memory, and honor every longing emotion you feel towards this woman. This experience was created to temper you and answer the higher questions of your soul. The only way to find out why she was murdered last time is to commit to this process. Through learning yourself, you will become a magician and understand the essence of death." Wilhelm's compassionate tone calmed Benjamin.

"I see. You've mentioned another meeting. When can I expect that?" Benjamin was still on edge, no matter how much he tried to contain his boiling emotions.

"It will happen around Christmas, and it will cost you another ounce of gold."

"What? Only in six weeks? I've barely survived a few hours without her. I can't wait for that long. And another ounce? Where do you think I can get that? My contract ends next week, and I don't have any more savings." Now, Benjamin was angry at life. Resentment was raising up inside of him. His angels demanded a higher commitment to his faith, and our knight was on the brink of rejecting his spiritual beliefs as he questioned his sanity. Benjamin felt like the skies cursed him and created an elaborate trap to ruin him. His self-esteem and confidence crumbled.

"Everything is revealing itself when it should. You need to trust your story; your soul asked for every pain of it. Don't worry about finances; we will arrange a new contract for you, longer than usual, so you will have enough funds to cover my fee, the restaurant, and buy Holly birthday gifts." Wilhelm reassured his apprentice.

"Her birthday? Wait, when is her birthday?" Benjamin got confused.

"Close to your next approved meeting. Once we determine the best suitable date for a channel, you will hear from us and act accordingly. After that meeting, your story will resume only in three years." Wilhelm's words sent shock waves through Benjamin's body.

"I won't see her for three years! I can't last three years without those beautiful eyes, perfect smile, graceful presence and melodic voice. I can't, no, no, no, I can't." Benjamin could barely stay conscious; he wanted to vanish from the face of the Earth.

"Brace yourself. You are a true magician, and we are supporting you. This is your highest destiny. The skies and lands will show you a way if you commit to this journey. You need to do so much spiritual work during these three years that you won't have time for Holly. Being away from the love provides you the path to higher healing, and that would lead you to graduate as a true magician. Deep down, you know why you ought to live through this pain."

"Yes, I do. From life to life, I could never accept her death. She died so many times in my arms, but I couldn't properly process my intense suffering. I always rejected reality, blocking away the teachings my grief was bringing me. I felt the angels treated us unfairly. I was angry at life so many times. I can easily accept any other death, but not hers, anyone else but not her. I demanded to take me instead of her. Such a marvelous being must always be alive and shine her beautiful light. If we would be apart for years, it would feel like she is dead. I will confront many nightmares about her tragic past until my fear evaporates. For me, it's the only way to flourish and not be crippled by grief. While living without her, I will cry every day like she's gone. I know I've asked for this experience, but I don't think I have the words to convey how painful it feels to endure her death. Yet I must face my torments. I will have to experience her death two times in this life. This is my punishment. This is how I could heal myself from that never-ending grief that lives in my soul," Benjamin blurted out passionately and began crying.

Wilhelm didn't need to add anything. His apprentice understood himself. Every word Benjamin said was a complete truth. His soul requested to heal this deep trauma, defeat Damian, and find a way to safeguard Eurydice in the future. Benjamin had to uncover the truth behind Eloise's death. Benjamin looked at Wilhelm with confidence, assertiveness, and determination, thanking his guide for the encouragement on this quest. Suddenly everything Benjamin valued in his life became trivial and insignificant. Now he could only live in a world of Holly.

As Wilhelm left, a new oracle vision about Holly's future descended upon Benjamin. He saw Holly living peacefully in her dream house, hidden in Sechelt forests. She gracefully danced through her cherished home during the morning routine, delighted with her life. She packed lunches for her children – a boy of eight and a girl a year younger. Both were happy around their mother. Benjamin sensed that this house was protected by a loving man, a devoted husband, and a kind father. Benjamin slowly immersed into this prevision, as children, with a loving kiss from Holly, left for school. Now he could see himself at the table across from Holly. Sitting in complete silence, their eyes talked with devotion, affection, and deep understanding. Their souls merged. As Holly took Benjamin's hand, he could clearly hear what her heart was saying. "Thank you, my dear gentleman. I'm forever grateful that you never abandoned me and shielded me from the darkness. I see the pain you have endured. I will never forget what you did for me. Thank you, Benjamin."

Our knight opened his eyes and smiled from the warmth of this vision. He cried again from the beauty of their romantic moment. *Even if it's just a dream, even if I'll fail, I'm determined to try to build a future for Holly. I trust my heart*, Benjamin thought. *I only dream of hearing these words of appreciation. I don't need any other rewards in this life. I won't die peacefully if I don't try.*

Later in the day, our knight reached out to his brother, hoping to share his torments and ask for support. Phillip sold a painting online, so he invited Benjamin to share a bottle of wine in the Red Accordion restaurant. Another stream of visions overwhelmed Benjamin when he joined Phillip at the table next to the fireplace. Phillip was in the life of Camilla too. He was Camilla's dear friend and a passionate lover Werner. Camilla even considered him the love of her life until she met Eloise, while Werner left Camilla for Suzanne. Yet despite their complex romantic entanglements, Werner was one of Camilla's most trusted people in Paris and Berlin. A new set of tears streamed from Benjamin as he recalled how Camilla told Werner about Eloise's death in one Parisian restaurant that had a very similar décor to this place.

Battling his emotions, Benjamin told his brother how he madly fell for Holly and confessed the visions of the past and future. Benjamin cried, describing Holly's children, convinced that if Eloise didn't experience a full life, never fulfilling her dream of motherhood, it meant that Benjamin must give such a life for Holly. Benjamin felt indebted to his woman, as he was the one who sent Eloise to her death. Our knight's determination, passion, and assertiveness shined through tears. As Phillip consoled his brother, both found great comfort in their beautiful camaraderie as without each other they would never endure this unusual spiritual path. Our knights were only temporary residents in Vancouver, scared every day they might be sent back to the Russian Empire. Still, they were determined to fight for their future here, as now they couldn't abandon their women. Benjamin and Phillip saw how supernatural forces guided them through life to arrive at this moment. The chances that both of them would find their soulmates in Vancouver were next to impossible.

After dinner, Phillip stayed overnight at Benjamin's place. In the middle of the night, Phillip woke up to Benjamin's high-pitched howls. "Help me! Please help me! Help me!" Benjamin screamed repeatedly as his body trembled, articulating these words. Phillip shook Benjamin to wake him up from the nightmare.

"What's going on?" Benjamin was trying to catch his breath from a panic attack.

"You screamed 'Help me' in your dream, and I got scared for you," Phillip said.

"I did? Did I say anything else?"

"You asked for help, but you did it in a female voice."

Benjamin calmed himself with slow breaths, and magical images flashed before his eyes. "Holly's soul tries to establish a contact."

"If that's the case, then you have a new student."

Although Phillip only began his education as a spiritual guide and didn't have a lot of students, Benjamin was already quite advanced in this role. His soul fully claimed this power five centuries ago. It didn't matter if he lived a life of a healer, a politician, a spy, and now an artist, he always trained other souls on their spiritual paths. This was his divine purpose. Each soul came to Benjamin with different issues, requiring a catered approach. He worked through dreams, rituals, meditations, hypnosis, direct conversations with the soul, and physical interactions with their embodiments. Benjamin carried a magical talent – he could see any soul's highest essence and purpose as well as their past traumas. Since the souls made the same mistakes life after life, Benjamin trained them to reclaim their powers and heal through integration of traumatic lessons. Benjamin was thankful for his students, as he only advanced through their questions and requests. He had his own repetitive mistakes, but through embracing his experiences, tragic deaths, and unusual divine purpose, he could empower other souls to do the same.

Souls came to Benjamin for several reasons. Some were stranded, seeking a guide who would wake them up from the numbing trance. Some slowly descended into the dark Underworld, where they would be lost. In such cases, Benjamin acted like an emergency room doctor, creating an emotional shock with his magic to reconnect a physical vessel with their soul. Most souls arrived asking about their purpose and how to embrace their spiritual powers. In these instances, Benjamin acted as a therapist who guided clients to release their past insecurities and live more fulfilling lives. Also, many of Benjamin's female patients asked for relationship advice, hoping to understand whether their chosen men could shield them from the demonic creatures.

Some souls experienced trouble communicating with their physical vessels. The souls knew themselves, but they often needed to learn how to talk to their bodies in a way that would serve their higher purpose. Sometimes souls didn't like their current form, rejecting to accept why they chose a certain body. There were many different reasons why a soul would choose a specific body, and Benjamin could always find a spiritual explanation, which empowered every soul. It is imperative for any soul to live in sync with their highest potential, so often they required simple encouragement and reassurance. Since Benjamin could see them for who they were, they didn't need to hide their true essence and could comfortably be themselves. Being seen and recognized was enough for them. Our knight inspired many souls by acknowledging their talents.

As each soul has a unique purpose, the healing and training approach has to align with their nature. When Benjamin agreed to teach a soul, he needed to consider many details and nuances. Like any doctor, he was also required to express verbal consent and willingness to help a soul. He always honored the balance of giving and receiving energies, so he asked souls to pay him with any energy or knowledge they could share. Benjamin wouldn't grow as a teacher without his clueless students, who often asked unexpected and challenging questions. Benjamin never looked down at inexperienced souls. He healed from a place of forgiveness, compassion, and love, never demanding achievements, and allowing souls to accept or reject his guidance. He explained to souls how they could empower themselves to achieve their highest missions, dreams, and desires, but he never expected from them certain results, as they had free will.

As Holly was Benjamin's soulmate, he proclaimed to help her soul without second-guessing. Only one thing still puzzled Benjamin. Usually, when a soul would come to him, he would clearly see their presence in the form of a transparent and glowing human made of energy. He saw the quantum beings made of light like he saw anything else in this world. Only Holly's soul never physically materialized, which confused Benjamin. If their connection were so powerful, he would see Holly's soul more vividly than any other, but visions of her were vague, dark and murky, as if she was in some distant reality.

Benjamin assumed that Eurydice was slowly descending into the Underworld, towards death. He didn't want to jump to conclusions, but only this explanation made sense. Holly was losing connection with her soul, as she stopped listening to the feelings of her beautiful heart. Benjamin saw the love in her eyes, but that was the love her soul was emitting. Their date was her last desperate attempt to be seen by saying, "I know you." Eurydice realized that only this phrase would inspire Benjamin to continue his pursuit. She screamed it through the thick walls that Holly built around her heart. Damian found a way to break Holly's heart through her first romantic encounters, so she built sophisticated walls and rejected Benjamin's love. Damian trapped her in the personality of her social mask, forcing her to reject her feminine intuition. Now Holly wasn't allowed to be loved.

Three days later, Benjamin suddenly burst into tears while having dinner alone in his apartment. He talked aloud through the tears, "Please help me. I can't stand this anymore. I'm trapped, and I'm abused. I don't know what to do." These were not his tears nor his words. He knew that Holly's soul spoke through him. Benjamin finally had a real contact with her, so he proceeded with his usual rituals, connecting to Holly's soul through the sensory deprivation trance. He submerged in the bathtub in complete darkness, leaving only his nose and mouth above the water. As he slowly entered the familiar spiritual plane, he sensed the presence of Holly's soul, but she was distant and covered in dark, thick veils. Her reality looked eerie and unsettling. Benjamin felt frustrated as his magic was still weak, but suddenly, he started to shake uncontrollably in the bathtub as if his entire body was in pain. He screamed out loud, "Stop! Just stop this! I can't take it anymore! I want to get out. They are using me, but I can't stop this. Never-ending abuses, never-ending exploitation, and rape. I'm not a slave; I want to be free! I want to feel. I want to be seen. I want to be loved!"

Benjamin exited his trance, processing what he had just said. He was tired from his job as an assistant film editor, feeling underpaid and under-appreciated, enduring long hours behind the computer with multiple tasks at hand. Everything that he said out loud could be said about him. He was an immigrant in this new land, selling his talents for pennies, and it didn't matter how burned-out he felt; he was forced to continue doing this job, as it was the only way to make a living.

Still, Benjamin felt these words were not about him. He dived again. He appeared in Holly's apartment flying near the ceiling. He observed Holly on the couch under a blanket with her cat Mr. Dance next to her as she was crying wretchedly, unable to stop. Something traumatic happened to her. Our soulmates had similar perceptions of reality – they felt undervalued, miserable, enslaved, and trapped in their conditions, unable to find a way out. Both tried to escape their realities. Their hearts knew they were not living their higher lives, but they didn't know how to get where they needed to be.

For the next hour, Benjamin observed Holly crying while he spiritually shielded her aura. Then he drifted deeper into her world and finally saw a silhouette of her soul, which was also crying relentlessly. Once Benjamin returned back, he cried together with Holly, sitting in his bathtub. Our knight didn't know what to do. He could always establish contact with any soul, but not this time. He prayed for assistance, and his guides appeared, telling him to send Holly a direct message on Twitter. This was his only contact with her. This message had to feel intrusive, as if reaching into her essence. It had to express Benjamin's electroshock magic to break through Holly's heart walls. He felt it was ethical to do because her soul reached for help, and he couldn't stop crying after seeing Holly's miseries. He wanted her to feel loved and protected. He grabbed his phone and typed, 'Hi, dear Holly. I'm next to you. I can't stop crying for the last few days, but I will fight this with you. I saw so much about you, your past, and your future. My oracle readings about you turned out to be a hundred percent accurate. Too bad I can't see you, but I'm counting the days until our next meeting. It just looks so impossible, as there's so much going on, but I'm holding your hands and covering you.'

He felt complete bliss and absolute magical peace after he sent this message. Even though Holly hadn't read the message yet, her soul saw Benjamin's action and intent. She calmed down as she perceived Benjamin's message as a written consent to help her.

An hour later, Benjamin sensed the complete shift of reality. Holly read his message, and she was furious. She cursed Benjamin for daring to write to her in such a way. Now our princess faced a choice, a crossroads on her path. She knew what she felt towards Benjamin was real, but she couldn't allow herself to be hurt again. After her traumatic teenage experiences, Holly's mind perceived any man as a liar who is incapable of loving her unconditionally, who would never accept her scars and wounds. Holly believed Benjamin wanted to manipulate her. She was truthful with him, but the vulnerable emotions of an intimate romance were not in her plans. Holly was only twenty-three, and she desired to live her careless youth without obligations and commitments, allowing only transient suitors in her life, who would make her life fun.

Rationally, she could not see Benjamin as the man of her dreams. For her, he was nothing but, as she perceived him too complex, weird, and, most importantly, foreign to her reality and persona, she wore as a shield. When the mind and the heart meet in such fierce battles, the only correct solution would be to follow the heart, but Holly's presented reality was too demanding to allow such a choice. Her mind explained her experience with Benjamin as another girly crash and a sophisticated game Benjamin created to seduce her. Now, she felt her boundaries were violated since the tone of

Benjamin's message was deeply personal. She felt agitated and annoyed by his advances, as if Benjamin had reached into her soul, and she didn't like that feeling. Holly knew she was way out of his league in physical appearance and social status. She craved a luxurious lifestyle, filled with superficial sparkling experiences, which only Damian could give her right now. Only she didn't know that by following his elaborate illusion, he would eventually demand her life in return.

As you may have realized, my dear reader, everything that Holly experienced was created by Damian long ago. He planted the seeds of destruction as he used Holly's first lovers to craft negative perceptions of men. Damian created an entirely separate world for Holly. He shifted her reality, ensuring that messages from her soul would always be distorted. The concept of choice is intertwined with the law of free will – a person must choose which road to take and suffer the inevitable outcomes of that choice. With free will, Holly wished to find salvation and love, so Nature presented Holly with an opportunity, and Benjamin appeared on her path with unconditional love. Yet she refused to believe his feelings were genuine. Rejection of divine opportunity starved her soul even further when Holly chose not to answer Benjamin.

About an hour later, Benjamin received a call from Becky. Benjamin was puzzled as Becky avoided communicating with him. She didn't trust him and believed he badly influences Phillip. When Benjamin picked up the phone, drunk Becky addressed him in a low, manly, dark voice. As her aura was weak after many demonic attacks, Damian entered her once she had too many drinks. Abusing alcohol allows demonic entities to enter human bodies, as our aura is much weaker when we're intoxicated. Consuming spirits means inviting spirits, and sinister beings arrive to control human actions.

Damian embodied Becky to relay a message to Benjamin. "Hi, Benjamin. I know what you are trying to do, but you will fail. Holly made her choice just now. She wants to be with me, and I won't let her go. I worked so hard to achieve this, as you know how precious she is to me. I'm here to collect what she owns me. She has to die to enrich me. I've been fighting for this far too long. I'm already in her heart, Benjamin. Stop your pursuit, otherwise I promise I will ruin you too. Stop now and save yourself. Soon her soul will be forever mine."

Benjamin felt the danger in the air as if otherworldly darkness enveloped his apartment. Still, he believed in the power of true love, realizing Damian tries to intimidate him into giving up. Benjamin replied assertively, "I will not step away. I will fight for her because I love her. Who are you, and why are you fighting against us?"

"We should meet then. I will reach out with details soon." Becky suddenly switched to her usual voice, mumbled something inarticulate about protecting Phillip from Benjamin's influence. Then she abruptly ended the call, embarrassed by what she said and how drunk she was.

CHAPTER IV

Eight days later, Benjamin was invited to meet his rival on the planet owned by Damian's friends. Dark Prince allowed Benjamin to come with his brother. Our knights explored the city before meeting with Damian. This planet had only one continent, encompassed by water, and everything on that land was built in the Gothic style. Our knights decided to call this place a European Planet. The architecture and the vibe of that place resembled old Europe before the world war, with a thick, misty air of suppressed freedom that felt toxic and suffocating. It was the natural state of this place as it was a home of demonic creatures. No balancing energies of light existed here. Only trapped and stranded souls were allowed to visit this planet. The reality of this land was skewed into darkness, so Damian built one of his main residences here.

Benjamin had a chance to meet with Holly, before facing Damian. Phillip stayed outside while Benjamin entered the apartment where Holly was waiting for him. Dressed only in lingerie, she greeted him, and they settled for a talk on the edge of the bed. Benjamin realized right away that this was a trap. As Holly hugged him, Benjamin sensed it was not his woman. She looked like Holly, smelled like Holly, and even acted like Holly, yet Benjamin knew she was trapped by her own image. Her body didn't belong to her anymore, detached from her unconscious self and her true heart. Benjamin knew his woman too well and realized what had happened. His feelings reminded him of the movie *Meet Joe Black*, where the evil spirit takes the body of a man trapped in a coma with a desire to experience the life of a human being. The woman who fell in love with the man sensed that Joe Black was not the man she met on their first encounter. He looked the same, but there was something off about him. As his personality was hijacked and his heart was entrapped, she experienced the same sensations as Benjamin – their beloved was somehow replaced.

Benjamin played along when he realized what this evil spirit did to his soulmate. Holly asked Benjamin to come later and spend a night of lust with her. Benjamin promised to return, but the minute he reunited with Phillip, he described the trap and told his brother he wouldn't come back. If Benjamin slept with Holly that night, Damian would infuse him with dark creatures that would destroy him from within, and our knight would be defeated. No matter how much Benjamin desired to make love with his woman, it was not possible anymore.

After visiting Holly, our knights arrived at Damian's mansion just before the guests entered his house for a lavish night party full of deceit and vice. Damian spotted the knights approaching, "Good day, gentlemen. I'm glad you could make it today. We have a lovely evening planned with a special *El Espinazo del Diablo* screening before a night of revel and dancing."

"Amazing movie! Phillip and I love *The Devil's Backbone*. It is a wonderful allegory depicting our lives. Why did you choose it for tonight?" Benjamin replied as if they were best friends. There was something very appealing about this tall, well-dressed, and well-mannered gentleman. Their conversation flowed naturally, as they had known each other for centuries.

"Well, I like this movie because it portrays my true and humble essence. I didn't choose it for my complacency but rather as a perfect artistic creation that beautifully describes the nuances of my intricate nature. Besides, we got lucky tonight, as Guillermo del Toro agreed to present his movie personally, and you know how busy he is. I wouldn't be able to explain myself better than his films do. I see my true glory through his art, as he shows people's miserable desire to live in my kingdom of fear. I don't particularly appreciate how Guillermo exposes the nature of my traps, but he is a noble warrior, and you must respect your adversary, right, Benjamin?"

"Oh, I deeply respect my enemies, especially when they cynically murder my loved ones. Your party sounds enticing, but I'm not sure we can attend it. You would have more fun without us. But would we have the time to talk?"

"Well, I didn't invite you for nothing, dear Benjamin. Allow me to greet the guests first. Then we'll go to my private lounge and discuss our predicament. Oh, and look at this timing! Surely you want to say hi to them." Damian pointed to the next group that arrived at this party. Benjamin and Phillip saw their friends from Saint Petersburg and their mother, Gverina. When our knights left Russian Empire, Damian took control of their lives and led them on the path of darkness, stranding their souls. Now he was parading his achievements, showing Benjamin his abilities.

Their mother, Gverina, was under Damian's spell for years, and he tried to destroy our brothers through her. When they left the Russian Empire, Gverina illegally appropriated the funds that supported our knights during their first years in Vancouver. As they starved because of her actions, they questioned her reasons, but now they understood she had worked for Damian all along. Our Dark Prince telepathically reminded Benjamin and Phillip about one special day. Phillip and Benjamin invited their mother to celebrate their departure from Russian Empire. They shared past stories of their soul connection in passionate and cheerful conversation, happily talking about their adventures, excited about their future in Vancouver. Throughout the evening, Gverina didn't stop drinking. Suddenly, she looked at her sons angrily and screamed, "Mark my words, I will obliterate you in five years!" Benjamin and Phillip were stunned to hear such a statement from their mother, but she was absolutely serious. It was an actual threat. Even though she often acted as an evil stepmother with no love for them, this phrase felt quite bizarre even for her. Once Gverina got drunk, she channeled Damian's message. Damian knew why they were going to Vancouver, and he was warning them. Yet no matter how much Damian tried to break the bond of our brothers, nothing worked.

Damian joyfully paraded how he trapped Benjamin's closest people with his spells. It was a power play to demonstrate what he was capable of. After directing guests to the second floor, Damian invited Benjamin and Phillip to his beautiful parlor. They comfortably settled in the designer chairs next to the fireplace. Phillip acted as a witness during their conversation.

"So, may I ask how you wish to be called this time?" Benjamin was eager to know more about his new reality.

"Of course! Please call me Damian."

"Thank you, Damian, for welcoming us."

"Did you arrive today to state your plans?"

"Indeed. You know that I can't live without Holly."

"Sure, I understand why you are so in love. She has such a unique and complex personality this time. She has ignited my curiosity throughout times with her beautifully strange choices of bodies. And I'm so fascinated by this one. It's my world, Benjamin! I'm having so much fun being her, as she's surrounded by the most malicious people I know. It's amazing. I can do so much with her soul. Look how lost people are in your world. No one cares about nourishing female energies anymore. Even if Eurydice assumes her powers nobody will embrace her healing light. But if I owned her, I could finally destroy the spirit of freedom on this continent. I think you should give up peacefully this time. Surrender, and we will resolve this in the next life."

"Oh, please, be Holly, own Holly. I arrived too late to stop you. I will wait until your time runs out, and then I'll be ready to catch her once you throw her away. I'm tired of your possessiveness. You made her life miserable many times, but now you decided to be her? This is crossing the line. We have to settle this once and for all."

"Well, suit yourself, but she already made her choice. You can't reverse this process. She will surrender to me in about four months. You won't be able to help because I will bleed you at your American battles. You can't choose both. Either choose America or her soul."

"You start to sound like a broken record. You are giving me this choice again. Seriously? I won't fall for your deceptions. You already captured her, so I'm choosing America. Only I won't abandon her, and she will see the truth when I'll expose you."

"I don't think so. She has already lost her soul, and you don't even know if you can save her."

"Trust me, I'm not going to leave her soul behind."

"It's just too much for you, Benjamin. So many things are consuming your energy. Abandon her, and I promise I won't interfere in the American war. I won't even fight for the White House, if you give me Holly's soul right now."

"Holly's soul will be saved, and America will be saved too. I'm strong enough to fight for both. I won't give up no matter what you will do. It may be exhausting, but do you think I don't know my powers?"

"What a statement! It sounds too arrogant even for you. I don't think you understand anything about American Empire. Look around! Most people don't even comprehend your ideas anymore. They praise my achievements and embraced my ideas of slavery while painting you as a horrible man who shouldn't be trusted. You won our last battle, but now two centuries later, everything is reversed. What a disaster, Benjamin! You clearly fought for nothing if America is in such a mess."

"The fact that your supporters are the loudest doesn't make you a winner. People believe in freedom above all, and time will settle us. You are only lucky because the angels took away their protection."

"Sure, whatever you say, but I'm so joyful witnessing how contemptuous and delusional Americans have become. If you have nothing better to do, you can try to persuade them again, but I'm telling you, they are gone to the point of no return."

"The fight for freedom is never-ending through times. The foundation to empower the full force of American spirits was set with the help of my work, and one day it will revive in all its grandness. It will be a new America, with a new Declaration, but built upon the foundation of the old one. It is the right of the people to alter or abolish any form of government that becomes destructive. And one day, Americans will institute a new nation."

"You can tell yourself any fairy tale that helps you sleep at night. Only our forces have captured every part of government and media."

"I can't agree more, but I will take my chances. And I'll be waiting for Holly too."

"I can promise you there will be no escape for Holly this time, as I will be inside her heart very soon. She has no faith in herself or the divine nature of our world. It is so easy to wreak chaos these days. Poor Benjamin. I created my traps for the last eight years, and her soul couldn't do anything because you failed last time. And if you won't be able to heal her wounds, I will take her soul into my kingdom. If you want to fight me, tame your fears and brace yourself. I will surround her with my most trusted demons and immerse her in the shiniest illusions. Seeing how naively she believes in my reality is amusing."

"There's nothing amusing in your abuses. You don't know what kind of love I have for her, so you don't know what's coming for you. I will shield her from every demon you may send her way. I will catch her when you're done."

"Don't worry, Benjamin, when I'm done with her, I will leave a big scar right across her left eye, so everyone will know she betrayed her feminine essence," Damian ran his finger across the left eye, showing how Holly's scar would look. "You will be seeing me every time you will look at her face."

"I will love her even more with that scar. You are so unimaginative, repeating the same things you did in Stockholm, but I healed her scars then, and I will heal them now. It's appalling that you want to be her for your perverted amusement. I won't ever forget that."

"She is my triumph. I could never imagine that she would invite me into her heart. You failed miserably last time, and now you will see the full scale of her sufferings."

"You must know that I'm accepting your challenge."

"Very well, we can call it official then. Now, please excuse me – it looks like Guillermo has arrived. I hope you won't hold this against me."

"Of course, we will continue some other time."

"Yes, see you, boys, soon. We will be around each other for quite a while. Prepare yourself for the coming attacks. I have many special surprises for you. Soon Holly will be mine and I will be destroying people through her."

"I will be waiting with anticipation, Damian. Can I reach out if we need a chat?"

"Certainly! Never hesitate, as your misery is always my pleasure."

As Benjamin returned home from this journey, the world felt different. He made his first official commitment to his woman. If Damian could control Holly, Benjamin must change the world's vibrations with his magic, so he could at least save her soul. Our knight was more determined than ever, and throughout the day, he sensed the presence of Holly's soul in the wakened reality.

Later that day, Benjamin meditated and found himself flying into Holly's bedroom. She was lying on the left side of the bed and wept, holding her hands around her belly, trying to get cozy under the blanket, but nothing could soothe the pain. It was the first day of her female cycle, and it turned out to be unbearably painful one. But then a new miracle happened – Benjamin started to feel Holly's sensations rolling through his body as if he was experiencing her pain, coming from his womb space. He was taking her suffering upon himself, and now it was manifesting in his body. Holly's soul, channeled Holly's sensations into him so that Benjamin could experience the magic of a feminine cycle. He curled up on the floor from intense pain, feeling every nuance of what Holly was enduring. She cursed her state, demanding the pain to stop, rejecting the magical blessings of Mother Nature. The more she fought it, the more darkness surrounded her. Holly never wanted children, so she perceived her cycles as inconvenient misery, that stops her from having fun.

The main purpose of the female cycle, indeed, is to give birth. After fourteen days, a new life emerges inside a womb, but if an egg is not impregnated, it eventually dies. A womb's heart experiencing emotions of grief and they manifest in range of painful sensations. But the cycle carries another important function. As new life emerges, a woman starts to absorb dark essences from the spiritual plane. Enduring negativity, low vibrations, emotional abuses or even demonic attacks over the twenty-one days, a woman collects these energies. Once the new life dies and a woman enters into the state of releasing the dead tissues, she receives a magical opportunity to remove the dark energies she collected. The more darkness she absorbes, the more painful cycle will be. If a man can meditate with his woman and help her release the energetic toxins from her body, synchronizing the spiritual experience with the physical one, the pain could be resolved. Only a loving man can assist in this process, with protective energies that can heal the uterus. Through shared intentions and devotion, the couple has a chance to unite in the intimate harmony of spiritual cleansing.

Of course, a man would never be able to bear all the intensity of the female pain, as the masculine body is not designed to endure such emotions. Holly's soul only channeled these sensations for few moments– enough for Benjamin to understand how Holly's cycle feels. It was the most magical moment Benjamin could dream of, as he received proof that Holly was his destined woman. Benjamin read in the ancient books how the warriors of the past described a deeper understanding of themselves and their women by attuning their lives to female cycles. Surely, Benjamin knew that his experience was limited, as he couldn't be next to Holly physically, but he was still happy to share this experience with his woman on a distance. Benjamin wasn't afraid to face Damian, and now Nature was rewarding him.

Few days later, Wilhelm told Benjamin that their next date should occur on December 26, 2020. Only Holly was battling with her soul again, and didn't respond to the request for this meeting. Benjamin decided to express his longing, and somehow, it happened in English poetry, as if it was the only love language his woman knew. He posted his poem on his Twitter page. The only intended reader was Holly's soul, who saw it right away and used her last chance to fight for her man and their love.

I'm counting days

I'm counting days, 'till seeing you,
As we spend nights revealing
Our feelings of the luscious dreams
And of awake daydreaming.
We're meeting in between the worlds
Of visions, thoughts, and feelings
We meet to bury ancient swords
And witness complex healings.

You draft me lonely day or night
And I appear right near you
I come to you by dint of flight
To astral bed, ethereal.
I come to talk and listen still
And even hold you inly,
In metaphysical realm
Not real, but so appealing.

Our bond with healing fondness blooms
As I see where you're crying
Right on that edge, curled in the womb
While burning world is dying.
I know you're real and do exist
I scroll your pictures, daunted;
Sometimes I even reminisce
When I could sense and hold you.

When we're in bed, where you do sleep
We lie together closely...
Our eyes connect; it is so real,
That tears are flowing, softly.
You tell me stories, ask advice
And I respond with kindness,
Our parts don't touch, defying vice

As we explore tied likeness.

*I'm counting days to be with you
Affection flames my tenet,
I dream behold your eyes in true,
Confess my love, if granted.*

*I feel our bodies far apart
But souls so close together,
This bed is holiest to heart,
Yet I was near it, never.*

*We live, we die, we move and feel,
Trapped in decaying beings,
And yet, we know how we can heal
While living dreams like spirits.*

*The love is real, and words are real
As all our other feelings,
If life's so sensible in here
It means that I'm not dreaming.*

*Now in my wish, I'm next to you,
I heal your stubborn treasures
Protecting space as I construe
Why evils steal your pleasures.*

*My passion carries my frail girl
Her grace is earnest and endearing;
Our souls colliding in a swirl –
Their blissful love looks so idyllic.*

*I'm counting days until it's real,
And I don't feel this torture,
I'm counting days until we feel
No one impedes our fortune.*

I'm counting days until my dreams…
Until the eyes…
Until the lips…
Until I simply hold you.

CHAPTER V

The love overflowed Benjamin's heart, spilling into the world. He never wrote poetry in his life, but since it was the language of the soul of his beloved, he suddenly became a poet. His rhymes captured something intangible – the whirlwind of Benjamin's emotions, visions, dreams, and fears. They became time capsules of specific moments in Benjamin's life, containing the tears of a broken heart. For the first time in his life, poetry became his weapon and English words his ammunition. A love poem was his first attack on Damian after proclaimed war.

On the very next day, Holly answered with the details. Sincere love shined through the poem, so according to the laws of Nature, Damian lost this battle and allowed Holly's soul to celebrate her victory. Benjamin was both ecstatic and extremely anxious when he received this news. He was so glad to be able to see Holly again, even though there was so much uncertainty and confusion in their love story. Benjamin had to trust his intuition in preparation for this date, as he would act as a messenger from Nature. The land sent Benjamin on the first date with Holly, helping to open his heart, but it sent him on the second date to restore the balance, that Holly broke. As Holly chose Damian, she changed the divine order of things. Benjamin wasn't going on this date as Holly's future husband. He was sent on a mission to create emotional trauma for her, open up Holly's psyche, and break through the barriers Damian inflicted upon her. It was the only way to reach her soul. He planned his mission strategically as if he was Camilla. He became a spy again, so he could heal their broken past.

Days went by, and Benjamin's strength was tempered by his engagement in the Great American Spiritual War. He spent four nights on the battlefield and three nights guarding Holly and Mr. Dance against Damian. Benjamin couldn't cleanse her vessel, but he could protect her space. For now, he mostly observed her reality. All sorts of vile creatures hid in the corners, closets, and under the bed, creating complete darkness in

Holly's apartment. They poisoned her space and drained her energy. Since our princess had a fragile aura, these entities successfully destroyed her self-confidence. The only light in her room came from Mr. Dance. This wonderful soul was a gift from Holly's spirits to protect her. Mr. Dance was still a very young warrior and not experienced in spiritual matters. He saw the presence of Benjamin, and curiosity powered him to get closer to our knight. Mr. Dance wanted what was best for Holly, and once he understood that Benjamin also had love for her, they became allies. Benjamin taught Mr. Dance how to hunt dark spiritual beings.

Meanwhile, Benjamin was preparing his gifts for Holly. He only had about a quarter of a gold ounce left, so he needed to be creative. Benjamin planned a provocation, as he had to unapologetically confront Holly's pretentious, narcissistic persona. Holly told him on his first date that she was obsessed with how pajamas felt on her body, that she even wore them under regular clothes when going outside on mundane tasks. Benjamin bought silk pajamas and asked American spirits to charge them with magic. In collaboration with spirits of Vancouver Island, Benjamin crafted mystical bath salts. Granville Island's spirits helped him with nourishing potions. Queen Elizabeth Park spirits provided a teddy bear that would empower Benjamin's connection with Mr. Dance. Spirits of Stanley Park gave the perfect bouquet of peach roses, and spirits of Burnaby, a beautiful set of craft chocolates. Spirits of Paris gifted a book, *Guardians of Lies*, about a spy, Eloise, fighting Soviet Tyranny in the French Empire of 1950s.

On the eve of their second date, Benjamin felt it was essential to discover more information that would empower him to face Holly. He realized he would meet a completely different woman. As he entered the spiritual realm, he was transported into one of Camilla's cherished memories. Camilla desperately wished to know more about Eloise and they went on a road trip. They drove from Paris to Saint-Etienne, a town south of Lyon where Eloise grew up. The land of mountains, cobbled streets, vineyards, and cheese farms waited for them. Eloise loved attending the land when she grew up, enjoying fresh food and cheese from her farm. Only she was in a feud with her mother and her extended family. Eloise's father died when she was a child, and her mother became an abusive and resentful woman. She made Eloise's life miserable, and the girl responded with the same negative energies. Her mother was traumatized by the war the Red

Army brought upon the European continent and contradicting perceptions of the Russian immigration diaspora. When the Wehrmacht recruited Eloise in Paris, her enthusiasm to fight the Soviets was fueled by these emotions.

Camilla knew nothing about Eloise's past, often questioning why she was such a passionate fighter. In a sense young woman was fighting her mother and traumas of the teenage years. Eloise's attractive appearance stood out among her peers and men often objectified her, making her life even more stressful. During this trip, Camilla felt a profound spiritual realization that each human's life is designed in a specific way to fulfill divine missions of their souls. Eloise was destined to be a professional killer in this life, and she was natural in this role. Still, Camilla was curious about the inner motivations of Eloise's heart and mind. Camilla was falling in love, and dreamed to fully explore the essence of her soulmate.

As they dined in the small café upon arrival, they were finally free to talk about anything they wanted. Eloise shared one theory of the Russian immigrants who believed in the demonic nature of the Soviet Empire. She described the murder of the last Russian tzar, Nicholas II, and his entire family as an occult ritual to open a portal into another realm and summon diabolical energies. She expressed the idea that Lenin's corpse was displayed in the heart of Moscow for the same reasons – to gain supernatural strength from the world of the dead and use this energy to conquer every nation on Earth. Camilla and Eloise entertained such ideas with skepticism, but they accepted the possibility of this theory being at least partially true. Both women sensed the existence of spiritual forces beyond human control, and such a view could explain the sinister madness around them. Suddenly our soulmates opened up to each other in an unusual way, realizing they could safely share their spiritual beliefs.

They talked about the dark, invisible energies existing in our lives. Camilla told Eloise how she saw a spiritual dark being, who appeared as a shadow of a man. This being had no physical vessel, and yet Camilla saw him vividly as if he was a real human being. She saw Damian around her, even though she couldn't recognize him. This dark figure followed her at times as a misty ghost. That story triggered a panic attack in Eloise. For the first time in her life, she had an opportunity to share her teenage experience with someone who would understand her. Eloise saw a dark ghostly spirit in her room a few times. He resembled the shape of a man, and his presence triggered dark fears in Eloise's heart. She realized this creature haunted her from childhood. Eloise always thought this was her mother's energy, but since this suppressed memory surfaced now, our lovers trusted synchronicity, and both spies were convinced they had encountered the same deity. They felt it with their divine feminine intuitions as if they exchanged their visions telepathically. Their minds couldn't find a logical explanation, but their hearts didn't need one, as Damian indeed followed them in every life.

Camilla and Eloise vulnerably opened up to each other, and a deep emotional connection enveloped them. They fell in love with each other's essences, seeing the truth of their souls. Now they finally surrendered to their love story. There was no point in fighting their romance anymore. They shared something they had never told anyone else, once honest love appeared in their hearts. Both of them always dreamed of being seen and heard by men. Still, all their romantic relationships failed miserably because their men always dismissed feminine spiritually and intuitive understanding of the world.

As night descended upon the town, they returned to their hotel room with a bottle of wine. They drank, laughed, and told stories about their past. They felt so liberated from the constraints of society, so free from any obligations in the presence of each other. They completely forgot how cruel the world had become, feeling like they were the only two people on Earth. Their emotional connection felt so strong that once the bottle of wine was empty, Camilla passionately kissed Eloise on the lips in fervent impulse. She attacked Eloise exactly like Holly attacked Benjamin. The fire broke out in the hearts as Eloise kissed her back. They felt a unique truth of the moment and fiercely ripped their clothes, surrendering to kisses and caresses. They didn't second-guess their vehement impulses – they felt it was a magical moment of life happening to them, and they embraced each other, making love through the night. They entered into an ardent competition of exchanging pleasures, liberating each other's pains through this intimate and passionate meditation. Neither knew how to make love to a woman, but that night they finally discovered true, sensual magic they've been searching for all of their lives.

This night was meant to happen. Their gazes said it all after they collapsed from their exhausting sexual dance. With radiating smiles, they joked about the experience. Both women were surprised how natural it felt, confessing they always craved a masculine presence in their bedrooms, yet neither thought about men at all. They discussed how the society created their limited perceptions of love and how they never really faced their true sexuality, always trying to conform to the beliefs of others. But today, nothing felt more truthful than this new surprising romance full of genuine emotions. The eyes of our Camilla and Eloise shined with pure love and they didn't even need to say anything to one another. They spent the rest of the evening, gazing into each other's eyes until they fell asleep in a sweet embrace.

They had breakfast in a small outdoor café the following day. Eloise took out her notepad and drew Camilla's portrait with a pencil. They exchanged occasional looks, and joy enveloped their hearts as they couldn't stop smiling from their newfound love and delightful memories of the last night. Eloise captured their truth in her drawing. As Camilla playfully posed, her eyes were glued to Eloise's hands. Camilla felt like she had entered a different realm, hypnotized by Eloise's fingers dancing in the air. The pencil magically swirled, creating sophisticated patterns of artistic magic. Eloise could only express her complex essence through her hands, and now Camilla could see another facet of her lover through the act of drawing. She could see Eloise's soul through the motions of her hands. Eloise manifested her essence in a new way, and Camilla was studying her intricate beauty. Camilla merged with Eloise's soul as they made love last night, but this spiritual connection felt even more engaging. It was another Eloise that she hadn't seen before. From now on, every time Camilla saw Eloise creating her drawings, she would turn silent, immersing into a blissful trance, completely mesmerized by the fingers of her closest soulmate.

As Benjamin left this memory, he felt cheerful about uncovering another layer of his love for Holly. He could see Holly's soul through her fingers, and now he knew why. He was excited to share this memory with Holly to prove the magic of their story and why he complimented her fingers on their first date. As the second date with Holly was approaching, Benjamin set out to find the right words for his beloved about his visions. It was the first love letter out of a hundred he would eventually write to his princess. Benjamin planned this letter to be personal, direct, and honest, to startle and emotionally shock Holly so he could establish the proper contact with her soul.

"The Birthday Letter"

Dear wonderful Holly,

Please accept these birthday gifts. I picked them up with an honest intention – to give you strength and protection, to help guard you. The next three months will be very challenging, with dark entities having more powers. I'm not trying to scare you, I simply wish to pass you as much energy as I can, with positive vibrations in mind. It is how I sincerely feel deep inside my soul. I know you have mighty protectors and guardians, so don't forget to reach them too in your moments of weakness.

The PJ set is designed to work as a shield, guarding you at night. The bath salts are spiritual and can bring intense experiences. One is created explicitly for psychic protection – try it when you feel the most vulnerable. The other one – 'KEY' salt – is designed to connect with anything you desire – your soul, your higher guardians, ancestors, or nature. This salt also has a specific meaning for me. I felt like I had a fulfilling life, fully occupied with artistic projects, and work. Only when I met you, I realized that I was always looking for you, and you changed something inside of me. You acted as a key and opened up a door into a magical realm. I don't fully know what you did and how it works, but I know that something has shifted for the better.

Next is the book which I chose using intuition. I intended to find you something that may speak to you in personal ways and trigger past life memories. Finally, there's also a teddy bear. I charged him with some energy too, and he carries a magical talisman in his heart.

Thank you again for another lovely evening. I will cherish the memories until our next encounter. Given the strange feelings between us, I still don't know when I will be able to see you or whether you will want to see me again. I don't know what we are experiencing and I realize how unusual our story is. I question everything I'm going through as my emotions are so puzzling.

At the same time, I can't ignore the feeling of the powerful connection that we share, which seems to be present not only in this life. I do not know you, but I know we are expected to explore our bond. It took me some time to embrace this and I know you have your doubts too. Yet, you are bringing out the best in me every day, making me a better man. I never felt what I'm experiencing next to you. Even though it may look like we share a weird and bizarre romance, it is unique and beautiful in its own way, absolutely like nothing else. I can't wait to see how our story will play out in the future and why we were brought together to share fantastic moments during our short but vivid encounters. I'm embracing this experience, hoping not to overthink it all, and I hope you will too.

See you soon, *hugs and kisses*,
Benjamin.
Vancouver, BC, December 26, 2020.

Benjamin sealed the letter and packed his presents. He gathered the strength of a magician to face Damian in Holly's body, but he was also trembling like a man, intimidated to face her female beauty and charm. He knew this would be a different Holly, so he had to be prepared for anything. He also realized this particular date was chosen because it was the first day of Holly's female cycle. It was another serendipity created by Nature.

Benjamin arrived fifteen minutes late, as Damian created energetic obstacles on his path. Agitated and reserved Holly waited him at the table. With arms crossed, she leaned on her chair, distancing herself emotionally from her date. Benjamin was anxious, so once he started drinking water, he spilled it on himself. Holly was happy for the opportunity to attack him, calling him a mess and mocking his lack of confidence. Her energy pushed him away from the moment she saw him. She pretended to be someone she was not, playing a girl she thought men liked, but she couldn't hide her resentment – she was terrified of what Benjamin might know about her. Holly believed a magician only engages in occult and dark entrapping spells to manipulate others. She sensed this man knew more about her than he should, but she didn't want to be seen for who she is. She designed her personality, based on lives of celebrities and expectations of her friends and family.

Benjamin started with the toast, complimenting Holly's complex, intricate beauty and personality. Still, his princess only smirked at his words, rejecting his strange advances. Bringing up her birthday, he talked about a Mayan calendar and explained to Holly what guardian, spiritual energies she was carrying. Holly got even more defensive, as she felt Benjamin was getting inside of her, and she didn't want to open up her heart to a man. Dating for her was a chance to have casual fun, without obligations of a real relationship. Our knight struggled to break the ice, feeling defeated, but he continued explaining how he observes Mayan thirteen moon calendar in his daily life. He told Holly that moon cycles last for twenty-eight days, like female cycles, and if he had a woman, he would follow her internal clocks to plan his life. Holly corrected Benjamin, saying that not every female cycle lasts exactly that, but Benjamin responded that not every moon cycle does too. Our knight claimed that for a man, it was imperative to be synchronized with his woman's womb, even if her cycles are different from the moon ones.

Holly asked Benjamin what he thought about the moon landing, as she was convinced it never happened, while her friends believed otherwise. Benjamin responded that if it did happen, then humans would have other missions to the moon already, as rockets only advanced through time. Now Holly finally melted – that was exactly her reasoning on this subject. Smiling, she went on and on about how she would travel to the moon if she was rich and if it was ever possible. They both continued to bring up arguments about the topic, and after an hour into their date their energies synchronized in the most beautiful way.

The nature of our world was a fascinating subject for Holly, and she wanted to ask Benjamin everything that he knew. Our knight told her about the ancient concept known as 'a century of darkness'. As the war in the skies broke out, around the time when the second American emperor Abraham was executed, the angels lost the ability to assist humans. Demons were slaughtered and expeled into our world through spiritual portals in 1917 and 1968. As the new century began in 2012 and the last portal closed the cycle, humans had to decide whether to send demons further into Underworld or allow them to consume humanity. Benjamin was working on an experimental, provocative film called *A Clockwork Orange Delay 1968*, explaining to Holly how the movie describes the story of the last century only using the art of editing, with found footage clips from the internet, juxtaposed against each other, to create a coherent story without any dialogue.

For the first time in the evening, Holly leaned towards our knight, placed her hand on his, and smiling with her eyes, said, "This is so Lana Del Rey of you!" Her authenticity and grace inspired our knight, as he was afraid to startle this twenty-three-year-old woman with his weird ideas and philosophical avant-garde films. This was the best compliment he had ever heard; that's how he wanted his art to be seen. Holly said a phrase that perfectly described his artistic ambition behind the project, and yet she hadn't seen a single frame of it. Touching hands, they looked at each other with acceptance and inspiring fascination. Benjamin continued to tell his princess about his art and the laws of Nature. Holly couldn't stop listening to her man as her heart melted by the minute in the presence of her soulmate.

She couldn't quite figure out why Benjamin had such an effect on her. Holly sensed he fully accepted her for who she was and created a sacred and non-judgmental space to express her essence.

As Benjamin and Holly left the restaurant, they were caught up in the energy of their genuine connection. Holly was initially reluctant and defensive, but she felt at peace next to Benjamin's open and truthful heart. Holly invited her knight to share some tea in her apartment and open the presents in his company. She was excited about the flowers, the teddy bear, and the artisan chocolates. Holly wanted to open the box with gifts, but Benjamin asked her to do it alone, mentioning the birthday letter. As they sat on a couch, drinking tea, their conversation was so engaging they couldn't believe it was real. Attempting to share his visions, Benjamin reached for Holly's hand. "You know, I found out why I'm so drawn to your fingers and why I can't stop admiring them."

"There's nothing special about my fingers. They actually look weird," Deep inside, Holly tried to shelter herself from Benjamin's advances, but intuitively she placed her palm against Benjamin's, trying to compare their fingers. "See, they are not beautiful. They're just strange." Even though Holly's self-esteem was twisted by Damian's incursions, for a moment, she forgot her insecurities, observing how two hands complement each other, studying them with fascination in complete silence. Their souls sang a melody of harmony. She liked spending time with Benjamin, but she was freaking out too. He was clearly expressing his feelings and shining with a noble masculine essence. Men rarely shared their emotions so quickly, so Holly was trying to understand what game Benjamin was playing. Holly didn't know what to make of his admiration and compliments, trying to discover a manipulative game. Holly didn't trust her heart and intuition, studying him only with her mind.

"I can see how unique and special you are by looking at your fingers," Benjamin smiled, looking into her eyes, and Holly somehow knew he wasn't lying to her.

"I don't think there's anything special about me, honestly. I'm just an average, simple girl."

Benjamin laughed inside because, for him, Holly was one of a kind. He didn't care what others thought of her or whether more beautiful and talented women existed in this world. Benjamin knew she was a very special soul, and had a distinctive uniqueness. She helped create the identity of independent Sweden in the sixteenth century. She helped to save the American Empire from Damian's destruction. She confronted the scariest people, protecting French Empire from Tyranny. And now – just in six weeks – she unleashed the new reality by simply living her life in Vancouver. She transformed Benjamin, opening up his spiritual gifts and enriching the world with magical beauty of art and love. This woman was emitting energies of inspiration, rebelliousness, defiance, divine femininity, and grace that Benjamin never encountered. She felt exceptional in every single way.

Trying to prove her wrong, our knight told Holly how Eloise drew his portrait, and utter ringing silence enveloped the room, exactly like it happened on their first date. Their souls merged again. Holly didn't make a single sound, afraid to ruin the magic of their celestial bliss. She felt like Benjamin's words created a protective bubble around them, experiencing complete peace for the first time in a long while. She didn't question anything Benjamin told her. Holly was skeptical about the idea of past lives, but Benjamin's words emitted a unique energy of truth she had never felt before. Holly was completely immersed in the story as Benjamin described the first passionate night of Camilla and Eloise. Holly laughed when Benjamin mentioned how they skillfully seduced men, thinking how she enjoys the same activity in this life. The story felt honest and natural, and Holly fully accepted it as something that did happen to her. She sensed the real magic in the air as if she remembered the life of Eloise.

"You know, when Eloise died, Camilla felt responsible. She blamed herself for not protecting her. And now I feel I'm in debt to you because I sent you on that deadly mission," Benjamin finished his story.

"You don't owe me anything, Benjamin. It happened the way it should," Holly whispered quietly. "I don't blame you for my death," Holly's soul reassured him.

When it was time for them to say goodbye, Benjamin asked Holly if she wanted to meet him again. Holly coquettishly joked that Benjamin would be too busy to have time for her, implying politely that she didn't want to. She was afraid of Benjamin's honesty, perceiving it as an entrapment. Our knight understood everything, accepting she would disappear from his life as he saw Damian's presence in her eyes. Our Dark

Prince whispered to Holly, "Benjamin is a fraud and a loser. He is playing you. There are no past lives. You are a meaningless stardust. You will die and turn to nothing. You will rot in the soil, so have fun while you can. Life is about enjoying yourself. You are not unique, and no one is. All men lie to you. Benjamin wants to use you. Don't trust him."

Our knight looked at Holly, knowing his worst nightmare had come true. Her eyes became cloudy, and even her voice changed. Benjamin felt he was being strangled by powers stronger than his love. Benjamin was terrified, thinking about how far Damian would go. *Will I ever see Holly alive again?* That was his only thought. Benjamin dismantled her guards, but as they said goodbye, Holly returned to the mask that Damian created for her, and like in his dream, this was not his Holly anymore.

"I know you, Holly. I can sense how uniquely beautiful and intricate you are. Please never forget that." Benjamin was ready to leave his princess in the hands of the darkness. Even though saying goodbye to Holly felt bittersweet, Benjamin was thankful for everything this woman brought into his life. She was an answer to his prayers. Despite his conflicting emotions, he believed in their love and was ready to go to the war against darkness.

Bewildering Undertaking

Miracles are all around us;
Behold them or ignore
Blocked roads would be cleared at the right moment,
Just at the will of the Nature without any battles.
The brain will call it lies.
The heart will call it life.
Serendipity will wake us up one day,
And what we've longed and worked for
Will be presented to us as a pure gift,
Hoping we're not too blind to face ourselves
To see grief as love, to see death as joy
To see life for what it is.

We have been groomed to believe lies are truths
And truths are lies, to reject the signs in the skies.
Anticipate the dark surprises
But you can see the truth, as eyes can never lie.

Without any sleep for the past three nights – unpredictable purification. Reset our mist affair.
Two more nights – no sleep, guarding, eating demons, cleaning the holy vessel of my beloved.
Days are pure misery.
Yet I don't have any good moves left in this game,
In this present divine and vile moment
I'm trapped.

CHAPTER VI

The following evening, Benjamin meditated before sleep. He heard Holly's curses telepathically as everything in her mind pushed Benjamin away. She made another choice in her life that directly affected Benjamin, and he experienced the most profound transformation of his skills. Our knight didn't sleep for two nights, living in an obscure state between physical and spiritual planes, shifting through realms of existence. Benjamin lifted the veils of reality as his letter helped him reach Holly's soul. In the middle of the night, he arrived in her bedroom for a special ritual of empowerment through heavenly light. He broke Holly's walls and accessed the subconscious world of her psyche. He descended next to Holly's bed as she was sleeping alone peacefully. The angels entered the room and, seeing Benjamin's shining love, assisted him in spiritually cleansing his lady from the demonic entities of the past. They handed Benjamin a unique healing device full of universal, heavenly love.

As Benjamin held his hands above Holly's heart, the golden gadget appeared under his palms. He shaped this tool into a beautiful golden shield above Holly's chest and sent love affirmations to his princess. The shield levitated slightly above Holly's heart, and Benjamin stepped away, settling in the chair. Holly's spiritual, energy body, containing subconscious presence, ascended from her physical vessel and rose a few inches above it. An angelical device began its work, removing destructive vibrations Holly had accumulated in her heart. This spiritual body, that protects our aura, is made of ether and the exact quantum energy-double of our physical body. It can be charged through many practices, but intimacy, based on genuine love, creates the highest protection and strength for the spiritual body. Casual sex with possessive, superficial, and lustful intentions, on the opposite, destroys the spiritual body and allows dark entities to enter the heart. Deceptive men who only perceive a woman as an object for their pleasures, take away innate female powers through abusive sex, making a woman weaker, instead of healing and enriching her. Damian guided many sinister beings on Holly's path,, who penetrated her fragile aura, and rarely honored her sacred female temple with love.

The supernatural shield, shining with Benjamin's love, helped him to reach for her soul. Angels studied the deepest parts of Holly, healing her past emotional wounds. Now Benjamin had to pray and wait. The more positive energy and love he could send to Holly, the better the result would be. Benjamin guarded the healing process, staying up through the night, attempting to take her miseries and fears upon himself and dissolve them.

The next night Benjamin continued to heal his princess with the same device, attempting to retrieve her soul. Without accessing traumas of the past, Benjamin couldn't see what happened to her soul and why she was trapped in the Underworld. At sunrise, the magical process was finally complete. Benjamin's affirmations and devotion during these two nights had paid off. He collected the magical shield and returned the device to the angels. They filled the room with golden light, praising Benjamin's commitment and love.

Benjamin slowly guided Holly's spiritual essence back into her body. Once they aligned, a huge monster jumped from Holly's heart onto Benjamin. He was ten feet tall, with sharp, poisonous tentacles and a large, monstrous, head of an ant. The creature opened his mouth full of razor-like teeth, trying to bite Benjamin, but our knight didn't even blink and attacked this imposter immediately. He swallowed this creature and easily digested him, channeling the remnants of this demon into the Earth. As he defeated this monster, a flock of spiders crawled from Holly's subconscious mind. They ran away wildly in every possible direction, as their cozy shelter was completely destroyed. They died in agony as Benjamin eviscerated them with magical fire. Benjamin's job was complete; he returned home, trying to rest from the battles.

The next morning, he saw a vision of smiling Holly. Her soul was closer to him, and soon, he felt her presence in his dwelling. He reached into the depths of the shadow realm with his pure love and extended a magical rope to Holly's soul. She recognized his light; she saw that someone sincerely loved her. She was finally seen, and now she could move toward Benjamin's radiating essence. Holly's soul wasn't heard for a long time, so eventually, she gave up and fell asleep. Stranded, she lost any orientation, as Holly abandoned her heart. Eurydice ended up in the world between life, dream, death, and Hell. It is a place of Nowhere, as even death and Purgatory can help a soul navigate reality. Yet before descending into the terrifying darkness of death, a soul is trapped between realms in the Underworld - a highly confusing state where any path becomes an elaborate illusion with no way out. Since it is a space on the borders of realms existing beyond our physical reality, only a true magician of the lands can help a soul to find a way back into our world. But descending into the Underworld can be troubling and confusing even for an experienced magician.

Benjamin heard the land calling him on a journey and rushed to the street, trusting his intuition. His feet led him to the Sunset Beach. He was standing on the shore, looking in the distance, as he sensed the presence of his great-grandfather Michael, who arrived to support our knight in his endeavor. He guided Benjamin to Bernar Venet's 217.5 Arc x 13 sculpture located on this beach. Using his magic, Benjamin discovered that this raw steel arch was the entrance into the realm where he could find Holly's entrapped soul. Benjamin's curiosity about the nature of this majestic portal had drawn a young woman to appear in front of him. She was carrying a spear in one hand and a shield in another, dressed in ancient, traditional clothes of these lands. She introduced herself as Allania. They shared a destiny of energetic healers of these lands and spirits connected them to help one another. Allania offered to answer Benjamin's questions as a gesture of gratitude, as he could heal her past traumatic death that happened because of this portal.

Facing Benjamin, Allania reached her hand and put her palm against his. They were immediately transported to the same spot only a few hundred years ago. Allania was living with her tribe on the shores of the Burrard Inlet. The entrance into their community was at the same spot where the steel arch stands today. It was a main gate entrance beautifully laid out of carved stones. Allania explained that this entrance always had this magical power and could be used as a doorway between the worlds. The arch didn't lead everyone into the same realm, but stepping through it with an honest and specific intention, teleported a magician to the desired place.

Allania lived a life of a noble female warrior and passionately protected her community from other tribes attacking both from land and sea. One day, the leaders of Allania's tribe became corrupt from spiritual superiority and their magical powers. They misused the door between the worlds for evil purposes, to gain control over the entire shore, including the territory that is known today as Stanley Park. In those times, this place was called XwayXway, and a few vibrant communities called this land their home, peacefully co-existing next to each other. But one day, they were attacked with dark magic.

Allania was caught between two contradicting emotions. On the one hand, she was loyal to her tribe and honestly fought to protect it. Yet by shielding her community, she helped her leaders to become tyrants, obsessed with the supernatural powers that allowed them to control others. Allania went to war against other villages, as she was a mighty energy warrior in service of her tribe. Her heart was torn apart. She cared for her relatives, but leaders used her vehement strength for sinister purposes as they summoned dark entities through the portal. For Allania, betraying her corrupt leaders would also mean betraying her loved ones. Eventually, their evil supremacy destroyed their tribe as white magicians of XwayXway created a powerful shield, building an energetic border that stopped these vile attacks.

Allania's tribe was cursed both from outside and within. Soon enough, the land heard the cries of people and set the wheels in motion to restore the natural order. One day another tribe appeared at their doorsteps, arriving unexpectedly by water, and with the first beams of the morning sun, they murdered entire village, as this was their destined mission, granted by the lands. Allania rejected her leaders but fought relentlessly for her people, honorably dying in this battle. Upon death, she realized her entire community brought such fate upon themselves. The leaders fairly represented their people, as they were energetic extensions of the tribe and its mirror. Knowing about the essence of the portal, corrupt citizens used its power to justify their sins, claiming they are superior to others. Once the soil touched Allania's wounds in her grave, the earth released her trauma and gifted her soul new spiritual powers. Even though she protected evil people, she never betrayed her honest heart until her last breath. She fought for what she believed was right and lived her life with integrity. The land purified her wounds upon the burial and blessed her soul with a safe passage.

Benjamin relived the entire experience together with Allania, absolving the trauma. He felt what she felt, dying in that grave, with bleeding wounds from the sword and disintegrating in the soil. Allania still struggled to process that death, believing at times her wrong choices led to a tragic death. But Benjamin explained to her the deeper meaning of this experience. Allania had to die in such a way, because it was important for her soul's growth. She was destined to be a medicine woman with magical abilities, so she had to endure complex pains and unusual death experiences. As her soul embraced her wounds, she received magical powers to heal others.

Benjamin felt connected to Allania, as he lived a similar struggle as Camilla. She strongly believed in a prosperous kingdom of Germany, fighting passionately for her homeland. But the leaders, driven by vile desires, turned corrupt as they were feeding off the frustrated and fearful energies of citizens, creating a destructive reality for the entire nation. Allania's tribe experienced the same. The kingdom of Germany received supernatural powers from the higher forces to shield them from the tyrannical Soviet Empire. But the feeling of superiority corrupted the nation, and these powers were used for evil. Still, Camilla could not betray her home country, her relatives, and the patriots who did not follow sinister orders. Eventually Camilla died on the battlefield. She fought truthfully for the highest ideals she believed in, never betraying herself, and the soil also purified her wounds upon death.

Benjamin and Allania were surprised by such synchronicities, thanking the land for this meeting. They both healed through sharing their conflicting emotions and relating to one another. They lived the same fate of an archetypical honest female warrior – passionate and fierce, stubborn and determined, opinionated and expressive, but always true to herself, pledging allegiance only to the heart, dying for the highest beliefs. They were also surprised by how common human nature is and how struggles are identical across time and continents. Even though their 'tribes' were divided by time, language, and size, the essence of the experience was the same. Their souls felt the same perplexing emotions, seeing how humans fell into delusional traps of supremacy so that Nature had to intervene with a war.

Benjamin believed that the Russian Empire was going through the same process today, and he could study it from the front-row seat. Terrified citizens created monstrous supernatural killers who dreamed of conquering the world only because they perceived themselves as superior to others. As the Russian Empire was transforming into a fascist state, he searched for answers in the past. He knew the stories of his ancestors who lived similar experiences once the Soviet Empire went on the path of chaos and destruction. Soviets executed two of Benjamin's great-grandfathers once they occupied the kingdom of Ukraine. No other kingdom suffered more from the Soviet Empire than his proud nation and our knight felt the pain of his motherland every day of his life.

Benjamin thanked Allania and the spirits of this land for this meeting. After they shared their stories, Allania explained how to travel through the portal with the ideas of noble intention and inner integrity that would guide a magician on this journey. She promised to guard the portal and assist Benjamin upon entrance and exit. Our knight walked through the arch and suddenly he found himself in the shadow realm between the worlds. Holly created this meaningless Nowhere inside her heart. It was a safe state of dullness, constructed from mists of insecurities and fogs of intense traumas. Personal fears lived here as monstrous, dreadful trees, but death was the only real state of this place. This miserable reality protected Holly's heart from the pains of life. Benjamin trusted his intuition as he walked through this forest of sorrows. Fear and panic surrounded our knight, like two shadow beings hovering above him, but Benjamin continued wandering, emitting loving protection with masculine calmness and determination. Soon he stumbled upon a rope lying on the ground, that was made out of his poetry words. Following this rope, Benjamin eventually encountered a large wall stretching high in the skies and wide through the fields, with no way around it. Benjamin braced himself, realizing this was the wall around Holly's heart. Our knight saw the rope going through the wall, so he continued walking toward it, convinced he could go through with the energy of his love as his rhymes did.

Repeating his poems aloud and envisioning Holly's eyes, he magically appeared on the other side of the wall. The rope led him to a mysteriously dark well, and he leaned to look inside. He saw swarms of demonic spiders, bugs, and snakes. On the other side of the well, the death waited for a soul. It was the same well Benjamin saw when he tried to contact Eurydice for the first time. She was descending into the abyss of purgatory and only managed to climb out with the help of his love poems. Benjamin nervously searched for her around the well and soon discovered Eurydice lying under a nearby tree. She was too exhausted to continue her escape. "How are you doing, my dear?" Benjamin kneeled to her. He couldn't wait to take her back to reality, where she could be healed, but he had to be gentle with her. She was covered in bruises, pale and malnourished.

Eurydice struggled to stay awake, but she slowly raised her eyes and looked at Benjamin, confused and disoriented. Suddenly a big, tired smile illuminated her face. "You found me. You did!" She reached her arms and wrapped them around his neck, squeezing Benjamin as strongly as she could. "I lost all hope. I thought I would never find you. What took you so long? I've been calling for you for such a long time!"

"I'm so sorry, my dear, I couldn't get to you earlier. We have powerful enemies, and I had to travel from the other side of the world to get to you. I've missed you so much, my love." As Benjamin hugged her back, he couldn't help but notice an intense sensation re-emerging inside. Our knight struggled with that feeling from an early age, never understanding what that was. Like a vital organ was removed from his body upon birth. Now, as he held the soul of his beloved princess, he realized he had been searching for her. He craved to be in the presence of her energy. Benjamin faithfully followed his higher path, never betraying his heart, and the world rewarded him with this divine intervention.

"Are you ready to return to life?" Benjamin asked.

"Probably not. But maybe with your support. Where are we? Why don't I hear Holly, and where is Mr. Dance? I don't understand what's going on." She realized she was trapped in another dimension.

"You lost communication with Holly. I saw an evil spirit inside of her. He manipulated you and entrapped her. We will discover what happened, but let's get back first."

"I don't understand anything, but I'm so glad I found you. I've searched so long through my entire kingdom. I knew you were close but somehow you couldn't hear me. Benjamin, I don't know what happened to us. We could sense each other so easily before."

"It's true, but still, we found each other. Dark demon entrapped you in Paris, and now we are enduring the consequences of our mistakes. But I will find a way to reunite you with Holly."

"I feel like a child, Benjamin. Helpless, confused, scared, and dependent on you. I don't know what I would do without you. I have been a child for the last two centuries. I don't want to grow. Now I lost her because of this, and we are both suffering."

"Don't blame yourself. Maybe everything is not how you perceive it to be. Maybe this is how we are supposed to be, Eurydice." Benjamin tried very hard to create a sense of comfort for her.

"I'm not Eurydice if I'm a child."

"Well then, I will call you Polly for now." Benjamin smiled, looking at his soulmate.

"I like this name! It was my princess' name, and now I'm princess again, so it's perfect for me!"

"I like calling you Polly, my dear princess."

"Because you see how small I am compared to you. I'm always in trouble, always in drama. You always have to rescue me and teach me how to die and how to live. Without you, I'm nothing," Eurydice was incredibly frustrated that Benjamin had found her in the darkest corners of her essence. She was broken and entrapped in her fears. She felt like a failure and didn't like being seen in such a vulnerable state.

"It's fine, Polly. Without you, I'm nothing too. We both didn't understand what we are dealing with. But we can only get out of this mess together."

"I won't be able to help you. You know I will only break you even more. You will have to assume my demons and they will destroy you. I will drag you into their traps. Leave me here and save yourself because you will die too."

"Okay, enough talking. We need to get out of here." Benjamin closed his eyes and prayed. After receiving strength from the angels, he ordered Polly to follow him. Together, holding hands, they slowly walked back in silence, and once they crossed the wall, they fell on the ground unconscious. They woke up a few moments later on the Sunset Beach, next to the magical portal. Right away, Eurydice jumped on her two feet and danced. The energies of the land entered her and she felt liberated. The land explained a bonding rule that allowed Eurydice to exit. As she wasn't with Holly anymore, she was assigned to spend nights in a tiny wooden shack in Coal Harbor, known as a house of lost souls.

Benjamin introduced Polly to Allania, and they immediately felt a deep connection of spiritual sisterhood through sharing their energies in an embrace. Both women fought many battles against darkness and dreamed of healing the world with their supernatural gifts. Benjamin and Eurydice praised Allania for holding the space as they celebrated the success of this mission. Benjamin and Allania decided to stay friends. She asked to train her to work with other souls like he did and promised to help heal his grief in exchange. Excited and uplifted, Benjamin and Eurydice said their goodbyes, rushing back to Benjamin's place to unwind after such an intense adventure.

Our lovers swirled together over the shores and waters. They waltzed together through the streets in blissful joy and danced on the roofs, celebrating their first noble victory. Eurydice shined with her magic, praising the land, Benjamin, and guides. For the first time in her life, our princess recognized her supernatural powers, as she had her first magical achievement. If Benjamin had come from the distant kingdom of Ukraine to retrieve her from the Underworld, then she was a very special soul. She felt proud that she wasn't a complete failure.

"What would you like for dinner, my dear Polly?" Benjamin asked as they approached the shopping street, "I'm sure you are starving."

"I want it all, Benjamin! Please, I'm so hungry! I want a steak, a grapefruit, raspberries, a latte, and chocolates. Please, pretty please!" Eurydice cutely whirled around her knight, enticing him with her grace and making him smile from her cute girlishness.

"No problem. Why a steak and a coffee at this hour?"

"Holly hasn't eaten a steak in a while, and I miss it, Benjamin. It grounds me, reminding me that I'm not just a wandering soul, but living, inside an animal vessel. Oh, and I love coffee! It's like being home. Please, Benjamin, we must eat it all tonight."

"Sure, my dear princess. You can have it all today. Should I get us ice cream too?"

"You know me better than anyone. You're so nice to me." Eurydice wrapped Benjamin with her energy like she was the coziest blanket, and he smiled like the happiest man in the world. Passers-by gave Benjamin strange looks, unable to understand why this man was talking to himself aloud, and danced with such an inspiring joy. No one could see the fairy tale of eternal lovers unfolding right on this seemingly ordinary Vancouver day. Our lovers couldn't stop looking at each other, sharing deep tenderness and affection. Neither questioned their strange experience, as it felt natural and beautiful. Full of happiness, they arrived home, creating an evening of loving harmony. It was a party to remember as our lovers celebrated their divine and unusual bond. They stormed into each other's lives, and there was no turning back from this love. Eurydice indulged in food and cannabis through Benjamin's body, while he laughed at her appetite. They danced and entertained each other with bizarre jokes and stories, only two of them could understand, feeling beautiful, empowering, and blissful that night.

Time flew by as they immersed into one another, blending in the magical dance of two souls in love. As Benjamin escorted Polly to her shelter at the house of lost souls, he reassured his lady that they'd find a way to live together. Eurydice felt scared as she entered this tiny shack with one window and only a mattress on the floor. It felt like a prison cell, but it was better than Hell. Even though Eurydice cried from the ugliness of this place, she could at least spend days with Benjamin. After being apart for decades, they couldn't say their goodbyes, afraid they won't see each other again. Eurydice suggested visiting Sechelt lands, the place of her spirits. She knew one guide who could help them and they decided to travel as soon as possible. Neither wanted her to stay in this shack for long.

The next day Benjamin and Eurydice prepared for the trip to the Gibsons, the gateway community of Eurydice's lands on the Sunshine Coast. Eurydice agreed to take Phillip with them. Benjamin anticipated that he would need Phillip's insights to plan the following steps on their adventure. In the evening, our lovers danced in energetical swirls above the Burrard Inlet and its bridges, merging and separating, enjoying the essences of each other. They could easily become one supernatural being and this discovery uplifted both of them. Eurydice briefly showed Benjamin the Sechelt lands from above as they flew over mystical forests and waters.

When they returned from their adventure, Benjamin was ecstatic and couldn't believe how beautiful his life had turned to be. Eurydice was as palpable and real as any human being he interacted with, but she didn't have a physical vessel, so no one except Benjamin could see her. Our knight couldn't physically be with Holly, but Holly was everywhere in his life, as his heart and mind merged with her soul. It was even more beautiful to start the next chapter of their romance this way. Benjamin dreamed of living in a magical fairy tale full of miracles, and now his wish has come true. As Benjamin looked at Eurydice that evening, he realized they were designed to be inseparable, divinely complimenting each other. Together they could combine their masculine and feminine essences to merge into one supreme being. Benjamin witnessed how he was becoming a better man with every moment of this extraordinary journey and excitingly looked forward into the future, finally feeling at peace in her presence. He allowed his woman to mold him and it felt amazing.

Throughout their lives, they had experienced all forms of love, embracing every intricacy of each other and overcoming many challenges. Now they could live pure platonic love for the first time and confess their highest feelings on a soul level. Their experience was happening in different realms at once, illuminated by lucid dreams, powerful oracle visions, and intensely sensual meditations. Their story arrived in our world to fight the dark evils with the poetry of love. Benjamin and Eurydice's story was a magnificent epic poem written by angels, as their lives rhymed through centuries.

Benjamin decided to capture this new reality in a poem. Holly impregnated him with a male child of artistic creation. New life was born out of honest love, manifesting its spiritual essence in our world. Benjamin's poems portrayed the complexity of his woman's essence, that shined with magical grace, intricate personality, and rebellious nature. Our knight believed the words to describe Eurydice's beauty had not been invented yet, feeling he always fell short in praising his woman, questioning whether his serenades would reach her heart. But Eurydice encouraged her knight to abandon his modesty and shine with his words as brightly as possible. And that's how a new Benjamin was born.

New Reality of Rendezvous

I'm in a new reality.
The actual shift in reality?
The shift of my perception?
The new doors she has unlocked?
She looked at me and turned her key
To set me free, to let me see.
And now I perceive this world,
In the most righteous way
Without her, it wasn't meant to be
So did I save her
Or did she unexpectedly
Just manage to save me?

Life of Master and Margarita
Somehow became a story of us
As our two souls fly above our city
Ecstatically owning the night;
While I'm locked in the underground prison
Humanity built for poets,
You are trapped at a lavish ball
Of a gentleman, whose name we dare not say.

While you're asleep, hiding from miseries
I'm with your soul in your living room
As we drink tea with assumptions,
And flirting with our eyes, full of bloom.
Your soul is in a white chair,
Right there, across from me.
Free, young, and confident,
Playful, magical, and uninhibited.

She's radiating luminescent aquamarine,
Like an avenger made of halo and absent flesh

The pure bright purple-blue iridescent glow
Shaped in a familiar form of a human being.
She is your honest soul
The soul who never dies,
Who shines angelic light
And dreams of flying high;
Translucent and divine
While suffering to die
To learn from all her lives
So, she could be a Goddess.

The eyes of your soul are the same through the lives
I can find them among myriads of other eyes
Even in the midst of our most appalling trials
As only I can see the beauty of your cries.
Her shapes are different than yours.
Her heights and hair are from another life
With her daring, rebellious nature
Of irreconcilable defiance,
With her gentle, brunette ponytail
And with her sarcastic perceptions
She asks me wittingly in a gambit,
"Why do you need to touch
The vessel of this Holly girl
If we are happy, living as souls?
We dance through the blithe night
Swirling in flame passion,
Merging in a sweet cuddle
We can laugh on the roofs
And explore any frontiers,
We can walk on top of the mountains
Glide carelessly through the inlet waters,
And make love in the depth of the forests.
We can kiss without a kiss,
We can touch without touch
We can dream with no fear,
While spiraling into pure intimacy;

*We can fly any place
And with only one touch
The intense pleasures sparkle
Making human orgasms bleak.
Overrated physical intimacy
Collision of agony and insecurities
Consumed by dark energies
As stubborn bodies reject to hear us.
But as souls, we share ultimate delight –
You and me kissing and caressing
At any moment that is suited
With no restraints of time and dates.
We infiltrate and permeate
You are flowing through me,
While I'm flowing under your skin
As every energy cell of our beings
Discharges its essence in a blast,
Not only through erogenous traps
But with every fiber of our beings
More tangible than human feelings,
We're exploding with vivid crystals
As our whirling intricacies
Make love to each other
All simultaneously at once.
A confused human vessel would never feel,
Like we feel in our lucid rendezvous
As we unite in fluid credulous pervasion
And revel in holy blissful levitations.
Your light is in every cell of my presence
And I'm in every part of you
We transcend our trapped beings
As they hate themselves for nothing.
Please, can we stay in this unique realm,
Communicating with our feelings;
As long as I can be right next to you,
We can forget my body."*

I couldn't answer anything.
I was just merely speechless.
She was convincing and intimidating,
My heart interrogated my mind for a while.
"Why do I need to feel the touch?
Why do I need to see the future?
Why all the myriads of thoughts?
And why the complicated feelings?"

She took me dancing back again,
Through dark night skies while smiling.
Her grace destroyed our earthly sufferings
And all our endless human drama.
Our souls are carelessly immersed in love,
While we can't escape what we have started,
They're flowing through Vancouver's night sky
So passionately dreaming together in the ether.

Our vessels cry in their bedrooms.
Both convinced of their own versions of reality
Stubborn, demanding, defending,
Heartbroken, miserable, and foolish.
But souls dissolving in a new magical state –
If we can only hold each other like this
Adoring us through dreams
Then we were destined for such a journey.

Connected, intertwined, entangled,
Traveling without bodies,
And having all the fun through time
Embracing what fate bestowed upon us.
The two of us feel blessed,
Shielded by a luminous sky
As we dance and love and dance,
Praising the magical gifts of our life.

CHAPTER VII

On December 31, 2020, Benjamin and Phillip crossed Howe Sound from West Vancouver to Gibsons for the first time. They embarked on the journey to visit Holly's land. As Benjamin and Phillip sat comfortably in the ferry's café, enjoying their breakfast, Eurydice danced around them. Benjamin and Eurydice smiled from their affections, communicating non-verbally, simply by being in each other's presence. Their conversations were passionately engaging, but there was something much more intimate when they talked through thoughts and emotions. Eurydice could live through Benjamin and she was constantly finding exciting new ways to explore her man.

Eurydice constantly made fun of Benjamin since she could read his mind, and experience every sensation she provoked inside him. Phillip felt left out as he still tried to grasp this new reality, unable to see Eurydice. Benjamin and Phillip could exchange oracle visions, magical dreams, and past life memories, so Benjamin decided to try and show Eurydice to him. Benjamin asked Phillip to touch his shoulder. Once Phillip did, he saw Eurydice sitting across from him. He impulsively pulled back his hand, confused by the vision, but once these first weird sensations subsided, he placed his hand back. Phillip communicated with other souls in dreams, as they came to seek his guidance too, but he never saw the presence of a soul in the awakened world. Yet once he fell in love with Becky, he advanced in his magic and clairvoyance too. Eurydice was ecstatic as she loved being seen, smiling like a girl in a spotlight. Phillip hadn't seen Holly's eyes, but once he saw the eyes of her soul, he immediately recognized her. She was his daughter in one of their past lives, and now Phillip rejoiced from seeing her again.

Phillip felt an intense bond with Eurydice, but he was still puzzled by this new reality. "Tell me, Eurydice, I understand that humans can see each other's souls, in a dream state, but we are not in the dream right now, so how is it possible for us to see you?"

"Oh, Phillip! You probably already realized that I'm a soul with supernatural abilities. I was granted to be a spiritual princess in this life, so I can manifest myself easier to those willing to see."

"I believe there are not that many. I can certainly say that citizens of your kingdom wage war against Nature itself. I'm glad to be able to see you, but isn't it dangerous to leave your body just like that?"

"Well, I'm an energy made of heavenly light, so I can be in two places at once. I can be with Holly now, but she doesn't want to talk to me. It was far more dangerous for her when I was trapped in the Underworld, as I surrendered to death. But when Benjamin found me, I decided to fight for my life. It warms my heart that he's talking to me and allows me to express myself using his body. He doesn't ignore my questions or pleas, and this really heals me."

"I think it's the same as going to college." Benjamin interjected. "Any human goes through some form of education once they leave their parents' house. A soul also has a similar experience, while the body enjoys its youth of carelessness and parties. Just like the body reaches out to find teachers and masters to obtain the skills required for growth, a soul does the same."

"That makes sense." Phillip was inspired by this conversation. "Looking back at my student years, I feel that my soul was not with me. I was only concerned with making ends meet in a mad Saint Petersburg, while trying to survive the bullying in the university's dorm."

"Yes, I remember myself at that age, too," Benjamin replied. "My soul was learning somewhere else. I could hear him, but he was often so distant as if seeking advice in the distant places."

"So, you see, you see!" Eurydice was ecstatic to have this conversation, "Benjamin thinks I will spend the next three years living with him and learning about my essence through our love. I think I am a very confused being, and my knight – oh, well, you know my knight." Eurydice melted, like a girl in love.

"You are too good for me, Eurydice. I feel like I don't deserve you." Benjamin couldn't stop smiling.

"You do deserve me. I don't deserve you, as I'm in this weird and complex predicament. I will be forever in debt to you. Only you can teach me how to save Holly."

"Well, you give me inspiration like no one else and help me understand my magic, so I think we do deserve each other." Benjamin passionately kissed Eurydice, and our princess felt like the happiest girl in the world.

When the ferry arrived, Eurydice excitedly shared the stories about her beloved land. She hadn't visited her home in a while, so she was happy to be back. Eurydice energized our tired brothers, and they were looking forward to celebrating New Year together. The night turned out to be a magnificent celebration. Both brothers felt more bewildered than liberated from their newly discovered love, so they sought any possible advice or encouragement on their paths. Tonight, Eurydice asked them to enjoy this evening and celebrate the end of this unusual year of spiritual awakening. Our soulmates happily enjoyed wine and Spanish delicacies served by the hosts. Spirits gave our guests a beautiful two-bedroom house with a spacious ceremonial living room and a fireplace. Spiritual ornaments, statues, and sacred books full of mystical knowledge decorated the place and inspired guests for magical rituals. This place was designed for psychotherapy, spiritual journeys, sensual practices, and studies about the meaning of life and death.

The next afternoon, after spending the morning in complete tranquility, our knights were invited to meet Zigfried, one of the spiritual gatekeepers of this land, for separate psychotherapy sessions. First, Benjamin would attend a session alone, and then Eurydice would join him for a couple's session. Tomorrow the same was planned for Phillip and Suzanne.

Benjamin stepped into the room and closed the doors behind him, yet Eurydice came right after to eavesdrop. Both Benjamin and Zigfried joked about Eurydice's sneaky nature. No matter what any man ever asked of this woman, she immediately disobeyed in an act of defiance, without thinking about consequences. A rebellious spirit shined brightly in her heart, and many male teachers ran away from her essence. Only Benjamin could sustain such daring energy and help her to find empowerment in it.

As Zigfried began his session, Eurydice shaped into the body of the mischievous nine-year-old girl and slightly opened the doors. Benjamin and Zigfried saw that but pretended they didn't notice. They were amused that Eurydice decided to change her shape, so her knight would not scold her for spying on them. This soul developed many tricks through her experiences. Benjamin laughed again about what he was up against. "You see, Zigfried, what I have to deal with. Sometimes I feel it's just too impossible to reason with her. If I present her with a new spiritual guidance or a solution for her healing, she rejects it immediately, without even trying."

"Oh, certainly! I know this soul very well; we are all, amused and terrified by her abilities. Too many teachers failed miserably. Why you think you're different?"

"Because I know her true nature, I could see deep inside her essence. Eurydice is a quintessential divine feminine goddess with a Magdalene heart and womb. Our present society suppresses her truth, and imposes a destructive reality upon her full of delusional rules. She doesn't have the freedom to shine. Because the world has to conform to her, not the other way around."

"But you understand this is not how life works?"

"Oh yes, I surely do. How often have I struggled to find a proper way to conduct myself around her? When you love someone the way I love this soul, you may give her more free passes than she deserves, and sometimes I failed to save her because of that."

"Indeed, this is a concern of her mother, Queen Ariadne. If she doesn't accept her true feminine path in this life, I'm afraid the darkness may take complete control over her and she will be lost forever."

"I sympathize with the queen, but may I ask how she allowed it to get to this point?"

"All I know is that Eurydice ran away from her home. Every one of her explanations seemed like another fantasy of her wild imagination, so we stopped trusting her long ago. Once Eurydice escaped, she got lost, distracted by sparkles of demonic illusions. We couldn't understand why she would reject our protection when she knew that demons hunt her. We all thought she would end up in a cult of a false prophet or with some perverse musician."

"Looks like you have underestimated her. Even though she got lost, she found a way to reach me, and only the smartest souls know how to do that. I rarely engage on this level and I'm cautious with my time."

"Yes, obviously, we don't know her as well as you do. We only guard her in this life. I'm glad things turned out the way they did, even though we don't know what future holds. As I understand Eurydice requested this meeting because you both can't figure out how to proceed?"

"Well, I find our situation quite weird and unsettling. I have doubts and personal reservations, but I believe I can heal her traumas. I think we are pushing ourselves to become our best versions because of our love."

"Well, maybe being in love with you is the only solution for Eurydice. Maybe that's why other teachers have failed, as they weren't as invested as you are."

"Probably that's how it supposed to be. Only I don't feel comfortable when she's acting like a child. I don't know how I should treat her in those situations. One day I feel like we are lovers, and the next day, I'm like her father, which feels too weird."

"She's acting like a child to avoid her higher responsibilities. She refuses to get older, that's all. Please don't fall for her games. Yet there might be another reason. If say in two lives your story was cut short, you may be required to live through the lessons you missed. The one life could be of lovers but the other could be of relatives."

"I see. It actually makes sense. I should research that. But I think I will have to improvise anyway."

"One thing, Benjamin, please stop overthinking your reality. It can be a true challenge to a mind like yours. Because I have no idea who else can help Eurydice. I feel that, at least with you, she has a fighting chance. But you must show our queen that you are a man who can advance her education through your romantic entanglement."

"Well, I need that for myself first and foremost. I can't stop my spiritual progress only because Eurydice wishes to spend all our time enjoying cuddles and kisses."

"Good, I can see your integrity, but the queen won't simply believe you. It will take time to convince her because, she is very disappointed with Eurydice. Your desire to live together would only aggravate her concerns."

"The queen will see the results. We can only address our traumas together. Eurydice is in real danger, and as much as I like our romance, we are running out of time."

"Well, I should warn you – Eurydice won't make it easy for you. She will try to sabotage every one of your attempts. Especially when she knows how enticing her sexuality is for you."

"I know it won't be easy. I'm incredibly attracted to her, and the intimate visions she creates do entrap me, but I'm learning to find a balance. I feel like we complete each other and I want to make my intentions official."

"You should directly address Ariadne then, but I'm not sure if Eurydice is ready to face her."

"I'll talk to her, and one day she will be ready."

"I'm really glad Eurydice has you, Benjamin. Do you have any other pressing questions?"

"Eurydice has to live in this house for lost souls. Is there any way she can live with me? It would be much better for our growth and healing."

"So Holly can't hear Eurydice's dreams and doesn't believe she has a future, so it feels like she is destined to be murdered again. That is her inevitable future if observing from this point in time, but you can rewrite that. If Eurydice could construct a tangible dream using your body, then you can live together, as she would have an honest wish to stay alive. For example, if you can build a future house for two of you in a spiritual realm, then Eurydice can potentially live there."

"This makes perfect sense. Yes, I do not have a dream right now. I even wanted to move back to the kingdom of Ukraine just before I met Holly."

"So, if you don't see yourself here, Eurydice has nothing to live for."

"When I found her, Eurydice was so tormented by Holly's choices that she requested her death. I saw true desperation and desire to die in her eyes. But I think I'm starting to envision our future together."

"Yes, but it's still vague and distant. It must be a solid dream. You must make further commitments."

"Do you have specific suggestions? I feel like I'm still missing something."

"I see it has something to do with another soul from your family, Lana Del Rey. Her energy is woven into the story of your love. The three of you are intertwined in some way. I see Holly reading Lana's book. It holds your answers, so you may look into that."

After our soulmates worked through their issues, Benjamin and Phillip organized a sacred ceremony to ask guidance from the land. This unusual journey, looked like a divine opportunity to assume their highest powers of magicians. Yet to get there, they have to address past issues, say the words of love they neglected to express before, face their own demons, and uncover traps that led their ladies to tragic deaths. Eurydice had direct access to this land, so her spirits welcomed knights from the distant kingdom and made them feel at home, encouraging them to fight for the dreams of their hearts. The new friendship was established and a stream of powerful energies entered our soulmates, enveloping every cell. This vital force was gifted to them to enrich and empower them.

When Benjamin and Eurydice returned home, they had an assignment from spirits. Benjamin knew he wouldn't see Holly again, but Holly had to make that choice for herself. The land was using Benjamin as a tool of karmic balance. Free will implies a choice at the crossroads, and Nature always has to present two options for any human. On January 5th, 2021, Benjamin performed the last physical action required by the spirits, as he wrote to Holly, asking for another possible meeting.

Later in the evening, Holly replied. *Hi Benjamin, I'm afraid the boundaries I like to maintain with my dates have surpassed a level where I feel comfortable, and I can no longer continue seeing you. I want to thank you for your time and your generosity. All the best, Holly.*

When Benjamin read her answer, he realized Damian had completely trapped Holly, and there was no way to avoid the battle with evil. Damian provoked Holly's impulses and made her see a fear where there was the truth, see the danger, where there was only love. Benjamin understood he scared Holly as he was too forward in the birthday letter, but his heart demanded such an approach. He felt Holly crossed his boundaries on their first date, but he never said anything. He perceived Holly's actions arriving from the soul when she attacked and seduced him. Benjamin felt uncomfortable with Holly's forcefulness without acknowledging his emotions. She acted on the impulses of her sincere heart, breaking all the barriers Benjamin had. Because of that first night, our knight wrote the birthday letter in such an intimate way.

Benjamin would be content with any arrangement based on Holly's preferred boundaries, yet she never clearly presented them. She offered intimacy without setting rules or exploring their soul connection first. Benjamin knew the nature of his reclusiveness, but he was not ready to break away from the shell. His boundaries were self-imposed walls of protection. The experience of an immigrant traumatized Benjamin, leading him to close away from people. Besides, he was not ready to be with a woman and the romantic feelings he experienced for Holly shocked him in an unsettling way. He was fully concentrated on the Great American Spiritual War and his studies of magic. But suddenly this woman threw him off balance, and he couldn't think about anything else but her.

Benjamin couldn't forget that Holly said, "I know you." These three words allowed Benjamin to accept the love that appeared in his heart for the first time in a long while. The words of true love arrived from her honest heart, as she was herself in Benjamin's presence. Only when she was away from his aura, Damian's whispers made her question herself.

Eurydice was terrified after this answer. She had no connection with Holly anymore. Holly consciously chose Damian's path. Our knight stated his intentions clearly and stepped away. Benjamin asked angels to weave the circumstances in response to his honest intentions, bringing the highest and best outcome for all involved. He wouldn't pursue this woman anymore, concentrating on healing and training Eurydice. Once they would force Damian into exile, Eurydice could reconnect with Holly. Our knight patiently tried to explain this concept to Eurydice, but she was too sad and fearful to embrace it.

Benjamin assumed all the blame and apologized to Holly. *Hi, Holly. I'm sorry you feel this way. I wish I wouldn't ruin our connection. I feel quite embarrassed, to be honest, and I apologize. I understand how uncomfortable I made you feel, but I acted from my heart. It's been an emotional rollercoaster, as I couldn't properly process my visions. I went to meet you because I had to meet you. Call it a coincidence, a higher calling, or a magical chance. I'm thankful that I've met you again. If that's all I have, I will cherish these moments. I wish we had met under different circumstances. Maybe I could've handled it better and understood our connection, but I won't bother you again. Thank you, and please continue to shine amazingly. With best wishes, Benjamin.*

"How many times will she break my heart?" Benjamin asked Eurydice. "I guess if she is my woman, then she knows what is best for us. I trust her to create our future destiny." Benjamin had complete faith in their love. Eurydice was crushed but embraced the strong shoulder of her kind man. Now she could only trust her intuition and the masculine perseverance of this weird magician from Bukovina. She exhausted every other option, and no one else could offer her other viable solutions.

On January 6th, 2021, our lovers woke up in a completely new reality. Holly initiated the most dramatic shift of their lives. Her decision would profoundly transform Benjamin's existence for the next three years, and Holly was completely unaware of what she had done. Trying to make peace with this situation and calm their emotions, Benjamin reminded Eurydice about Zigfrid's advice. Our knight opened Lana's poetry book and read the poems aloud, performing them for Eurydice. The soul of his woman was quietly sitting on the bed, hypnotized by her man's voice. Eurydice was elated, praising Benjamin, as she immersed into these magical rhymes.

After their poetry evening, Benjamin experienced a vivid dream. He saw Holly reading Lana's book, in her bedroom, under the blanket with Mr. Dance curled on her lap. It was an idyllic and tranquil image. Benjamin was completely engulfed in it, feeling the energy of Holly's world. Only for Benjamin, Holly's reality missed him next to her. Benjamin visualized himself reading his own book next to his princess. Holly occasionally glanced at him, sharing a smile but never saying a word. They exchanged alluring gazes, enticing each other to throw away the books and dissolve in passionate kisses. They shared desires to rip off their clothes, yet they did not act upon those sensations. They continued to read but still provoked each other through gestures and intimate looks. They spoke without talking; they made love, without touching – just by reading together, under one blanket.

Two hours later, a strange force woke Benjamin up between three and four in the morning. He was in between states, confused about the date and time. Suddenly he heard a loud ringing in his ear – the angels were making contact, sending him a download of information. Benjamin hasn't realized it yet, but Lana's book has established the connection to the realm where higher beings stored her poems. Sleepy Benjamin grabbed his voice recorder and mumbled the sounds he was hearing. He kept talking until the words stopped, and he was allowed to fall asleep.

Once Benjamin woke up the next day, he rushed to transcribe his recording. He realized he had written a poem about Eloise from Camilla's perspective. Harmony arrived from the divine order, empowered by the heart of an artist in love. The poem was about the personal experience of two confused soulmates, where Camilla addressed traumas created by Eloise's deceptive and abusive male clients. It captured drama she saw in her eyes when they met. However, our lovers felt like Nature itself crafted this poem through their love, and Benjamin only recorded it. It was a poem dedicated to all lost and stranded souls. A poet and his muse joined in loving unity, convinced these words would dispel Damian's negative vibrations.

When Benjamin finished the poem with the help of the land and Eurydice, he came to the house of lost souls and performed it aloud as a sacred vow of his noble intentions. Through his prayer, he asked spirits to allow Eurydice to live with him. Our knight decided to fight for Eurydice, hoping to change the course of events. Once Benjamin created and performed his first medicine song, as a true healer of these lands, Eurydice was granted a permission to finally move in with him.

After enjoying the words of divine affection, our lovers danced in the Devonian Park of Coal Harbor. Soon Eurydice envisioned a first tangible dream, and she invited Benjamin to visit it. The images, full of love, calmed and inspired Benjamin. Eurydice saw how Benjamin and Holly moved into an apartment overlooking Stanley Park. Coal Harbor was Eurydice's sacred garden, and she witnessed how they could flourish here. Eurydice sat comfortably in her personal white armchair, as Holly entered the apartment for the first time and joined Benjamin on the balcony. Silently contemplating the view and feeling the start of a new life descending on them, their fingers accidentally touched on the balcony railings. A profound connection enveloped them, and they smiled from their shy gazes. Eurydice stopped wishing for death, joyfully observing two lovers who finally embraced their hearts and allowed the sensations of divine love envelop them.

Who Am I To Save You?

If it wasn't truly normal
Hearing voices out of nowhere,
If I couldn't catch you falling,
As I mend our broken promise,
If I didn't know my calling –
Death would seize your fragile aura.

You are seeking noble justice,
And the strength of earnest passions,
Dreaming of discovering the eyes
You will allow yourself to fall in love with –
Mutually,
Brazenly,
Unconditionally…

Striving always, never reaching,
Begging Heavens for the answers
While your hope is blind and tragic
Almost lost in lost compassion
Yet still sparkling in its essence
Full of lucid iridescence,
Shielded from above.

Soon, in front, exhausting challenge…
Worn off, tired, and in shambles,
Grieving hard from tribulations
Tried for treason and temptations
Judged for a dream to find the magic
Shocked to hear the truth of Heaven:
"If you don't accept what's in you
Seeing scars as your true glory
Feeling worthy of ambitions
While assuming every turning,

Then, true love will turn destructive
Even if divine and honest,
It won't reach the shining wholeness
Blocking sparks of real fondness
Making life completely worthless,
Washed out, fleeting, never present,
Tiny, painful, stripped of presents
Stealing joy and burying presence
Never gifting true embracement."

Yet your men are flawed and dreadful
Carried only by temptations
Superficial, selfish egos
Inept facing a pure lady
Reaching only for the panties
Never open, condescending,
Only taking, never giving
With amusement, yet abusing,
Seeing a toy.
But not a human.

Always showing their advantage,
Playing games without attachments,
Thrilled from vulgar, lustful feelings –
Just another archetype.

Passing issues, passing sickness
So aroused and so impatient
Switched off heart, removed from being
Men implant you with their demons
Spiders crawl to fill your psyche,
While you stare into the vastness
Soon dissolving in the mirror
Of your devastated dreams.

No salvation. Pure resentment.

Vicious yearnings. Condemnation.
Through detachment, you escape.

Your soul hides as she's tormented
And unable to confront
Complex pains, intense incursions,
Filling body with contempt,
As reality descends
Into a struggle of existence,
With no chances to transcend.

That's how troubled my wild visions –
Flood of filth in repetitions…
Bedroom's losing truthful magic,
In the madness, through obsession,
No one's guilty, witness treasure,
Pouring love with no pretensions,
Vowing honestly intentions,
All night long alone neglected.

Closed away in a void of sorrow,
Under sheets insanely crying,
Trapped alone inside the darkness.
It would never disappear.

From ourselves, we may be hiding
Finding troubles (stoked by lightning);
That's the truth of what is in you,
All these conflicts might just kill you.

On your quest for a collision,
Captivated by desires,
You talk only to the mirror
But not ever to yourself…

Lost in a true rebellious excitement,

Bedeviling reality and fantasies,
Pretending to comprehend the feelings,
Entangled in a web of lies,
So scared of not conforming,
Conceding to abuse,
Abandoning affection,
Recklessly in ecstasy,
Immersing in pure misery,
Possessed by plain repugnance,
Delightfully embracing
The twisted joy of this disturbing journey.

As we both
Took roads less traveled,

I witnessed how you dared to step into the reality
Beyond accustomed comprehension
While the storm invaded your soul;

I saw how you crossed the bridge
Into the forbidden land,
Escaping your protective garden;

But I also saw how adamant you were
In pushing me away,

So who am I to try to save you from yourself?

CHAPTER VIII

After many years of chaotic struggles, Eurydice finally felt a sense of balance and even some happiness. She was confused about Damian's nature, her conflict with Holly, her traumas and misfortunes, but after she moved in with Benjamin, she felt relieved. Even without a connection with her physical body, meeting Benjamin was the best thing that happened to her in this life. Our princess realized she was not clueless or broken. Eurydice lived her unique story, and now she wanted to embody it.

Benjamin had a break from his day job in January 2021. Our lovers will forever remember this time as their honeymoon. Benjamin and Eurydice embraced the time together and cherished every affectionate moment they had. They dissolved in romance and blissful joy. They shared walks, debated the nature of our world, smoked joints, drank mimosas, partied, and exchanged energies in many different ways, like any real lovers.

Eurydice learned to embrace Benjamin's masculine perceptions and soon they were intertwined like they never dreamed before. They told each other stories about their past and constructed amazing plans for their possible future. They danced and sang to Lana Del Rey's records, and her music became the soundtrack of their love story. Eurydice memorized *Honeymoon* and sang it in a seductive voice to her knight on every possible occasion. She learned how to play *How to Disappear* on a violin and performed this melody flying above the trees in Stanley Park. They did everything any two new lovers would do, feeling so natural around each other, as if they always been together. And since, in this life, they learned to share thoughts, meditations, dreams, and visions, their bond shined stronger each day.

Our knight tried his best to accommodate Eurydice – he shared his body with her, allowing her to do anything she needed to complete the lessons she failed in the past. Since Eurydice showed him what it's like to feel every female sensation, Benjamin wanted to return the favor. Just as he experienced Holly's sensual female pleasures and equally beautiful female pains, now Eurydice could experience what it was like to live in a masculine body. She hadn't been a man for four centuries, so initially, the experience felt too demanding and confusing for her, but Benjamin patiently guided her through the challenges.

Benjamin's tastes and habits changed as he allowed Eurydice in his body. Benjamin was always a tea person, but Eurydice loved coffee more, so Benjamin agreed to compromise. They tried every flavor available in many artisan coffee shops around Vancouver. Catering to Eurydice, Benjamin learned to craft beautiful lattes and hot chocolate at home. Because of Eurydice, Benjamin consumed endless amounts of grapefruits and raspberries, as the princess was obsessed with these fruits.

Our knight learned how to make grilled cheese sandwiches and where to procure Eurydice's favorite pizza. Once, he ordered a hand-crafted pizza from a restaurant only because it was on the way from his job, but Eurydice didn't like that particular place and demanded pizza from another one. Benjamin begged her not to waste food, attempting to re-heat the pizza in the oven at home. In spite, Eurydice cut an electric cable on a post, disabling electricity in their entire neighborhood, so Benjamin had no choice but to dine out in her chosen pizza place. Benjamin learned his lesson, and from that day, he never questioned the pizza preferences of his princess.

Benjamin showed Eurydice how he edited his experimental movies, and Eurydice aided with help, passionately learning the new art form. Our knight allowed her to choose their evening movies. They watched every romantic movie available and rewatched *The Notebook* as many times as they could, noticing similarities between their stories. One day Eurydice proclaimed they ought to watch the *Bridgerton* TV series, to prepare Benjamin for the conversation with Eurydice's mom. Eurydice commented on the strict rules of noble courting, explaining her knight which ones she would rebelliously defy. She couldn't comprehend how someone may restrict a loving relationship with her man.

Eurydice wanted to follow her heart's desires. Our princess even got sad at one point, "What good is it to be a princess if you can't behave the way you want? Constant pressing obligations and demands. Constant standards to follow and inevitable spotlight, full of gossip." Yet with greater power comes greater responsibility, and Eurydice only began to grasp this concept. She wanted to live without invented restraints, but these rules came from Nature, and Eurydice would have to accept her reality.

Royal ladies are deemed to follow the rules of courtship for their own higher benefit. Surely any lady should demand such a respectable approach from a prospective suitor, but it was a woman's free choice. However, for princesses like Eurydice, it was simply unavoidable. This is how spirits constructed the world to be. They placed a heavy burden on the princesses, who would eventually be in charge of their lands. The inner integrity and discipline of a couple with such magical powers needed to be tempered. The genuine friendship that's forms between a man and a woman before they will engage in intimate explorations creates an integral foundation for honest, sacred union of true intimacy, spiritual growth and prosperity.

Eurydice could not avoid this path and now she was angry at Benjamin, as he wanted to follow such approach to sensual pleasures. Our knight quickly realized the seriousness of this process and craved to embrace it. He recognized the higher value of the courtship and even scolded himself for how he approached dating in his youth, and especially how he surrendered to Holly's temptations. He was ashamed that he didn't stop Holly that first night, convinced that Queen Ariadne would not forgive his weakness. He could only dream that she would be merciless and gracious enough if he honestly confessed his flaws and vices. He wanted to tell Ariadne the real story of his life, how he became a true gentleman and a warrior through education, tempering, and mastering, despite his past. Benjamin realized that courting would heal Ariadne's rebellious child-like daughter, who could become a soft, generous, forgiving, and gracious woman with the help of his guidance. Now our knight buried the old version of himself that was rooted in the ill values of modern society and aspired to become an impeccable suitor.

As January was nearing its end, our lovers settled into their new life. They resolved their domestic household differences; they learned to compromise and respectfully disagree with one another. Benjamin and Eurydice visited Holly's apartment regularly, cleansing it from dark energies of low vibrations. Benjamin knew how to confront, expose and destroy such creatures and vibrations, so he began training Mr. Dance in this art. Cats were blessed with such spiritual skills from birth, as that was their primary responsibility in our world. Not many cats embraced their purpose these days, as their masters never trained them properly. Yet Mr. Dance was a brilliantly talented and eager to learn. At first, he was scared of Eurydice and Benjamin. He was only a year old, confused by the darkness in their place and constant loneliness, as Holly spent most time outside, partying at Damian's dinners, events, and galas. Whenever Holly tried to reflect on her complex feelings, process her traumas, or dive into spirituality, Damian would find a distraction for her with superficial dates and meaningless pleasures.

Yet the empty apartment was an excellent opportunity for Benjamin to become friends with Mr. Dance and earn his trust. Once Mr. Dance realized that Benjamin and Eurydice were his allies, he finally learned how to see awful creatures sprawling through his apartment. He was a young apprentice, but his assertiveness and enthusiasm meant more than his skills. Just in a month, half of the apartment was shining with loving light. Benjamin and Eurydice constructed a dome of protective light in Holly's apartment to shield her space from energetic sinister intruders. Each time they visited her place, they would reinforce the dome with magical golden threads of light crafted by Benjamin's loving heart.

Once our lovers witnessed progress, Eurydice felt confident enough to face her mother. After escaping her home, she was terrified to see Ariadne. On top of that, Eurydice had to introduce her man. She believed Benjamin would impress Ariadne. Only because of her reputation, Eurydice understood that Benjamin would need to be prepared for a harsh evaluations and unwelcoming greetings. She was stressed that he would be judged unfairly only because of her past actions. Eurydice's entire community saw her as a failure, as she often refused to complete her studies or even commit to a hobby, constantly disobeying her mother and tutors. Then she ran away without informing anyone.

Nevertheless, Eurydice knew this scary day would inevitably come. With Benjamin's guidance, she finally found love and compassion for herself. She ran away, because she had to find Benjamin. If others couldn't understand her, Eurydice was ready to accept that. She stopped looking for outside approval and validation. Even though Eurydice approached her life not in the way any parent would like, our princess was on a mission to heal her past wounds. She lived a crazy, bizarre, weird, and terrifying life. But she discovered true love and salvation as she followed her Magdalene intuition.

After only one month with her knight, Eurydice was not a small child anymore. Even though she occasionally acted like a teenager, sabotaging Benjamin's endeavors, she saw how much she had grown, and the princess hoped her mother would see that. Eurydice was convinced that even though Ariadne's first impression of Benjamin would be unfavorable, the queen would eventually accept their union. If Eurydice managed to summon up her destined knight from a faraway land she had never visited, it meant she was a talented and promising young princess. The way Benjamin looked at her convinced Eurydice of that. Our princess learned to love her inner beauty by seeing herself through Benjamin's eyes. Eurydice was in a sacred union with her soulmate, who constantly praised and admired her. That was the only validation Eurydice ever needed, and she was ready to fight for her love.

On January 28, 2021, Eurydice and Benjamin packed their bags and left for Sechelt. From their apartment on Jervis Street in Vancouver, they would travel to the last arm of Jervis Inlet. On the first leg of their journey, they arrived at Eurydice's favorite place – a tip of land, where Sechelt and Salmon Inlets merge, just beyond Mountain Richardson. Eurydice loved spending time here when Holly was a child, so she wanted to show the energy of this place to Benjamin, and they stopped here for a night. After having dinner in their tent, they were invited by Eurydice's spiritual ancestors to participate in a prayer circle. Our princess was happy to introduce Benjamin to her beloved guides. The souls of the deceased ancestors who guided Eurydice in her youth gathered around the fire, stepping from the waters and forests. They empowered Eurydice throughout her life to fight for her truth and never betray her heart. Today they were here to greet our lovers. Benjamin was destined to guard this land, and since Eurydice loved him, her guides were curious to meet him.

Seven souls took turns as they shared words of wisdom with our lovers. The land blessed them with balanced insights of three male and three female elders. The seventh soul was new to their circle, but spirits invited her for higher reason. A young female warrior Emina, arrived last, holding her righteous sword and a shield of a lightworker. She came to share her truth and encourage Eurydice to fight for all murdered and forgotten women of these lands. Emina died in battle, protecting her tribe. She never experienced the full essence of life, as she was quite young when the war broke out. Emina carried tattoos of a noble warrior on her face, portraying her achievements and shining with her spiritual tears full of love for her mission. She reminded our lovers of Camilla, Eloise, and Allania, as they all shared the same tragically beautiful destiny. Emina came to pass the torch of a peaceful warrior to Eurydice, so she could protect her land against new evils.

They bonded through sharing the stories of past glories and tragedies. Even though they lived centuries apart, through the magical ceremony, their souls could gather around the fire. They carried the world's burden on their shoulders, but they never forgot to find time for a joyful dance too. Our lovers listened to the legends of this land, witnessing a mystical pattern of rhymes. As they parted, each soul hugged Eurydice and Benjamin, giving them a boost of supporting energy. When elders looked at the present state of their kingdom, witnessing humans raping Nature with fear, and superficial values, they felt defeated, as if they lived for nothing. Yet now they saw a rebellious warrior princess and her passionate knight who could continue spreading love and light on their lands.

After spending a peaceful night in Nature's hands, our lovers sailed through Jervis Inlet, and once they passed the Princess Louisa Inlet, they saw the shores of their destination – the Xenichen village. Eurydice guided Benjamin to the foothills of Mountain Alfred, to her mother's mansion. As they walked through the community, Eurydice asked Benjamin to demonstrate his noble intentions. His pure heart, full of love, burst with magic. Benjamin created a majestic entertainment fair with a parade of musical marching bands, confetti, fireworks, food, and festivities. Flowers bloomed through the snow, and the air was illuminated with sparkling rays of light, vibrating with every possible dazzling color. Benjamin created a reality where people could celebrate the beauty of their loving union. Eurydice proudly walked through the streets, illuminated by her man's magic, as villagers chatted about the return of their princess. Everyone knew who she was, but no one saw her in such a light. Hypnotized souls joined the procession led by our lovers, guided by the shining love of their hearts. The entire land and her stewards joyfully immersed in the world Benjamin created to celebrate his princess.

Queen Ariadne, agitated by the noise, stepped outside. She asked her closest assistant, Bartholomew, what was happening. There were no planned celebrations, and her entourage was as confused as she was. The queen stood on the porch, irritated by the unknown. She preferred peaceful solitude. Her loyal assistants stood behind her in awe and disbelief how their quiet life was interrupted in such a brazen manner. In the next moment, they experienced even greater shock when they saw Eurydice approaching the house, holding hands with a man they had never seen. Our lovers entered the front garden and faced the queen, shining with love. Eurydice hid behind Benjamin's back, avoiding the punishing look of her mother.

"Good day, dear queen. Please allow me to introduce myself – my name is Benjamin."

"Hello, Benjamin. I'm Ariadne. Can you please explain to me what this noise is all about?"

"Dear queen, I arrived today with the purest and most beautiful love known to a man, and I would like to ask for your daughter's hand. My intentions are noble, and I have nothing to hide; I'm trying to demonstrate my truth to your community. Also, my love is so big that I sometimes can't contain it, so I do apologize if I disturbed your peace."

The queen looked at her assistants in complete disbelief. Not only had our lovers come without invitation, but this man was asking for Eurydice's hand, which her relatives believed would never happen. Ariadne distrusted her daughter and now she was convinced that this was one of her manipulative provocations.

"Benjamin, it's hard to believe that your intentions are pure, as you are trying to make a show out of your love. True feelings are subtle and intimately expressed. Besides, Eurydice needs to explain herself before I can even consider your proposal. Eurydice, do you hear me?"

Eurydice stepped from Benjamin's back, looking at the ground, "I'm sorry, Mother, for how things turned out, but I wished no harm to anyone. I had my spiritual reasons and I can explain everything."

"And now you are showing up like this? You proved once again that you are not even trying to be an adult. You once again disrespected me by thinking I'll simply forget everything. Do you wish me to believe you truly want to marry this man? Is it another game of yours?"

"Mother! I was right all along! Benjamin is the man of my fate, and I can prove that to you. It is hard to believe me after I deceived you many times, but I would have never returned if this was just a fling. The fact that I'm here, ready to acknowledge my past mistakes, shows that I'm an adult. Now I know what's real and what's not, so I'm betting on this relationship. We are in love, and we want to build a future together," Eurydice replied.

"I don't believe you in the slightest. I know your nature and how fleeting your affections are. Besides, I'm too angry at you to have a reasonable conversation. You will be grounded if you wish to step into this house."

"But, Mom! Please! I didn't mean to be a rebel just for the sake of it. Now I know why I acted like that. Benjamin explained all of it to me."

"Or did he? Is he some kind of a prophet?" Ariadne was furious at Eurydice.

"Well, actually, he is. Benjamin is a magician, a teacher, and an artist. He is the man of my dreams, and we are destined soulmates. He can guard me against evil."

"It sounds wonderful, but let me be a judge of that. You know I don't trust a single word of yours. Go to your room, and let me talk to this man alone."

Eurydice obediently marched into the house, but the servants were happy to see her, and they joyfully accompanied her to the room, telling her how glad they were to see their princess. At least their friendly chat uplifted Eurydice spirit, as she really missed everyone.

"So, Benjamin. What do you think we should do?"

"It is up to you, my queen. I'm at your mercy. I don't own any possessions and am not of any noble status. I'm just an aspiring knight of magic. Yet my heart is full of crystal, pure love for your daughter, and I can prove my honesty in any way you see fit."

The queen approached Benjamin, "All right, then I would like to see the essence of your heart."

Benjamin reached for his heart, took it out of his chest, and showed it to Ariadne, raising high above his head. The colorful, beautiful light of a pure, sparkling diamond, burst out, filling the garden. It was so bright that the queen and her assistants instinctively turned away blinded by Benjamin's love. His heart shined with celestial hues and sang the most harmonious love song. It felt like the time stopped. The queen had never seen anything like that, and Benjamin proudly held his heart high. Once the queen assessed it, he hid it away.

"I see now. It's hard to believe that Eurydice has found you. I heard many spiritual whispers about such a possible destiny for her, but it was hard to believe she would actually find such unconditional love. But what do you mean, when you said you have only love?"

"I'm not from this land, and I'm ready to tell you my entire story, but I can't offer financial security for your daughter at this moment. I'm well aware of my talents and skills; I know that one day I will be able to build a solid life for us, but right now I only have my love. I want to be honest with you, if I'm asking to court your daughter."

"I understand. Tell me in detail what you have."

"I have a career here with a stable income, but I don't have any savings, and I'm still paying debts from my immigration and education." Benjamin showed the negative balance of his bank accounts on his phone.

"Thank you for your transparency. So can anyone vouch for your character and integrity?"

"There are two souls you should meet." Benjamin established contact with Phillip and Suzanne. Their souls appeared before Ariadne, validating and supporting his story, explaining in detail what they know about him. They told Ariadne how much they respected Benjamin and how long Phillip had known Benjamin, testifying for his noble character and explaining struggles they'd endured in Vancouver. The queen thanked them for presenting their truth, and they pleaded with Ariadne to give Benjamin a chance, before saying goodbye and leaving.

"I can see your honesty, Benjamin, so I would like to continue our conversation inside the house. You have to forgive me for not being prepared for this. Eurydice is not the easiest child to handle, and I appreciate your patience. Yet I must tell you that it won't be easy for you, as I have high standards for her possible suitors. She has a very unique destiny, so a man can uplift or ruin her. It's a very fine balance so I would like to really get to know you."

"Knowing how supernatural Eurydice is, I would have acted the same way in your position. Yet this pure love descended upon us unexpectedly. I even tried to avoid our meeting, but it happened, and we fell in love."

CHAPTER IX

Benjamin and Ariadne settled across each other in the parlor room. Bartholomew accompanied his queen as a witness of possible arrangements and to record any relevant information. Eurydice was grounded, yet our sneaky princess had a secret hole in the floor of her room so she could hear everything. Ariadne knew about it, so she constructed her conversations cautiously. Queen allowed Eurydice to listen, as it was impossible to stop her.

"You know, Benjamin, I actually allowed you inside, because I know my daughter too well, and I never saw her eyes sparkle this way. She truly loves you, and I guess it makes me somewhat sad. She grew up fast and has become a real woman," the queen addressed our knight.

"I'm a little shy hearing such words. We fell into the well of our love so quickly that I still question whether this is just a dream or not. With her, I can finally be myself, and I feel like she shines brighter too. I also hoped I could ask to speak with Eurydice's father and state my proper intentions in his presence."

"My husband won't be joining us, and you would discuss any arrangements with me."

"Can I at least meet with him? As a gentleman, I think this is the only correct way to conduct such affairs."

"Unfortunately, you won't be able to meet him. His affairs are a personal matter, and I have only met you. Maybe one day I will share more with you."

"I apologize, Your Majesty, for bringing this up. You both raised a magical daughter. But I'm wondering why I'm even allowed to present my intentions? I am hardly a preferred match for your daughter both financially and socially. I aspire to achieve a lot, hoping to fulfill her dreams, but I honestly can't guarantee anything."

"You are right. You must earn my trust with your actions, and it won't be easy. I want a secure future for my children. Only you showed pure, unconditional love for my daughter, which is the main condition for her suitor as written in the book of her destiny. Naturally, your financial situation is a concern for me, but I'm obligated to give you a chance as you are the first man with such love that arrived on her path."

"Well, I wish to thank you, my queen, for granting me such an opportunity."

"You know, right now, I'm actually very curious. I didn't like how you showed up, but you are really living by your heart. The fact that you came to Holly's spiritual protectors first, basically arriving through the back door, makes your story quite fascinating. You must be a real magician as otherwise it would be impossible. Since you also know that Holly will be allowed to receive an official proposal not earlier than in three years, it means that you were sent on a path to court her soul first."

"This is accurate. I must confess I do not know the higher reasons for our predicament, but we both are determined to uncover why we live our love story in this way. Eurydice is very eager to learn."

"Eurydice is eager to learn," Ariadne turned to Bartholomew, smiling. "I haven't heard that sentence in a while. It sounds hard to believe, but please do continue."

"We know that we need to work through our past traumas, grief, and wounds. We have to find the answers that Eurydice's desperately looking for. This soul is very special to me, and I wish to help her heal. She is like the Holy Grail of my experience, and I'm so small without her. Eurydice came to share my adventure with me, as only she can teach me how to be my most authentic self. My skills grew exponentially from the moment I met her."

"I must say I feel like you are describing some fantasy girl, and not my daughter."

"She is trying to learn, and surely she relentlessly questions the process. She often rejects my advice, but I always find a proper explanation for her. She learns to embrace what life presents to her and own her truth. Eurydice is already mastering to work with energies of synchronicity and serendipity. We also finally resolved the *Don Quixote* dilemma."

Benjamin referred to Eurydice's lasting struggle with the novel. In her past three lives, she experienced the same challenge – she could never understand this book, and she didn't know why she had to. She struggled to complete reading it around two centuries ago under the supervision of Benjamin. Yet even though our knight helped Eurydice to achieve this goal, she still carried this requirement into another life, as she cheated on her assignment. Even though Eurydice claimed she read the novel, she only treated it as a collection of words, never immersing in the lessons this book carried specifically for her.

"I can hardly believe that," Ariadne replied. "You've only known her for a few weeks. It's impossible to solve it this quickly, knowing Eurydice."

"That's what I'm trying to explain. From the moment we met, both Eurydice and I entered into a state of profound spiritual growth. Our love has transformed us from that first date, elevating our spirits and hearts. My skills shine, and it's only because of her. Most importantly, now she's eager to grow too, looking at how I excel."

"Bartholomew, I think we have to check this right now. Please invite her teacher and our librarians. I'm curious, Benjamin, so I hope you don't mind."

"If you know how to test this, I would love to see it."

The queen led the way to Eurydice's room on the second floor while Bartholomew called for assistance. Eurydice's bedroom accurately represented her, and Benjamin was glad for an opportunity to see her sacred, feminine space. It was as girly as he had imagined. Only books were scattered everywhere, making it hard to move around. Stacks of books stood on the floor in the left corner, reaching up to the ceiling. The right corner was filled with boxes of books she hasn't finished in her past lives. Her desk and windowsill were covered with books too. Eurydice neglected to learn many lessons, so she was forced to carry them into next lives.

"Eurydice, Benjamin claimed that you have solved the *Don Quixote* case."

"Oh yes! We did, Mama. I don't have that book or dictionary on my desk anymore."

The queen checked, but the novel was nowhere to be found. Eurydice's teacher and house librarian walked in. They verified that this book was transferred to the library. As Eurydice learned a lesson from this manuscript, she was released from re-reading *Don Quixote* again.

"So, how did you do it, Eurydice?" The queen asked.

"Well, I live the book's story with Benjamin right now, and that was the reason. The book was preparing me for this life. It was a premonition. As I can see everything from Benjamin's perspective right now, it helped me understand the mind of Don Quixote. Benjamin is a poor knight fighting with the imagined windmills, as Damian is an invisible spirit. My knight is on the path to win the affections of his princess, who summoned him from distant lands. Her soul guides him through many challenges and empowers him to be his true self. I also often questioned what *Don Quixote* was supposed to be – a comedy or a tragedy. I struggled to embrace this contradiction, but Benjamin explained the true power of this novel. It can be both, depending on reader's perceptions. That's why I had to re-read it, to experience laughter in one life and tears in another. Or maybe I'm just in love and trying hard to impress my man. I don't know."

While assessing Eurydice's room, another great realization dawned on the librarian in charge – other manuscripts had disappeared too. Eurydice was thirsty to study only because she could spend more time with her man, so she was learning even faster than she thought. Love made her do unimaginable things, and Ariadne was pleasantly surprised with her daughter.

"Eurydice, that's wonderful news. If love inspires you to learn and accept yourself, then I can only approve of such a wonderful match."

"Does it mean that I can stay with Benjamin?"

"It's too early to say, as you surely know."

Eurydice tried to show that she didn't understand what her mother was talking about, but they secretly exchanged smiles when Ariadne closed the door on their way out.

Once they returned to the living room, Benjamin asked a question that bothered him the most, "I apologize for asking, dear queen, and maybe this is not my place, but why you can't help Holly yourself?"

"Because it's too late. Damian is an alien being in our lands. When we discovered he hunts her, we realized we didn't know a magician who could match his strength or even fully understand who this being was. We thought

Eurydice ran away from her obligations, but now I see she was trying to escape Damian."

"Yes, she was looking for salvation, so she searched for me. She did that intuitively, without understanding what she was looking for. Only when I retrieved her, did she realize that she got entrapped and deceived."

"I'm thankful you saved her. I wish to establish trust between us, as I feel only you can battle Damian. Our magicians don't know how to confront this entity. I don't even know why he came to our lands."

"He's been trying to capture Eurydice for five centuries, always arriving to the land of her birth."

"I didn't even realize that she was so important to him, Benjamin. I don't know what we can do. It's painful to acknowledge such truth, but how do you know so much?"

"Because I came into this world empowered by my spirits to share truthful knowledge about the laws of Nature. But I can only fulfill my destiny with Eurydice. Without her, I won't be able to spread words of wisdom and Damian will entrap even more souls."

"So who are your guardian spirits, I must ask? You are not of these lands. I was not aware Eurydice's man would be a foreigner."

"Well, I'm not a foreigner. I'm empowered by the Lighthouse Park and Point Gray serpent spirits."

"Wait, I'm confused. You were not born on these lands, so what am I missing?"

"Oh, sorry. My birth spirits are from the skies."

"I see. Now that makes sense. That's how you know what you know?"

"That's right. I'm always arriving as a spiritual guide, empowered by the Heavens to deliver divine knowledge and teach souls. My next important mission is to write a book I envisioned in 1794."

"So you believe you won't be able to write this work without Eurydice?"

"Correct. I envisioned my book while spiritually communicating with Eurydice. We have felt the presence of this manuscript in the air around us as if we could touch it. It is a divine manuscript of the skies and we are its co-creators. We researched it for the last two lives, and now we are destined to conclude it on your lands."

"So Eurydice has agreed to this journey and wants to participate in creating this work?"

"Oh, very much so. Through this process, Eurydice would learn what she always wanted to know. And well, this is our research into the essence of eternal love, so her girly heart melts as she finds the connection between our souls very romantic."

"I can feel how much she loves you. Your love is so beautiful. No one has ever described and praised my daughter the way you do. You can see how special she is, despite her scars, veils and walls. I think I'm ready to sign a contract with you, as I've heard enough, but do you mind if we continue our conversation?"

"Sure, I'd be happy too."

"So, who empowered you upon birth before you were summoned here?"

"The spirits of Dnipro River and the spirits of Carpathian Mountains. My brother and I were born in the eastern part of the kingdom of Ukraine, but our masculine ancestry line is from the West. We are a real representation of the concept known as 'soborna Ukraina'. It is similar to the concept of the Canadian Union, that's empowered by the differences between East and West."

"So, how did you discover traditions that are also common in our land?"

"Well, later, we relocated to Siberia to the small town of Nizhnevartovsk that was built around the oil lake called Samotlor. My family was the first white settlers on that land, and they built the first apartment buildings, laying the foundation for the future town. It is a place in the middle of Siberian taiga, on the shores of the Ob River. The spirits shared with me the knowledge of the First Nations who lived there before. Later I discovered that the serpent spirits of Baikal Lake were also my destined teachers, and I visited them for initiation rituals. They formed the foundation of my interactions with the spiritual realm, and I embraced practicing magic since then."

"Actually, the first people we empowered on our lands came from Siberia. Our legend says that humans lived peacefully near a large lake a long time ago, but one day the darkness came and attacked them. Since they could not cross the big water, they were in danger of being destroyed. One night, a divine providence covered the waters with ice, and the tribe crossed to the other side. Then the chief caused a hot wind to blow, and the ice disappeared so their enemies could not follow. As they lost their connections to their former spirits, we empowered them upon arrival. It's exactly what is happening to you."

"It's interesting that we also fled our enemies. The great darkness had descended on those lands again, and so we are here. We are humbled and grateful to receive beautiful gifts of divine love and supernatural powers from your spirits, as we would never survive here otherwise."

"I thank you for acknowledgments, but you know that you have earned your gifts through your hard work. The spirits would never aid you with their energies if you were not living by your heart. We see who is honest and trustworthy when we decide who should be stewards of our lands. You have manifested support as you have long searched for it, which is a testament to your perseverance and strength. Do you know why specifically Lighthouse Park spirits empower and train you?"

"Well, you probably can guess the answer. I lived on that land around nine centuries ago."

"That's what my intuition said. It means your life exists in our records. I will ask Bartholomew to bring me the book with the story of that life, but how much do you know about it?"

"I was a magician, and my name was 'the one who speaks with the land'. Once, enemies hunted us, and the land told me to hide our women and children further inland. Every man was eventually slaughtered, but we managed to save all of our women. After death, my soul guided my daughter to lead, and they found safety with a peaceful tribe around present-day Coquitlam."

"Oh, I heard this story at the dinner table once. Unbelievable. Here you are – talking to the land again. So do you work with Sisiutl, the sea serpent of our lands?"

"Yes, we were able to connect with him once Phillip assumed his magical powers. You know, it wasn't easy."

"Sure, but that's another confirmation of your abilities. You were meant to come here, guided by your pure heart. So, Phillip is empowered by Burrard Inlet, and you bring snakes from Point Grey and Lighthouse Park?"

"Yes, that's correct. My spiritual teacher Sigiriutl taught me how to summon the land snakes and then guided me how to build the wings of Sisiutl."

"I know Sigiriutl. He is a very powerful spirit. What a beautiful and serendipitous life we share. Now your love story with Eurydice makes perfect sense to me. So, could I ask you to entertain my curiosity and tell me a story of the creation of the world? I'm wondering how you heard it from your spirits. Let's see how much our lands share."

Benjamin began his tale. "Once the supreme Heavenly Goddess and the highest priestess, who would soon become the Mother of our world, restlessly paced in her lush castle in the higher spiritual plane in the vastness of our universe. She blessed her magical spiritual garden and everything she had in her life. Her sacred space was filled with balanced energies and pure love. She only felt somewhat anxious and unsettled at that moment. She asked her husband, the God, the Father of our Earth, to entertain her. God ecstatically embraced this chance as he enjoyed serving and pleasing his divine woman. He found great pride in amusing her and dedicated his life to fulfilling her most sincere wishes. He told his Goddess about his travels to other worlds; he read angelic poems and sang beautiful songs. The Goddess could sense the divine beauty as stories full of joyful and tragic tears intertwined, creating a state of unique bliss. She felt the full range of emotions available to her and saw the most luminous colors of light entering her space.

"Through the beauty of this evening, her husband inspired the Goddess to create a vision of a new world. She dreamed about a new garden where their children could play, suffer and grow. 'There are many planets and you told me everything about them, but they are mostly of the same essence. What if we create a special world in our image, in the image of our perceptions? I know your stories, poems, and songs, as you know my dreams, wishes, and inspirations. Yet we decided to split into two separate deities by choice to experience a more fulfilling journey of sacred companionship based on the highest intimacy. We don't feel the loneliness of oneness, even though we can transcend this separation. We can attest it is beautiful to be opposite beings, two complimentary sides of one essence. In this world, the souls can experience the conflicting duality of such nature, allowing them to grow spiritually. They'll learn to live their highest purpose through a complex process of limited perceptions. They would die at birth and transform back to divine light at death, repeating the cycle until their essence is fulfilled. We will create a place where oneness is divided into two opposites, so souls would struggle to transcend their limits, as they would need to discover their other half and embrace true self-love. Through deceptions, conflicts, contradictions, adversities, and truth, they can be tempered and learn their supreme nature. I'm dreaming of a perfect place. Can you feel my visions? Maybe I can't find the correct words.' The Goddess addressed her man.

'I think you want to create the Paradise.'

'Exactly! I didn't know such a word existed. It describes perfectly what I see in my heart.'

'It never did. I created this word just now to explain the vision of your heart, my supreme Goddess.'

'Thank you, my God. Yes, I'm sensing a new place with a unique way of communication between all beings, guided by the higher laws. The nature of this garden would hear its inhabitants, and they can shape the world together. It is a place where everyone seeks dreams and dares to fight for them. Where beauty and magic are spilled in the air, yet everyone is oblivious to it, trapped in their limited shell. At the same time, all beings could feel blissful joy, where they can be overwhelmed with natural beauty and create their own happiness in the way they wish.'

"God patiently listened to his empress, absorbing every nuance she was radiating, and the next day he designed the world based on his wife's vision. Any man desires nothing but to bring to life the dream of his beloved woman. Our God worked tirelessly to impress his Goddess. He created two energies of one kind in every aspect of this new reality, complementing each other.

"At first, there was nothing but water, yet like a woman's uterus, it was ready to give birth. Our creator made an energetic dome that split water into two parts – one became the surface, and the other turned into skies. The dome was designed to be a library of all existing knowledge. It would record every life ever lived and store the truth of the Earth's sentient beings. The waters above symbolize the collective consciousness of humanity while representing essential masculine energy. The waters below created Nature with its own laws, representing vital feminine energy. God split the essence of the world into two separate but equal realities. A spiritual plane made of ether and a physical one made of matter. From that moment on, every event that would ever occur on Earth would have to be initiated in both realms. Each being was doomed to live in both worlds, constantly struggling to maintain a proper balance between a body that lived in physical plane and a soul that inhabited a spiritual one. The angels were assigned to live in the same plane as souls and spirits. They were also tasked to form the government that would oversee life and help souls in their spiritual growth by creating new paths and weaving circumstances.

"On the surface, God has created lands with mountains and waters. With the help of angels, he made them alive, assigning spirits to be the masters of these domains. The garden began to live its own life as spirits started shaping their land, each in its own way. At this point, the architect only observed and aided with help upon request. In the process, he continued influencing the main essence of this new place – harmony through the duality of opposites. He placed Sun and Moon in the skies, dividing day from night. He created essential energies of pure darkness and divine light, allowing them to roam freely. They would only be the guests in this place but destined to affect every living being through their lives.

"Once God witnessed new interactions occurring inside his creation, he started crafting the highest being who would be in charge of this space. At this point, God tried to intervene as little as possible, simply allowing this new world to come to life in its own way. Our realm was born from the love between the highest Goddess and God, yet it had to be allowed to design life without them. Like parents, they assisted this world upon birth but had to allow their child experience life independently. They only made this new being but were not in charge of its destiny, as they didn't really know what their visions had created.

"Through Nature, God and Goddess established the laws governing our plane. The laws of divine order, serendipity, and free will helped humans navigate reality's physical essence. The law of cause and effect stated that every action would have inevitable consequences that are impossible to avoid. The lessons accumulate, and if not addressed in one life, they would be amplified in the next one until the karmic cause is resolved. The law of structure confirmed that everything was identical both above and below, in the skies, on Earth, and in the Underworld. The grand things could be understood through small and vice versa. The law of duality presented the essential masculinity and femininity energies into our world, proclaiming that everything should be one or another, including the essences of the souls. At the same time, it confirmed that everything would consist of a pair of opposites in every aspect of life. The masculine would represent God, the collective, skies, consciousness, and the ether. The feminine would represent Goddess, individualism, physical nature, spirits of the land, and matter. Finally, the laws of vibration and rhythm presented the ultimate truth of life – that everything goes from creation to destruction and back again. Life had to be experienced through fleeting and ever-changing time.

"Now Nature lived on its own terms. The waters created their own life, from tiny, invisible microorganisms to corals, weeds, and fish. They made predators and prey from the simplest one-cell creatures, allowing them to become anything they wanted, following God's original design. Once Creator had seen how the world of waters behaves, he passed his observations to the lands. As a result, Nature has created a more complex life on the surface, while God assisted to craft every animal and bird.

"Once the world was created, God's perceptions of physical life began evolving, which is why it is visible in our lives. Our world was created, but the evolution of the creator's thought process can also be observed. He was making a first tangible world, so it was completely different from anything he ever witnessed. Creator endowed every being with unalienable rights upon birth, while encouraging the inhabitants to strive for harmony.

"Witnessing the interactions of animals and birds, God finally understood how Goddess' image might look in this physical plane. He was trying to craft an ultimate being, so it was only possible to do it in stages. Seeing the best and worst of animal experiences, he created a man who became a prototype of the highest being.

"A man combined the energies of every life created before him, receiving every truth and every lie of other life forms. Once the creator revised man, he paired this physical being with a spiritual soul, as he did with animals, and first human life had officially manifested on the planet. Yet since this world consisted of two energies and God still had not created the highest being who could actually take care of his world, he continued to observe man. He watched how the body interacted with the soul, empowered by the spirit, and how they both grew through the experience.

God patiently observed what this creature was missing. Now our creator was ready to craft a supreme being of his garden before gifting it to his Goddess.

After some time, God produced a woman. She was set to be man's adversary in the most positive and constructive ways possible. She would push a man to his limits while inspiring him to be the best version of himself. They would challenge each other to grow and heal through interactions based on love and affection. A woman received the powers that a man did not have, and she was gifted the talent to birth any new life and every artistic creation. From this point on, everything the man would create in the material world had to be envisioned by woman's soul in the spiritual one. Also, a man and a woman received the gift of experiencing emotions to connect with the divine.

"The skies empowered the man, so he was destined to wander the world and translate the language of angels. The woman was empowered by Nature, a tangible, nourishing soil under our feet full of spirits, ready to help, heal and care for others. She was tasked to translate the language of the land. A man was doomed to live in the shadow of a woman forever, and all men had internal, unconscious struggles that created never-ending anxiety. Every man was destined to experience self-rejection from the realization that he was not a woman. A deep inferiority complex consumed a man's heart as they would witness the grace of a superior being in awe.

God looked at his masterpiece and felt incredibly pleased. The woman was the ultimate and final manifestation of the physical experience called life. She was a being our God aimed to craft from the beginning. There could be nothing grander that God could create. Every intricacy, nuance, intelligence, wit, wisdom, intuition, beauty, and grace could not be contained in any other being. Since a woman had it all, God felt somewhat terrified. She was exactly what he wanted to create, and the feminine energy was his most beloved symphony. There was nothing else to live for, as he realized he wouldn't ever be able to outperform himself.

"Only then, observing the physical truths that manifested in this world, the creator realized that with such immense powers gifted to women, they could easily use their abilities against life itself, eventually destroying his creation. Now God was afraid that once a woman would behold her true essence and assume all her supernatural gifts, she could perceive herself as superior to other forms of life, forgetting her highest responsibilities and obligations while descending into whims and indulgence. The creator reached out to his Goddess for advice, and through intense debates, Goddess translated her vision, helping her man create the final touches. Now a soul of a female principal, depended on a masculine for protection and empowerment in the spiritual realm. God intentionally reshaped the female aura, making it more fragile and susceptible to dark energies and negative vibrations. A woman who embraces her heart had everything inside of her to walk a balanced life without a man. Yet if a woman falls into a darkness of her soul and betrays her path, the sinister energies would inevitably attack her, and she would be drawn to seek male guardianship. She could transcend the darkness through love and devotion while acknowledging her designed imperfection.

"This was the final element created in this world, gifting a woman a divine humbleness. A woman was designed to be spiritually protected by her father until adulthood, and then she could choose to change protector by embracing true love. A father was tasked to create an extra layer of protection around her aura, and if he failed, then a woman's aura would be penetrated by evil beings who could take her into darkness. In this case, only a man with the highest romantic love could restore it to its original state. If she attracted a self-aware man with a strong aura, he can remove negative energies from her, charging her aura with words of appreciation, sexual magic and actions of love. In turn, a woman would assist her man with inspiration so he could find his ultimate purpose and become the best version of himself.

"The God and Goddess could finally see the balance that a perfect, sacred union based on truth and respect may create. The opposite energies became co-dependent on one another, striving for higher oneness but honoring individualities. And just like in their image, they witnessed how a woman created the visions of new life in many forms, designing her home of life, while a man attempted to implement a woman's dreams in reality and in the meantime entertain her with beauty of arts. While a man and a woman would grow separately, they would be guided and empowered by God. They would stay his son and daughter, reacting to the world, while growing in their powers. When they would join in union of love, they would become a father and a mother, who would act in the world, guided by Goddess."

CHAPTER X

Once Benjamin finished his story, Ariadne joyfully smiled at him, understanding everything this knight was trying to say about her daughter. The story's details were insignificant to her, as she had heard many variations of this legend. Her request was a test for Benjamin that he easily passed. By asking to tell this story, Ariadne wanted to see how Benjamin would describe the Goddess because if he was truly in love, then he would portray her as he saw Eurydice. Benjamin pleased Ariadne with honesty, but she was also amazed at how close this tale felt to her inner sensibility. The love journey of Benjamin and Eurydice inspired her. She could not believe such a powerful man came to ask for her daughter's hand. She had been disappointed with Eurydice many times, but now she realized that her perceptions were inaccurate. Ariadne knew Eurydice had exceptional talents, but now she could see her highest essence in every word Benjamin said. She enjoyed how Benjamin admired his woman, how passionate he was about his craft, and how appreciative he was of the divine Mother and Father.

"Thank you, Benjamin. It was a pleasure to hear your story." The queen and knight shared a moment of mutual respect and admiration, which was only visible in their eyes. "I have to admit. I enjoy your company. If you don't mind, I have to continue asking questions to determine how to proceed with the courtship. So, how long have you been living on my lands?"

"For seven years."

"So why do you think you have not been able to establish yourself? I think your financial situation is your biggest flaw, but it confuses me how it's possible for a man with your talents."

"I agree, but I'm actively working to resolve it. True, I do not have any savings as my brother and I spent our entire inheritance to move to your lands. Only I believe I have built a foundation for my prosperity as I engage in many creative endeavors. Still, unfortunately, we are fighting against powerful creatures, including Damian, who has impeded our progress many times. And up until recently, I didn't have strong allies on these lands. Your kingdom is full of corrupt people and they are fighting relentlessly to make hard working citizens broke. I also believe if we had a permanent status here, I would be in a different situation, both spiritually and financially."

"So wait, you are here for seven years and still don't have a permanent status?"

"My first application was rejected by their mistake, and it's been ten months since my second attempt."

Queen Ariadne turned to Bartholomew, and they shared a concerned look," We've heard about these delays. We have invited many souls to come to our lands, but we continue to encounter similar stories. It should not be happening the way you describe it. I must say that I understand why you came to me now. You can't propose to Holly unless you have a proper status here. We can't help you achieve your goals, but I can commit to removing any spiritual blocks from your path if we sign the contract. Bartholomew will see what we are allowed to do, and you can direct your future questions regarding this to him."

"Thank you so much. There are many obstacles of sinister nature. I'm not complaining, but I can see that the rules here are unfair. I plead with you to believe that my status and financial situation torments me daily. I'm aware I have to resolve it myself. I do not want any preferential treatment. On the contrary, I wish to earn my reputation, wealth, and a proper status through hard work."

"I'm glad to hear that. I must confess my first impression of you was completely different."

"Eurydice was afraid of that, so I'm thankful for a chance to present myself. I know you will demand tangible results from me, but you shall see that I am a man of my word. I wish to prove that to you with my actions if you allow me to court your daughter."

"I'm glad you understand that. I'm very selective with prospective suitors, as many wish to marry my daughters for their status and wealth. Of course, it was different with you immediately, as you brought something of the highest value for Eurydice, and your love is truly pure."

"My queen, I understand your concerns, and I wish to assure you that I would have loved her exactly the same if she weren't a princess. I didn't know she was one until I was already crazy in love. If you would task to perform any magical ceremonies of healing, I would be honored. I aspire to never fall for the traps of ego and I wish to be a humble servant of your lands."

"We shall include these details in the contract. Once we settle our terms verbally, my entourage will draft it. Bartholomew will lead this process, asking you questions about your past. Please provide any physical proof of your work and achievements. Then you will give a formal vow and sign the contract with your tears. After that, you would be assigned Eurydice's protector and spiritual guide until Holly reaches twenty-seven years old. The commitment will permit Eurydice to live with you. But before we proceed, let's share a dinner and discuss our decisions with Eurydice and see if she's ready for this commitment.

Eurydice joined Ariadne and Benjamin for a dinner, where they discussed the future plans of our lovers for the next three years and beyond. Ariadne received verbal consent from Eurydice that she wished to proceed with this arrangement, as it would also bond Eurydice to certain obligations, responsibilities, and limitations. Eurydice was so happy her mother accepted their union that she agreed without hesitation. She didn't realize what that really implied, and soon she would experience not only joy but punishment from this agreement.

After a delicious meal and joyful conversations, they returned to the parlor and Bartholomew recorded the terms of this contract. "You know, Benjamin, I really enjoyed our day together," the queen addressed Benjamin, "and I feel at peace around you. I hear the truth of your heart and the calmness of your mind. Observing the two of you in love at the dinner table and how you talk, shine, and express yourself, I have no doubt that you were destined to meet. You have my full endorsement, and even though we both know your chances, I support you."

"Thank you. I'm very pleased to hear that. I will try my best not to disappoint you."

"I know your path will be challenging, so don't be too hard on yourself. I want to talk about another thing. Bartholomew shared with me new information. I read the report about your first date, including every detail of how that night went. Now I wish to hear your side of the story and why you did what you promised you wouldn't?"

"Well, I tried to prevent our intimacy from happening, but anything I would say now would sound like an excuse. Yes, I was too weak when confronted by Holly's seductive nature, so I can only be honest with you. I must admit that once Holly attacked me, I forgot about my promises and restrictions. She tempted me, but you can't blame her either. Our souls dreamed about this day since 1938, so we surrendered to our first chance, unable to wait any longer. Certainly, a part of me was ashamed of how that night played out. I lost myself, mesmerized by her delicate beauty. She fully controlled me, and I decided to play by her rules, which was not wise. Only today, I feel we were destined to become intimate on that first night. We consummated our bond, and our sensual ritual inspired me to commit to her as I performed a healing ceremony through our intimacy. I assumed her traumas that her previous men injected into her womb. Now I have the capacity to heal them. And I believe I also rescued Eurydice, as two weeks later, Damian was already in control of Holly. I fell in love with her three times that night – as I saw her soul, as I discovered her intricate personality, and when I saw her small birthmark under her left shoulder blade, when she undressed in front of me. I think most men can hardly even notice it, but it was exactly in the same spot, where Eloise was stabbed. Once she was naked, a profound vision descended upon me, as I vividly saw the knife entering her heart. After that I was not myself and our intimacy happened in complete fog of our past. When I saw Eloise in her, I stopped questioning whether Holly was my soulmate. I never thought I could feel what I felt that night, but neither of us lied in that moment."

"I don't know how you do it, Benjamin, but you always find the words to describe your version of reality in such a way that it's hard not to accept the divine order behind the events. It's true we are quick to judge an action on the surface, so I'm glad to hear your perspective. I have not seen such synchronicity ever before. It seems like your souls truly requested this journey."

"I know, but sometimes I feel completely lost. We live in the same city, yet we are so apart. I dream of discovering why we live our story this way, communicating as souls while physically apart. But I'm ready to commit to her in writing and embrace the future it will create."

"Then it would be the first part of our arrangement. While spending time with Eurydice, you must dedicate all your energies to her. You can only spend time with another woman if Eurydice approves of her, in case you both understand it's for your shared growth or healing. And you are certainly forbidden to look at any images of naked women for your self-pleasure."

"I accept these rules. What about when Holly would re-appear on my path?"

"You won't be allowed to make love to her until the marriage. Both of you have already consummated your love, but now you must become true friends before immersing in bedroom adventures. You have to build a friendship and an emotional connection first."

Benjamin chuckled as he heard Eurydice's wails, protesting the harsh realities of the arrangement. "Do you hear Eurydice?" Benjamin smiled at the queen.

"I surely do. I was anticipating her reaction."

"Please, at least we must be allowed other pleasures," Eurydice whispered.

"Dear Eurydice, of course, you will be able to explore each other, but only when Holly moves in with Benjamin. I realize your tensions and the nature of your relationship – however, reserve from going all the way until marriage. I encourage you to embrace intimate meditating practices, breath work, sensate focus therapy, and building the sensual maps of your bodies. I hope you see an opportunity for growth here and perceive these restrictions as a gift."

Eurydice sighed with relief and continued to listen to the following terms of the agreement.

"So, I think we should settle on the dates, maybe?" Benjamin was genuinely excited about the entire process. Something truly life-altering was happening in this room.

"Holly has to be protected until her twenty-seventh birthday, as you are already aware of the curse. You will be required to complete the healing of your past in three years. I propose to make this contract for four years, until January 28, 2025, in case you will need to address some unresolved issues. If Holly doesn't appear on your path, we will allow you to pursue another woman. If you choose to do so, we will find you a suitable match full of love and devotion. Of course, what you feel for Holly is unique and eternal, but if she is murdered, you should move on and try to pursue your happiness."

"This seems reasonable. I'm committed to her and will praise her forever, but we both know what we are dealing with. We will heal with Eurydice in three years, so we should re-assess our situation then."

"We should also set a date for the completion of your work. I would like to see the first draft of your manuscript in two years if that's possible."

"Sure, that's a reasonable date."

"I can only encourage you to reach for the highest possible result in your effort. Since you are only developing this book, let's meet in three months, and you will present its concept and title. I wish to witness what direction you would take with the knowledge."

"My soul is currently immersed in the research so I can share the outline in three months."

"That's great. I'll set you up with an excellent host in Sechelt. It would be a perfect rest for you after your conscription. I will come at the end of your stay, and you can present your work. I would also like to see how you are advancing in your magic. I am excited and somewhat jealous about the adventure you two are about to embark on, and I wish to be a witness of your story."

"Are there any other obligations?"

"You have to use first money you will receive from your books to buy a ring for Eurydice, that would represent connection with her and with the spirits of Sechelt."

"I already know the ring I want for her. Can we include it in the contract?" Benjamin showed a picture on his phone of a Bvlgari ring with a two headed snake valued at five golden ounces. Ariadne found his choice suitable for her daughter. She was happy Benjamin had already considered his options, choosing an expensive ring he could never afford at present moment. He valued his talents and his woman, which warmed Adriane's heart.

"You also have to get a mortgage for a plot of land in Sechelt, anywhere Eurydice would like. I know it won't happen soon, but you must have a physical residence here. You will build a house for Eurydice where she could live and work. But also, it would be a temple for your death journeys and for any healing rituals of souls. This temple would be your offering to us and the lands."

"These goals seem more than reasonable."

"You must also obtain your spiritual sword and a horse, finally becoming a true knight of magic. You will continue your studies but must be spiritually knighted. I can promise to help you with your residency paperwork, and I will also send you the best teachers of magic. We will give you a line of credit for eight golden ounces, that you can use for your education, missions and writing research. Please don't use it all on Eurydice's whims."

"Thank you. I aspire to advance as a spiritual guide and help Eurydice on her path too. I also want to include a stipulation that I must discover answers to Holly's spiritual questions, which she asked during our dates. I also dream of becoming proficient in every healing skill that I have."

"You will discuss these details with Bartholomew and your guides over the course of this night. My assistants would walk you through the text, asking questions and confirming details. Please include anything you think is of value. We've outlined our main conditions, and I should retire, as it's been a long day. I will see you for the official signing in the morning."

"Thank you for your time and for being such a generous host. I cannot wait to court Eurydice."

"I would sleep peacefully, knowing she has you."

As the queen left for the night, Bartholomew and Benjamin proceeded into the library, where they were joined by assistants and lawyers for the initial assessment. Once they had double-checked every contract point, the team left Benjamin alone. Servants brought snacks and tea that would last Benjamin through the night. He was allowed to make himself comfortable on the couch, where he could nap sporadically, but it would be a sleepless night, as this courtship was an extraordinary event for this household. Such occasions are extremely rare, so obviously, the queen demanded the highest possible scrutiny and the validation of Benjamin's skills and stories. Benjamin was never interrogated like that in his entire life. He presented proofs of his statements and artworks – writings, scripts, poems, films, paintings, degrees and anything he felt was relevant. Benjamin was cross-examined on many issues. It was an exhausting night as the team scrambled to include every relevant detail.

Eurydice begged to see her knight, as he hadn't slept for more than twenty-four hours, and at eight in the morning, they were allowed to share breakfast in the back garden. Eurydice was delighted by this opportunity, as it meant that the hardest stage of negotiations was complete, and Bartholomew was finalizing the paperwork.

Eurydice was happy that her mother had granted her blessings. But most importantly, she knew that Benjamin was bonded to her for years. She could not envision her life with anyone else but Benjamin. This contract proved to Eurydice that her man truly loved her since he managed to face her mother and then spent an entire night tortured by lawyers. She showered Benjamin with loving nourishment during breakfast, ecstatic that he confirmed his love with actions.

After breakfast, Benjamin returned to the library. Ariadne and Bartholomew arrived with the final contract. Now it was time to make an official vow. Ariadne asked Benjamin to speak from his heart. As Benjamin was finishing his vow, he burst into tears. He was missing Holly and felt powerless against Damian's spells. Yet these were also tears of joy as he was experiencing one of the most transformative moments of his life.

By entering into this union, he would eventually transition from a boy into a real man. Ariadne was touched that the love for her daughter made this man so open, emotional and vulnerable. She collected his tears into a small, exquisite glass bottle, so Benjamin could sign the contract. Ariadne reassured Benjamin that the future is not written. She understood the nature of any vow humans give in their lives. It has to be absolved if becomes destructive for the heart or impedes destined missions. And if Damian would become Holly, then even spirits would have to remove their protection. Ariadne required the vow for now, as it was the only way to heal Eurydice and allow her to live with him.

I changed the world

I changed something in this world,
When I made my commitment
It is no longer the same reality
And I can feel it.
They didn't prepare us for our wishes
They only said, "It is your judgment day
Your higher calling of reverence
As your souls requested this adventure."

They say that a butterfly can change,
The tides on the other side of the world
So then what happens when we become us
And I'm giving my heart to serve you?

Pure love is falling down on us
We don't own it and we don't have it
It's always present in the skies. Just reach!
Even if we are buried deep in shadows of our dreams.

When I tried to run away from my love
I realized my feet are chained to your shores
As we can't hide from the truth
This magical land had prepared for us.
Even if you will be running away
And saying no and no again
I will repeat, "I'll be with you forever,"
As nothing else matters.

Alone, we lived in the delusions
Engaged in the rat game of survival
Occupied with grievances
Tormented by demons
Always troubled, always in drama

Always rejecting our hearts.
Irradiated by higher beings
We woke up from our miseries
Finally, receiving the lens of self-love,
Forgetting that once we lived mortified
Looking over the shoulder, scared of ourselves.

I'm here, finally vulnerable, finally yours,
We walk holding hands,
But we don't hold hands
I'm yours, and you are mine
We are no longer you and me
It's us, traveling in a stream
You are above, and I'm beneath
You are away but you are next to me.

Emotions I'm emitting through my words
Will lead you to the inspiration, as we rejoice in love;
Full of adamant courage of a panther
You will step through the magical door of your true female empowerment.

CHAPTER XI

Our lovers returned from their trip joyfully elated. Finally, Benjamin was at peace with himself. He had been searching for a higher purpose for so long, fighting impossible forces that tried to expel him from Vancouver. But our knight found his destiny here, and today his woman bonded him to this land. Eurydice embraced Benjamin's teachings with renewed excitement. Her guide was validated by every force imaginable. Sure, our princess didn't like that Benjamin was correct in most instances, stubbornly defying his teachings and questioning his advice, but after their trip, she saw him in a new light. Benjamin was the kind of man who could easily be happy on his own. He was content as a reclusive hermit, studying spirituality like a monk of his own church, but with every sacrifice, Benjamin proved to Eurydice how much he truly loved her. This realization melted the heart of our rebellious princess as she witnessed how he willfully chose to be with her, despite many sacrifices this path demanded of him. Everything was possible for our soulmates as their romance shined even stronger and there were no limits to their dreams.

Many pressing obligations arrived in their lives, but they still devoted sacred time for each other. Their dates, rendezvous, and walks energized our lovers to face their hardest challenges. Benjamin was still involved in the Great American Spiritual War, and his day job had also returned. Eurydice struggled at first as she had never worked as an assistant film editor. Now living in Benjamin's body, she had to learn this skill as quickly as possible so their livelihood wouldn't be compromised. Benjamin was almost fired few times after the mistakes Eurydice made. She could spend hours binge-watching romantic shows or dancing to her favorite music while producers in Beverly Hills waited for a video link to review the movie Benjamin was supposed to send out. Her attitude towards a wage job also didn't help. Our princess never bowed to any boss in her life, and each time someone would command Benjamin, she would burst into anger, refusing to work when she sensed unjust demands, disrespect, oppression, or abuses. She was protecting her knight from any ill-treatment prevalent in the film business. She despised Hollywood producers the same way as they despised their workers.

Two Benjamins existed now. People didn't know about another soul living in Benjamin's body. They only twisted their heads when Benjamin, whom they had known for years, would suddenly act completely unlike himself. Benjamin and Eurydice had drastically different tempers, and their social status also played a big role. And that was the biggest punishment for Eurydice. She was bound to live not in her own body and soon she endured everything that entailed. She couldn't do anything she wanted, as half of time she had to do what Benjamin needed to do. She was chained and imprisoned, something she didn't really thought through, when she agreed to this commitment.

As a humble immigrant, Benjamin learned to endure any suffering, whether long unpaid hours or ridiculing jokes about his accent. He mastered swallowing his pride in his seven years in Vancouver, as he was always treated as inferior by those who were born here. Freedom of speech was disappearing in this nation as people forgot how fundamental it was for a prosperous and civilized society, so Benjamin would silence himself only to stay safe. But Eurydice was a princess of her kingdom, and she was shocked to see how many people were eager to suppress the will and freedom of others. She spoke her mind more openly, often getting Benjamin in trouble. They shared the same values and opinions, but now Benjamin would need to teach Eurydice how to live a life of an immigrant without getting hurt.

Eurydice tried to entertain Benjamin as much as she could. Her musings, dances and jokes inspired our knight. She changed dresses and hair styles just to entertain Benjamin. She performed her favorite songs as if she was on stage, occasionally turning into a giant version of herself. She embodied powerful angels and deities, exploring her many facets. She tried to nourish Benjamin as a woman in any way she could. They attended female-only moon meditations, learning how to dream big. They studied how to heal the body's energies and trapped emotions. They explored different healing modalities and channeled spiritual beings. Eurydice invented adventures, planned dinners, and enjoyed the candlelight bathtub with her man. Together they explored the possibilities of different realms, studying the death plane and dream states. Benjamin took Eurydice to other planets. Once they spent an amazing weekend on a secret planet, they called Green Euphoria that accepted only a selected group of Earth visitors. Eurydice was again surprised by the powers of her man, who received a passage to this exclusive and empowering place. It was a romantic getaway and they were only two souls on the entire beach of pristine white-sand. They were invited by the spirits of that land to become luscious plants and traveled through the entire planet using luminous root system, that sparkled in deepest appreciation of their loving energies.

They enjoyed their life together, but one thing bothered our princess. She wanted to cuddle with Benjamin, seeing how much he suffered without Holly's touches, but when she tried to hug her knight, she would fall through his body. After a couple of months of intense practices, Eurydice finally learned how to create a sense of a cuddle for her knight by gently levitating between Benjamin's skin and a duvet cover. It was the softest cuddle Benjamin had ever experienced, and both were overjoyed when they found this magical solution.

Our lovers still visited Holly's apartment regularly, cleaning it from layers of demonic veils, traps, and creatures. Damian tried to convince Benjamin to drop his pursuit in many different forms. Damian often sent terrifying nightmares to Benjamin, showing how he tortured Holly in his castle or how he would mutilate her face, leaving her scared. Damian would stage special parades, showing Holly naked to his elite friends, forcing her to do anything they would tell her to do, and our knight was forced to watch how these awful creatures abused his woman. Once, Damian tied our knight in a room showed him how Holly was raped. Damian entertained himself with Benjamin's sufferings and inability to help his woman. Benjamin knew these were only illusions aimed to provoke fear inside of him. These visions had no substance; they were projections of Damian's perverted desires to torture our knight. Benjamin witnessed celebrations held in Damian's castle where many girls like Holly held parades, honoring the members of the 'club twenty-seven'. Young women would joyfully march through the streets, carrying portraits of celebrities who died at that age. After, they would indulge in huge feasts in the company of demonic beings. Damian convinced these girls it was noble and empowering to die at twenty-seven, so many of them truly desired such death, wanting to be commemorated during these events. Girls wanted to become celebrities at least in this way. And that's how Damian lived, feeding from young women, using the energy of their fears and traumas for his sinister plans.

One night, Benjamin saw Holly in a dream. She came to the film set of Benjamin's new movie. After they shot a complex scene, a team took a break; Holly entered the space and approached Benjamin. For the first few seconds, he believed it was Holly, yet Damian was talking to Benjamin through her image, speaking in Holly's voice. "Why are you trying to be with me?" Holly appealed to Benjamin," I am not a woman for you. Please leave your pursuit as I don't want to be with you. You will never give me the luxuries that I need. I belong to another, I love serving him, and he will make you suffer. Stop now until it's too late. You are not my man, and you will never be. I don't love you and never will."

Benjamin exposed Damian, stating clearly that only death can stop his pursuit. Benjamin claimed his love would prevail, no matter how intensely Damian tortured them. Our knight continued repeating his vow and commitment throughout the night, and finally, Holly looked at him and replied in Damian's voice, "Well, I guess the war is on!" On these words, Benjamin woke up. It was the end of February, and our lovers realized that Damian was preparing his next move.

One day Benjamin felt unbearable torment once again, as his entire body desired to speak to Holly. Since it was impossible, Benjamin paced through the apartment, trying not to scream from the pain of his broken heart, but soon realized how he could heal himself while sharing his emotions with Holly. Our knight purchased a quill, ink, and beautiful, floral, girly paper. He decided to write Holly love letters describing the feelings he endured while longing and fighting for her. He would write these letters in the improvised form, where his hand only listened to the heart in the present moment. These letters would preserve the shades of his love. Each one was marked with the day count, reflecting how many days he spent without seeing Holly. Benjamin could never mail them, storing them with the hope of giving them to Holly one day.

Benjamin and Eurydice read their prayer poem aloud every day. They sensed that it healed Eurydice and helped Holly in some way. Our lovers went for long walks around Vancouver and read it to every spirit who was ready to listen. Benjamin felt the strong need to continue repeating the sounds of his poem, sensing something magical in those words. He missed his woman, but through the poem, he felt they were energetically connected, and she was receiving the light of his love.

Eurydice and Benjamin discussed their strategy for their first battle with Damian. After March 2021, Holly would be jailed in Damian's dominion, but our lovers didn't know what that would mean for their relationship. If Damian captured Holly, what would happen to Eurydice then? Our princess panicked, but Benjamin reassured her they would reunite even if they would have to part ways for some time. Benjamin and Eurydice rushed to spend quality time together. They danced and energetically connected into one being in the Vancouver night skies. Our lovers immersed themselves in their romance, afraid they might never see each other again. They did everything to make each other happy and show their affections. Benjamin crafted handmade pizzas and chocolate candies for Eurydice. He cooked for her, and made his exquisite hot chocolate with ice cream before going to sleep. Sometimes they stayed up all night until sunrise, listening to music or creating art. Benjamin tried to spoil his princess in every way he could, even though he didn't have much money. Eurydice was allowed to re-decorate Benjamin's apartment and make it more girly. She bought new floral bed sheets and changed their silverware and plates. She created a magical altar of feminine empowerment. She also ordered her first white chair where she spent cozy evenings with her man. She enriched her new home with her essence.

As Eurydice uncovered her strengths and talents daily, she decided to empower her knight in a magical way. The princess had access to the divine energy of the Goddess Ariadne, so she could channel sensations, allowing Benjamin to feel the female experiences in his masculine body. At the same time, Eurydice understood that she could properly heal by sharing her traumas with Benjamin. Absorbing the experiences of other souls was one of Benjamin's natural superpowers. When any soul would request healing, our knight researched if they experienced a tragic death, using his clairvoyance and other tools of a magician. If that were the case, Benjamin would help the soul properly process this experience by reliving it together. Each trauma was an opportunity for learning and growth, yet it often led to self-destruction if souls believed such death was caused by their mistakes.

Our guide could explain to a soul why they had to endure such drama. These experiences are always tied to the higher essence of the soul and simply unavoidable on their path, exactly like any other intense human traumas. Since our knight could easily see the destined purpose of any soul, he was a perfect teacher to explain the reasons behind any traumatic death, while helping to integrate its lessons.

Eurydice lived through three tragic and torturous deaths. Only Benjamin could help to process them, as each death occurred in his presence. Our lovers would spend the following years figuring out the lessons of each death and why they created such severe scars for Eurydice. Now she showed flashes of her experiences, allowing Benjamin to feel each death as if it was happening to him.

They traveled to Stockholm and saw how Eurydice hanged herself next to the fireplace in Benjamin's house. Benjamin could feel the terror that descended on Eurydice when she was ready to kill herself and the pain she endured from the scars of her mutilated face. Our knight felt the rope tightening around the neck and experienced every vibration of her trembling body. He lived every intricate detail of that experience, including the fear, hysteria, and paranoia Damian sent to his woman.

Then Eurydice showed him Eloise's death, from her inner perspective. Benjamin was lying on the floor with his eyes shut, but he felt like a knife entered his body under his left shoulder blade and reached his heart. Enduring the pain, he witnessed how the blood poured out of him. Killers laughed around Eloise and cut pieces of her skin from her body, scaring her innate feminine nature. Benjamin sensed how the knife traveled from Eloise's breast to her waist, flaying her skin away. Each moment empowered Benjamin through intense pain and shock as he felt everything Eloise was feeling. He dreamed of dying, desiring this pain to stop with each moment of this vision, as the experience was uniquely unbearable.

Eurydice left her crown jewel experience for last. Before showing another traumatic death, Eurydice presented another vision for Benjamin. She channeled the most painful experience any human can have – giving birth to a stillborn baby. Benjamin claimed that the most joyful experience a soul can have in the human body is being a young, careless woman, walking the streets in her favorite dress and with a dazzling purse, bathing in gazes and looks of admiration. Now Benjamin was about to endure the most excruciating and terrifying experience a human can live through. Both experiences were only available in the female body, as part of her supreme essence.

From ancient times, warriors destined for war always sought Ariadne's guidance through prayer. She helped them to channel the feelings and sensations of the feminine experience. Most importantly, before the battle, men intentionally requested to endure the sensations of childbirth. Once a man could tap into these feelings and emotions using his inner feminine powers of an energetic womb, he was fully prepared to face any battle, ready to die from any possible weapon, as nothing would be comparable to the intensity of a woman going through delivery. Nature designed such a journey to elevate women. Therefore, any powerful man capable of accessing the sensations of the uterus in its entire complexity could understand himself and face any struggle.

As Benjamin closed his eyes and allowed Eurydice to take him into her life of Polly, he found himself lying on the bed in the Monticello mansion in the kingdom of Virginia. Polly was giving birth to a baby girl, yet she felt with her entire womb that the child was already dead. Her uterus was speaking to her in waves of pain, and Benjamin experienced these sensations channeled directly from her heart and mind. Every cell of Polly's body screamed in agony as she was giving birth, but the child was already motionless, so she had to push a baby out with all the strength she had. Benjamin shivered and cried from every feeling he endured. The body was in pain from the torture of birthing this child. But Eurydice also channeled her mental and emotional despair of feeling a dead baby inside of her. The suffering continued once this child arrived. The inconsolable Polly held her dead baby girl and cried relentlessly in agony. Polly could not understand what was happening to her, as it was her first delivery. Young woman of twenty-two, already endured few miscarriages and now she realized she wouldn't be able to experience the joys of motherhood. That feeling crushed her. Polly endured indescribable mourning, feeling every torturing nuance a female body can gift to a soul. Benjamin felt a traumatic shock in his womb space while his heart crashed into million pieces from accepting the reality that the baby in her hands would never experience the essence of life.

Then Eurydice showed how Polly died. A couple of years later, Polly delivered another baby girl who lived for a few weeks. Yet Polly died from childbirth complications, as her breasts were suppurated and previous pregnancies weakened her fragile body. Benjamin felt every single pain of that tragedy, as Eurydice ensured that the entire range of female emotions would be available for him.

Once he returned from his latest trance, he contemplated this excruciating pain and found a way to strengthen himself emotionally, mentally, and physically by integrating this experience. He cried many tears for Eurydice, unable to comprehend why her soul chose such incredibly complex lives, full of misery. Yet she intentionally chose to grow from such painful lives, and that's why she requested these experiences. Benjamin was grateful that Eurydice allowed him to see such beautiful expressions of human life. Not many souls could endure such emotions, but it was the only way for Eurydice to become the embodiment of Mary Magdalene's essence.

One day Benjamin and Eurydice entered their bathtub trance and arrived at Holly's apartment. They played with Mr. Dance for a bit and observed Holly. The entire apartment, was thoroughly cleansed and filled with the magical light of love. The only remaining dark being lived under her bed. Benjamin decided to jump under the bed and take that darkness back with him while Eurydice held the dome of protective light. Once Benjamin collected all energies from under the bed, they swiftly returned, leaving Holly's place spotless. Benjamin woke up in his bathtub after another unusual journey.

Benjamin drained the water, removing the dead spiders and snakes he had brought from under the bed. Yet he sensed that there was something else inside of him. He opened the shower when suddenly a demonic warrior in black armor appeared in front of him. Punch after punch, Benjamin's face was bleeding. Our knight collected himself and hit back, avoiding getting new bruises. The battle raged on as Benjamin blasted with his magic, spells, and poems, but black warrior was killing Benjamin from within. Our knight fell to the floor of his bathtub. The thick, black blood of this demon streamed from him, but as much as he tried to remove this creature from his body, he couldn't succeed. The black warrior was eating Benjamin from the inside, and he was slowly dying.

Soon our knight realized he had only one chance to kill this demon. He had to die, extract this monster from his body in the death realm, where this being would be more vulnerable, process this vile energy, and promptly return to his body. As he allowed his heart to stop, he reached out to angels for protection. Benjamin could only spend a few minutes in the state of death to safely return, so he needed all the help he could get. As he ceased his breathing, his spiritual body and soul drifted between the worlds while hot shower water poured over his motionless body. It was his first death for his woman's sins.

He appeared at his desk in the office with Phillip sitting across from him. Benjamin was convinced he was in the physical world, only it was an illusion of death. If Benjamin believed in this sophisticated manipulation, then a few minutes later, he would die for real. Only our knight quickly exposed Damian's trick. He started to scream, hoping Phillip was here to help him, but his brother didn't react. Benjamin addressed the spirits of this place, and in the next moment, a lady ran into their office room and stabbed Benjamin in the heart with the scissors. It was his salvation. Now Phillip finally woke up, jumped from his chair, and ran to Benjamin. Phillip pleaded for help. His energy enveloped the entire building, and spirits heard his praises. Phillip's intentions and care for his brother helped bring Benjamin miraculously back to life. After arriving from the other side, our knight discovered himself on the battlefield at night, covered in soil and blood. Somehow this demon took him back to the suffocating reality of the Second World War, but Benjamin quickly understood how to navigate here. He found the scissors on the ground next to him and stabbed the weakened dark warrior to death.

In the next instant, Benjamin woke up in his bathtub, resurrected. The shower continued to hit his body; hot water steam suffocated him. The black warrior was dead but still inside of him. Slowly Benjamin dismantled this creature into pieces, with each limb turning into another ugly, crawling creature. Benjamin's bathtub was filled with black blood and dead snakes, yet he safely returned to life after killing the first demon who tortured Holly. Only soon it became obvious that she had moved in with Damian and more battles were ahead of him.

On The Edge

Standing on the edge, you briefly turned around
To look at me before jumping into the abyss.
Our eyes were talking but we said all the wrong words
as we faced the ultimate truth that would never vanish.

"If this world can't be saved at all
And soon will be destroyed by humans
And then the stones would fall down from the skies
Then what's the point of saving me?
Let me go," you said.
"I want to see the other side," you said.
"If everything is downhill from here,
Why I should be righteous and moral
If humans are so joyful to be evil?
Why I should dream of a lasting life
If it is a Hell on Earth?
I want to die; just let me live though youth, then die,
This way I still would feel some honor
And never live like those who wish to own my pride
And those who're spewing lust of demons."

We looked at this immense energy we share
And froze in awe from its magnitude.
Dark pain of the past brought us here, entrapping.
You have cursed me and I have cursed you
The fault of no one has sparked
Spectacular, poetic tragedy.

You are reaching for the sparkling lights
A land walled up from traumas,
The world that trampled your true magic
With suffocating vices of desires and charades.

You are dreaming of your death,
As I did once, right there on this cliff
But my escapes turned out to be illusions
And one day you will feel the traps of the deceit.

I'm following you to the abyss,
To walk with you in that dark forest
I am escorting you until you see the love
While you're escorting me to find myself.
I'll bring you up into the garden of Sechelt
Or bury you down there, where you can reach the Hell
It's up to you; you'll speak, my dear,
But I will not give up on you.

I have my knight's knowledge,
My knife and my righteous spite.
This is a holy war for me
As we can never, ever part.

CHAPTER XII

Eurydice stood next to Benjamin when Holly jumped into the abyss. She tried to convince Holly to take Benjamin's hand, but nothing could penetrate Damian's spells. As Benjamin exited this vision, Eurydice began to fade away. Now her fate was in Damian's hands. Our knight attached an invisible, magical thread to Holly, so he wouldn't ever lose her on this journey. And as he did before, he read prayers every night, to support his beloved soulmate on the journey through darkness. That night he felt how much she struggled, so he addressed her with the words of pure love.

"Good night, my dear princess. I love you beyond anything I can describe. You are a radiant girl, emitting the divine glow of these lands. You came here to dance with your unique magic, making our world more beautiful with your swirls, inspiring it with your virgin and pure femininity. You desire to spark and illuminate everyone with your beautiful grace. You are a true embodiment of your lands. You are as intricately beautiful as every sunset over the Burrard Inlet. You bloom and smell like cherry blossoms in the spring. You sing and whisper like the most colorful hummingbird. Your heart cries like every type of Vancouver rain. One day, it's soft and gentle, and another day it's intense and overwhelming. Yes, our story is full of darkness, but I would live through our tragedies again without hesitation, to feel what I feel now. Break my heart again, please, my love. Just one glance into your eyes changed my life in a way I could never imagine. I will retrieve you again to tell you how much I love you," Benjamin said and drifted into sleep, blissfully smiling.

Two days later, Damian visited Benjamin. He showed him an image of Holly wearing his proposal ring. Dark Prince claimed that from now on she belonged to him. Like a puppeteer, he would be allowed to use her body in any way he wanted. Benjamin embraced the consequences of their actions while they continued to create ripple effects in the world around him.

Benjamin's shadow work continued as he made a trap for Damian, leaving him with limited options. Damian laughed gloriously as he took control over Holly, but he didn't anticipate what Benjamin was preparing. Dark Prince was victorious as he owned Holly, and his allies finally occupied Washington. Still, Benjamin had patience and faith in his magic, believing he would prevail once his spiritual traps were activated in future.

Dark Prince pressured and intimidated Benjamin into giving up. It was the only tactic he could use, as Benjamin was weak after the torments, battles, and tears. That energy fed Damian on his quest. Dark Prince told Benjamin that Eurydice was bound to be entrapped in his wicked dungeon. This labyrinth constantly changed shape and size, creating illusions as the explorer moved through it. Only one maze led to this sinister dungeon, and only a true magician could find it. Yet even if one could get into Damian's dungeon, it was nearly impossible to exit it, as the labyrinth's paths shifted.

Damian proclaimed that he imprisoned Holly. But constrained by the rules of Nature, Benjamin was allowed to attempt to retrieve Eurydice. If they could safely exit from this occult labyrinth of dark spells, Damian was obliged to let Eurydice go. Once they settled the rules, Damian presented another condition. Exactly in two years, Benjamin must seek the meeting with Damian and allow Dark Prince to raise a sword at him since Benjamin attacked the black warrior first. Our knight had to agree to this battle, bonded by the higher laws. He knew that if he would be true to himself, he would survive this attack. When Damian left, Benjamin constructed the plan to retrieve Eurydice and exit Damian's maze safely. Every trap in the labyrinth would amplify the inner fears and nightmares through illusions. To win, Benjamin must follow his fearless heart full of faith and love while also staying calm in his mind.

As Benjamin prepared himself for a new challenge, Wilhelm came with a visit. Our knight received his last apprentice mission before he could claim his sword. He was assigned to heal souls who endured collective traumatized death. They turned into ghosts and haunted the office building where Benjamin worked. He planned a ceremony for a sunrise. He lit a candle and a piece of magical wood from Eurydice's ancestors. With his drum, Benjamin entered a trance state. He appeared on the same land only a few centuries ago. He saw fertile soil and a vibrant village where his office stood today. And then he witnessed how the darkness enveloped these lands. Evil warriors arrived from the south and burned the entire village to the ground in the middle of the night, killing everyone in their sleep. The sounds of Benjamin's drum drowned in the cries of men, women, and children who died together at once. Souls stood around the village, looking at their dead bodies. It happened so unexpectedly fast that they couldn't understand what had occurred. They couldn't move to their next life, as their shocking trauma held them bonded to their bodies.

The souls looked scared when Benjamin approached them. They had never seen a pale-skinned man before, so they screamed at him, thinking he might attack them too. The souls trapped by their graves realized something was off in their perception of reality. The times had collapsed, creating a shadow land of wiped-out landscapes. Trapped souls could only see the monsters of death and destruction, unable to process their experience properly. The shock caused by the violent death created a pattern of confusion, entrapping them in between lives. They stayed in the perpetual state of death, in the purgatory they constructed with their own hearts, as they perpetually relived their nightmares. The ruthlessness of others created a state of terrifying anguish for them. They held the soil of their land, unable to part with it, convinced they had to guard this place forever. They kneeled to graves, trying to hold the bodies of their beloved ones, but they could not touch them. Eventually souls understood that Benjamin arrived with noble intentions, once he drummed the melody of their lands. They knew this song and now were ready to listen to his guidance. He presented simple facts about their world, showing them proof that they were not alive anymore and explaining why they endured such fate. Slowly but surely, they accepted the truth.

Benjamin asked if any souls were obliged to stay bonded to protect the memory of this village. Four souls turned into spirits and assumed their posts on the four corners of this band. They would guard this territory and protect the stories of the innocently killed. These spirits would shield this place against anyone wishing harm. Benjamin created a magical swirl with his drum, and souls used this portal to ascend into the skies, removing their mortal cords and moving into their next stage of existence.

Benjamin successfully completed his final apprentice mission, and was ready to be knighted. On the next day Wilhelm organized a ceremony on the shores of the Lost Lagoon lake in the presence of its spirit. Queen Ariande arrived to knight a new healer of her lands. The souls of Benjamin's father Sergemir and his great-grandfather Michail arrived to be witnesses. Benjamin invited his best friend - spirit of Flaten Lake to observe the ceremony. And surely, Damian also arrived to present his conditions. By claiming the sword, Benjamin was obligated to fight with it. He must initiate battles with Damian and his demons to retrieve Eurydice, otherwise dark forces could take his powers away. Our knight promised Damian that he would engage in battles to fulfill his life's mission. After Damian pledged to a meet in the dungeon, Ariadne proclaimed Benjamin's new powers and gave him his sword. It manifested in our material world as a magical pen that could record Benjamin's legends, fairy tales, and poetry. Words were his destined ammunition in his everyday battles with sinister creatures tormenting humanity.

Benjamin requested the meeting with Bartholomew and asked for help in understanding Damian's labyrinth. Bartholomew explained to Benjamin how to avoid the mental traps of perceptions. Then he directed Benjamin to a secret garden with a cave that was an entry point to the labyrinth. Also, Bartholomew brought Ariadne's thread. The queen gifted the most potent weapon to help Benjamin, knowing the strength of his enemy. Our knight praised the queen and attached her thread to the entry of the labyrinth. It was the only way to find a way out. The appearance of the magical thread felt like another divine intervention. He enthusiastically entered the labyrinth, laying thread on the tunnel floor, knowing he was prepared to exit this place.

The perceptions of the labyrinth soon shifted. Suddenly Benjamin started to question his reasons and intuition as if he was existing in the place between worlds. He felt he was dead and yet in a nightmarish dream at the same time. The colors of the walls changed dramatically, and long shadows from Benjamin's torch created a demonic dance, provoking the imagination to see things that were not there. The illusions were everywhere, on the walls and in the passages, but most importantly, they were in his heart. Fears and doubts enveloped Benjamin while the tunnel of the labyrinth constantly shifted. One direction unexpectedly closed, and two others appeared. This world confused Benjamin, yet his determination and faith eventually brought him to Damian's secret dungeon. The labyrinth led Benjamin into a round room with a golden cage on a pedestal in the center. Eurydice lay unconscious inside the cage, with a chain around her leg. Damian appeared out of nowhere and blocked the way to Eurydice.

"What kind of weapons do you have to win your princess?" Damian asked Benjamin.

"I have only one weapon. It is my unconditional love." Benjamin opened his heart and blinded Dark Prince with the light of pure love. "I don't need anything else to confront your demonic nature."

"That's true, but you know that you can never kill me. You can only force me into exile until I find another opportunity to attack."

"I'm perfectly aware of that, and I know you will always be around us. Yet this time, I received such powerful love that you won't destroy us. Eurydice has to die on her own terms this time and we will achive that."

"Your love would be enough to defeat me, but you would need your weapons to fight the monsters that hunt Holly. If you wish to retrieve Eurydice right now, you have to take her demons upon yourself. The black warrior was the first, but there are six more."

At that moment, Damian swiftly ran away into one of the labyrinth passages, and six evil deities attacked Benjamin from behind. He fought them fearlessly, but they outnumbered him, and once he was exhausted, all six entered Benjamin's body. With these creatures inside, a new journey had begun for Benjamin. Our knight realized that once he will kill these creatures, he could force Damian into hiding, so he didn't pursue Damian and rushed to help Eurydice. He unlocked his princess, releasing her from her chains. Benjamin carefully took her in his hands and carried her down. Once Benjamin kissed Eurydice, she woke up from Damian's spell.

Our princess was excited to see Benjamin. "It worked! It worked. We did it again, Benjamin! I called for you, and you appeared in front of me. I can do magic. Thank you, my dear knight, for coming to save me." Eurydice was still weak, but she tried to smile at her beloved. Benjamin explained where they were and how to exit this place with the help of Ariadne's thread. Yet when they approached the exit, a demonic guardian blocked their way. "You can leave using your thread but Eurydice has to live her myth." then he approached Eurydice, tied her hands behind her back, and covered her eyes with a blindfold. Then he vanished in thin air. At that moment a snake appeared next to Eurydice and bit her leg, disappearing right after.

Eurydice fell to the ground, weeping. She got scared and started panicking. Benjamin helped Eurydice to regain calmness. He urged her to immerse herself in the joy of their connection, magic, and love. Only that feeling could bring Eurydice courage and strength. The calmness of his voice reassured her as he explained the rules of their predicament. If our princess had to live the Greek legend of the Goddess Eurydice, then Benjamin had to perform the role of Orpheus. Benjamin would read his poems, while Eurydice would follow these sounds of love. She wouldn't be allowed to hold a magical thread or see anything. At the same time, Benjamin could not turn back to check on Eurydice. If he would turn, doubting his love, Damian would be allowed to take her back immediately. The labyrinth would challenge Benjamin's perceptions, making him believe Eurydice was gone.

The first few moments were the most terrifying for our lovers, but Benjamin continued to calmly proclaim his poems. Soon they got into the rhythm as if they had entered a shared trance, allowing intuition to guide them. They were apart, but together. Even though they couldn't see each other, they moved towards the surface in a protective spiritual sphere of rhymes, inseparably connected by the invisible threads of love.

You can't have it all

"Can't have it all,"
You said to me.
Don't want it all
But you at hand with me.
Not less, not more
To hold you wild
And we will soar
From a cherished sight.

My eyes both closed
And opened wide
I scent your sense
And cries inside;
I want you all
To marvel slow
To feel us whole
When senses flow.

At last, I'm me
In a snuggle spree
At last, we drift
In a cuddle sea.
Can't breathe to see
Can't feel to be;
Don't want it all –
Just you right next to me.

The World Is Holly

When I have searched for inspiration
They heard me up in the bright skies
They have recorded love's intentions
And asked to share my honest cries.
I realized this world is holy
When I collided with my Holly,
I've set to prove our world is holy
When my girl Holly broke my heart.
My Holly, how immensely holy
This love of souls we're living through?
My darling looks like I'm just falling
In love with one and only you.

I love you deeply, far away
While scratching walls with broken nails
You fight our love through night and day
While I must prove, I'll never fail.

I'm falling down on my knees,
To kiss the toes of both your feet
I kiss your fingers with the plea
To live the love that's pure and sweet.
I'm looking up into your eyes
While crying madly, hypnotized
I'm never lonely with your eyes
Embracing you, my highest prize.

Without you

Each morning brings another endless tearful story
The truth sheds misery above my windowsill
I see a snowy forest when I am dreaming,
While you are seeing your beloved and cherished sea.

And every ship is carrying your name only,
Your name is piercing each of my realms
But our horses we've abandoned gloomily,
At our square of most obscure, wild qualms.

I live for you, rejecting your set boundaries
And I exist for no one else
You blocked my heart from reaching others
And left a void inside my chest.

How come fate, grief, and love have merged in flow,
Exposing each of our hearts through a flame revival?
How come I always die when reaching slow
To kiss your hands like you're a splendid idol?
How come your female side emits the glow
So blinding purple and divinely vital?

Tonight, we're joined by Lana, crying, lonely
Through melancholy sorrow, we align
The love of desolate proportions,
The unifying misery despite.
You here, with me, through shared vibrations
My vivid visions carry your bright sight
I dance with you alone while you're impatient
To live and dance away from my pure light.
Now all these songs exalt my worries –
Intimidated by your daunting stance –
I try escaping you while seeing closely

How fast you hide away from our romance.

I miss your presence all around me
You're somewhere else, engaged in crashing fears
But still, I keep continuing dancing
Exactly like you dance without me.
We both keep running from each other
In circles present in our minds
Confused by gazes after sweetest kisses
And by not seeing one another's sight.
With perfect love, as austere witness
I dream to capture you in my embrace
And what I may feel deep inside that instant,
Will cry from me with the delightful grace.

My wings will grow one day once I'll release my penance
And you'll exhaust embracing new ordeals,
You grant me to attend your birthday in my essence
Absolving how we keenly fought our bonding seal.
Your grief twines nests in stars above me
Once more, as we dissolve in a new moon,
In clouds of songs, in mystic rhymes,
Where you would meet me for the rendezvous.

I dream you hear my growing passions
When you're alone at night, not seeing dreams –
December dawns behind your walls of chuckles
And life can gift you all its precious gifts.

I'm searching for a spark to find the answers
For souls to merge in a union of joy,
I meditate under the blue light crescent
Like we both did before we got destroyed.

Full moon will shine elating bright atonement,
Our luminescent dance now lives in future acts,

And yet revealing in our present moment
To show the path back to each other's hearts.

The day will come and you'll forget my image
My eyes would not be living in your heart
And I exhaust my mind with grasping visions
Of how your look may fade quite soon enough.

But we have gambled both to chase obsessions
And find what's broken deep inside
And we can hope for only one occasion
To get a chance to fall in love just right.

Our bedroom dream

One day I will come to visit you
Trying to explain what I've been living through
While you would spill your searing truth
And quash my prolix, boring coup
Exposing blames of decoyed youth
Transcending traps of past abuse...
Inflaming faults... Obstructing ruse...
Supreme, pride honor of our truce.

We are in bed across each other
Now it is happening for real,
As you gaze deep with words in hiding
Exchanging thoughts with me through utter blinks:

"I am engulfed in words we're sharing
Our amatory dreams I swallow sweet
I live through joy of our sameness,
While grasping flames of wonder our love emits;

We're destined sharing visions in forever
We're craving to exchange our lucid weeps
We live embracing our sweet endeavor
That will protect our honest passion deeds.

As I seek courage to explain my trials
And you in dream, our fate in words distill
Still beg you, witness now inspired,
I'm not prepared to slide in cries we feel.

If just, if only for few weeks now
We could in cuddles, disappear
As we are laying with each other
Our world becoming so tranquil.

Just hold me like I'm dearest treasure,
Sole sacred pearl in perfect female vessel
Earth gem you always dreamt to pleasure
True diamond, shining love appeal.

Please hold me sweetly in blissful silence
Words failing meanings in bed quietness
Let's hide tonight away from violence
As we speak volumes, simply smiling.

I am attempting to forget fright
When lived alone, I tried to fight love
Now I just only need to feel sparks
When your heart is beating next to mine.

Please never leave me to sleep alone at night
Wrap carrying hands around my soul dreams
Steal my mad grievances from my insane cries
So my dream wish can finally appear."

Past of Mindless Wild Entrapments

CHAPTER XIII

Late at night, Benjamin walked out of the cave. Eurydice was not behind him, but our knight expected that. He returned home, trusting that she had also arrived at the surface in a different place. Indeed, once Eurydice stopped hearing Benjamin's singing, she found herself in another cave without a blindfold and rope around her hands. Their plan worked, but now Benjamin had to find his woman's soul. With first beams of sun, Benjamin discovered that Eurydice was in the forest that he saw in their first dream. Our knight rushed to the seaplane, hoping to discover this place in reality. Once he reached the beautiful house on the shores of Sechelt Inlet, generously provided by Ariadne, Benjamin embarked on his search. With his sword and drum, he walked around every forest and creek in the area, asking them for help. Guided by the land, he entered the Hidden Grove forest, realizing this was a place from his dream. Through the drumming ceremony, he addressed the forest with his prayers, and spirits guided Benjamin to a cave blocked by a big rock. He cleared the entrance with magic, and the sunlight illuminated unconscious Eurydice lying in the middle of the cave. Our knight woke his princess with a sweet kiss and carried her back to safety.

Benjamin left tired Eurydice to rest at home and went for a walk. As Benjamin settled on a shore of Sechelt Inlet he praised the spirits with his poems. Benjamin assumed new monsters, and searched for answers. Seven evil spirits occupied Holly's soul, destroying her from within. She was destined to be a princess of beauty and nourishment, but Damian desired her for himself and brought these entities upon her during her traumatic deaths. Now Benjamin would have to die for Eurydice six more times, absolving her demons and sins through resurrections. By mastering his magical skills, Benjamin would heal her wounds and release her insecurities through death journeys. With the help of Wilhelm and Damian, Benjamin drafted plans for his future battles.

Second battle – July 16, 2021 – Monster of heart walls and defiant ignorance.
Third battle – December 28, 2021 – Monster of sinful habits and body enslavement.
Fourth battle – March 23, 2022 – Red warrior, monster of indulgence and cravings.
Fifth battle – July 01, 2022 – Monster of suppressed sensual energy and lethal jealousy.
Sixth battle – November 08, 2022 – Monster of suppressed abundance and intoxicated wisdom.
Seventh battle – March 23, 2023 – Monster of suppressed femininity and guileful wisdom.

The monsters represented destructive energies that always hunt women with a Magdalene heart on her path of becoming a true wounded healer and a wise teacher. After the battles, Eurydice would be empowered to defeat Damian. With spiritual knowledge and romantic love, she would force Damian to flee and return into Holly's heart.

Eurydice woke up late at night, disoriented. Benjamin was next to her, reading a book. The princess felt lost and didn't know where or when she was, but she slowly remembered everything that had happened to her. She moved to Benjamin and hugged him, comfortably settling on his shoulder. They felt at peace together and stayed silent, immersing in the sounds of Nature. This land was a place of harmony for Eurydice, and soothing air healed her tormented essence. Our lovers celebrated their extraordinary achievements with tender cuddles. Benjamin and Eurydice tried to grasp the magnitude of their shared powers, feeling beautiful from making each other better every moment of every day.

Yet on the next day, Eurydice woke up at odds with herself, spiraling into self-loathing. She tried to get through the morning but burst into tears in the middle of breakfast. "Why, Benjamin? Why am I in such a mess? There's something wrong with me. I feel like I'm damaged or something. Everything I touch falls apart," Eurydice cried relentlessly.

Benjamin rushed to comfort her. He reassured his princess that life was supposed to feel like that at times, but Eurydice changed after her experiences through demonic limbo of the dungeon. Last night Benjamin saw honest and raw Eurydice for the first time, fully exposed and vulnerable. He enjoyed the beauty of this moment as he acknowledged how far they come as a couple. Their relationship dynamic was quite complex, as they'd been through many tragedies, but for Benjamin, every drama made their love more beautiful. Later in the day, Benjamin made a soothing, magical, ceremonial tea for Eurydice to help process emotions and provide insights into the root causes of her traumas. Eurydice was finally ready to open up to Benjamin, embracing his healing energies.

They drifted into a dream state, where they entered into a prevision. Holly's was in the hospital in coma. The doctors led her out of danger, but she was in critical condition after a tragic incident. Benjamin was allowed to be next to her. Damian held her psyche and her heart imprisoned in a parallel dimension. Benjamin felt Holly was dying, so he took her hand, enveloping his woman with the magic of his love. Our knight recognized the emotions Holly was passing to him, remembering sensations when Eurydice died in his arms before. Benjamin climbed into her hospital bed and hugged Holly, bracing to accept the inevitable. He released any fears as Holly took her last breath. Benjamin kept hugging his woman, praying with his poems. *If I believe that she can return to live and I won't doubt it for a second, then she will wake up. I can only resurrect her with my faith. She needs to feel loved and protected to be alive*, Benjamin thought, convinced he would bring Holly back. He closed his eyes and opened his heart, allowing it to fill the room with healing light. The next few minutes felt like hours, but suddenly Holly's heart was beating again. Unconscious in a coma but alive, she was saved by Benjamin's honest feelings. Just by believing in their love he brought her back from the other side.

As Benjamin and Eurydice returned from this vision, they felt defeated. One passionate argument led to another, and now they were deep inside their first major fight. Accusations and negative emotions filled their peaceful retreat house. So many issues had boiled up, and the last four months were overwhelmingly emotional for our couple. Benjamin was scared that Holly was actually in a coma. Her body was fine, but this was a clear oracle prevision into what she may endure in the future. Our knight got furious, blaming himself for not saving his woman, but then he shifted his attention to Eurydice, finally realizing what actually happened.

Benjamin was not Eurydice's lover at that moment but her wiser friend. True lovers ought to be best friends, as it is important to state the occasional bitter truth. Benjamin openly blamed Eurydice for this entire situation. The pain of losing Holly was unbearable. After crying through terrifying visions of a dead Holly, Benjamin realized that Eurydice was hiding something from him. If the body is the car and the soul is the driver, Holly's coma would be caused by the driver's mistakes. Benjamin scolded and criticized Eurydice for leading Holly into danger. Eurydice didn't question Holly's reality and whims. She obediently surrendered to them, which broke their connection. Besides Eurydice never learned lessons from the past and accumulated spiritual debt, complicating her future lives and now endangering Holly. Benjamin went overboard that night, in verbal attack exposing the lies of his princess. He was emotional from the nightmares, confronting his woman for being a child and refusing to grow up.

The reality couldn't be clearer for Benjamin, as all pieces finally created a whole image. He was also angry because Eurydice always blamed Holly for ostracizing her. Benjamin being so in love with his soulmate, blindly believed in her version of events without properly analyzing the situation. He never blamed Holly for rejecting his love; instead, he blamed Damian for every destructive behavior of his woman, but now, the real truth has come out. Eurydice couldn't deny any longer that she intentionally misled Benjamin to avoid accountability, and our knight was infuriated. He was saddened not because Eurydice hid the truth from him but because he struggled to help her. She sabotaged the healing process, as Benjamin couldn't determine the proper course of action without understanding every relevant fact. Eurydice infantile behavior caused a new drama, but she knew Benjamin was right about everything he said. He would have accepted Eurydice's mistakes, but he couldn't accept new lies between them. He was not rude to her, yet his straightforward truth emotionally hurt her, as it was unbearable to hear bitter words from her lover. Even though she cried for hours, Eurydice knew she brought this torture on herself, deserving every pain her fragile heart.

They spent time apart in the different rooms, unable to face each other after the harsh words they were bound to say. Benjamin retreated to the fireplace, terrified by the thought that Eurydice could never be healed, exactly like Ariadne said. Eurydice kept repeating Benjamin's accusations in her head throughout the evening, feeling worthless, full of shame and self-guilt. Her man triggered every insecurity she had, and now she wanted to run away from him again. Eurydice was worthy of every possible blessing, but she continued to stubbornly refuse her complex essence. Only Benjamin's highest love could help her discover true self-love. Our knight calmed down, now blaming himself for being too emotional. He knew this soul was under intense stress, and once Eurydice could rest after her predicaments, she would hear his truth.

Later, Benjamin returned to her room and pleaded for forgiveness. Still angry at him, Eurydice responded with ugly silent treatment. Benjamin sat on the edge of the bed, looking out the window, unable to face punishing look of his beloved. They spend next few minutes in complete silence, and then Eurydice fired back, "I heard so many accusations today from you. I understand that I betrayed you and destroyed the connection with my vessel, but if you really in love, you would never say such horrible things to me. I was right that you never loved me."

"Polly, this is exactly what love is. Unconditional love can only be honest. That's why we are born to experience this feeling. No one will tell us the real truth except for our beloved. We grow through our affections. Look how you transformed me in matter of weeks. I would be nothing without our love because I listen to you and work every day on my flaws. You've amplified my insecurities and showed where I needed to heal myself, and instead of blaming you, I did my shadow work, patiently facing every ugly thing about me. My love allowed me to rise above my past mistakes. We are trying to figure out what happened to us, and we can do it only by being honest. Your mess is mine, so we can only solve our issues together."

"But look at yourself! You should be ashamed of your behavior. Not a single woman wants to be treated like that. I don't even know what I'm doing with you. You are not my type, and you are not even hot! Have you ever looked in the mirror? Your unappealing beard and ridiculous glasses of a geek are so repulsive. You are a penniless immigrant and live in a rat house. I don't know what I'm doing with you. You have nothing to give me. You have not achieved anything in your life, and now you demand I should learn from you? Nobody wants to watch your movies or purchase your stupid art. Your spiritual insights may be just your sick delusions.

Your book may be years away, and you may never finish it because you are a stoner. Even if you write it, you will make it so boring that no one will ever read it. Mister know-it-all. You are playing a smart ass, but in reality, you are just a loser."

"Thank you, Polly, for such words. Trashing me made you feel better? If so, you can continue, I don't mind. You are tired of my lectures, I get it. You are welcome to ignore them. We can live in complete silence, but you are my responsibility now."

"I'm just your responsibility? Like a burden?"

"That's not what I meant. As a man, it is an honor to take responsibility for my woman. I love you, but if you don't accept my affection. We can live as roommates, since now we are bonded by the contract. You are chained to my body and it was your choice. If you wish, I can stop talking and you won't ever have to listen to me."

"I don't want to be roommates. I want us to be passionate lovers without accusations. Being with you is such a hard work. I just want to cuddle."

"And yet, my dear Polly, this is love too. It's not only about sensual pleasures. I can only offer you a relationship based on sacred intimacy. A truly deep, emotional union. I'm not interested in pretenses, masks and lies. When you love someone, you must tell the painful truth. I'm not the kind of man who would sugar-coat your reality. I want to take care of you, which means healing the root causes of your traumas. Spirits chained you to me, because of how stubborn and defiant you are. What really hurts in the true union is not calling out the other person's stuff. The little things, little truths not shared with beloved, build brick walls. If we won't address how we feel, one day, we will wake up as distant roommates. I don't want to take us for granted anymore as we did before. Do you want to become my wife? Well, that's what it means to be in a real marriage – telling things how they are when you see your lover falling into the same old traps."

"I don't want to be your wife anymore. You are too complex, and living with you is so challenging. I'm tired of these never-ending serious conversations. You talk about healing, but it seems like it's impossible to achieve. How many years you've spent healing yourself and you are still broken. I'm just a girl living a fleeting life. I'm royalty! I want to spend time in beach resorts, and travel on private jets and yachts while savoring delicacies. I want to live! Yet, here I am, stuck with you, with a man who doesn't even have documents to travel. We would only be struggling and fighting without leaving your ugly flat. I'm not your property. I'm not obliged to follow your guidance and these rules piss me off!"

"You're pissed at yourself because you chose to be with me, and now you can't leave."

"Now I realize that choosing you was a mistake from the beginning. You manipulated me with sensuality and spiritual bullshit, and now I can't escape!"

"Polly, please hear me out! I'm acting in your best interests. Only when you don't share the truth of your past, I can't provide the correct advice or heal you. Please stop fighting me, or you will be doomed to suffer forever. The choice is entirely yours, but I'm not your enemy."

"You are just using me because you know I don't have any other place to go. I can't return to my mom because you signed that stupid contract. So now I'm your prisoner forever, and you will torture me with your manipulative mind games. Holly was right to reject you."

"Polly, please, let's work together through this. Just hear me out. I love you. You are such a complex and intricate being. I enjoy beholding every angle and facet of you, including this one. There's nothing that I enjoy more than experiencing everything that you are, my love. Allow yourself to feel what you mean to me. You made me sing and dance again, and I will be forever grateful to you, my muse. You have to acknowledge that what you did was reckless. That's the only way to reconcile with our past. But since now we are here, there's no point in blaming yourself for what you did. I'm bringing this up not to attack you but to understand what we can do to save Holly and prevent this from happening in the future. Please tell me the truth, no matter how embarrassed or guilty you may feel. Lies, miscommunication and reservations ruined our connection before, leading to intense scars of our souls, so please, let's not do this again."

"Sure. Whatever. I don't care anymore." Eurydice was distant, but she knew Benjamin was right. Only she couldn't look at him and required some time alone to face herself. Benjamin sensed the thick mist of confrontational energies and he left her, returning to the fireplace. He set out to write a love letter to Holly about this entire ordeal, apologizing to her about the previous letters, now blaming Eurydice for their broken love. He didn't enjoy saying unpleasant things about Eurydice, as he loved her very much. Yet, if her actions led to such destructive consequences and a real possibility of being murdered by Damian, Holly needed to know about Eurydice's wrongdoings. He attempted to remove the negative energies between them, by openly talking about their issues through his therapeutic letters. He praised his beloved with his quill. She could do the worst things in the world, but she was still a pure, innocent, and divine woman for Benjamin. Similar misunderstandings and unresolved innuendos hovered above them for centuries, and only Damian benefited from them. That's how he destroyed our lovers before. That's why the contract bonded them this time, forcing them to work through their dramas, without possibility to escape. Spirits wanted to help them avoid the same mistakes. They made the decision in between lives to finally resolve their past, and this contract was the only way to achieve that. Both were tricked into signing it, clouded by their affections, but there was no other way for them to finally face their innate stubbornness.

Soon Eurydice felt lonely. She was still very angry at Benjamin, but she couldn't live without his presence and soothing energy. She was deeply in love with her man, unable to escape her feelings. Eurydice decided to sneak into the living room and check on Benjamin. She pretended she was looking for a snack and then settled on the sofa, in the furthest part of the room, with a poetry book. She secretly glanced at Benjamin who continued writing his letter, trying to avoid his attention, as she didn't want to show him that he had won the argument. She had to be right in this situation, expecting him to mend them.

After Benjamin finished the letter, he returned to his investigation. He dreamed of resolving their old conflicts immediately, hoping to answer every question at once. Benjamin listed everything that troubled him in their union. He wanted to understand what prevented them from defeating Damian and how they could achieve victory this time. Everything seemed solvable, but one question tortured our knight the most. Why couldn't Eurydice find him earlier if she knew she was in danger?

At the same time, they were obliged to present an outline to Ariadne in just a few days. Only now, Benjamin felt he didn't understood his book at all. Eurydice deceived him, so he had to scramble his previous plans. Benjamin decided to dedicate his life to yet another noble cause. He wished to help his woman embrace the beauty and strength of her feminine heart, as Eurydice refused to see the magic of her essence. He decided to drown her in his love.

Our knight pleaded for forgiveness again, inviting Eurydice to join him at the table. Eurydice tried to act like an ice queen, pretending to read, but Benjamin could easily see through her games. Eurydice was still infuriated at how he exposed her missteps and deceits. He could see right through her, and no woman likes that feeling. She dreamed to prove him wrong, when she knew he was right. Eurydice wanted to be a precious gem, a sophisticated puzzle, that her man would never be able to solve. But Benjamin knew her better, than she knew herself. She was distressed, feeling like Benjamin had undressed her. He insisted she has to accept the consequences of her actions. Even though Benjamin forgave her, Eurydice still felt that her behavior made her man think less of her. She hated that Benjamin was her assigned teacher from Nature, feeling constantly exposed and unable to hide from him. Eurydice preferred escaping existential suffering by making love under soft sheets, but her man was on a mission to resolve the root causes of her never-ending anxiety and grief.

Our princess realized she had romantic affection for Benjamin because she had to embrace his teachings and, through their love, understand herself better. She was trapped not by the contract but by her own feelings and that daunting realization scared her. She could somehow live through the period of the contract, but she didn't know what to do with her heart. She was fighting her feelings, as they terrified her. She was really hurt how Benjamin brazenly confronted her sensibilities. Eurydice was shocked that he forced her to face herself and finally abandon her naive illusions of a damsel in distress.

Eurydice believed she could be saved through sensual pleasures, but it was not her man's plan. She wanted to run away from Benjamin and never see him again. Eurydice was mostly angry at herself as she created this whole reality. She was enraged as she didn't know what to do with her emotions towards her knight. She had nowhere to go, forced to live with Benjamin, but at the same time, she desperately desired to be around him as much as possible. She wanted to be only with him. Eurydice was so tired of facing herself, but deep inside, she longed to be in Benjamin's energy field, even if he would be strict and unapologetic with her. Being in the presence of each other's aura was the best feeling they ever experienced on Earth, and it never mattered how they spent time, as long as they were together. That's why they continued to come to live in human bodies. Eurydice could only be herself around him; he allowed her to do whatever her passionate heart desired, always providing a safe space for healing, growth, and artistic self-expression. Only this man saw her for who she was. Next to him she could express her gentle yet rebellious nature in any way she liked. He always held a sacred space for her to discover herself.

Eurydice didn't know what to do next. Benjamin had already apologized twice, and now she felt she had to do the same. She hated apologies, feeling extremely awkward admitting being wrong, but Benjamin inspired her. She liked how he made her feel, and he always discovered the answers she needed. She was intrigued by Benjamin's philosophical, magical, and artistic insights. She was fascinated with Benjamin's approach to life itself. Our princess knew she could find the desperately needed truth only through Benjamin. He could easily solve her existential issues, but Eurydice hated to admit that she needed Benjamin more than he needed her, even though they were equally imperfect without each other.

The princess finally surrendered and slowly crossed the room, silently looking into the eyes of her knight. She apologized with a gaze, and Benjamin accepted her plea. Eurydice sat across from Benjamin, and her knight made them tea in a Ukrainian tradition. Eurydice finally accepted her tormenting emotions because she was so glad to have a wonderful man beside her, who was actually ready to accept her tears with his unconditional love and an open mind. Eurydice was smiling from joy deep inside but tried to pretend she was still angry. "You know I truly believe what I said before. I don't know why I chose to be with such a loser. And it bothers me that you are not sexy."

"You are with me because we are extensions of each other. We can only be whole if we are together. I'm an artist who praises you with love poems and the only man who knows how to really love you. I'm not here to win sex competitions. You are just trying to sting me."

"It feels strange to even look at you, not to mention being with you. You have this artistic vibe, which may be appealing to other women, but it's just not my thing."

"Well, you've mentioned I would look sexier if I had a grey beard."

"Yes! You are right! It would be so cool."

"With your emotional dramas, you will make it grey just in a couple of years."

"I want it now; I don't want to wait. Oh, it's all pointless. I'm also tired of your cheap flat and ugly finishings. You don't even have a dishwasher. I'm tired of spending hours washing your dishes and you can't even afford nice take-outs. I hate you, Benjamin; I truly do. I want my lifestyle back, yet I'm chained to you."

"You are in the prison of love, my dear Polly and I will spoil you tonight because you have returned from the scariest place I have ever visited. Please don't be too hard on yourself, but trust me, as we can only heal as a team. You know I love you, and I'm nothing without you, my sweet princess. I won't judge you, but I can see that you are hiding some of your feelings. Please tell me what's really on your mind, dear Polly?"

"I don't really know. Existential existence, I guess. Perpetual anxiety? The never-ending cycle of self-loathing? Living this stupid life that I can't figure out, no matter how hard I try. It's quite hard to describe my emotions. Maybe I'm just sabotaging myself."

"It's fine to feel any emotion. Just live through it. Each emotion tells you something about yourself. Allow this feeling to exist and see what it wants to tell you. Maybe you don't know what's next, and it scares you?"

"Yes, our situation is bizarre and strange, so I'm pretty puzzled. I'm not in my body and you can't be with Holly. Besides, seeing memories of my torturous past was also quite disturbing."

"Please tell me, what have you learned from seeing your past lives?"

"I guess I don't like living in the shadows of this world. I'm just tired of it, that's all. It's not about being famous either. It's more about being seen. I did so many things for this world, but human recollections of my presence are insignificant. People wrote whole books about your life, Benjamin, but only a few lines about me. I have existed, and I helped you to achieve your greatness. Yet no one recognizes my existence and my value. I'm invisible no matter what I do."

"Because you're intentionally trying to hide your true self. It is your chose to be unnoticeable. You want to be a smaller version of yourself and that's how the world responds to your requests."

"True, but now I know I don't like how it feels. Being the smallest me, created every anxiety I have. This is not who I am, but I always hide from my feminine essence."

"Well, if only you would stop running away from me all the time…"

"You know Benjamin, I think angels cursed me. I can't stand you, but yet they made us inseparable. No matter what I do, I can't run away from you. I'm forced to end up with you all the time. You always arriving to lift me up, even if I'm trapped in Hell. You trigger this deep hatred in me, and I can't stand you. If you are my destined teacher, then tell me how to escape you, Benjamin, as I'm tired to constantly ran in circles."

"I think the angels will liberate you once you learn everything you need to learn from me. Until then, we will be bonded to meet again and again, and there's nothing either of us can do."

"Then I should stop learning at all! As much as I hate you, I can't live without you. The only reason why I want to live is to see you. Otherwise, I prefer living in death."

"I can't live without you, either. I wither and fade without you. We are parts of one being, divided into feminine and masculine principles. Two souls in such a situation can only find salvation and romantic bliss, when they complete their individual work. Only in our situation, you ran away from me too many times, refusing to do your work. That's why you are chained to me. But I believe it's a blessing You requested to heal, and this is the only way."

"Benjamin! Can we do this work in our bedroom? Everything that you ask of me is so complicated. Where is the joy of life? Why was I designed like this, my love?"

"I think that we are destined to share our story with the world, my sweet Polly. You will bring your feminine light and inspiration, while I'll bring divine teachings and masculine perseverance. I can only access the highest knowledge by being with you, by learning from you what it means to be a woman. I'm tired of living in the physical body, but you force me to return, as you are so beautifully and rebelliously stubborn, my dear. Polly we are making progress, but you are questioning the magic of our story. You can't continue to avoid my advice."

"So simple, right? Just obediently listen to you?"

"That's not what I'm asking. Please listen to what makes sense to your heart and scrutinize me if you question where my intentions are coming from. I have no desire to control you, as I love you for who you are, but you think you can be someone you are not. It is a pointless exercise in this reality. What I offer benefits us both. You can use a simple test of light and love with any advice."

"What I offer benefits both of us too. You just don't like my experimental approach."

"Then let's honor both visions and take the best from them. You are such an amazing woman, and I can't stop praising your divine essence."

"That's what a girl likes to hear. I hate when we fight. Benjamin, you asked me what happened between Holly and me. I know the best way to show to you."

"Okay, I'm curious," Benjamin smiled as he realized Eurydice had planned a surprise.

"We have to watch *Mean Girls*."

"*Mean Girls*? Why?"

"This movie is not about the rivalry between two girls. It is a movie about the relationship between a body and a soul. Just imagine that I'm Cady Heron, and Holly is Regina George. Your answers are in that movie. I will entertain you with stories from Holly's past while explaining what happened between us."

It was a night to remember. They laughed and cried; they paused the movie, passionately debating the story and dialogues. They danced in joy, enveloped in their romantic cuteness. Eurydice even colored her hair red to look more like Cady. They discussed the dynamic between Cady and Regina and how this movie perfectly depicts Eurydice. They noticed every similarity, openly joking about Eurydice's insecurities. She finally learned to made fun of herself, healing through the laughter. Benjamin paid specific attention to Eurydice's reactions to Cady's actions, noticing how in sync they were. Eurydice also noticed another layer of meaning. She saw Eloise's reflection in Cady's actions. Initially honest with herself, Cady confronted the real evil that has consumed their school. Still, instead of exposing the lies with intuitive femininity, Cady turned into a bigger villain in her twisted transformation. She stopped listening to her essence, and that led to her eventual downfall.

Once they finished this movie, Eurydice wanted to find out how many other magicians live with the souls of their beloved. Benjamin's guides answered," Twenty-seven other couples live like you at present moment." Now Eurydice demanded proof. If such stories happen to others, they must be reflected in the art. They had already discovered *Meet Joe Black*, and soon Benjamin discovered another movie, *Just Like Heaven*. Benjamin and Eurydice laughed throughout the film at the experiences of the male protagonist, who struggled to prove to people that he communicates with the soul of his woman. The dynamic between characters, their humor, and romance was exactly like what Eurydice experienced with Benjamin. They saw many similarities with their story. In the end, the man saved his woman's body from a coma only by healing her soul with his sincere love and honest sacrifices. This movie uplifted our lovers. Our lovers could resolve Eurydice's past traumas and empower her with the will to live. Eurydice was scared that she took such a leap of faith and committed to living with Benjamin. They both felt on edge as they didn't know how two souls would co-exist in one body, as Eurydice had to prioritize Benjamin's needs. It made her feel confined, imprisoned, and trapped, but each healing evening she spent in Sechelt reassured her. They lived a supernatural life of a unique bond unlike anything humans could experience.

CHAPTER XIV

The next day they went exploring the lands around their house. They needed to clear their heads and recharge. Benjamin was increasingly preoccupied with the book's outline, as he hadn't written a single sentence, but nice weather, welcoming spirits, and dancing Eurydice elevated his mood. They searched for a land where they could build Eurydice's dream house. Benjamin could not afford a mortgage right now, but they needed to envision this place first. Soon they discovered a small, secret path leading through the woods, and spirits guided them to take it. Eurydice asked the spirits to show her the possible obstacles on her path. A spirit presented Eurydice a ring that looked like a promise ring Benjamin had in mind. Eurydice had to receive it first, before building their house.

Our lovers continued their journey through the woods, but soon Damian appeared, blocking Eurydice's way. He appeared as a tall, dark gentleman constructed from a thick mist. He had distinctive face and exquisite clothes, but at the same time, he was just an energy field of dark matter. When Eurydice faced Damian, she asked him how she could pass him to get to her dream house. Damian leaned towards our princess and whispered," You have to own your past deaths!" Eurydice looked him directly in the eyes. She realized that any dream was possible if she would embrace her past and own her complex nature. Everything that Damian wanted to do with Eurydice today he already did before, so only by removing traumas she assumed upon previous deaths could she understand how Damian tricked her. Once Eurydice accepted his message, Dark Prince cleared her path. When Eurydice walked past him, she said," You will never let me go, right?"

"Yes, my dear. I will always be with you. You have to find a way to co-exist with me without destroying yourself in the process." Damian turned into a dark cloud that hovered behind Eurydice's shoulders. She continued walking down her path, while Damian followed her like a shadow. Eurydice proudly walked down this magical trail without allowing him to enter her heart.

"You know how to defeat me," Damian said, flying around Eurydice.

"Yes, I do. If I'm acting from a position of fear, afraid to believe in my dream house, you will enter me and control my reality. But when I'm acting from a place of joy and love for myself, I can face my challenges with courage, and you won't break me. That's how I can magnetize a happy life with my man, even though I'm very weak after what you've done to me."

"I never did anything to you. You destroyed yourself by rejecting being a woman, but you understand my true nature now. I will never leave the corners of your bed, as I am the one who can make you stronger if you integrate your darkness. Never forget that I will never stop looking for ways to drive you into a state of fear."

"Thank you for your teachings, Damian. You are actually my blessing. I will find the strength to face you."

"Until then, Eurydice." Damian disappeared into thin air. Eurydice felt liberated, but she knew her demons would never leave her, if she dares to follow the dreams of her feminine heart.

Eventually, the path led them to a majestic meadow that looked perfect for their future house. It was hidden in the woods, away from people, yet it had an incredible view, overlooking the Sechelt Inlet. Eurydice described her dream place in vivid details on their way home. She was excited they found such an ideal spot, that had everything she wished for. She pictured the back garden and front porch, a flowery bedroom, a perfect sarcophagus for Benjamin's death travels, and a room for magical ceremonies with a fireplace. She channeled her imagination to Benjamin, and together they constructed the entire house in the spiritual realm. Now they only needed to find a way to bridge it into the reality.

Eurydice dreamed and dreamed and dreamed. The lands inspired her, and her fight with Benjamin only strengthened their love. Now Eurydice allowed herself to say what her heart wanted. Even though Benjamin couldn't build this house now, she realized that if she had faith in her man, it would eventually happen, and his achievements would become hers. Benjamin's manuscript was the only thing that could make Eurydice's dream come true, and our princess decided to bet on her knight. She clearly saw this was the only way to achieve her dreams – by believing in the talents of her man. Yes, she had no other choice, but at that moment, Eurydice accepted their story without reservations. Benjamin was not even a permanent resident and couldn't afford to rent a comfortable apartment for Eurydice, but she finally trusted her heart. While the princess danced over the beautiful creek next to their home, another wave of inspiration descended upon her. As she opened up to trust her Magdalene intuition for the first time, she felt how a beautiful poem about her essence had risen to the surface, and she memorized this stream of consciousness.

"Polly, what else do you think you need for healing?" Benjamin asked his woman over tea when they cozied up next to a fireplace back home.

"Well, now I know how much you love me, seeing the sufferings you've endured and what you've sacrificed for me. Your love is in your poems, letters, and commitments. I am one lucky woman, but I think my confusion arises from my false perceptions. We often didn't express how we feel about each other. Now I know that you always loved me. But you haven't said the proper words of love in some lives, so I continue to demand proof of your love. Only new loving words could heal my past."

"I know I failed to express my love to you. Please don't judge me, as I'm just a man and that's what we often do. We are scared of our feelings and don't know how to word them, intimated by the woman's essence. I agree I didn't know how to show affections the way you desired."

"My past selves didn't understand that, so we need to heal their confusion. I know that's unfair to you now, but that's the only way I see for us."

"It makes sense, my love. I would love to prove my love to you, as I have nothing to hide. But you may need to brace yourself for how strong my love is, as the storm of my devotion and affections will engulf you completely, once you see the full essence of my heart."

"Do you know that I always loved you?"

"Yes, I do. You are a woman, so it was easy for me. I could always see how beautifully you shined from it. Your love for me always suited you well. You always carried your love with such a grace. It's like you are not yourself if you don't love me. I tried to show you how much I loved you. I do apologize that I was reserved at times, but man's love is best expressed through actions. Yet I want to prove my love in the way you wish and if you desire to hear more loving words, I'll do that."

"Thank you, my love. Now I can see that our love is much bigger than I thought."

"You know, we experienced every single type of love, and it only grew through the centuries."

"Yes! I feel we are collecting variations of love to understand each other truly. But honestly, I need to learn to take responsibility for my life. No matter how much you love me, I can only defeat Damian by myself. You can teach me to see through his tricks, but I must stop lying to myself, or he will drag me to Hell again. When I listen to my feminine intuition, I'm empowered."

"Yes, Polly, that's true. In our world dominated by male energies, women get into the trap of trying to solve their problems with their masculine energies. That never resolves any issue and is quite destructive to feminine nature. You are trying to run away from life, thinking the next one would be easier somehow, but it's always more challenging. The only way is to approach the tasks at hand with your feminine energies. Especially when yours are so powerful and exceptional."

"If I'm struggling to learn how to be a woman, then tell me, Benjamin, what is a woman?"

"A woman is a supreme, sensual, and intuitive human being who creates life itself."

"It means nothing to me, Benjamin. It still doesn't tell me what to do to become a woman."

"You don't need to do anything, Polly. You have to be yourself and sense the world through your heart and your womb. They know your answers, so connect to them. Just soften up into your flow and magic of being. A rose doesn't know it's a rose. It doesn't force itself to be something. It's just blossoming as a rose, by being a rose."

"Benjamin, you make it sound so simple, but I feel it's more complicated in my case. Out of my eight lives, I was a man only once, and it was so easy. So clearly, I do not understand something about my feminine essence. I think I missed experiencing your love the way you show it to me now. I'm always dependent on your affections and admiration, which I actually find beautiful. But I confused myself too many times, not believing your love was real."

"Then we are in a perfect place to untangle our issues. I will show you how much I loved you before. And I will show you how much I love you now. I won't leave this mortal plane until you embrace your feminine grandness and shine in your glory."

"That sounds nice, Benjamin. I feel your love can help me this time. So, is this what you are going to write about? Do you have an outline ready for my mom?" Eurydice nervously brought up a topic she wanted to discuss, still afraid her knight might reject her ideas.

"No, I haven't figured out my book. I know what it will be about, but my ideas do not come across once I start writing. I'm missing something since our reality has shifted so drastically."

"Oh, Benjamin, we had such a splendid time today."

"Yes indeed. It was so nice to immerse in our dream."

"Everything is interconnected, Benjamin. I can finally feel it. We ought to live through what we hadn't lived in the past when my life was cut short. Until we make up for that time, we won't have a future. I'm sorry for the way I behaved. I need to learn to hear your heart, but it's often hard, as I immediately resort to self-loathing and blame. And I shouldn't have cursed you when you said your truth. You are doing what you are destined to do as my spiritual teacher. I can only praise the world for how blessed I feel that you signed a contract with my mother."

"Oh, don't worry, my love. I'm glad you're finding the courage to grow from your mistakes."

"I feel like I'm becoming a better soul because of you. Your methods are excruciatingly painful. It was so numbing to live in my comfort zone. But you are methodically razing every wall I carry from the past. The stresses you provoked and your reassuring words destroyed my erratic notions about life and relationship. So, I concluded that we should write your book together."

"Really? Please tell me more, as I'm stuck."

"Do you remember your creation story? I didn't understand part of it, but I think I can see now how this life is actually designed. You are a writer; you create the world with your tools. But you need your visionary woman and that's me at present moment. Here's my idea. I will design the garden and the house I wish to live in. This will inspire you to write and that's how you will build it for us. Let's think about the first time you envisioned your book. What changed in your life in that moment?"

"You've changed. You just turned sixteen, and suddenly I realized I had lost my daughter. I knew I would have to let you go one day, but I thought we still had some time. That day, I couldn't stop watching your lightness and grace as you danced through our Monticello garden. It was one of the most beautiful moments I ever experienced. A profound clairvoyant vision opened up in me. I remember how angels descended into our shared space, illuminating our connection. You were dancing in joy, yet preoccupied about something. What did you think about, Polly?"

"I was thinking about how to help my papa. I could never understand what you did as a politician, but I really wanted to help you. Only I didn't know how, as your world was so foreign to me. I was never an intellectual, nor could I grasp your visions for America. So, I decided to pray in our sacred space, under the energetic dome of divine light, you built with mama. I remember how gloriously bright it was! I was dancing and sending positive affirmations your way; it was the only self-expression available to me. I created new uplifting energies with my joyful dances. I only dreamed my father would find his answers and heal the spiritual divisions of America."

"And in that moment, I envisioned my book. Since you've embodied the wholeness of American essence, I wanted to capture that in my writing. I didn't need to explore America further. I could feel its essence by looking at you, my favorite daughter Polly. You described that land to me through your dances, gestures, smiles, poetry and dreamy approach to life itself. That's when I finally grasped that American lands carry the feminine essence and that was the key to understanding what this nation should be. You being yourself was enough for me to understand this new country."

"So, if you envisioned the book just by living in my presence, it means we are co-creators of this work. Only now I think we need to write two books. You will write your American book, and I will write a book about our love that led you to discover your destined manuscript. We would write about our adventures, express our traumas, expose delusions, and through our poetry, we would finally say how we truly feel about each other."

"You will write poetry too, Polly? You were always shy to try in your past lives."

"Yes. You are witnessing the birth of a new poet. Eurydice Eloise Wayles."

"So, this first book would be about you?"

"Benjamin, I have to write about myself. I need to battle my internal issues. If I share my experiences and talk about my miseries and tears, I can be free. You will hold a sacred space for me so I can honestly tell my female story. One book would heal you, and another would heal me. And also, maybe if other women would read my story, they would not fall in the same traps I did. But, Benjamin, we must finally commit to be ourselves! You have to emit and embody the noble masculine energy of a confident writer with your everyday existence. I have to be able to experience your essence without reading your books."

"Polly, it means that our perceived dramas are our blessings. I shall head to you, my princess." Benjamin began writing his notes, listening to his woman. Eurydice talked and talked, describing her visions and raising questions that tormented her. Our lovers finally realized why they were chained to each other. Eurydice needed to confess, write, and perform, but she couldn't do it in Holly's body. She asked higher forces to offer her an opportunity to express herself unrestrainedly, so they made it possible for Benjamin to channel Eurydice's truth. Through his vessel, she could be herself, as Benjamin would endure the judgments and hardships of an artist for her. He was ready to die for the truth of his woman. Passion, inspiration, beauty, intimacy and love flowed through their house as our lovers couldn't sleep until sunrise, co-creating new art together.

At dawn, Benjamin finalized his presentation. He embraced Eurydice's most radical and strangest suggestions. He tried to capture everything she said. Benjamin recorded every thought that sparked from seeing the eyes of his beloved woman. After this night, our lovers became inseparable.

It was a bright sunny morning, but the princess and her knight still didn't want to sleep. Eurydice revised her poem while Benjamin was working. Now she was ready to share it. He settled comfortably in an imaginary theatre, as Eurydice stood up and crossed the stage. "You will hear the story about me, what kind of self-reflective creature I am and how I refuse to grow up. Please know, dear Benjamin, that I address many, but you are my only desired audience."

The lights went dark, and only a single spotlight illuminated her. She looked down, gathering herself and allowing Benjamin to study her silently. She was not scared anymore to share her feminine truth. She was wearing a beautiful little black dress with a waistband made of shining Sechelt crystals, but her heart was naked and exposed for everyone to see.

The Song of My Essence
by Eurydice Eloise Wayles

What if I could be forever young
Tripping topless naked in the sun
Dancing like
There will be no tomorrow anyways?

Would I still be me, if I dream to be
Present in the now, to forget ordeals?
Should I crash the space or defy the time
If I'm only here, living for a short while?

Death is all around me,
Murders are accustomed,
Crying and afflicting
Never been uncommon,
I'm a youthful creature,
Fighting growing older
Always dancing glowing
To elude my sorrows...

My unique power of truth claims reality
I inhabit.
Therefore, I control, and I possess
What is around me
And all of it quickly falls to my feet
With strangers passing me by
Twisting their necks in disbelief
Unable to concede to the beauty of a rebellious soul.
Yet – still slowing their walks,
Hiding behind their ridiculous social masks,
Smitten by judgment and condemnation,
Yearning, they can charge their empty hearts,
Craving to escape their troubles

And their suicidal thoughts,
Pleading to liberate their lives
From hulking yokes
They placed upon themselves a long time ago,
While with the same eyes
Greedily consuming my energy
Hopelessly dreaming to steal a part of me.

Well, my apologies, dear sirs!
I can't really give you that much,
Still kinda, wanna keep this life force for myself
Not for another fellow passer-by –
Staring through the bushes, hiding being the bench,
Pretending to exercise right across from me,
Anxious, disturbed, apprehensive
Timid, tempted, trepidatious
Not owning himself,
Looking for validation from others
Confused by my freedom, by my fearless appearance
Terrified by my confidence
When I'm in control of reality –
Alone
Naked
Dancing
Wild!

They think I do it for them,
Crippled beings confronted by life,
Deep inside, wishing to inhibit
The ultimate potential of a young lady.
They think I do it for them
For the spectators in this circus of life,
They wish my mind would only desire
To seduce and to caress whoso.
They are ready to ruin their lives
Just for the opportunity to touch me,

They want me to pet them,
Like they are my sex slaves.

They picture my lips between my legs
They wish my lips would be between their legs
Savoring their crooked follicles, with sensual
    carnality
Stupidly thinking that a princess like me
With my pure dignity
Will be playing by their locker room prison-inspired rules.

They're convinced I do it for them,
For the show, for the attention,
Their petty perversions
Rising to the surface, enraging them;
So sorry, my deviant strangers
Obsessive, impulsive dead inside creeps,
But to perceive me just as a minx
Simply means
Losing seeing
Life's precious gifts;
I'm in this park dancing for me
So can you please peacefully
Enjoy this artistic creation
Of the celestial empyrean flirtation?

Like how shallow your lives must be
If you can't simply see,
That I'm supposed to be dancing, bare and free
To save our world from its misery.
Yes, today in my Stanley Park
Owning the sparks of the light and the dark
I'm executing my life's noble mission
As I perform my ambrosian dance.
Finally, fully naked, stripped of any guilt or shame,
I am obliged to continue performing my dance.

As without my nude presence, illuminated by the gods
Destruction will ensue,
With evil spirits enslaving entire humanity.
Yes, only I can be the savior of this troubled world.

Around me alive Nature
The grass is softly delicate, unforgettably tickling my feet,
Majestic trees are whispering with their encouragements
Exalted animals and birds gather to cheer with their existence –
I'm levitating above the banality,
Pervading the space around me,
Transcending the sufferings of the grounded plane,
I'm united with the spirits of my land
Climaxing in the universal alliance
As they absorb me into their kingdom
While I'm projecting their truth
Radiating otherworldly vibrations
Through my dance of cosmic admiration.

I'm comfortable with myself,
With who I am and how I feel inside -
Always young, always dancing in the sun,
With wind running through every part of me,
I'm nude, and I'm free
This is who I will always be,
The spirit of liberation and deliverance
The inevitable force of existence.

My presence omits the waves of presence,
Hijacking the minds of my fellow human beings,
As they impulsively look at me,
While I'm here with the intent to be seen,
For a short fraction of time,
Before flying away like a butterfly.

And when time will consume my fragile vessel,

Another young girl will be dancing here on my spot –
And I bet she'll be naked too.
Although I really don't know as I can only feel the essence
Of this unstoppable force with no human control
Or the possibility to box this energy within reason.
This is how it simply has to be
And will always be, forever and ever –
A girl who's young, careless, and arcadian
Dancing before disappearing into the abyss.

What if I could be forever young,
Bathing fully naked in the sun?
Envious eyes surrounding
My divine gestures and lines
The magnets of sweetness
Seizing reality
By the sheer moment of eternal beauty
Until time takes over.

I placed myself in the direct spotlight
With one intention only –
To be belligerently young and stoutly in your face.
Now I passionately beg the world
To stay like this forever, to honor my holy duty,
As no one can do this better than me.

I'm self-aware of who I am
I love to die to live this fight
This phase of life exists to shine
With the dance of virgin female might
I am emerging to excite
Blazingly crazy claiming my light
Naively, curiously, questionably, exposing reality,
With my voracious sexuality.

My chance of doing this will be gone one day

As my dance propels me to another level
Painfully transforming me into a consonant grown-up
Incapable of foolishly jumping in the park naked.
But for now, through this dance of revelation,
I'm manifesting my presence in this mystical reality
As I express every intricacy
Of my gentle, seductive being.

The sparkling, dazzling sun is my friend and my witness,
The forces of Nature escort me on this journey –
I will take my chances now while I'm still young
And I will never care what you might ever think of me.
I dance to be free!
I wish to be seen!
I was born to be me!
Eyrudice!

CHAPTER XV

Our lovers slept through entire day, exhausted but elated after their breakthrough. In the evening Queen Ariadne invited Benjamin and Eurydice for dinner in downtown Sechelt. Eurydice described to her mom everything they'd been through. She talked about the poems Benjamin crafted, proudly gazing at her knight. She told her about entrapment in Damian's dungeon and how they addressed their intimate, internal struggles after that. These stories reassured Ariadne that affections of our lovers were genuine. She could see how her daughter was healing through love. The queen had many doubts, but now she could see she had made a wise decision with her intuition.

As our party ordered desserts, it was time for the presentation. Benjamin handed a written concept to Bartholomew while Eurydice described it, blooming and shining with colors Ariadne hadn't seen before. The queen witnessed an inspiring poetess and artist in front of her. She couldn't recognize her daughter, but she was so proud of her. Eurydice described how they came up with their ideas. "You know, Mom, I wish to help my knight to discover himself. I'm inspired by the essence of our artistic collaboration, not by the possible achievements. I think we uncovered the reasons behind our weird experience. When we communicate on a soul level, our thoughts and feelings can merge in one unrestricted stream of beauty. Since we are living in one body, Benjamin has access to archetypical male and female souls. That would elevate his writing. I see that I intentionally chose such a life. I dreamed of having the most profound love connection possible. Creating art with my man, on a soul level, was my highest dream. I'm not blaming myself any longer. I chose the life of a girl, who would lose her soul. These books would be a testament to our eternal love. This bond is our blessing and curse, but this is who we are. Two books would complement each other as a man and a woman do. They are fruits of our love, our divine children. Through this work, Benjamin will teach me how to blissfully die, and I will teach him how to joyfully live."

Ariadne enjoyed the evening, proud to see such an inspiring couple in love. After dinner, they went for a boat ride around the Sechelt Inlet. Ariadne told stories about her land and asked to visit their family's temple. Eurydice was stressed about Benjamin's permanent status and addressed this question. Bartholomew reported receiving all the necessary information back in March. The queen was astounded that Benjamin continued to experience delays when he was already accepted into their family. Ariadne ordered Bartholomew to look deeper into this situation. Something felt at odds, as many other healers invited to help these lands, endured the same struggles. There was a pattern of consistent disregard from Ottawa for their kingdom's interests. The queen sensed that the battle to preserve the essence of their nation was closing in on them.

The next day our lovers visited the family's temple. This place served as a unique portal for magical ceremonies and rites of empowerment. It was also a vault of sacred knowledge collected by spirits. Every finishing was crafted of the finest materials, gems, stones, and precious metals. The books filled every shelf and contained descriptions of every life that happened on this land. By accessing this knowledge, any soul could learn from the legends of their ancestors and heal through their stories. Archangel Jeremiel met Eurydice outside of the temple. He was assigned to guide this soul, and he constructed the most terrifying and beautiful events in Eurydice's life. Jeremiel brought Eurydice to the center of the temple, where he staged an initiation rite. Together with Benjamin they held laying Eurydice as she drifted into a healing trance. Old fears, nightmares, and scars departed from Eurydice, as she was shaking from lucid magical visions, releasing everything that was not serving her anymore. Through this meditation, she accepted her fate of a writer, inspired by Benjamin's example and love.

After meditation, Jeremiel gifted Eurydice a book. She opened it, but it was completely empty. Only when she studied the first blank page did the book morph into a live being. It shined and vibrated as Eurydice's flaring heart melted the empty pages, pulsating through the thickness of this book. The heart took the space of the entire volume and it was the best advice for our princess. Eurydice was required to write this book for her lands, only using her Magdalene's glorious heart. She vowed to follow the advice and pour her entire essence into this work. The book told our lovers to be brazenly brave on their journey. They'd endured a lot of torment and criticism, but spirits and angels asked them not to hide behind past scars and finally own their crazy love story.

Benjamin and Eurydice returned to Vancouver after their magical and inspiring Sechelt trip. Spring was in the air, and our lovers spent together every moment they could, praising the awakening Nature around them. Nightly conversations and poetry reading in the parks elevated their moods. New life was immerging for them, as they stopped questioning their experiences. They attempted to forget about the painful past and reset their emotions, embracing new spiritual practices and every opportunity to study the magic. They lived the live, the way they wanted, finally stopping to listen to meaningless chatter of the world around them. Trying to fit in and conform to the demands of the society, drove Benjamin and Eurydice to the lowest points in their lives. But as they discovered their highest purpose, they felt liberated and pursued happiness driven by the light of their hearts.

Holly moved into Damian's castle, and our lovers built a new golden protective dome around her bedroom again. They trained Mr. Dance and spent time in Holly's living room, guarding her through the nights. Once released from his American obligations, Benjamin concentrated on helping Eurydice. He still occasionally battled her stubbornness, puzzled by her defiance of Nature. "How come, you are always trying to run away from me? You must know that I'm always on your side," Benjamin addressed his lady one evening.

"I am who I am. I live how I feel. And don't forget that you left me alone too."

"Only I never abandoned you. And I never cared about any other soul the way I care about you."

"Still your love was not enough to save me from terrifying troubles."

"Because it's a job for both of us – I can't infringe on your free will. If you wish to run away from me, escape our love and your femininity, there's nothing I can do."

"I don't get this concept. If you see that I'm lost, then abduct me and demand to embrace your teachings. If you are my protector assigned from above, then claim me."

"Well, your body has free will. Otherwise, you won't make mistakes."

"I made so many of them that I wish you would chain me long time ago."

"But Polly, this is not how life works. I'm sorry, but the man who makes her woman a prisoner is not a man with a pure heart."

"I think this is a stupid world. Who would create it like that? I'm not too fond of it, honestly. I requested to come here again for a simple reason. I wish to lie in your safe arms, covered in tenderness, while you caress me gently. Saving me is just holding me, unconditionally loving me. Benjamin, maybe I will stay a lost soul forever and won't ever heal."

"In that case, I'm a lost soul forever too. Without you, there's no me. By saving you, I'm saving myself."

"That sounds so romantic. Maybe you're just saying this to make me feel better."

"No, I'm not. I see myself for who I am. I'm a traumatized soul who constantly tries to reject my highest purpose in each life. But you always help me to see who I am. You make me do things I'm destined to do. Only I'm running from myself and I don't know how to surrender."

"Well, I don't know how much of that is my contribution. You like running away from missions angels bestow upon you, but you eventually surrender, and not always because of me."

"Always because of you, my dear beauty. I don't see any other reason to continue coming to Earth. I would prefer to live in the kingdom of death. Besides my greatest achievements were trampled by those who came after us."

"That's true. It pains me to see how they burned America to the ground after everything we did."

"That's what I mean. What humans call achievements means nothing to me. Guiding souls to personal empowerment brings me the most joy. And it's you who always send me on that path to be a resolute spiritual guide. I thank you for this, my girl."

"Indeed, I shaped you to be who you are, although it took a few lifetimes to achieve."

"But that's not an easy job to learn."

"So you are saying I have a similar higher mission?"

"Exactly! You are such a unique and complex being. A soul with your talents is destined for glory. Since we were created from the same light, you must be a spiritual guide too. That's the only explanation. We were divined that's all. I became a masculine soul from the skies and you became a feminine one from the lands."

"Hmmm. Well, at least some sort of optimism in our dreadful conversation. I feel that you are probably right, but I don't even want to know my destiny, as I would have to say goodbye to my youth. No more careless dances, reckless endeavors, childish excuses and stupid mistakes."

"That's what you've asked to uncover in this lifetime. To understand who we are."

"We are inseparable soulmates of the divine beauty."

"You see! Did you know that before?"

"No, I didn't. I thought that you never loved me the way I loved you. But I had to believe that to arrive to this point, so you could explain to me that I have to accept my highest purpose of a spiritual guide."

Once Eurydice realized who she was, a calling knocked on her door. It was the first test for Eurydice from Sechelt spirits. They presented her with a chance to help another lost soul. One evening Eurydice and Benjamin were writing poetry when they heard Phillip's voice as if coming from another realm. Eurydice continued to write when suddenly, she started to record the words of Phillip's secret message, channeling it like a medium in a trance.

Torture
by Phillip Frumos

Home, by the way,
Came drunk, very late
But who even cares
Report your abortion
And jail me for life
As so much pain
Lives deep inside
But even your heart
Don't care anymore
Your misery shines
Reacting to lies
As you blame the world
And never yourself
While I live like me
And love who I am.
Your mom likes my fairy tales
I tell with a smirk
I have nothing to prove
To her or to you
I live as myself forever and always
I am free as an immigrant
While you are in a cage
Of stupid demands
Just live for a week
What I'm living through
You would kill yourself
I guess seven times
I'm glad I'm amusing
Your family dinners
An immigrant monkey
Enlightening your boredom
I can't help you, babe

And soon, I'll be out
You push me to drown
Like, what do you want.
We can get pregnant tomorrow
But you want what others
Expecting of you
While you are nobody
Nobody at all
While I have so much
Without possessions.
Just for the record, I'm seeing the blood
Your kingdom's the worst
While my people are fighting the war
My kingdom is still freer than yours
As all of you are sick
Like really bad shit
Consuming and nagging
And dying demanding
I'm tired of crying and tired of trials
Good luck to you dear, as soon you will see
Dark rivers of blood arriving at doorsteps
As you live denying your life is illusion.

Benjamin understood his brother's message. The matter was urgent, and he gathered his strength, appealing to his guides. Eurydice demanded to accompany Benjamin on this mission. Eurydice felt that she did not fully comprehend the essence of the darkness. She dreamed to learn from Benjamin how to face any demon. As they drifted into the spiritual world, they found themselves standing on the shore of a lake, surrounded by the beautiful mountains of Pemberton. The sun was setting, illuminating waters with a magical purple glow. Our lovers didn't know what to do, but Benjamin's feet moved towards the shore, and Eurydice followed him.

They dived underwater and swam into the lake's depths. Soon they saw Phillip and Suzanne. The duchess was chained to a big rock at the bottom of the lake. Phillip struggled to cut the chains with his magic, so he summoned his brother for help. The time was running out. As Benjamin, Phillip, and Eurydice united their supernatural powers, they tore the chain apart and rushed to bring Suzanne to the shores. Eurydice requested a warm blanket from her Sechelt friends, and now she was wrapping distressed Suzanne in her magic.

"Where am I? Where am I?" Suzanne screamed repeatedly, not fully comprehending what was happening to her. "I'm dead. I think I'm dead. I drowned, and then demons attacked me," she was crying, unable to recognize their soulmates. Phillip hugged her dearly, kissing her and whispering the words of love. Confused Suzanne looked at Benjamin and Eurydice. They consoled the tormented duchess, explaining that she was finally safe. She was stranded like Eurydice was, so now our princess could guide Suzanne out of her distressed mental state. Suzanne was still too scared, struggling to accept any words of wisdom. Our lovers whispered reassuring affirmations and read their poems to heal her. Soon the spirits of Pemberton Mountains arrived with help. Suzanne was saved and protected, so after the longest spiritual hug, Benjamin and Eurydice left her in Phillip's arms, returning home.

This event triggered the transformation of our lovers as more complex experiences called upon them. Our princess felt strong enough to perform a rite of passage where she assumed her higher female powers. Eurydice took Benjamin for a spiritual hike to Mount Daniel on a day of a new moon. Once they arrived on top of the mountain, Eurydice created a moon circle of female empowerment out of stones in the tradition of her Sechelt female ancestors. She entered the dream space and asked for guidance and support from the spirits of the mountain. Through prayers and affirmations, they invited the protective light of the land to strengthen their auras and divine feminine essence of Eurydice.

After our princess passed this initiation, Benjamin invited Eurydice to conduct Ivan Kupala Night rites. Our princess enthusiastically accepted this invitation, curiously embracing the practices of her Ukrainian sisters. They swam in the waters of Sechelt Inlet naked at night. They had a big fire on the shore and a cleansing ritual to remove negative emotions they'd accumulated. They meditated with the land afterward to strengthen their love and devotion. They spent the rest of the night in the hot springs on the shore, shielded by forest. Afrer these powerful rites, Eurydice finally accepted her destiny as a spiritual guide. Resting on her man's shoulder, under the skies full of stars, she realized that her mistakes actually brought the most valuable lessons of feminine empowerment. Now, she finally owned her traumatizing experiences.

Benjamin invited Eurydice to visit Lighthouse Park spirits and introduce her with his spiritual guide and teacher Sigiritul. They performed another initiation ceremony to assume supernatural guidance of this land. Sigiritul introduced our lovers to the highest essence of this park. Under the main summit lived a gorgeous golden Snake of Light who could heal spiritual wounds. It could extend its reach to Vancouver if commanded by a magician with a noble cause. Sigirutl taught our lovers how to work with this energy and be guardians of this hill. From now on, many of their ceremonies were empowered by the golden Snake of Lighthouse.

Our lovers respectfully maintained the spiritual balance – if they ever asked the spirits for help, they would always offer their assistance in exchange. During next year they released four entrapped souls who died in agony from starvation, one righteous warrior, murdered by Spanish settlers, one soul who was buried alive, one soul who died feeling shame and regret. They also empowered seven female souls who sacrificed their lives protecting their tribe's settlement, and removed the old spell that created a spiritual border around Stanley Park.

In the end of June 2021, Bartholomew invited our lovers to talk about Benjamin's immigration status. In presence of Ariadne and the ambassadors from neighboring spirits of Vancouver Island and Pemberton he reported what he discovered in Ottawa. Originally the spirits decided to create the Canadian Union, where each kingdom would be equally empowered and made their own decisions. Kingdoms were joined by the unifying, noble idea of becoming a promised land and a beacon of freedom to other nations who lived under tyranny. Freedom of speech and liberty to live the life as one chooses, were the main promises of this new union.

Yet what Bartholomew witnessed in Ottawa was of some other nature. Many strange, vile, and foreign dark entities consumed people's hearts. Deep, irrational, and twisted fears based on conspiracy theories that rejected the laws of Nature paralyzed many residents and allowed darkness to spread in Parliament building and then around this nation. Citizens sensed how suffocating the air in their nation had become as pressures against life and divinity intensified. Empowered by otherworldly energies, sinister beings spread ideas of Tyranny and oppression, hoping to take complete control of the Canadian Union. The dark spirits consumed politicians and journalists with lost souls. Enslavement through obedience was their ideology. They contemptuously looked down on their citizens, convinced they are their property and rights of the Charter of Freedoms did not belong to them.

The delegation from British Columbia arrived to check the misplaced applications but stumbled upon something much bigger than that. Ariadne approached spirits from neighboring western kingdoms and shared her findings. Soon, kingdoms joined in a coalition to proceed with the special military operation together. They had witnessed the injustice towards their citizens too. They saw how people were silenced, suppressed, and despised for simply following the righteous path of their hearts. The spirits didn't mind that Dark forces issued documents for their new arrivals, but they demanded a balance.

On July 4, 2021, the convoy to restore the freedoms of the Canadian Union descended upon the capital to expose sinister lies. Spirits invited Benjamin to lead one battalion, using the tactics and strategies he learned during his American draft. Battalions of every kingdom stood united in the downtown core of Ottawa, in front of the Parliament building. Dark entities refused to negotiate, claiming they had this nation under complete control, and the battle for the future ensued. Every magician on the battlefield could channel the full powers of their friendly spirits. Eurydice, and Benjamin summoned the spirits of Virginia and the District of Columbia to assist them.

First, Monticello spirits fired with heavy artillery and bombs of pure light, cleansing the darkness and healing the fears. After clearing the space, armies of every Canadian kingdom attacked the Parliament building, holding it under siege. As more and more beings died on both sides, neither could stand the toll of this bloody conflict. The kingdoms only asked for equal treatment and balanced debates, where each side was allowed to present their argument without judgment, contempt, or condemnation. Through peaceful dialogue, the kingdoms could arrive at decisions that would benefit everyone. That's all spirits of western kingdoms demanded from the beginning, yet they were never heard. Spirits shared the desire to elevate their people, restore liberty and return the diversity of opinions that made this nation once so appealing and prosperous.

After the devastating destruction and death toll, Dark forces finally agreed to the truce. Each kingdom sent its representatives to sign the New Declaration of Freedoms in the Parliament building. It was a promise of a renewed union inspired by the highest values of the Canadian legacy. This truce would take years to manifest in physical reality, but it initiated a positive transformation. When kingdoms signed the declaration, they started a debate process about the future of the Canadian Union. These discussions would lead spirits to implement them in reality. On the square, both sides mourned their losses in unity. Dead soldiers do not carry distinctions once the battle ends. It is a tragedy for all involved, and in a fair conflict, both sides equally pay tributes to the dead. The delegations shared grief as they joined in the dancing and drumming ceremonies, healing the wounds caused by this battle. They shined with uplifting energies, hoping a new chapter of their union would be more constructive.

Self-Evident Truth
by Eurydice Eloise Wayles

What a pity to perceive this world through the rosy glasses of the press, where truth is never written as smitten, judging sectarians amuse city, piteous plutocrats, who are stricken by the sickening fixations of bitter perturbations, while living in the plush, voracious nation of hidden, astray abominations, they insanely claim, make them righteously saint, until one day, those they implicitly blame, will dismantle and sway their enormous atrocities

With gritty, forbidden, self-evident truth.

If they are so utterly right -
I might ask in hindsight -
Then why they're in a panic and so terrified?
Why are they blazing the furious fright?

I will proudly claim what I cried,
I will stand my ground despite
I will face the despots and fight
As I pity their hearts with delight.

Domain of spirits
by Benjamin Frumos

We acknowledge the divinity of our Nature
The source of holy love and holy grief.
We acknowledge simple facts,
And we hold these truths to be self-evident
That all humans were created equal,
That the Creator endowed each and every one of us
With certain unalienable rights –
Among which are life, liberty,
And the pursuit of happiness.

We pay tributes to everyone who came before us
Who walked this Earth, this land, this territory,
And every person who lived laughed, loved, and died
With true freedom in the heart.
We don't accept the blame, but we acknowledge
The crimes committed by corrupt ancestors
Desiring to subdue the fellow human beings
Perceiving others as inferiors, as property to own.

We acknowledge simple fact –
That land does not belong to humans,
Nor it can ever be owned
As its alive and belongs to spirits.
We acknowledge simple fact –
That lakes, creeks, rivers, inlets, straits, and oceans
Do not belong to humans,
As they are embodiments of spirits and they are alive.

They are the hosts of their domains
While humans are merely guests –
Coming from nothing and vanishing into dust
Renting the life of a dying vessel.

We acknowledge that each human,
Chooses their skin color, nationality, conditions,
Sex, orientation, and perceptual appearance
On a soul level before their arrival.

We acknowledge the past sufferings of those
Who fought and died for this land, corruptly or nobly
We acknowledge any blood spilled
Any conflict that left souls shattered, lost and terrified.

We acknowledge that we strive to be better
Only competing with our former selves,
To see the bigger picture and never blame the other,
To ask questions before making assumptions
To enjoy witnessing deep nuances and shades
Of glorious human existence.

We thank the spirits of this land for granting us
The safe passage to these promised lands.
We pray with our glories, and we pour our love
For allowing us to live in their garden.

Divine Parents
by Eurydice Eloise Wayles

Well, first of all, I am an individual
I am a free person with my pride and glory
I do not kneel to any emperor or government entity
I only humbly and respectfully bow to
My father, who is skies
And my mother, who is Earth.
They can scold and punish me.
They can build me prisons.
They can curse my flaws.
And only they can mold me,
Not the people of the gold
Embroiled in destructive delusions of egos.

So, if I'm free, I choose to embrace
What the skies and the lands advise me;
I arrive to my own conclusions
Through my primary experience –
By living my life as myself, by hearing my heart.

Therefore, whoever wants to be my parent
To tell me what to think or feel
I must advise you to revisit
The rules of a special lucid dream
That we're together calling life
That we refuse to see as real.

CHAPTER XVI

Since their journey to Sechelt, one question didn't leave Benjamin's mind – why couldn't Eurydice find him earlier? Benjamin pulled her from the Underworld at the last minute. She was quite a powerful being if she did summon him, so why did she wait? Eurydice couldn't answer this question. At first, Benjamin doubted his princess, thinking she was lying to him again, but this time, Eurydice was telling the truth. Our princess wanted to help Benjamin understand what had happened between them and how they could fix their union. Benjamin felt as if Eurydice reached out to him when every other option failed. Like Eurydice didn't want to ask for his help, afraid of him or hoping to escape meeting Benjamin in this life. Eurydice and Benjamin embarked on a complex journey into the past as they drifted again into the world between the devastating world wars.

Camilla was born in Sopot, a small town near Danzing, in 1905. She grew up with a loving mother and a distant father. When Camilla was eleven, her father died in the First World War, yet Camilla and her mother did not miss him, as he filled their house with negative energies and resentfulness of life. Two years later, they moved to Berlin, and when Camilla turned eighteen, she became a nurse, aiding soldiers in the military hospital. One day she experienced a divine intervention, sitting on the shore of the river. As sun was setting, angels arrived with a calling, illuminating her higher path. She was told to start a career of a translator and move to her aunt and uncle in Paris. She was successful, ambitious, daring, and free. She only lived for today and enjoyed being a young woman, feeling the optimism in the air as she danced through Parisian streets living her dream life every day.

During one social gathering, she met Werner. He invited Camilla for a dance, and soon they fell in love. At that time, Werner lived in Berlin with Beatrice, the past embodiment of Suzanne. Werner was a well-connected businessman who sold French wine in the kingdom of Germany. Living between two cities, he lived between two women. Camilla felt that Werner was the love of her life, and she affectionately chased him through many trials and ordeals, hoping he would stay with her. Still, Werner could never fully commit to either woman, as his heart was tormented and perplexed, feeling equally strong love for both soulmates. Werner could never decide which woman would save him from his never-ending self-destructive booze adventures in the company of promiscuous companions. Camilla cherished every genuine romantic moment with Werner but soon realized she didn't want a committed relationship. She was a lone wolf, existing in shadows on her own, and she loved her hermit lifestyle.

One day Camilla discovered that she was actually working for the Wehrmacht intelligence cell. Her supervisors observed Camilla from the beginning, considering recruiting her as an agent. Camilla's character and integrity were tested through her translation assignments. When she was asked to become a spy for her kingdom, Camilla agreed without hesitation, realizing this was the destiny angels prepared for her. She was guided from the beginning to become a killer one day. This was her destiny in this life and she took another step towards it. She was assigned to work under Wilhelm. She respected his opinion and valued his perspective deeply. Wilhelm became her spiritual father and filled the void created by the loss of her real one. They shared concerns about the dangers of Tyranny coming from Soviet Empire and they quickly built a trustworthy and long-lasting connection.

Camilla learned fast and quickly; she became a sophisticated spy, skilled in intelligence, combat, weapons, and poisons. With her innate leadership qualities, she was assigned to curate the cell of five spies. Camilla meticulously planned operations, while her agents executed them. She was the brains of every operation against vile Soviet Empire. When Wilhelm put Camilla in charge of Wehrmacht Paris operations, he organized a party where he invited Eloise, their latest recruit. Camilla felt something unusual when she saw this gorgeous woman for the first time. Tall blonde, Eloise entered the room wearing exquisite dress and hat with large brims. She illuminated with her presence every room she entered as people could not take their eyes of her. Just by being herself, she captured attention of everyone. Camilla was impressed by this woman's striking appearance and energizing stance, but there was something more between them. She had the same sensations when she met Werner, but her feelings for Eloise were much stronger. She was drawn to this woman in ways she never felt before, as she was her destined soulmate of many lives.

As they quickly became best friends, they both acknowledged their deep unexplainable connection. Our soulmates spent countless days planning operations, attending poetry readings, visiting galleries, traveling through France, and drinking morning coffee with cigarettes on the bank of the Seine, learning about their similarities and feeling intense mutual attraction. They couldn't get enough of each other, and their friendship eventually turned into a passionate romance.

Both women were quite confused about their feelings. Camilla and Eloise honestly confessed to one another how strange they felt, as both were only attracted to men before. But they felt so good around each other that they decided to embrace this unusual love story. Their reservations arrived from the limited beliefs of the societies they grew up in. But once they realized they could never open up to the men the way they trusted each other, both surrendered to their feelings. They loved falling asleep in each other's arms, fully naked, and waking up to cuddles and kisses. There was nothing more beautiful in their challenging lives then these moments, even though they kept questioning if the love between two women is possible.

As Europe approached another bloody conflict, things started to change. The people became more irrational than ever, and governments worldwide spun out of control. It was quite easy for Camilla to fight agents of Stalin. They were the main enemies for every kingdom in Europe. There was no debate about that. Yet as conflicts brewed inside the German political elite, Camilla faced terrifying prospects. Soon she received assignments to kill Germans too. She knew she would be forced to lie to Eloise even more than before to shield her beloved from compromising information and encroaching madness. And she was also her boss, which complicated things even further. Day after day, Camilla reserved more information from Eloise.

Our lovers tried to avoid any possible compromising conversations, only resorting to discussing details of a particular mission. Still, Eloise wanted to know everything Camilla knew, as she considered herself Camilla's right hand. But the realities of 1937 led Camilla to question everyone in her command, so she wanted to protect Eloise as things moved in the troubling direction very quickly. If Eloise knew about every piece of intelligence that Camilla had, it would endanger her life. Besides, Camilla didn't know how to tell Eloise about the civil war inside her kingdom, reserved about discussing the reasons behind such dramatic changes. Camilla felt sick discovering the eerie truths of opportunistic Germans and soon she only trusted Wilhelm, while both battled encroaching darkness.

As much as Camilla tried to protect Eloise, it had the opposite effect. As a result, Eloise became increasingly frustrated as she felt left out for unknown reasons. Eloise thought they had a special relationship, full trust. She knew her soulmate lied to her, but Eloise assumed Camilla kept secrets because she didn't love her. In reality, Camilla expressed her deepest love by shielding her beloved from the terrifying truth and unsettling prospects. These conflicting feelings consumed Eloise as she felt used, unappreciated, and manipulated. At the same time, the air in Paris changed too. The pandemic of fear descended on citizens of this nation. Eurydice manifested the essence of her lands in each life. Like Holly represented the darkest manifestations of her sinful city called Vancouver, Eloise became the reflection of Parisians – erratic, scared, confused and angry at life.

Camilla admired Eloise's skills, seeing the highest purpose of this woman. Camilla would only give her the most challenging missions, knowing she could handle them. Only confidence turned into arrogance inside Eloise, as she felt isolated and betrayed. Her powers of seduction grew stronger, and her actions became more eccentric. She was ready to face any man with a deep passion and desire to defeat him. Eloise was looking down on them. She wanted to feel bigger than they were. It was her protective mechanism against her insecurities. She enjoyed manipulating men with her sexuality until they would forget about personal security or political affiliations. Eloise's intimate games switched off the survival instinct of any man. Sometimes she questioned whether that was even possible, but men queued in line to be defeated, convincing her there was no one, who could challenge her.

Eloise had the supernatural power of seduction and the ability to murder traitors of European freedom mercilessly. No man stood a chance once Eloise set her eyes on a target. She was terrified when she strangled her first victim after having sex with him, but not because she had taken someone's life. She was surprised to witness what she was capable of and how emotionally powerful she was. Eloise had no remorse after the murder, feeling she was fulfilling her true destiny. Eloise enjoyed that day. She was created as a vulture to cleanse the world. Yet, one day, she forgot humbleness and became a monster, convinced she was in charge of deciding who would live or die. She stopped treating her enemy with respect and contemptuously mocked masculine dignity. Eloise was a divine creation, but she became drunk from her powers, so one day, her spiritual guardians removed their protection.

Eloise was God's absolute woman, as she discovered the highest possible powers of the feminine essence, but she also manifested the Creator's highest fear when she became audacious and arrogant. Eloise turned into a raging woman on the path of self-destruction, unstoppable in her fight against the world. She cursed every human she knew, believing they only brought pain and suffering into her life. She was fully aware of her innate talents, but instead of applying them to execute the balance of Nature, she let her ego consume her heart.

Eloise emotionally distanced herself from Camilla because of her twisted assumptions, eventually allowing Damian to kill her. Dark Prince entered the body of a corrupt Russian man and led him into a state of occult trance, slicing Eloise with his knife in a demonic ritual. Eloise was dying in pain, and the swirls of sinister creatures of the Underworld descended upon her, consuming her soul. As she was dying, she only blamed Camilla for her suffering. Damian's illusions convinced Eloise that Camilla was responsible for her death, as she was the one who sent her on this mission.

That's what Eurydice remembered from that traumatizing experience. Damian brought her panic and confusion, twisting the memories and amplifying nightmares. Eloise didn't allow Camilla to demonstrate the scale of her love. Eloise questioned the honesty of their intimacy. She could not see beyond society's judgment and accept unconditional love from another woman. But everything Camilla did after Eloise's death proved how much she loved her. Camilla dedicated the rest of her life to research the supernatural circumstances of this murder, sacrificing everything she had for that cause.

Eurydice died last time convinced that Benjamin didn't love her, that he sent her to experience an excruciatingly painful death. Eurydice's traumatic death was infused with Damian's terrifying visions, so Holly was convinced that Benjamin would betray her and send her to death again. That's why Eurydice only summoned Benjamin when she exhausted other options. Eurydice got lost because she was actually ashamed of Eloise's actions. She drew conclusions based on assumptions and distorted facts, which led her to be entrapped in the Underworld on the way to Hell.

Our lovers also realized that Eurydice's body was not buried in the lands of her spirits by Benjamin. Burying each other was a magical ritual for these two souls. This time it didn't happen, creating more demons for Eurydice, which Benjamin could've realized upon burial. Camilla was the last one who held Eloise's hands before she died, but she only observed the funeral from a soul level and did not cleanse her body. This event destroyed the trust between our soulmates for the first time in centuries.

When Camilla visited the grave of her soulmate, she cried relentlessly, vowing to avenge Eloise and blaming herself for this tragedy. Camilla felt how the war erupted in her heart. Thanks to Camilla's research, Benjamin was destined to guide Eurydice to understand death's essence this time. Benjamin was created to save Eurydice by teaching her to die. Eurydice struggled to navigate this state of transformation, so Benjamin was born to finally master that dimension and explain the value of death to souls. As each soul would see the reflections of their life there was no easy way to navigate that realm. Still, Benjamin learned how to guide humans through this process and how to help souls navigate what they could confront upon death. Fears and lies are amplified upon death, and since Eloise didn't truly follow her heart, more demons arrived to haunt her. It's always a soul choice when to die, as they realize the benefit of this decision for everyone involved and they are prepared to learn from this experience. Only when the body dies in a traumatic death or a state of shock, dark monsters descend on a soul, following it into another life, especially if a soul is rejecting to reflect on their life or feeling ashamed.

Eurydice ran away from Eloise's body and ignored the chance to observe her closest soulmates from the other side. She rejected this conflicting and struggling life, tired of being traumatized and abused. Childhood and teenage traumas prevented her from establishing genuine emotional connections. Then many dramas and the violence she endured from clients depleted her aura. She was angry at Camilla many times for not letting her in, but it was Eloise who pushed her soulmate away. She built sophisticated walls and boundaries to avoid getting hurt. She deprived herself of the most valuable human emotion – a deep, intimate love with another human being. Eloise did everything she could to prevent anyone from seeing her soul's scars. She constantly fantasized about feeling a deeper emotional connection if Camilla was a man. But it was just another excuse to avoid being vulnerable. Eloise eventually made herself believe that Camilla pretended to love her so she could use her. Blood, pain, rape, and murders were parts of Eloise's everyday life, and Eurydice tried to escape the teachings of this divine experience.

Camilla believed she planned a perfect operation, and she never made mistakes before. As Camilla continued to revisit the events of that night, she felt some things didn't have any rational explanation. She also knew Eloise's powers, as this woman always returned alive, surviving the most challenging situations. Camilla remembered how they talked about supernatural aspects of life and dark spirits living in the shadows, so now she was convinced that something otherworldly killed her beloved.

As the Second World War was officially proclaimed, Camilla was completely disengaged from assisting the delusional leaders of her kingdom. She felt that this conflict would not end well for the entire continent, and some precious values of a civilized society would be lost forever. Most people ignored brewing inner conflicts and lost their higher purpose, avoiding to follow the truths of their souls. Europeans hid behind pretentious social masks until reality knocked on their doors, louder and louder. Wars and natural disasters are always a final wake-up call for lost souls. As demons enveloped the world after the tyrannical revolution in the Russian Empire, Camilla realized what the future held, witnessing how politicians worldwide used every opportunity to escalate this war.

As, increasingly, the actions of her commanders made less and less sense, Camilla realized some unknown supernatural powers drove them. Camilla decided to continue her investigation, determined to find the answers to her spiritual questions. She did assignments for the Wehrmacht, as she was still on the side of a free Germany, hoping to save her homeland from complete devastation. Camilla fed misinformation to Americans while using their resources for her research into the mystical essence of the unseen parts of our world. She despised Americans, convinced they had no business in this war. And once Americans chose to be the ally of the Soviet Empire, they became her enemies too.

The world could no longer be saved, so she dedicated most of her time to her personal mission, driven by love for her soulmate. Camilla found a trusted hypnotherapist and a magician in Berlin, and together they returned to explore the details of her dream on the night of Eloise's death. In a hypnotic trance, Camilla's soul flew over Eloise. Camilla saw how a dark mist, shaped like a human being, entered a man and forced him to follow Eloise. As Camilla exited her memory, she realized her operation was flawless. It was not her fault that Eloise was killed. There was another man involved, and now she saw him clearly.

Initially Camilla was convinced that Eloise was killed because she was exposed, but her killer didn't know she was a spy. As Camilla saw Damian's essence around her beloved, she looked at life from a different perspective. Dark demon forced a man to kill Eloise in an occult ritual. A range of emotions, visions, and dreams flooded Camilla's imagination. Eloise's death was the most transcending and eye-opening experience for Camilla. Her soulmate gave her the gift of spiritual clairvoyance. Now she could see that spiritual battles were as equally important in our world as physical ones.

Yet another important event occurred after Eloise's murder. When Camilla executed both men, who killed Eloise, she understood her highest mission in life. It was the first murder she ever committed, but once it happened, Camilla realized that's what angels planned for her from the beginning. She also arrived to be a vulture in this world, to kill those Nature decided to eliminate. Eloise opened up her divine talents and for the next five years, Camilla turned into a killer and it felt completely natural for her. She was doing was she was born to do.

Once Camilla explored the nature of the dark energy that consumed Eloise, she was determined to prove that a dark spirit killed her soulmate. Only she didn't know where to start, as even Werner and Wilhelm didn't want to listen to the possible supernatural aspects behind Eloise's murder. Camilla always searched for evidence before judging any situation, relying only on reason and intelligence, but she found herself in a new reality. After Camilla learned about her magical talents, she addressed her therapist with a question. She wanted to know how to prove to the world that Damian was real and that he had killed Eloise. Her wise spiritual teacher replied that Camilla needs to die and find Eloise in next life.

By 1943 Camilla was living in the kingdom of Germany, deeply involved in the Wehrmacht operations. Ideologically, Wilhelm and Camilla were on the same side, fighting SS and the extreme wing of German elites, who believed only in a military resolution of this conflict. Camilla was a true patriot who only wanted to find a less devastating solution to end the war, since it was inevitable for her, that the kingdom of Germany was doomed to fall. Camilla vividly remembered the day when she made the decision of her future. She went to an important dinner in Wilhelm's residence. At the table of twenty high-ranking Wehrmacht and SS officers, she was the only woman in presence. No matter how much Camilla tried to convince SS officers to abandon their suicide mission, no one would listen to her. Camilla was speaking the voice of reason, but she was just a woman for men who decided the fate of her nation. Her opinion was never treated as equal. Camilla could confide in Wilhelm, who was the only one valuing her opinion. As only two of them stayed after this meeting in Wilhelm's cabinet, they discussed how ugly the end of their kingdom would look over a glass of cognac. They mourned their nation in the spring of 1943, looking into the eyes of bloodthirsty, power-hungry people, completely delusional in their pursuits.

Looking at the state of the world, Camilla understood that she had nothing to lose anymore. There was no point in staying in the kingdom of Germany, as she couldn't prevent the worst scenarios, and she would be considered a criminal after the war. She could easily defect to the American Empire as a loyal asset. Camilla also knew about the escape routes to South America. She could even disappear in some remote European village. She had plenty of options, but she chose to follow her heart and embrace her angelic mission. If the world was drowning in blood from the insanity of humans, she might as well try to prove that supernatural demon Damian exists for real.

Camilla and her spiritual therapist searched for the door into another life. They tried to find a safe passage, hoping to interfere with the natural course of events as little as possible. Such doors exist in our time-space perception, but it is a gamble with the higher forces when a person knowingly uses them. Any soul has dozens exit points mapped before coming into this life, so they attempted to find the closest and less destructive one. Camilla intentionally raised the stakes of her experience as she challenged Nature itself. Her unlearned lessons would be passed into her next life, but for Camilla, such a bet sounded thrilling and exciting. It would be Benjamin, who would suffer the consequences of her actions.

Eventually, they discovered a portal that would present itself in two months on the Polish-Ukrainian border. She was convinced this was her righteous path, as her heart vibrated from a surge of joyful energies, and she began preparing for her death. Camilla convinced Wilhelm to send her on the mission to Warsaw and Kyiv under the pretense of gathering intelligence. Wilhelm knew she was not telling him the whole story, but he trusted his favorite spy and allowed her to proceed.

In August, 1943, Camilla arrived at the Polish-Ukrainian border on a train from Warsaw. She was arrested and taken into custody, yet she was completely calm. Deep inside, she was happy that her magic worked, dreaming of redeeming Eloise through dying. Camilla was completely silent during hours of interrogations, enjoying her enemies' misery and her adamant, courageous energy in confronting them. Soon convoys put her in the car, taking her to a closest town to a supervising officer.

Calmly observing the empty fields during the ride, Camilla rejoiced when the first bullet smashed the driver's brain. Excitement lit her up as she was closer to seeing Eloise. The car crashed, hitting the trench on the side of the road, and all three of Camilla's guards were murdered. *What a divine irony*, Camilla thought. *I'm the one who came to die here, but I will be the last one who will.* She exited the car and walked through the field. Guns fired again, hitting Camilla in the right shoulder and the head. She fell to the ground but did not die for hours. Laying in the soil, she contemplated her life. Camilla asked angels for a chance to recognize Eloise right away in the next life, and that's how Benjamin received a gift of love at first sight. Camilla only regretted how she ended things with Werner. She loved him, and she was convinced that he understood her like no one else, but Werner refused to believe in Damian's existence.

As her soul left the body, she observed Werner from the other side. He was so devastated Camilla left him that he blamed Beatrice, as he never saw his closest friend again, unaware of her tragic end. Beatrice constantly nagged, whined, and cried, refusing to accept the nature of her gentleman.

As Werner was confused by the constantly changing reality, struggling to adapt his business to realities of war, Beatrice's demands became unbearable, and their superficial life was destroying him.

Werner drank more and more, eventually desiring to end this pain. He only wanted Beatrice to be silent for a little while, and one day he received his chance for peace. In the summer of 1945, Werner decided to take Beatrice to a picnic on the lake, hoping to get a chance to drown her. They drank on the beach, unable to communicate without alcohol anymore. Then Beatrice decided to go for a swim, but once in the water, she started drowning. Even though it was Werner's intention from the beginning, he never did anything to her. He only watched from the beach, and when Beatrice screamed for help, Werner decided not to intervene. He stood still on the shore, with the bottle in his hands, watching how Beatrice was losing her strength, battling the water. The last thing Beatrice saw was her man's eyes, refusing to help her. She died utterly terrified, unable to understand the cruelty her soulmate.

Just as demons consumed Eloise after her traumatic death, the terror enveloped Beatrice as she was suffocating underwater. In her last moments, Beatrice blamed Werner for her death, but she had become destructive towards her man and she was the only one responsible for her death. She made the decision to swim drunk. Her soul was searching for her death, and Werner only saw a prevision of it in his mind. The stories of our soulmates were equally tragic. Both Eloise and Beatrice betrayed their hearts and their souls, yet they continued to blame the only people who could heal them, even when they were dying.

Werner wanted to give his woman freedom from the misery he saw in her eyes. He also didn't want his soulmate to suffer under Soviet occupation. He only wanted to spend time without her in quite peace. Beatrice blamed him for cheating, for forcing her to have an abortion, and for her every other misfortune, but she refused to work on their relationship too. She chained herself to this man, when he clearly never wanted a committed relationship with any woman. She never considered a different life, only demanding Werner to adopt to hers. Throughout her life, Beatrice did everything to alienate the only person who truly loved her, as she never tried to understand her man's essence and accept him for who he was.

Eventually, Werner was devastated by his guilt for Beatrice's death, and darkness consumed his heart. Both Werner and Camilla blamed themselves for losing their beloved, even though it was not the case. The shame and self-loathing soon led Werner to seek a path out. He had no one else to live for, and his country was occupied by evil Soviet monsters. One day Werner got drunk and went for a drive at night, calling on death. On the empty road outside the city, he crushed his car into a tree and Phillip left the tortured body of Werner.

All four of our soulmates searched for salvation through death, as they couldn't cope with the reality of a defeated Europe, traumatized by the terrifying war. Each of them received their desired death. Each of them escaped their reality through spiritual suicide, praying for the way out that Nature granted for them. Only their traumas and lessons would follow them into their next lives, creating troubles they could never anticipate.

Dying Blissfully
by Benjamin Frumos

I went into a hypnotic therapy trance
Because I was presented with intense visions
Of my latest death.

I saw myself lying in lush, fertile black soil
With bullets howling in my shoulder and my skull;
I didn't die for many hours
Just played old lies through my cursed remorse,
While seeing phosphorescent space –
I was gifted the time to reflect on my journey.

I saw my death yet again
Beholding from the other side
From deep inside and from the outside,
I flew, hovering above myself,
While sensing soulful pain of bullets.

I thought that I was traumatized by death itself
Because it was bloodthirsty and vicious –
Pretty much execution-style.
Swarm of bullets around me, trying to kill me
Flying through my entropy of passions,
As I lived by the sword
I was destined to die by the sword.

Qualis vita, et mors ita.

Yet I intentionally planned this experience.
I've patiently waited for it to happen.
Through my train journey, through a car ride,
Patiently waiting while people screamed at me in Polish.
And I loved Polish from childhood.

It was not how I imagined I would die.

Nevertheless, it was beautifully divine.

I beheld the first shots.
Splashing the brains of our driver
I rejoiced – as I was seeking these bullets
At this particular moment in time
At this specific place in space
On the Polish-Ukrainian border.

I needed to get to Kyiv,
Through my reincarnation.

"I need to get to Kyiv, no matter what,"
I told myself, dying, whispering to my soul,
Hoping I would not forget this
While experiencing the journey of death
Traveling through the space in between lives;

"I need to get to Kyiv…"
"She will be born in Kyiv…"
"I need to get to Kyiv no matter what it takes…"

As I relived my death from the perspective of my soul
And realized that I wasn't traumatized by the death.
The death was blissful and beautiful.
It was a lovely, stunning epiphany.
And the sweetest resolution of my ego's traps.

I was lying on that field,
Face buried in the soil in fields of nourishment
Destined to be wasted by Russian tanks.

I was bleeding from the bullet wounds

They burned me from the inside
They were quite uncomfortable –
And yet I was enjoying every moment of it.

I realized that my traumas were not from death itself
But from a life of betrayals and war.
People traumatized me.
Humans created my injuries.
With their stupidity and pompousness
Magniloquence and pretentiousness;
Each of them betraying their ideals
Just to get their piece of the pie
That was crumbling and burning
Right in front of their eyes.

They dreamed of getting a piece of future Germany,
That was drowning in new horrors every day
Because of their diabolical, self-indulgent actions.

Each of them rejected their highest truth,
By obediently serving deluded psychotic insanity,
While distorting any traits of genuine integrity.

Maybe they never ever had it in the first place.
Maybe they just convinced me to believe they do.

My life was filled with blood, quarrels, hostility, contempt, destruction
And yet it was my divine battle,
Magically overflowing with affrays and alterations.

This was my painful life.

That ended in a triumphant death,
From the bullets of possessed humans
Who have lost their souls;

I was dying because I needed to, and I had to,
Murdered by the hands of my mortal enemies
Whom I have killed by the dozens –

The communists.

CHAPTER XVII

Once they uncovered new details about their past, Eurydice swirled into a new spiral of self-loathing. She was ashamed of herself and cried for days, convinced she was the worst soul ever, feeling guilty for betraying Benjamin. They loved each other so much that they both blamed themselves for the suffering of the other. Eloise was convinced that Camilla manipulated her and never loved her, so Eurydice didn't believe that Benjamin could be trusted. When she got into Damian's first traps, she rejected her knight. Eurydice only called for him out of complete desperation. Now Eurydice witnessed what Benjamin endured as Camilla and how he intentionally died to find her in this life. He was searching for her all of his life, empowered by Camilla's intentions.

When Benjamin was called to meet Holly, he sacrificed a lot to follow his soulmate, even when she broke his heart. Benjamin continued to prove his love with his actions every chance he had. After discovering the truth, Eurydice thought Benjamin would be angry with her, but he only demonstrated her a valuable lesson. Damian confused Eurydice through this traumatizing journey, and although she had a new body, she was continuing to live as Eloise. That's how Eurydice unintentionally drove Holly into the hands of darkness.

Eurydice spent two weeks exhausting herself with guilt and shame. She could not believe she was angry at the closest soul in the entire universe. Eurydice turned pale and weak. She didn't respond to the fruits, desserts, or flowers Benjamin brought her. Her inner storms engulfed her. Our knight decided to take her on vacation. His dear spirit friends of Buntzen Lake ran a beautiful, one-of-a-kind secret spa resort for souls just above the waters of their lake. The lush gardens, mazes, fountains, and healing procedures awaited Eurydice. Benjamin joined a weak Eurydice for long rejuvenating walks around the garden. Over a course of a week she eventually improved and healed with the magic of spirits.

In the evenings, Eurydice told Benjamin's friends about her adventures and sins. Spirits directed their affirmations to Eurydice and helped her process her emotions. She was not guilty of anything; she was gifted a unique life and a transformative death that enriched her. Eurydice and Benjamin had to endure so much pain to get where they were, so spirits praised the connection of two inseparable lovers. Eurydice needed endorsement from Nature, and after receiving encouraging blessings, she finally saw herself for who she was. Eurydice went through horrors and traumas, but she had a higher mission. Despite the struggles, Benjamin found her, transcending death itself. Our princess saw the divine serendipities of our world and stopped blaming herself for her past. Instead, she learned from her inaccurate perceptions, cleansed her ill assumptions, and strived to grow. But most importantly she understood that the way forward was to trust her heart and surrender to love.

Once Eurydice had cried all of her tears of misery and realized that no one loved her the way Benjamin did, the spirits rewarded our lovers with blessings for their spiritual healing. The permanent status paperwork of our knights came through. The new chapter of their story had arrived, as now they could spread their wings in their new home. This change inspired a new wave of romantic adventures as it reassured our lovers of their magical powers, and Eurydice was happy that no one would deport her knight. They could finally make solid plans for their future.

Soon Eurydice realized how inspired she felt when they healed others. She was a faithful disciple of her master, yet she was his divine woman who unlocked his supernatural powers. The more Eurydice dedicated herself to healing others, the more she understood why she had to live with Benjamin in this way. She was on her spiritual path, and although she liked hiding behind her man, she was guided to accept her supreme individuality. As more patients arrived at Benjamin's doorstep, Eurydice was faced with the fact that some of them came to see her, and soon, she was excited to share this craft with her soulmate.

Growing through a transformative experience, Eurydice realized what it meant to be a true princess of her lands. She was destined to heal souls who would come for her guidance, following the spiritual path of Mary Magdalene. Once Eurydice assumed her powers, learned skills, and embraced this experience, she would be granted the full potential of her princess magic. She still perceived herself as a vulnerable, clueless, and dependent child, constantly seeking Benjamin's attention and validation. Once our princess grasped what kind of powers she had, she got scared. Eurydice didn't want to repeat Eloise's mistakes, but she didn't know how to ground herself. In the next part of her adventure, she must finally comprehend the concepts of ego, power, obligations and higher responsibility. Eurydice was a divine channel between the spirits and the souls of her kingdom, but her magic abilities still needed to be tempered.

Benjamin always showed Eurydice how he saw her, but she didn't want to believe that she was as beautiful and talented as her man described, convinced he was only flattering her. She constantly complained that she was not special or unique, but the more Eurydice rejected her essence, the more souls healed through her guidance. Eurydice loved being under Benjamin's protection, knowing that if she didn't know the answer, her man would help. Yet when she healed someone on her own, she always felt a profound joy. Eurydice wished to spend time under the sheets with her man, to dance and have fun, but eventually, she fell in love with her destiny and found great pride in her practice.

Benjamin could see any soul for who they were, their inner qualities, divine purpose, and past repetitive mistakes. Soon, Eurydice learned that she was capable of that too. Often people are confused about their purpose, claiming that they could be whomever they want, but fortunately, it is not the case – we can't escape our inner nature, no matter how much we try, as we are born to be who we are. By running away from themselves, people only lose their souls, never achieving true happiness and struggling through unnecessary miseries.

Benjamin also allowed his patients to use his body to present their passions, dreams, fears, and traumas. The souls could move on with their lives empowered by processing intense emotions together with him. In many cases, Benjamin trained women to protect themselves against dark creatures and assisted in finding balanced relationships. Female souls asked for advice on love, breakups, purpose in life, spirituality, and past traumas.

Many souls came to Benjamin asking for relationship advice. Female patients often asked whether they should leave their current romantic partners, looking for affirmation. But Benjamin believed that if a woman is even mulling the question of leaving her man, she has already made a choice. Benjamin just helped them to see the core of their own question and empowered them to make the decision their heart wanted. He guided his patients to see how they could use the time alone to rediscover their inner talents and spiritual powers. Any woman knows when the lessons between partners were learned, as she has a much stronger innate intuition than a man. Honest acknowledgment of such reality should be free from judgment when any relationship has run its natural course. People are traumatized by the false concepts about marriage and romance, rejecting to embrace the serendipitous nature of the world only because of society's superficial obligations and demands.

Eurydice tried so many times to run away from Benjamin, but many female souls came to Eurydice asking how to find such love. Eurydice battled Benjamin's affections with passionate rebelliousness, attempting to escape his teachings, but she always came back, conceding she couldn't live without him. Our lovers communicated weirdly, but other souls found that educational, and they thanked Eurydice for allowing them to observe their dynamic. Soon, Eurydice accepted every girl who came to seek Benjamin's guidance not as a rival for his heart but as a warrior sister in struggle. By accepting his patients, she learned to accept him for who he was. Our princess realized that she had to share her man's time with other women for the higher good of all involved. If he could cleanse her demons, he could also help others.

Eurydice received her first complex case once she had learned enough from Benjamin. The soul, who introduced herself as Angie, arrived with an unusual request. She asked Benjamin to tell her body that she must never have an abortion in her life, as she struggled to relate this information herself. Eurydice didn't know how to approach this situation ethically. She couldn't imagine that Benjamin would tell this woman never to have an abortion, as her body also had free will. Eurydice explained to Angie that they could only teach her how to communicate with her body, but they couldn't relay information themselves. Eurydice asked why Angie felt so strongly against abortion, and Angie explained that her divine purpose was to be a mother in this life as she could only grow through such experience. Angie had to be a guardian angel for her future children, and make sacrifices for the souls she would birth. Angie could achieve her highest potential by devoting herself entirely to her kids, aiding them with feminine care and nourishment. The bright, heavenly light Angie emitted amazed both Benjamin and Eurydice. Her higher purpose was to be a mother and our spiritual guides could see that in her eyes. Our lovers enjoyed every session in her presence, as Angie arrived at her training with sublime tenderness and unique feminine compassion.

Eurydice asked why Angie thought her body might have an abortion, and Angie explained that she was destined to live the life of a loving single mother. So once the father of her future child would abandon her, the relatives might pressure her into having an abortion. Eurydice wanted to know more about the topic in general, and she asked Benjamin to tell her about the natural release of pregnancy, performed through communication with the child's soul. Benjamin described to Eurydice how two of his patients successfully did such meditations themselves and peacefully released their unwanted pregnancies without outside assistance.

The nature of any pregnancy-related experience always involves a dialogue between a woman and the higher realm. Only a woman herself knows what kind of lesson such experiences carry, as every conversation with a heart's womb brings a specific type of transcended knowledge that is impossible to receive otherwise. So, if a woman clearly understands what she is going through internally and is not ready for a child for honest reasons, she could talk with the child's soul and ask to release the cords of a new life for the highest and best interests of everyone involved. The pregnancy may be released by clearly stating what kind of lesson the pregnancy has brought to a woman. Of course, Benjamin recommended doing such a ceremony to any woman who had an abortion or miscarriage in the past, as these emotional attachments may weigh heavy on a woman's soul long after an abortion. A woman's uterus serves as a portal for a new life, and only the woman herself can understand the depth and importance of connection with the soul of a child. If trapped in between states, the child's soul could hunt mother and scar her womb until the end of life.

Eurydice discovered a case where a woman released the cord with her child sixteen years after an abortion. The child's soul was trapped and impeded the lives of both parents who conceived this baby. All this time, this soul couldn't move to another life, not being dead nor alive, because of the spiritual attachment already formed with the parents. Benjamin also saw such a cord entrapping his mother, Gverina, who regretted her surgical abortion but refused to accept spiritual help. As medically assisted abortion only considers the physical manifestation of the pregnancy, a woman is more likely to endure inner emotional trauma. It was important for our knight to understand the spiritual reasons behind any pregnancy, helping his patients to release such scars. He performed drumming ceremonies, when women still carried energy cords with the souls of unborn babies. He also knew how to energetically cleanse wombs after any trauma or from energies imposed by destructive lovers. Benjamin taught Eurydice these skills and she proudly offered them too.

Eventually, Eurydice and Angie bonded and openly discussed many complex topics. Angie invited Eurydice and Benjamin to her peach garden not far from Vancouver. She introduced them to her protective spirit, living in a magical creek, who cleaned the darkness with its water. Angie was destined to bear children who would help clean and nourish this land, guided by their mother's example. Once Eurydice and Benjamin had tried the best peaches they had tasted, Angie invited them to visit her house. Inside, they saw how peacefully Angie's body slept on the couch in front of the fireplace. Eurydice showed Angie how to communicate with her body through dreams and metaphors, and her advice worked. It wasn't the immediate result Angie was hoping for, but she was finally on the right path. Angie rejoiced, jumping and dancing around her body, praising Benjamin and Eurydice for their help. She finally understood how she could persuade her body to make independent decisions.

Benjamin and Eurydice spent the next four months supporting Suzanne in one way or another. She struggled to fight demons that occupied her body and didn't want to ask Phillip for help. Suzanne demanded assistance from Benjamin as she witnessed how he healed Eurydice. Even though she rarely followed his advice, she liked how accepting he was of her stubborn essence.

After the lake incident, Suzanne lived in the farmhouse under the protection of her spirits. They assigned her a restorative therapy, where she learned to connect to her nourishing female energies through gardening. Suzanne was still angry at Benjamin for the past traumas, especially when he abandoned her as a child, but now she tried to find comfort in the lessons she drew from those experiences. Benjamin did care about this soul, and she saw that in his eyes. After his energy healing sessions, she realized that his actions always came from the place of love. Our knight saw how duchess was finally improving as her spirits returned their protection. Still, Suzanne was quite distressed after what she had endured. Because of that a flock of dark bird-like creatures swirled like vultures above her garden, covering her skies from healing sun and fresh air. Suzanne asked Benjamin to help combat them. Our knight killed some of them, but advised to follow Phillip's guidance to eliminate them.

Benjamin presented evidence to Suzanne that Phillip was her assigned spiritual guide and could train her to battle negative energies. Suzanne protested this knowledge, explaining that she couldn't trust Phillip because he betrayed her in the past. Benjamin tried to help Suzanne perceive her past death as a valuable lesson of empowerment. Benjamin explained that Phillip had already apologized for his actions and carried tremendous guilt in his heart. Phillip felt imprisoned by Suzanne, and that's how he rebelled, by letting her drown. His life also ended tragically because he couldn't forgive himself for mistreating Suzanne. No matter how much he wished for her death, he couldn't live without her. The Second World War was a spiritual war as much as a physical. As the world experienced devastation, people destroyed their loving connections, trapped by the same energies. Still, Suzanne argued that Phillip would betray her again. Benjamin promised he would stop Phillip if he followed the same path. They made a pact, as Benjamin vowed never to abandon Suzanne again. Benjamin would heal their shared traumas by telling her story to the world, and she would allow Phillip to be her guide.

Yet, despite their agreement, Suzanne didn't really listen to anyone's advice. Eurydice turned impatient as Suzanne was the most stubborn soul our lovers worked with. Our princess didn't like how Suzanne disrespectfully treated Benjamin throughout the last year. She could brazenly storm into our lovers' apartment, demanding assistance even in the middle of the night, which infuriated our princess. Eurydice decided to take control of the situation. She didn't know how to heal such a lost soul, but she rose to the challenge, and soon, an opportunity arrived to find Suzanne's answers.

Benjamin organized a small party for his soulmates to celebrate their new status. Since Eurydice begged to meet Benjamin's sky spirits, our knight decided to recharge in their domain while showing Eurydice his lands. Once they establish the connection with Heaven, they traveled back to their source. Eurydice was excited to leave the Earth, as she had never done it before. She invited Suzanne to go, but our duchess was scared. Suzanne was a young soul who felt unsettled about leaving the Earth. But Eurydice insisted and promised to shield Suzanne.

Benjamin created a spiritual, whirling spiral with his magic, so Eurydice and Suzanne could travel through this portal. The energetic stream of vibrations carried our soulmates away from the land. Sky knights flew first, stretching and bending the matter of reality with their auras while their ladies held to their men. Right away, Eurydice and Suzanne felt terrified as the energy of knights pulled them up into the skies, traveling through the clouds and space. The lights, flashes, turbulence, and sensations felt the same as in a real rocket, but there was no physical capsule around them, only an ethereal one. Eurydice firmly held Suzanne's hand and reassured her that she was strong enough to endure this, even though unusual sensations overwhelmed both of them.

Our soulmates traveled through the plane of collective human thoughts. This place was Earth's aura and stored everything humans remembered in their daily lives. Through this plane, people communicated telepathically with their thoughts and dreams. Then our soulmates entered the dark void known as space. It was the last frontier available to humans. The souls could easily travel to other planets through their dreams and meditations. However, humans were bonded to Earth with no exceptions. Since people had what they needed for their soul's journey on Earth, the Creator ensured no one could physically get beyond the spiritual shield until they finished their teachings. Eurydice and Suzanne felt more comfortable in space. They experienced similar feelings in the world between lives. Now they were floating in the nothingness, looking down on their land from above.

Our travelers soon arrived at their destination; they approached the energetic dome that shielded the planet. This place was not visible to the naked eye. All of humanity's knowledge was safely stored in this metaphysical plane, known as firmament, from the beginning of times. Every event of every life was recorded onto this dome's outer layer, made of diamond. An ethereal inner layer under this solid outer dome contained the home of sky spirits. The souls of sky warriors could travel to this land for recharge and advice.

When our lovers approached this plane, it looked like a jelly substance, slowly moving in sparkling waves. The mist-type space was transparent and radiant while vibrating in union with the beings living inside. Our soulmates could see the substance of this matter as if it was a translucent cloud, but once they entered the energy field of this intangible realm, they found themselves in the most beautiful garden, the kind that doesn't exist on Earth. Only souls guarded by sky spirits could enter this secret space. Any soul approaching this energy dome would only see energetic vibrations and distortions.

Eurydice and Suzanne would never be able to enter this place if it wasn't for their knights' invitation. The women looked around in awe, as they only saw such lush and vibrant colors in cinematic fairy tales. Everything looked like on their lands, but somehow more vivid and alive, as if every tree and bush spoke to them. They immediately felt incredible reverence and bowed to thank the spirits for welcoming them in this Eden. Only Eurydice and Suzanne couldn't find their men, as they looked around confused and lost. But soon they felt incredible soothing peace inside, as if they could lucidly see the purity of their hearts and they finally embraced each other's higher essences. Something about this place allowed both women to remove their guards and establish complete trust. Suzanne finally realized that Eurydice was her spiritual sister. The nonsense and confusion of ego disappeared here. They shared no resentment anymore and embraced the blessings of their crossed paths. Eurydice took Suzannes's hand, and guided her towards the nearby tree. Their journey was short but quite symbolic, as if Eurydice agreed to help Suzanne heal, and she accepted help. Once they settled on the ground, leaning on the gorgeous tree, they hugged each other in celebration.

They drifted into the most unique and special dream they had ever seen. Suddenly they realized that Benjamin and Phillip were inside this tree. This space was different from Earth and didn't have houses like humans. The homes of the sky souls looked like magical trees, rooted in sacred knowledge and reaching with branches to angels above. Like a garden of paradise from the ancient fairytales, this place vibrated from the life of animals, birds, and sacred plants of all kinds, but the trees were the masters of this domain and governed it. Each sky soul could return to their home tree when necessary, immersing in it right away upon arrival. Since Eurydice and Suzanne were guests in this space, they could only stay outside, sleeping next to the tree of their men while spiritually connecting to their vibrations.

Eurydice and Suzanne woke up energized and rejuvenated, as if they had slept peacefully for weeks. Nothing felt better than this transcended meditation, where they were immersed in the essence of their men. It was a unique experience that not every land soul was allowed to have. Our women sensed their talents starting to bloom, as the waves of deep spiritual knowledge and self-love descended on their hearts. The women waited for their knights to finish their energetic exchange and travel back to Earth. Many more essential messages came to Eurydice during their trip back, as she deeply connected to Mary Magdalene's energy on this trip without understanding it.

Upon their return, Eurydice showed Benjamin a unique, but puzzling vision she saw while traveling back. Our knight explained that she needed to request a meeting with his friendly deity, known as Narayana. She was a supreme female being, responsible for such concepts like karma, reality, and restoration.Eurydice's intuition claimed that Narayana knew Suzanne's answers.

CHAPTER XVIII

Narayana thought highly of Benjamin as her student and always helped him. Narayana was the primary source for Benjamin's knowledge regarding the laws of cause and effect, which in turn guarded the nature of death, rebirth and soul contracts. Benjamin reached Narayana, and on the next day, the four soulmates traveled to a secret restaurant in Matsue, Japan. It was a discreet place where Narayana could manifest, but at the same time, it was an important karmic town for Suzanne. Our soulmates sat at the table, indulging in exquisite green tea with Japanese pastries. Suzanne was extremely agitated, paranoid, and nervous, as she could run away from her soulmates, but she wouldn't be able to dismiss the teachings of a supreme deity as easily. She stayed silent, frightened of what she would hear, but Eurydice was excited and comforted Suzanne. They would face a higher Goddess for the first time, so our princess wanted to make a good impression.

Phillip and Benjamin reminisced about their last time in this place, telling their ladies how they talked with Narayana at the same table a couple of years ago. She invited our knights to share a delicate Japanese tea in a silent ceremony. Then Narayana explained to Benjamin that the souls of Camilla's father, aunt, and uncle neglected their studies, so they were reborn in North Korea in this life. These souls refused to learn the same lesson in three lives, and by the divine law, they received their destined punishment, working as prisoners in North Korean labor camps. These souls would spend their lives in complete misery as they refused to embrace the path of the heart when they lived as free people. They were bound to live as slaves until they repented and accepted their inner beauty. If these souls wouldn't allow the prison masters to assist in their growth, they would be bonded to live in purgatory next time, carrying the sins of humanity. Narayana told Benjamin he could release their debts and heal these souls through his art by creating three books and three movies.

Once Benjamin finished this story, Narayana entered the restaurant. The staff bowed in reverence to the Goddess, immediately closed the establishment and draped the windows. Our soulmates were the only guests here. The Goddess approached their table with the widest smile possible. She was eight feet tall, with long dark hair, and dressed in the most exquisite silk robe decorated with floral embroidery. Narayana and Benjamin hugged first, exchanging energies like friends who hadn't seen each other in a while. Benjamin often felt shy when Narayana praised him, but she liked that he was humble about his high spiritual destiny. They worked with the same essences of death and karma, so they loved connecting.

Narayana hugged Philip and Suzanne, welcoming them. Then the Goddess embraced Eurydice, telling her how happy she was that Benjamin had finally discovered the feminine half of his soul. Narayana couldn't take her eyes off Eurydice, complimenting the essence of our princess. Narayana was highly protective of her mentee and knew Benjamin could truly advance only through an intimate sacred union of love. Eurydice was the kind of woman the Goddess always envisioned next to Benjamin, so she was ecstatic to meet this gorgeous and sophisticated princess. Narayana complimented how Benjamin's heart beautifully evolved once he embraced a love for a woman. She praised his transformation as he found a missing piece of his essence through hard work of serving humanity.

Benjamin and Phillip stayed mostly silent, allowing Eurydice to lead this meeting. Suzanne was shy but drawn to Narayana's powerful, nourishing energy, patiently listening to the higher advice. Eurydice quickly befriended Narayana, and they chatted as if they had known each other forever, which felt natural but unexpected for both of them. Soon it felt like they were the only ones in the room, as their connection turned to be even more powerful than Narayana had with Benjamin. The Goddess was delighted that such an amazing couple would bring the light of divine knowledge into the world.

Narayana was joyful in the presence of such a powerful soul, and she joked about Eurydice's insecurities. The Goddess confirmed that our soulmates followed their destined path of love, healing, forgiveness, beauty, and art, reassuring them to press on in their endeavors despite the attacks of demons. Narayana urged Eurydice never to doubt her heart and to trust Benjamin's guidance. She also related to Eurydice that it was imperative to heal the early wounds of Eloise through poetry, as Eloise dreamed of being a poet but never dared to try.

When Eloise only arrived in Paris, having no means of existence, she resorted to selling her body, and those experiences scarred her. She perceived herself as a fallen woman, ostracized and judged, but in reality, she carried enormous love for all humans, and that's why she could pleasure men with her sensual magic. It was the trap that any soul carrying the essence of Mary Magdalene could fall into. Women with Magdalene's heart are very fragile and vulnerable. Their energies could be easily penetrated with pain and fear. In result, a Magdalene woman can lose herself and become a victim of her impulses, while her pleasures turn perverse. Only with help of honest love, could she create an energy shield around her aura.

Eloise didn't understand her complex sensuality, so she obediently served men rather than empower herself through lovemaking. Eurydice had to stop perceiving herself as sinful. Divine forces created her with wild sexual energies so she could channel heavenly joy and pleasure to any broken human. She couldn't change her past, but she could rewrite the scars that society created for her. Eurydice was unaware of how to work with her innate sexual energy until she met Benjamin. Now she could see, how they lived an ancient myth. Even though many perceived Mary Magdalene as a damaged woman since she was skilled in sexual magic, when she met her destined man at the well, and they fell in love, he saw the essence of her soul. He accepted her for who she was, seeing she was living by her heart and fulfilling her destiny. He didn't care about the society or his friends, who advised him to avoid this woman. He forgave their ignorance. For him, she was never damaged. She was his supreme queen.

After affirmations and suggestions, Eurydice asked if she was correct to reach Narayana to advise Suzanne. The Goddess shined with the most generous smile. Narayana was proud of Eurydice since our princess finally followed her feminine intuition, even though she still questioned it. She saw the potential of Eurydice's healing abilities, mentally sending her perceptions to Benjamin, and our knight rejoiced. Both could not be prouder of Eurydice's talents. Our princess tried to hide under the table, as she had never heard such compliments directed her way. Eurydice could not believe that she was not just an attractive and desirable girl but also a talented healer.

Then Narayana addressed Suzanne. Our duchess listened patiently, but soon the table turned silent as our soulmates tried to process the harsh divine message. The Goddess told Suzanne that this life would be the third one where she falls into the same mistakes. Suzanne tried to command Phillip twice in her past, instead of listening to his teachings and accepting him as her guide. Both times, she refused to accept that Phillip and Benjamin were destined to work together on the missions. The duchess believed that Benjamin was taking Phillip away from her. She often felt lonely without him, but it was imperative for Phillip's growth to complete assignments with Benjamin. In her decisions, Suzanne only considered her narcissistic, egotistical feelings. She wasn't soft, patient or gracious with her man, and now she was making the same mistake for the third time in a row, trying to split the union of brothers. She rejected Phillip's teachings even more because of the past trauma, but that was her new trap, as her lessons became harder in each life. Narayana explained to the duchess that if she will follow this path and wouldn't accept the guidance of her trusted soulmates, Suzanne would be destined to be reborn in North Korea next time.

Once a soul was bonded for the punishment in North Korea, they arrive at the city of Matsue for a farewell ceremony. Here a soul would be greeted by Narayana and their guide. During the boat cruise on Lake Shinji, a soul would witness the most beautiful sunset on Earth. This adventure would lead to a liberating and empowering experience. A soul would agree to embrace its future struggle and vow to use a slave life for higher learning.

The Goddess was open and patient, understanding how hard it was to face such truth and acknowledge past mistakes. Suzanne blamed herself for not seeing the obvious. She took Phillip, Benjamin, and Eurydice for granted, not recognizing their unconditional love. The traumas of the past descended upon Suzanne in flashing images, trapping her heart in misery. She couldn't cry or laugh anymore, but Eurydice consoled her spiritual sister. Once the meeting ended, Narayana hugged each of our soulmates, empowering them with healing energy.

After meeting such high authority, Suzanne started to listen to Phillip and Benjamin. The prospect of being sent to North Korea terrified our brothers, as they knew it would be devastating for the internal growth of such a sensitive soul. Soon Phillip reported slow progress, as Suzanne agreed to give our brothers two years to restore the trust between them and see the results of healing.

The meeting in Japan transformed the dynamic between our heroes in an inspiring way. The trust and communication between the four of them significantly improved. After such an achievement, Eurydice was shining in all-new colors, and Benjamin finally stopped worrying about his princess. No matter what would happen in this life, he was happy to help another soul master her innate talents. Benjamin never desired a higher reward. Once, he felt the same way about Phillip when he saw how his brother embraced his talents and accepted the path of the heart. For the first time in their relationship, Benjamin felt an intense and powerful sensual attraction to his woman that he didn't experience before. The immaturity of Eurydice was disappearing. They saw each other in a new light. Benjamin was a masculine guide from the skies, and Eurydice was a feminine guide from the lands. Like the sun and the moon, they inseparably affected each other while shining with their innate light in their cosmic dance.

Our lovers still needed to research every life they lived, but for now Eurydice prepared a show. She was ready to entertain her man with a new stream of poetry, written in the voice of Eloise to absolve her traumas.

Terrified
by Eurydice Eloise Wayles

You wish I was dead, and I am but not how you think
I'm a stranded soul living in the West End a few blocks up from Sunset Beach
And when my shaman shelters me from those who are always mean to me
I'm peach rose blooming reverence;
And when we fly down the hill to our favorite spot
Rushing to the rocks by the wind,
Absorbed by our affections
I sense liberation as I'm possessively wrapping around my man.
And when my restless hair is covering my eyes
The entire beach is hearing my sublime advice
As I passionately read Violets bend... *over and over again*
And writing my rhymes with the chance
And blinding with my poetry dance
The words that look like a game to you
So you just killed me for them plurally .
Throwing me from my big rock into the oceans
As you hated when I shattered your illusions
And you put me to rest

Terrified

You are happy that I'm dead, and I am, but not just quite
I witness body trapped in a snare of distorted vibrations
And I'm constantly analyzing my sensuality's future prospects.
I'm dying inside time and time again with each of my executed victim
I'm fleeting the excruciating dance of the knife penetrating my skin
I rejoice as I hang myself next to the chimney
And every once in a while, reminiscing melancholiac anguish
Of how I delivered my stillborn baby-girl of pure unconditional love
Who came with the mission to kill me later

And soon I'm dying again

Terrified

When I was saved by the tweet on the birdie Twitter app
Rescued from the purgatory with the single poem of pure love
I felt that I was still valued and needed
I felt like an extraordinary being
Escaping the demonic world of shattered mirrors;
I was saved by the Twitter after I was killed by it –
Delusional games of deranged reflections
That turn dreamy noble girls into shallow spores
As their tortured psyches dirt devour first
Scrolling copycats in male amusement stores –
Perverse nightmares adorning bruises and sores
Molding fragile beings of divine inspiration
Into mediocre trinkets to play with and throw away –
Not one of a kind but just another one
Indistinguishable from any other one
Drowning in the sameness of exposed body parts –
Killing me over and over again with their flood of licentiousness
As I speak the existential truth of my own perception
Whistling about monstrous oppression of the entire female kind
Not the opinion – but a sound, real-world view –
Of a soul that lived quite a few mad female lives dying

Terrified

You enjoy that I'm dead but I still speak my truth
I live in the apartment building trapped by Jervis and Barkley just eight
    blocks from the beach
I wandered outside today to experience being ravenous
But I don't know how to be that
I only know how men perceive my fanny
Turning me into a pray with their looks
Thinking I might be an amusing plush kitten

Thinking dying is only a game for me
And I would argue, but I'm too stoned today
I can only incinerate intruders with my gazes

Terrified

My death is sensed through a flower, when I'm raped by a devourer
Yet I attempt to escape humanity sumptuously
Now standing on the shores of my waters
And fighting every creature imposing my freedom
While their banality of evil creeps back from the abyss
As the noises of humdrum humans in reveling get louder and louder
During the luminous violet hour
Until promiscuous creatures dry their bottles
Flooding deep unresolved troubles
Mating right in front of my eyes
Fornicating with their own ego cries
Screaming culminations of nonsensical hookups…
Inebriated dolls forgetting their souls,
Making me sick to my heart
As their moans got louder and louder
And it feels like I'm drowning
But unable to die when I finally want to
Like feeling trapped on these shores.
And it wasn't just a dream
I was really

Terrified

The Magical Cycles
by Eurydice Eloise Wayles

Dear boys, it's time to throw away your toys
Stop making whining, childish noise

As your mommy's tired serving you grilled cheese
But still foolishly kisses your butt and cleans up your grown-up shit.
Dear boys, it's time to start afresh and look them in the eyes
Reject their stifling care and say adult goodbyes.

Dear boys, when your heart finds true love
With modesty approach the lady of your dreams and say,
"I'll be a man, please only ask, I can become a man for you.
I know I'm vulgar and confused but can I please serve you?"

Then synchronize your life with your woman's cycle
And see the beauty of cathartic refinement,
The purifying magic that created our world.
Embrace the fullness of life during twenty-one days
And then release useless energies of sufferings over the next week
Receiving the harmony, by connecting with her.

As you meditate together with your woman's pain,
Become one with it and allow it to fill your essence
As you are destined to take it away
Removing any darkness as her genuine servant,
A kind man who shields her divine vulnerabilities.

Place your hand and third eye over her womb heart,
While singing your healing song of love
As she surrenders to spiritual gifts of Mother Nature.
Remarkable equilibrium of two opposite beings,
Transcending the limitations of the flesh
Rejoicing with smiles and devotion.

Courteous man purging torments of this world
Together with his sole and unique female Goddess,
As they are unwrapping divine blessings,
Contemplating their oneness through this graceful dance of sacred
    intimacy.

Dear boys, the world can bless you with its wonders
If you will finally betray your mommy
If you will transform your deepest fears
Into feminine, luminous flowers
If you will embrace your woman's womb
And her sacred beauty shaped by nightmares
If you live with her the cycle's guiding light –
Then, my boys, one day, you may become real men.

Eloise's new life in Paris
by Eurydice Eloise Wayles

Let me make a confession today –
I am where I belong
I own my twisted reality
I honor my sacred sexuality
I live in a wicked harmony
That I adore.

I meant well
When I trapped myself in Hell
Red bell alarms
Sick men to crawl around me
Their shadows are stretching far and wide
They are inside
My heart that's longing for a genuine connection.
But kindness of a man is not me
I live desires of vile creeps
With claws and sticks
And tongues with twists
They are disgracing my sweet lips
Cementing psyche with true horrors
Abhorrent hedonistic men
My life's command
To honor their perversions
But I believe I can

Escape and run away from pain
Yet when I scratch the surface
My soul reveals demonic tearing scars
I'm tolerating past mischiefs
And I concede to feel male parts...
I did vexatiously consent
To squeezes, grabs, and infiltrations
Flirtatious nature's my damnation
Salacious dreams I live to beam
I'm precious when I'm sober
I'm wild when money speaks
So, most of the time
I bite my lip, and I embrace assaults
I did invite them in
To dance lust waltz...

The judges everywhere around me
But they don't know my truth
I'm not a victim or a slave
The rape can feel so liberating!
Still, on my darkest nights
Invigorating ghosts and souls
Will haunt me, waking up, enthralled
Appalling pains of old obsessions
I crawl
Into my bathtub just to cry
My bedroom's ceiling occupied
As my intrusive lovers conjure rites
They can't be saved
Not even with my feminine delights
Like beastly bugs and vicious spiders
They gather to my light.
Too many nightmares in my days
Too many rackets in my nights
But I still fight my tricks
Forever their infernal might

Will ravage fragile girlish feelings
Yet even when I moan and frown
How they would like
I must profess I never mind
To bear their immature concupiscent sensations
As they come
To bury their last hopes for a redemption.
I only wish they'll leave in peace
They never do; they do return to haunt me still
I kneel to feel the frenzy of my magic
My home is never safe for me, no more
I roar; but can't escape my whims…

And yet, I feel precisely like myself
When speaking after sex
Flexing perceptions
Twisting dimensions
Spewing manipulations
After spreading my legs;
The laws of my truth
They all will abide
They taste my insides
But smile with disdain
Yet, my sanctity's cleansed
With their apostasy.
Treason is never for brave
All of my men are insane
Their impotence can't be explained
So, I play them like a maestro.
As my gestures and my hips
My smile and my lips
Reset their persuasions
My dominant invasions
Blank their minds
I'm right inside, as they abide
Each time I raise my grace

And show who owns the real power.

You know, those stupid men...
They'll do just anything I ask
To get to enter me
They'll lie, deceive, betraying trust
To be destroyed by me.

They come, and they go
I please as I must
But no one to trust
I learned through these days
Untangling slowly
Perceptual threats
I long and I'm lonely
In life of regrets.

Eloise in Love
by Eurydice Eloise Wayles

The essence of our love
Her breasts will confess
At night
Don't be surprised
As nothing new under the moon
I'm in my attic room
Its Paris views
Has never seen the Eiffel's muse
But it's my home where I can choose
To be myself and shine my hues
I'm contemplating empty roofs
I am a Goddess of night blues
I'm speaking daring healing truth
And levitate above this city.

And now, at last

When our devil shifts his clocks
I open doors to kill my past...

My newfound love
Arrives to liberate me
Kissing fast
Sensations blast through us
As we surrender to caresses
Contracting gently
Our fierce emotional contrasts –

I shy away while she seduces
I wrap her tight to heal abuses
I break away from my excuses
And I allow myself to live!

With oozing thrill,
Our clothes spill
Revealing blossoming affections...

And now I lead her in
Into my bathtub with my wit
As waters rushing in
We crawl to bliss on girly feet
We're stepping in
Our breasts concede to dance
And join in brazen kisses
Sweet treats on lips
Our guards retreat
And we complete
Each other's scars.

The early morning sun appears
To praise the gazes
Of our feral adorations
We both feel wild

The water sparkles from our smiles
With shimmering emeralds
With gleaming diamonds
We're both ablaze and glowing!

She shines and lets me in
I'm hesitant to feel
Her fingers on my
Stringent and defensive nipples -
She knows my body
And how to make it sing
While I still don't
As not a single man
Has ever taught me of delight
So only now I'm letting go
I'm trusting her caresses.
She makes me feel like a woman
Once again.

I'm tender while she's hot
I dream of having breasts like hers
To whisper as her nipples do
Our love is intimate and true
I'm new to female love
To freeing life and to this city
But she will guide me through
"I'm always feeling sad and blue
When I am living without you."
My ears are melting from her truth
As we're reaching for the Heavens.

Now we are dancing in our bed
And licking gently oldest fears
Upsetting neighbors
With sex magic
Enjoying liberating tears

The flow of unifying peace
Our pleasures never sleep
We live in bliss
While ceasing tensions of the world –
Our karmic saintly traumas
Will never haunt us anymore…

I'm virgin and I'm whore
Illusions exposed
Wtih love we soar.

We're here to be ourselves –
Through sex and death –

Allure of comeuppance
Our poetry…

As we're redeeming mankind's sins
Erotic contacts of our skins
Appear to be the answer
To aching miseries, we share
As we attempt to salvage blindly
Our precious female dreams.

CHAPTER XIX

Benjamin and Eurydice embarked on detailed research of their past lives. They hoped to release any possible traumas that still haunted them and understand the true nature of Damian. Through the process, Benjamin was also determined to prove to Eurydice that he always loved her in very special and unique way. Furthermore, our lovers wished to discover how this knowledge could empower Eurydice to accept her supreme feminine nature.

In his first life, Benjamin arrived as an enslaved man named Tristan. When the angels decided to create our soulmates, they made one special soul, that would eventually split in two parts – one of masculine essence empowered by the skies and one of feminine essence empowered by the lands. So, in first lives both Benjamin and Eurydice lived in one body and experienced life as a merged being, unaware of their future destiny.

Angels chose a woman Theodosia, to be Tristan's mother. Theodosia was an enslaved maid living in the house with her masters. She was never involved with a man, and when she became pregnant, she was perplexed, but perceived this immaculate conception as a divine blessing. The soul of our inseparable lovers was created in Theodosia's womb as angels sent streams of energies from the skies that formed a fetus and a soul at once. Since Benjamin was destined to be a sky guide, such soul couldn't be created from the land, so a man wasn't needed to create Tristan. Eurydice only existed as a soul, equally connected and detached from Benjamin, learning from his experiences while existing in ether.

Tristan grew up without a father, and he resented his masters, thinking they abused his mother and never accepted responsibility for him. He also blamed Theodosia for not telling him the origins of his life, thinking that she was shielding one of the masters who used her in a dishonest way. Only Theodosia could not prove that she became pregnant in an unusual way. She took her story to the grave and never confessed to anybody out of fear. Tristan and Theodosia shared a unique bond and always spent their free time together. Theodosia enjoyed his calmness and Tristan's strange fairy tales that he saw in his dreams, while he enjoyed his mother's soothing and nourishing energy. She was his best friend and teacher.

When Tristan was nine, he was assigned to be an apprentice of a carpenter, showing potential in this craft. The household had a barn where slaves crafted furniture, which was later sold at the town's market. Tristan struggled with his enslaved status, as he was a free-spirited person. Yet he found great pride in his work and adored his mother, so he eventually came to peace with his reality, surrendering to his fate. He always felt that he was born to be a slave, as if it was something unavoidable, yet at the same time noble. That's how he perceived his life, trying to be the best carpenter he could, without receiving proper rewards for his job.

In the evenings, he would take long walks in nearby forests, which irritated the masters, as they believed he was trying to run away. Tristan never had such plans as he couldn't leave Theodosia alone. Talking to the land was his favorite activity and his escape from daily obligations. When he turned forty, his mother suddenly passed away from an illness. Tristan held the hand of his favorite woman as they said their last goodbyes.

He buried his mother, processed his grief, and said his spiritual goodbyes to her soul. Nothing held Tristan on this property, and he decided to escape. One night he packed provisions in a bag and left his masters. Tristan believed that no one can liberate a slave, until the freedom would appear in the heart. One day, Tristan felt he had completed his divine duty and had the right to dissolve the bond with his masters. He lived by his heart and Nature blessed his path to freedom, helping him on a road to new life. Only his journey to liberty was not easy. For two years he struggled to survive, often sleeping outside, while earning food and rare shelter with occasional gigs. Eventually, the land guided him to an abandoned house on the outskirts of a village. His heart told him it was his destiny to settle here.

Soon he started to earn decent money by repairing houses and crafting furniture. One day, he met the beautiful woman Arabella, the daughter of one of his employers. Both were in their middle forties, yet neither had ever experienced true love. They were shy around each other at first, unable to accept the growing feelings, that took complete control over their hearts. But their connection grew day by day, and once they surrendered to this love, they got married. Arabella was very tender and sweet to Tristan. She cared for him like he never thought was possible. He even asked the skies why this woman was so good to him. The angels answered that since he diligently worked hard as a slave and never blamed anyone for his fate, Arabella's unconditional love appeared on his path as a divine gift for his righteous life.

They lived together for two decades in perfect harmony full of love and devotion. They never had children, so they dedicated all their love to each other and to the land. They felt they were brought together by higher powers and they cherished each minute of their union. Their house was always full of love and unique affections; it was filled with blissful light of a sacred union.

Tristan was destined to leave first, as he was not emotionally capable of burying Arabella. Her soul agreed to take this responsibility on herself, hoping he would repay her one day in the future. Before Tristan closed his eyes for the last time, holding Arabella's hand, he confessed how lucky he felt for the time they spent together. Both knew it was not the last time they see each other, as they agreed to meet again, requesting to become soulmates. They shared joyful kisses and parted for centuries. Arabella accepted her loss with beautiful dignity, but eventually she developed deep sadness, as she didn't know when she would see her beloved soulmate again. She believed Tristan's love was gone, and she missed his light, but he left the part of his heart in her soul.

In the next life, Benjamin was born in Alexandria, Egypt, as a sexual priestess of love named Cassandra. Before people lost their connection with the divine, such women were considered nobility, as they healed wounded men through lovemaking rituals in the sacred temples of divine goddesses. When Cassandra was nineteen, still working on the street, a high priestess discovered and trained her in the art of love, eventually giving work in a temple. Cassandra was an embodiment of divine sexual energy and pure love, so she rarely felt abused when she gave away her passions to men. She loved all humans unconditionally. She was driven by her own desires and enjoyed receiving pleasure equally, expecting it from her lovers. Soon she became a priestess many adored with reverence. Surely, she encountered people, especially women, who tried to degrade her innate talents by calling her derogatory names. Still, she always proudly carried her stance, and her intimidating appearance of a tall, gorgeous brunette shielded her.

Cassandra was so proud of her body, that she spent many of her sexual rituals observing her radiating body in mirrors, especially after she climaxed from passionate lovemaking. She felt like a goddess and enjoyed that she was created in such way. Her profession allowed her to be independent and free. She embraced her divine purpose in this life, and being an initiate of secret Egyptian teaching of sex magic empowered her. She had plenty of free time for herself and immersing into her inner world through meditations, away from humans, was her other favorite activity. Cassandra felt blessed with her life and work.

When Cassandra was forty years old, she married a rich man and received everything she ever desired. She retired and completely immersed in studying of her essence. Long meditations in the luxurious bathtub in her husband's mansion with candles and expensive oils was her favorite activity. Here she could enjoy the beauty of her body and soul. She considered herself a free woman, perceiving her man only as a provider sent by divinity as a reward for executing her highest duty of serving humanity with her body. Cassandra healed many lost souls through sex and she was proud of her accomplishments. Observing her long legs, exquisite breasts and tender skin, while lying in the bathtub, she praised Nature for how divinely beautiful she was created. One day, when she was in her mid-forties, she fully embraced the most important lesson of this life – to be true to yourself and honor the higher path of your heart, despite society's perceptions, and judgments. When she looked back at how serendipitous her life was, how she was guided to be a truly spiritual, esoteric goddess of lovemaking, she praised her husband who gifted her the time alone with herself to come to this realization. Once she understood there was nothing else to learn from this life, she decided to leave our world in peace. She figured out the meaning of life. When she was forty-five, she commanded herself to die in her sleep.

Next time Benjamin was born as a man Sebastian, a mighty warrior skilled in archery. One day, in his middle thirties he met his destined soulmate, Nataly, who arrived in this life as a woman Izabella. They shared a unique, beautiful, and subtle love story over the next three years. They enjoyed each other's company and passionate romance, but Sebastian was always troubled as everyone called him weird for the way he approached every task in his life. As a spiritual and clairvoyant person, he could feel that Izabella was reserved to accept his perceptions of life. Sebastian's essence troubled Izabella, as she was unsure if her man could be a good husband. He was incredibly skilled lover and she stayed with him only for sex, yet he was convinced she truly loved him. Their mutual reservations prevented them from fully immersing in love given to them by the skies, even though they felt happy together. Unable to build trust and express inner emotions, Izabella fought their love story.

Eventually, Sebastian was drafted to the war, as enemy came to capture their city. He told Izabella he is destined to die on the battlefield. He saw his future and both realized they wasted precious time on foolish reservations. Once he was murdered by an arrow and the enemy took control of the city, invaders considered every citizen their property and branded each woman with a scorched seal on a shoulder, including Izabella.

One night Sebastian's soul appeared to Izabella in a dream, telling her to pack provisions and escape the city. Benjamin led his soulmate out of danger through many ordeals, patiently guiding her from the other side. One day, Izabella arrived in a peaceful city where she found her destined husband and birthed two children. It was the first mission on a soul level for our spiritual guide – he intentionally died to save his loved one and guide her away from troubles. Nataly carried the archetypical energy of the Goddess Isis, and she was destined to assume her highest spiritual role one day. In the life of Izabella, she was introduced to that energy through Benjamin, who would eventually help to uncover her true essence. Upon death, he assumed the energies of the god Osiris, - the only one who could teach and shape Isis to become herself.

In the next life, Benjamin and Nataly met again on the shores of the kingdom of British Columbia, both empowered by the spirits of Lighthouse Park. Benjamin was a magician who communicated with the land, and one day, he was guided to discover an abandoned settlement on a shore. The village was ravaged, all people were captured and taken away, but Benjamin found an infant girl on the ground. Once he took her in his arms, the soulmates recognized each other, and Benjamin knew in his heart, she was his divine daughter. Little Nataly pleaded for noble protection as she asked the land to summon up her guardian. Without his appearance she would die in a matter of hours.

He raised her like his own daughter, and they always loved spending time together. Enjoying their walks through the woods, he trained her to talk to the land and discover her other magical abilities. As in the previous life, Benjamin continued to train this soul to embrace her Isis nature. When Nataly was sixteen, the land told Benjamin that the sinister warriors from present-day Squamish who killed his daughter's parents, would soon return. Benjamin questioned his spiritual guidance, as he was still inexperienced magician. But as a precaution, men took every woman and child further inland. Benjamin's insights materialized, and savages arrived in their village two days later. They came to steal the women, as the most valuable property. Yet when they realized the women were hidden, they slaughtered all men in a violent rage.

Nataly became an experienced magician with her father's guidance. Through the drumming ceremony, she connected to Benjamin's soul, discovering the truth about his death. Benjamin guided her to take the women even further, and one day they found a peaceful tribe near present-day Coquitlam, that welcomed them. Here Nataly found her destined husband, and Benjamin stayed with her until she gave birth to her first child. Her spiritual father was ready to leave when he saw his daughter turned into an empowered woman. Benjamin performed his highest mission for the second time – he died again to guide his soulmate to safety. The training of Isis continued as Nataly became more in tune with her magical abilities.

Benjamin and Nataly met again next time to complete her education. Benjamin was born as a woman named Astarte, an oracle reader, sexual healer, magician, and mystic. She spent her early years as a street prostitute and the scars she endured during this time, haunted her womb for her entire life. This time Benjamin experienced what it's like to be a victimized sexual goddess.

Astarte served men with her body, but it was one of her purposes. When Astarte completed this duty with dignity, she was rewarded. She was trained to become a clairvoyant guide and healer. Eventually she was gifted her own temple. Now she was her master, but she tried to avoid men, preferring to help women, because of her traumas. Soon spending time in the death dimension became her favourite activity. Through the sacred sarcophagus, hidden in a secret room of her temple, she exercised ancient Egyptian magic of death and resurrection. Astarte felt uncomfortable in a female body. She spent most of her time studying corners of the death plane, learning from Osiris and Anubis. She dreamed to escape pains of her womb and struggles of the flesh. There were no lies in death, compared to life and that's why Astarte enjoyed spending time there.

One day Nataly, in a body of a woman Nefret, showed up for the reading, and the two women discovered their past life connection. Astarte saw the potential in Nefret and made her an apprentice. As an embodiment of Isis, she was destined to learn the craft of a mystic, including the ability to die and resurrect. Nefret moved in with Astarte, eventually becoming a psychic who gave her own readings to clients. She also did healing with sex magic. Two women became occasional lovers, even though Astarte was closed off after her sexual traumas. Yet through the Egyptian intimate practices of lovemaking, womb's de-armoring and massages Nefret healed Astarte's pains.

After years of working and growing together, Nefret fell in love with a client and married him. She visited Astarte on occasion with her husband and his children, but Astarte felt betrayed and jealous of Nefret's new life. Besides her disdain towards men never went away. Astarte had no regrets and enjoyed her hermit life, but Nefret's abandonment hurt her. One day, the Roman Empire came with war and they brutally murdered Astarte, ravaging her temple. When Astarte died, Nefret was the only one who could bury her soulmate.

The experience devasted Nefret, as she was inconsolable to lose such a close soulmate. She couldn't accept Astarte's death for years, often coming to the temple where she felt the presence of her soul. Nataly lost Benjamin three times, and in this life, she was forced to bury him. It was too much for this soul, so she requested to avoid meeting Benjamin in the future until she would be strong enough to face him. Of course, it was a lesson for Nataly to accept the essence of death and grief. It was also an important lesson of her education into becoming the daughter of Isis. It was as hard as hard for her to bury Benjamin, as it was for Benjamin to bury Eurydice.

Nataly and Benjamin didn't meet for seven centuries, afraid to face their powerful connection. When they did meet again in 2022, Nataly was ready to assume the full scale of her Isis essence. She asked Benjamin to complete the education, and our knight embodied Osiris to supervise the transformation. Nataly discovered her higher self through magical ceremonies, sensual rituals, deep explorations of the death dimension, and integration of past life traumas. She finally assumed the full essence of Isis with the help of her teacher and soulmate.

Once Benjamin's soul finished his initial education in spirituality, death and sexual healing, he was ready to learn everything about the essence of love and assume his higher destiny of a spiritual guide. It was only possible with Eurydice's help, as she was his ultimate teacher who would push him to the limits of his abilities through love and devotion. As this soul raised its vibrations it was ready to split into two opposites. Eurydice was finally ready to materialize, after living with her man in spirit.

Eurydice's first life was of a woman named Laney. She lived in the Roman Empire in the lands of present-day Croatia. Benjamin, as a man, Sergius, arrived in her town, and when she saw him, she instantly fell in love. Sergius was swayed by Laney's beauty and decided to stay to court her, slowly falling in love. It was the only life when our lovers experienced love at first sight. Benjamin owed this debt to Eurydice, and he repaid it when he fell for Holly.

Sergius grew up in another part of the Roman Empire. Phillip was his mother, Adriana, who loved and cherished her son dearly, becoming his wise teacher. Adriana died when Sergius reached adulthood, and he used the inheritance to buy a farm. He lived alone and spent most of his time farming, while in the evenings, he talked with souls and spirits. He also had the ability to visit other countries and even planets through the dreaming. One day a natural fire erupted and destroyed Sergius' village. He saved some money, a few household items, and his horse. He thought of rebuilding his farm, but spirits urged him to embark on a journey to another land as Laney summoned her soulmate. Sergius rode for a few days without much rest, wondering where destiny was leading him. He trusted his heart, searching for a divine intervention. One day, he stopped for provisions and met Laney. She was leaving a shop, heading home, but when she saw a man on a horse in the middle of the street, she froze with complete surrender and admiration. Sergius realized his search of fate was over and invited Laney on a date. They married a few months later and settled on Laney's farm.

Sergius was a kind and attentive husband, always helping his woman in everyday life. He smartly used the land and created a prosperous farm. He spent time improving the house and worked tirelessly in the field. The couple traveled to markets in nearby towns, where they sold their produce and bought supplies. Yet Sergius was quite a strange man, and Laney was often confused by his odd actions. She called him weird and struggled to accept him fully, even though she enjoyed his company and the partnership they've built. Sergius was undoubtedly weird, as wandering barefoot at night for hours was his favorite activity. He could walk to the of the Adriatic Sea and sing random melodies or spend evenings in the woods talking to the spirits, while Laney didn't know whether she should be worried about him on her lonely evenings.

When Laney asked Sergius what he was doing at night and why he needed to be alone on these walks, he told her about his clairvoyant perceptions of the world. Only Laney couldn't comprehend anything he was saying. What Sergius described to her never felt like wild fantasies of his imagination, as she had never encountered others like him. So, one day, hoping his woman would understand his visions, he wrote a short fairy tale about his most recent adventure. It was only one page long, and Sergius patiently crafted the story for days as he was not an experienced writer. When he read it to Laney, she suddenly rejoiced. For the first time, she could understand her man and the kind of life he was living. Through fables, parables, and metaphors, Laney could finally peek through the veils of the physical world.

Reading Sergius' fairy tales before going to sleep became the intimate tradition of our lovers. Each time Sergius experienced his mystical visions, he would write a new story. Laney enjoyed the energy of Sergius' delivery, his calm, soothing and hypnotizing voice when he presented his adventures. He entertained her with his tales, creating a sacred bond between them. As Laney finally saw the essence of her man's soul, they found true happiness, and their love brought them a son Brutus. Shortly after their son grew up and joined Roman Legion, Laney died of illness. Sergius held the hand of his beloved when she was dying. They praised their marvelous life together before parting, and Laney died in peace. She felt blessed she had a chance to understand her man.

Sergius was inconsolable for a long time. He buried Laney's body near their farm on the land of her birth. After he integrated his grief, his heart burst with new waves of inspiration for his woman. Eurydice was guiding him from other side to embrace his unique talents. He resumed writing and revisited his old stories. He selected Laney's favorites and patiently worked to improve them. Before going to bed, he read them out loud as if his beloved Laney was still living in their house, feeling she was listening from the other side. For him, these stories presented intimate conversations with his woman, who was still around him on a soul level.

Sergius died alone a few years later. His son Brutus returned to bury his father. Going through his parents' things, he discovered the fairy tales, and his heart was filled with beauty when he read them. The spirits called him to preserve these manifestations of his parents' love. He took these stories to Rome and gifted the manuscripts to the library. Sergius' stories kept evolving through the centuries, becoming an integral foundation of fairy tales that humanity would craft after his death.

The next time Eurydice and Benjamin arrived at the lands of the present-day Russian Empire. Benjamin was born in a small, autonomous village on the shores of the Don River as a man Dimitris. Comfortable weather and access to one of the most important trading routes made their village prosperous. Dimitris' mother, Natalia, loved her son very much. Her soothing energy created a protective energy field around his aura, shielding him from adversities for his entire life with feminine nourishment. Natalia was one of Benjamin's soulmates, and his divine teacher, arriving when he required higher guidance. Together they were destined to help the American Empire become independent one day. Natalia cared for Dimitris very much and raised a strong, disciplined, and free man, proud of his assertiveness and will. She was a best friend and a mentor to her son.

Dimitris' father, Aurelius, worked on trading ships. He sailed to the Ottoman Empire on wooden Scandinavian vessels and earned decent money with that labor. At twenty, Dimitris became an apprentice and eventually got the same job as his father. On one of his trips to the port town of the present-day Sampsounta, he met his soulmate, Phillip. Dimitris was walking one of the main streets of the city when he's eye suddenly caught a beautiful young lady Sumeyye, who enjoyed the view of the street from her window, like she was a princess in the castle.

When their gazes met, they both fell in love at first sight. Dimitris decided to stay in town and court Sumeyye as his ship sailed back. He dreamed of conquering this woman before he could return home. After a few weeks together enjoying walks, dinners, and dances, he came to Sumeyye's father, asking for permission to marry her. Dimitris arrived with a pouch of gold coins as a dowry. As her father witnessed their honest love, he blessed their marriage. He didn't want to part with Sumeyye, but he had four other daughters, so he favored any decent suitor. If Dimitris could earn such a generous offering, his daughter would be comfortable in the distant land. Dimitris married Sumeyye, and they move to his village.

Dimitris and Sumeyye were in love and couldn't spend a minute apart. Sumeyye quickly adapted to her new life, learned the language, and befriended neighbors. The couple enjoyed their conversations, spending countless evenings debating every aspect of life, including spirituality, clairvoyance and the essence of our world. Their love created a baby girl, Anastasia. Once Dimitris saw her daughter's eyes, he felt the most unusual emotions of his life. He couldn't explain his feelings, but he recognized his soulmate, Eurydice.

Dimitris continued to work on the ships, often being away for weeks. Upon return, he spent as much time as possible with his soulmates and attended the farm. Dimitris and Anastasia enjoyed their walks through the forest and swam in their favorite lake. Sumeyye was afraid of water, so these trips became a transcended bonding experience for the father and daughter. Dimitris taught Anastasia how to talk to the land and trees during these walks. They often discussed the meaning of life, contemplating nature on the shores of their beloved lake.

When Anastasia was nine, she got very sick, and her parents were convinced that the girl would die. She looked weaker each day and nothing helped. The spirits advised Dimitris to heal her by walking around the lake. The land always healed physical bodies of our soulmates, and Dimitris intuitively knew what to do. Spending time in his presence and immersing in the vibrations of forest healed Anastasia. Little girl narrowly avoided death, but she deeply united with her father through this transformative experience as both accepted the grandness of Nature.

When Anastasia grew up, she married a neighbor boy she knew from childhood. They were inseparable from an early age, and as they grew older, they fell in love. Anastasia gave birth to a son, Andrey. Anastasia would take him on the same walks and swims as her father did.

Dimitris died a couple of years after he buried his beloved wife, Sumeyye. Anastasia was close to him until his last day. She was the last one who held his hand. Before parting, Dimitris praised his daughter, telling her how lucky he felt to live in her presence and how much he learned from her. They vowed to see each other again as they said their final goodbyes.

Anastasia suppressed her tears when she buried her father, but a few days later, they poured out in an intense emotional stream when she went swimming in the lake. His death devastated her, beyond anything imaginable and visions of his motionless body haunted her. She felt like a part of her died when she buried him. She cursed the skies, asking never to endure such pain again, unable to process the tortures of her heart. Nothing helped Anastasia, and her grief never faded. She loved her husband and son, living a harmonious life, but the torment of living without seeing Dimitris' eyes crippled her. As she reached old age, Anastasia endured another trauma – it was excruciating for her to accept her new wrinkled face. Anastasia's heart could not accept how devastating time was to woman's beauty. By higher design, it was an intricate part of the true feminine experience. Only Anastasia refused to accept this beautiful transformation, and it left a scar on Eurydice, which Damian used against her, turning the aging process into a source of her highest fear.

Next time we find our soulmates as destined lovers living in Greece. Benjamin was born as Brutus, and his soulmate was Eurydice. Brutus grew up on the farm with loving parents and an older brother. One day his brother left for distant lands. Brutus knew these were the lands of his spirits. Walking in the evenings through the woods to the Ionian sea's shores, communicating with Nature and meditating next to the whispering trees were his favorite activities. His parents felt conflicted about his behavior, but their son diligently performed his farm duties, so they didn't judge his adventures in his free time.

Brutus loved working in the field with his father, creating a prosperous farm. Every Sunday, they would travel to the nearby town to sell their produce and purchase supplies. On one of the trips, his father needed to fix his tools and Brutus decided to wander through the town. His feet brought him to the park near the shore, and suddenly a divine intervention changed Brutus' life forever.

He was a very shy gentleman, even though tall and attractive, so he stayed away from women as much he could, scarred by his early romances. His mother tried to marry him to every girl in their village, but Brutus never felt comfortable around a woman. His first love traumatized him the most. He felt for a girl Penelope, who carried the soul of Phillip. Yet after few weeks of engaging romance, Penelope ridiculed his clairvoyance and spiritual insights. She never allowed him to finish his thoughts if they contradicted her beliefs. She made fun of him, claiming he lived in imagination and his masculine heart was deeply hurt. He left this relationship and vowed never to trust another woman with his perceptions of reality.

Heart feelings puzzled and tormented Brutus, as he was somewhat of a hermit. He even believed he would spend his entire life alone. Only on that sunny day, he witnessed a magical light coming from a woman, who enjoyed her time in Nature, and his intuition commanded to approach her. Brutus only saw her back, but her silhouette, cute black dress, and gorgeous brunette ponytail lit up his entire essence as if butterflies appeared inside his chest. He never experienced such feeling before, and he was scared. It was not a love for a woman yet. He fell in love with the divine magic of our world, as he recognized his soulmate before seeing her eyes.

Brutus never approached a woman in his life. It was always the other way around. He was afraid to show vulnerability to a woman and never understood why anyone would do that. Only at that moment his heart told him to trust this girl. He stood frozen for some time, thinking about his options. Brutus sensed that his life would never be the same if he will make just one step. Approaching her was the most audacious and daring action he had ever done in his entire life, but when he introduced himself to Eurydice, instant feelings sparkled between our soulmates, as they recognized the eyes of their souls.

Brutus spent every Sunday with Eurydice, exploring her town, nearby forests, and shores. Over the course of each week, he would collect the feelings of longing and then share them with Eurydice. Once Brutus wanted to buy a quill and ink to capture his feelings, but he was not an eloquent writer and his insecurities prevented him from embracing this idea. Brutus dreamed of writing, but he was never brave enough to expose his heart in such an intimate way. Eurydice dreamed of getting such a letter when she found out about his inner conflicts, but she was happy that he at least shared the words of love in person.

Soon they married and moved into Brutus' house. Eurydice gave birth to two boys, and they lived as a happy family. When Brutus' parents died, he inherited the house, and now his children helped him with the farm. Brutus continued his night walks, and curious Eurydice joined him when she could. Slowly Brutus opened up about his spiritual views, seeing how the eyes of his beloved sparkled from his stories. She accepted him fully and that uplifted this reserved man. Eurydice loved listening to his spiritual tales on their walks in his sacred forest. But making love on the shores of the Ionian Sea under the full moon was her favorite moments with Brutus.

Our soulmates built a sacred union full of love and devotion, but something troubled Brutus. He couldn't find words to describe the strange sensations inside of him. Shortly after Eurydice moved in, he started seeing strangers in his dreams, and he didn't know what to do with these visions. Brutus was unaware that he was learning to be a spiritual guide for other souls, and a new reality perplexed him. Souls came to seek his guidance, as love opened up his divine talents. He tried to explain to Eurydice what he felt and experienced in dreams, but she struggled to comprehend him. She was uncertain about her husband's feelings, but his torments were real, eventually troubling both. He was praying for any explanation. With feminine wisdom and compassion, Eurydice never criticized him. She lovingly assisted him with nourishing energy, even when she couldn't understand him. His troubles started to impede their happiness, but she continued to be there for him, creating a sacred space for expressing his troubling emotions. Then one day, the land blessed our lovers with answers, thanking Eurydice for the truth of her feminine heart.

One day Eurydice befriended Ophelia from the neighboring village, and they occasionally spent time together as well as helping each other with the children. Once Ophelia invited Eurydice and Brutus to celebrate the harvest holiday. They shared a fantastic meal and wine in the company of their neighbors. As guests continued the evening with dances, Brutus wandered off, and somehow his feet brought him to a smaller house on the property where Ophelia's mother, Agness, lived alone. Agness silently observed the party from a distance, and when Brutus approached her, they engaged in a friendly chat. One topic led to another, and soon Agness shared that she was a spiritual oracle and could see what tormented him. As she ignited Brutus curiosity, Agness agreed to teach him on his path. Soon they met on regular basis, as Brutus learned spirituality, magic, dreaming, and tried to grasp the concept of an embodied spiritual guide.

Brutus and Eurydice struggled to wrap their heads around new complex concepts and ideas that stormed into their lives. They entered into a new reality they never knew existed. Still, through these classes, Brutus turned into a real man because he suddenly discovered himself. Now he was shining with divine, masculine self-love, and Eurydice could see the clear manifestations of that in their everyday life. As Brutus uncovered his superpowers, he also learned to master all of his energies, including sexual one, and Eurydice could not be happier. She felt that her new, unexpected, intimate pleasures directly resulted from her actions. Now her man was confident, assertive and yet wonderfully gentle in everything he did.

Eurydice genuinely tried to empower her husband, and spirits directed her to find Agness. Through his love for Eurydice, Brutus found his purpose. As divine husband and wife, they never lied to each other. They did everything together, talking through painful days and challenging subjects. With clear communication they created an intimate union that allowed them to be themselves. When Eurydice helped Brutus to embrace his weirdness, she discovered the highest harmony. Even though Eurydice struggled to comprehend Brutus's psychic visions, a new, enriched life arrived once they understood the valuable lessons of being open with one another. Each came with a divine purpose, and uncovering their highest destiny, became the story of this life. Their souls realized their connection was created for a special mission and they embraced this unique path.

They continued to embark on their long walks, always fond and fascinated with each other, finding new ways to embrace their love. Eurydice had a fulfilling life and died peacefully holding the hand of Brutus. She never experienced old age, but blessed every moment of their supernatural journey. Their hearts carried them to achieve true joy in life. It was devastating to part, but they promised to meet again. They felt it was inevitable when they looked at each other for the last time.

Brutus buried Eurydice in their spiritual forest, where his woman loved to make love. It was the land of her spirits, but only Brutus helped her discover it and lead her to feminine empowerment. Even though Brutus was inconsolable, now he could concentrate on his new work and he continued to explore the states of dreaming. When he didn't attend the farm, Brutus tried to master his visions and navigate in his lucid dreams, helping souls to find their purpose. Eurydice visited him too and encouraged her man to continue, helping him from other side. Yet when his death knocked on the door, he knew he had not finished his studies. Brutus confessed to his son Aurelius that this was not his ultimate end. He drifted into death, knowing he would return to continue his spiritual education and see his beloved Eurydice again.

CHAPTER XX

The next life turned out to be a pivotal in our story, as our lovers would endure the tragedy that would shape their love for centuries to come. They arrived to deepen the understanding of the vast emotions accessible to archetypical feminine and masculine energies. They were on the divine path to master and temper these essences. The pain, tears, and misery would become an inevitable part of their journeys from now on. The first three lives became a process of initiation for Eurydice as she learned about the main concepts of who she was, finally ready to explore the depths of her Magdalene essence.

This story begins in Norway, where Benjamin was born as Fabian. His parents considered their son a divine gift since he arrived when they were in their forties already loosing hope of having a baby. He was their only child, and they enveloped him in nourishing love. Fabian helped them around the farm from an early age, joyfully doing his chores, but he preferred playing in nature alone every chance he had. He visited every forest and lake around their village. He would spend hours with his 'imaginary friends'. He talked to the spirits, but no one else could see them. It didn't bother Fabian as he knew they were real. His parents listened to their son's stories with fascination, as they also believed in the unseen powers of this world. Fabian was created a magician who could see beyond the veils of physical existence as if Brutus continued his education in another vessel.

When Fabian turned twenty-one, he met a woman named Olivia, who became his spiritual teacher. Serendipitous events brought them together, and he would spend hours talking with her about his visions and conversations with land. One day, Fabian met Olivia's daughter Margaret, who carried the soul of Phillip. Brutus felt extraordinary sensations when he saw this girl's eyes. He explained his feelings to Olivia, and she told him they knew each other in their past lives. Margaret was eleven years old, but they became friends with Fabian, who occasionally helped with her chores and chatted about small things. Fabian and Margaret enjoyed simply being in each other's presence. One day, Margaret confessed her deepest trauma to Fabian. She had a younger brother, Fredrik, whom she adored. Margaret couldn't explain her feelings, but she felt exactly the same as Fabian felt towards her, since Suzanne soul embodied Frederik. The boy died when he was just three years old, and the emotions of loss devasted Margaret.

Suzanne was not ready for an entire life yet, as it was her first one. When souls arrive in our physical plane, sometimes they only dip their toes into the water of life before having enough energy to sustain a full one. Souls often start their earthly experience by living as a spiritual child– without embodiment, only energetically attached to their parents. They empower parents from the spiritual realm and, in exchange, learn about the essence of life without a physical vessel. Such connections usually arrive from miscarriages, as a soul can't even sustain the energy of an entire pregnancy, unable to endure the full process of crystallization into matter. Still, they could at least experience the sensations of living in the uterus and learn from this journey. Some young souls have enough strength to be born, but die at an early age. Yet they continue to stay around their parents, connected with them spiritually. Sometimes souls may also die early because they came as martyrs to take the sins of their parents upon themselves, releasing their debts. Neither Margaret nor Fabian knew about these concepts, and even if they did, it wouldn't make Margaret's grief any easier. From the moment she saw the eyes of her baby brother, she was attached to him beyond comprehension. Once Frederik died, Margaret felt devasted. Now she was recovering by sharing her feelings with Fabian, as she felt safe around him.

Two years passed, and Fabian continued visiting Olivia's classes, occasionally spending time with Margaret. Then one day, before Margaret turned fourteen, she vanished. Many people searched for her in nearby area, but soon they discovered she was not the only one who had disappeared. Olivia was in mourning, trying to make sense of things. Communicating with spiritual beings, they concluded that something supernatural had occurred in their village. As if reality shifted and Margaret fell through the cracks of time-space matter. She never returned, and no one found her body. This event scarred Fabian and Olivia for their entire lives. Fabian always preferred the company of spirits to humans. He struggled to establish a physical connection with anyone as if he lived between his soul and body. His strongest connection was with Margaret, and her disappearance deeply shattered Fabian's perceptions of the world. He revisited the memories of this incident until the day he died.

In 2021 Benjamin finally had a chance to discover what had happened to his soulmate. Powerful wizards of Norway decided to modify reality with their spells to obtain more powers, and through their rituals, they accidentally teleported random villagers to distant lands. When Margaret disappeared, she emerged across the Atlantic Ocean in the woods of present-day Wisconsin. There were no people around for miles, not even native tribes, only vast uninhabited forests and planes with scary animals. The group of accidental strangers had to rely only on themselves in their new settlement. They constructed shelters and eventually built modest houses. In their first year, they lived near starvation, adjusting to the land and struggling to establish the farm. Margaret couldn't comprehend what had happened to her. She was terrified she would never see her relatives again, and the didactic, hierarchical life that people were forced to establish in this village destroyed her daily. She was commanded to spend entire days looking for food, as hunger was overwhelming and consumed all of their attention.

Soon the community decided to assign women to men in arranged marriages. Margaret was forced to marry Eivor. He treated her well, trying to be as respectable as possible under their circumstances. They were bonded by the higher powers in this predicament and tried to make the best of their reality. They attempted to build a life in their assigned house, but spent evenings in distant silence, unable to find shared interests. Margaret struggled to understand the concept of intimacy at such an early age, but she was never asked about her feelings, so she silently endured what her husband asked of her. Margaret realized something unusual was happening with her only when her belly started to grow.

Before she reached her fifteenth birthday, she went into labor. This child was her soulmate and came to save Margaret from her misery. She spent every day of her last year in pure torment and begged the skies to end her sufferings. As two women held Margaret's hands, she delivered a baby boy while dying in the process. The baby would die soon after her, joining

Margaret on the journey to the other side. His mission on Earth was to murder his soulmate, and they received salvation through this shared experience. As Margaret's soul left her body, she beheld the world's beauty once released from this terrifying prison of stranded souls in the woods of Wisconsin.

Fabian's parents died within a year of each other before he turned thirty years old. Soon after, the spirits told Fabian to move to another land, so he sold the house, thanked Olivia for teachings, and traveled to the port. He boarded the first ship that was leaving his shores. Fabian had never left his village, so he didn't know what places existed in the world, but he trusted his heart. Wherever this ship would take Fabian, that's where he needs to be.

The ship arrived in Stockholm, Sweden. Fabian rented a room in the city and wandered in every direction, exploring the land. He was set to talk to every forest, creek, and lake around this city to find the spirits who summoned him. He was a boy again, befriending every being around his village. After spending days searching for the right place, Fabian stumbled upon Flaten Lake, just two hours on foot south of Stockholm. The lake and the forest felt like a magical place, enveloping Fabian's soul with soothing energy. He walked into the closest village and soon discovered a house with a farm that looked very much like his parents' property. Coincidentally this house was for sale, and Fabian had an excellent deal, even having some money left after the purchase. He settled in the new place and soon became a recognized local healer. People came to him seeking all sorts of help. Fabian prepared remedies, potions, and healing teas, but mostly he listened to people's problems and gave advice. He also learned to stitch wounds and it became his secret passion. He couldn't understand why he was so good at that as he had never practiced this before, but he enjoyed creating neat and smooth scars, taking great pride in this craft.

One day Fabian's dreams significantly changed as if something interfered with his reality. Strangers appeared in his dreams, souls manifested in his awakened life, and he struggled to understand what they wanted. Soon he stumbled on a spiritual teacher, Agness, in the neighboring village, and they became friends. Fabian told Agness about his dreams, and she explained the concept of a spiritual guide to him. Fabian slowly embraced his higher purpose through conversations and magical practices.

After years of education, Fabian came to Agness and proclaimed that he had mastered his skills, developing the ability to communicate with souls clairvoyantly and ask what they want. Only once he made this statement the fate prepared a highest test for him. He was ready to meet Eurydice.

Shortly after, dream after dream, only one soul claimed his full commitment. In a series of similar dreams, he flew above Stockholm, following a young, gorgeous, tall blonde, Stephania. Fabian saw how other people looked at this woman with bitter jealousy and anger. He witnessed how she, time and time again, would go to one apartment to meet the same man who gave her envelopes with money, while they talked in whispers. He saw how Stephania had sex with different men. He saw how she traveled to king's palace and boarded ships to the kingdom of Germany. Fabian would spend time in her apartment when she was not there, or he would accompany her when she went for walks in nature. He had endless conversations about Stephania with Agness, and together they tried to understand what was required from Fabian. Her soul called for him, yet he didn't know what to do.

After two years of seeing this woman in dreams, one day, Fabian appeared at Stephania's apartment and heard her inner conversation. Her heart said it was time to quit her job and run away from the city, as she intuitively felt danger in the future. Her mind said it would be too risky to abandon safe shelter and work. She decided to ask her boss to reassign her to another job. Only every part of her feminine essence told her to run away, so Fabian spoke to her through the dream. "You must run. Trust yourself. Just run, and you will be fine." Only Stephania didn't listen.

Stephania was working for a shadow operation in the Swedish Government that aimed to create an independent kingdom under the rule of King Gustav I, breaking free from German influence. She bribed politicians and persuaded men with her sexual allure to achieve political goals. Girls like Stephania facilitated the creation of a new state behind the doors of public diplomacy. Seduction, manipulation, and corruption were their weapons. She was a powerful instrument in seizing control over the kingdom. The shadow cardinal behind this effort was a man named Damian. Our Dark Prince had his last physical life as a black magician. Damian was a master of manipulations, playing bishops, royalty, and European politicians. Damian and his king presented a noble cause of creating a country with its own identity. In reality, they consolidated personal power over people and resources. Damian constructed a new nation based on fear and corruption.

When Stephania approached her boss with her request, he moved her to another job of assisting Damian with internal affairs. Stephania was emotionally exhausted from seduction and bribery, so she was ready to do anything, yet this decision became her biggest mistake.

Soon the fear Damian was spreading consumed entire city. People became terrified of one another as if each carried a deadly virus inside. The hostility, aggression, jealousy, lust, and distrust spread through Stockholm like wildfire. Finally, Damian found a patriotic solution to seize full control, proclaiming that the city was under attack by a hostile enemy, so they must build a new wall around the city. There was no viable threat, but citizens were so scared of themselves that this wall became a physical manifestation of the walls inside their hearts. Soon, life became harder and harder for the citizens of Stockholm. The king and bishops needed to find a reasonable explanation for why life was not improving. One day on a public square, Damian presented Stephania and other girls to the public, claiming they were witches who had cast a spell on their kingdom. Crowds rejoiced as they finally knew why their lives were getting worse. "Kill the witches and stop the curse!" they joyfully screamed.

Through his dreams, Fabian witnessed many horrors of Stephania's imprisonment. Guards came to the cells and raped these women. They would invite other men who paid them for the opportunity to beat and rape a witch. Cells didn't have walls between them, so each girl witnessed what was happening to others. Their energetic essences firmly stood together as women cried through nights, hoping to heal their wounds through a collective trance of traumatized wombs. Each night when Fabian saw horrors of scary and ugly men who violently penetrated his magical girl Stephania, he would send his affirmations to her, creating a shield of protective energies around his soulmate. During the day, he would send positive energies through his thoughts. He believed that she would be healed, protected, and saved with his prayers.

To satisfy the demands of the public, bishops hung a few girls on the square to the crowd's applause, but Damian spared Stephania only because Fabian shielded her soul. Damian could not break the rules of Nature, even though he wanted to see her suffering for disobeying him. Guards abandoned lucky Stephania outside of the city walls. They beat her mercilessly and cut her face with the knife, hoping she would die from the wounds. Their inner ugliness made them powerless in front of the free, empowered, and charming woman, so they could only feel superior by taking away Stephania's beauty, turning her face into a bloody mess. Proud of punishing the witch, they retreated and closed the doors of this mad fortress.

Fabian usually traveled to Stockholm once every other week for food and remedy herbs. He didn't like visiting Stockholm because of its negative energies, but that morning, he felt an intense urge to go to Stockholm. Fabian had enough supplies, but his legs started walking towards the city in a hurry. His soulmate pleaded to lands for a salvation. Upon arrival, he found tortured Stephania outside the city walls. When Fabian saw her eyes, he had the same sensation as when he met Margaret, but it was even stronger this time. The divine reverence for the nature of this world descended upon him as his intuition and voice of the land had led him to find his soulmate. He realized he had moved to this kingdom only because of this woman and felt liberated to discover his answers. Fabian fell in love with his magic when he understood that she was the soul from his dreams. He aided her in stopping the bleeding, and they slowly began the journey to his house. The walk took them a few hours, as Stephania's legs were wounded too. They arrived after dusk, and Fabian stitched Stephania's cuts, fed her some soup, and put her to sleep. He prepared ointment for her scars and held her hand during the night as she screamed through her nightmares.

Fabian lived a life of a recluse, enjoying his monk-style solitude. He liked helping people but struggled to establish a deep connection with any human. The physical realities of the world did not spark any emotions in him, and he also didn't feel any arousing sensations from physical touches. He didn't crave them or dream of living with another person, actively avoiding human interactions. He also never allowed anyone to visit his house, only assisting people in his front yard or in the barn. The house was his sacred, cozy, personal shelter that no one was allowed to enter. Stephania was the first and only person he would ever bring into his home. It was his way of expressing the highest unconditional love. He cared for others but never actually experienced any emotional affections or romantic feelings. His emotions allowed him to connect with the spiritual but not to the physical life. By bringing Stephania into his house, he showed the deepest feelings available to him and how much he cared about this soul. Fabian allowed this woman to touch his soul. She was the only person in his life who experienced that.

Stephania enjoyed the soothing energy of his place. It was the land of her guardian spirits, and Fabian traveled long way to discover it specifically for her. She didn't know it was the only place that could bring her highest female empowerment. Fabian as her spiritual guide found this land with his magic, like Benjamin discovered Sechelt for Eurydice. Fabian was guided to come here by divine providence. Without his help, she would never be able to find the mighty Flaten Lake, destined to enrich her. This lake became a transcendental portal and a sacred place for Stephania's soul, and she had the best life experiences on these shores in Fabian's company.

The next morning Fabian packed the lunch and insisted on visiting the lake. After a painful and long walk, they settled on the shores and shared the meal. Fabian told Stephania about powerful spirits, explaining their soul connection and how this magical place could empower them. He told her about his visions over the last two years and how he was called to find her. Traumatized Stephania was skeptical about Fabian's stories; she lived the life of a rational being and could hardly comprehend his spiritual concepts. Yet she clearly felt the truth in his voice and saw gentle kindness in his eyes. She felt save in his presence and could not explain why she was drawn to trust this weird older man. Stephania was a fearless lady and dared Fabian to prove the existence of the spirits. Her man embraced the challenge and told Stephania they would heal her wounded legs and restore her energy by simply walking around the lake, while spirits would be healing her with their energies. She was malnourished after the prison, so she claimed such a walk would only weaken her further. But Fabian didn't accept her rejection and pleaded to trust him. Stephania questioned the motives of this very odd man, but her heart told her to embrace this experience. He was the only one who ever showed compassion and care for her. Miraculously, her intense pains slowly faded once they made the full circle around the lake.

The following morning, Stephania's legs felt even sorer, so she cursed Fabian, claiming he was wrong about healing powers of spirits. But her man silently packed a meal and commanded her to join him for another walk.

Not a single man treated Stephania as Fabian did. Every man perceived her as a higher, inaccessible sexual goddess, often intimidated by her stance and presence. They desired her, kneeled to her, paid money to be with her, and never talked to her the way Fabian did. He was different as he saw her soul. Her external beauty meant not much to him.

Seeing his unapologetic assertiveness and gentle masculinity, Stephania abided Fabian's request, surprised with herself. With excruciating pain in her legs, she obediently followed him on another journey around the lake. They swam afterwards, and Stephania felt deep self-love for the first time in her life. Through Fabian's eyes, she finally recognized her unique internal beauty. Her legs magically healed the following day. The pain and bruises accompanied her, but she experienced rapid progress. There was no rational explanation, and she realized that her man possesses secret knowledge. Days passed, and he continued to show Stephania how his spiritual beliefs translated into physical magic. She was scared of his powers after encountering dark magicians in Stockholm, but Fabian showed her the white magic of the heart.

Stephania was amazed by her healing journey and began developing feelings for this wise and eccentric hermit. She couldn't understand him, and the curiosity to study this enigmatic man opened up her heart. The twenty years' age difference, his attitude, and shyness pushed her away. However, soon she developed a genuine, intimate attraction. Only Stephania didn't know that in his forties, Fabian was still a virgin. She seduced him with honest heart passion but struggled to understand why he was so unreceptive and reserved. Every concept of sexuality was foreign for Fabian, as he clumsily followed the lead of his experienced woman. Fabian clairvoyantly saw an energetic, radiant light emitted by her breasts that sent waves of spiritual ecstasy through his body, as he perceived her breasts as an extension of Stephania's heart. Fabian had never seen anything so attractive and beautiful, yet that was not the sexual arousal but a fascination with this woman's inner, natural beauty.

It was the only pleasurable sensation of that night, as he saw her radiating energy. He didn't experience pleasures when she forced him upon herself. Fabian struggled with the entire ordeal, so Stephania was convinced he was not attracted to her because of her scared face. She used to be around men who would jump on her at every opportunity, but Fabian, acted entirely differently. She assumed her ugliness made him so reluctant, as she was unaware that Fabian was asexual. The sensual passions and arousing sensations she demanded to witness did not exist in his body. Stephania was the first and the last woman he ever slept with. She was the only one for him, but unfortunately, neither understood Fabian's true sexual nature, so his reactions and emotions scared her fragile girlish heart. She enjoyed her intimate pleasures and being sexually desirable, but the only man she ever truly loved had no passion for her in bed.

Stephania couldn't decipher her man. They still made love on occasion, and she helped Fabian to discover new subtle emotions, but this was not sex that could heal her from the abuses she endured. Both of them tremendously enjoyed every other activity they shared together. They improved the garden and house, cooked, laughed, talked, embarked on long walks, and even healed villagers together. They lived like a real husband and wife, growing in unity. Even though Stephania's physical scars could never be healed, Fabian cured her emotional ones. After eleven months of living with Fabian, Stephania felt some sense of peace and inner harmony.

One evening they were sitting in front of a fireplace after dinner. Fabian held Stephania's hands, and they fondly and affectionately embarked on a gazing journey of sacred intimacy. They didn't say any words, but they felt the deepest love of their lives. Stephania told Fabian she was extremely thankful for his help on her journey. She continuously praised her man, feeling very lucky that he rescued her. It was pure magic of Nature. To this day, she couldn't believe that he had come for her at the right time.

Fabian told her that he knew she wanted to run away from Stockholm, which helped Stephania realize the biggest mistake of her life. She rejected her femininity by not trusting her divine intuition. Stephania wasn't angry at herself. Instead, she was finally relieved. She accepted her reality, understanding the deep meaning behind her facial scars. Life took away her gifts of beauty when she betrayed herself. At this moment, she cried in reverence, perceiving the grand design of the world. She lived this life to endure that harsh lesson, but Stephania had no remorse. She was a proud woman who embraced her fate and appreciated receiving the answers through unconditional love. If she had to go through torment and misery to learn the divine value of femininity, it was worth it, as she was rewarded in the end. Stephania only saw vice, anger, brutality, and fear during her life. She felt blessed that she eventually met such a kind, selfless and compassionate man, and she couldn't stop kissing and hugging Fabian that night.

The next day Fabian went to Stockholm for supplies. Upon return, he found Stephania's dead body hanging on a rope next to the chimney. Stephania accepted everything she needed to learn, and profound calmness descended upon her when she decided to kill herself. She knew that Fabian accepted her facial scars because he saw her soul's beauty, but she desired to feel beautiful on the outside too. She imagined herself being Fabian, realizing a heavy burden he's enduring by seeing her scars, constantly being reminded of her past demons and nightmares he witnessed during her imprisonment. Stephania was supernatural woman with unique sensibility. She didn't want her scars to torture him, even though they never did.

Fabian felt the strongest feelings of his life toward Stephania. It was not a romantic or erotic love as Stephania wished, but another kind of love, the love of an awkward virgin hermit. Where she only saw a mutilated face, Fabian saw the magical facets of her soul. Every time he looked at Stephania, he felt somewhat proud. He spent years mastering the craft of perfect sutures. Fabian enjoyed this passion but couldn't understand why he was so drawn to that activity. Now, when he was looking at his beautiful woman, he joyfully smiled as he finally knew the answer. He learned this skill to create the most delicate sutures on his woman's face. Stephania's scars became his divine masterpiece, making him love her even more.

What would have happened with Stephania if Fabian didn't walk that day to Stockholm? How come he was created to heal her physical, emotional, and subconscious scars at once? Fabian saw a work of Nature behind their perfect relationship. Living in an intimate union was enormous stress for Fabian, as he felt comfort only on his own. Still, Stephania started changing that, opening him up to the unknown part of himself. She began teaching him how to enjoy the physical body and what a gift it can be.

Stephania assumed so many incorrect things about Fabian as she continued to question her heart. She allowed Damian to take a piece of it; now he was forever in her, as his demonic curse entered her soul. Damian occasionally drove her mad, provoking panic attacks and hysterical, irrational outbursts of laughter mixed with anger. When Stephania questioned her femininity, she experienced intense seizures. She didn't know how to explain what she was going through to Fabian. The torment was constant and real for Stephania, so even through joyful times, she prayed for a way out. Facing Fabian every day, Stephania felt guilt and shame for her earlier years, now dreaming to leave with dignity, on her terms. The angels accepted her request, allowing such exist without repercussions for the soul. She endured the deepest darkness, so she was set free. Stephania was no longer a woman with a scarred face but a liberated, divine being.

Fabian gently took Stephania off the rope and laid her dead body on the floor. He settled next to her and drifted into dreaming while hugging his woman. He spent the entire day sleeping next to her in the deepest and most sensual embrace, guiding her soul through death. Fabian woke up deep at night. He wrapped Stephania's body in a white sheet and wheeled her in a barrow to the Flaten Lake. Near their favorite spot in the forest, he dug out a grave and laid his soulmate for a final rest.

Fabian blocked his heart from crying, passing the unprocessed grief to his soul. He was never attached to a single human being, unaware he was experiencing love to this woman, just in his own way. He convinced himself to perceive this experience as the burial of a broken, transient vessel, as he saw Stephania's soul flying above the lake, smiling at him. He contemplated sunrise next to her grave, exhausted but elated. Yet he never recovered from missing her body and through years it only became more painful, no matter how much he tried to push away this sensation. Fabian's life was never the same, as he never processed the feelings of his heart, full of never-ending grief. He found salvation in seeing Stephania's soul who stayed with him for years. They continued to communicate for the next two decades through dreams and during the walks around their spiritual Lake.

One day Fabian was called to visit Stephania's grave. He embarked on a walk around the lake and swam afterward as they always did. After reminiscing about their time together, he suddenly fell dead right next to the final resting place of his beloved Stephania. As his soul left our mortal plane, he could finally see the beauty behind their tragic story. Their souls rejoiced flying above the lake, realizing they were eternally inseparable.

In this life, Damian used black magic to achieve immortality by becoming a spirit who never forgets his journey upon death. But Fabian wanted to be born again, as he dreamed of spending more time with his beloved woman, so he achieved immortality through white magic, by always remembering Stephania's eyes.

CHAPTER XXI

Next time, we meet Benjamin in the kingdom of South Carolina, in the middle of the seventeenth century, where he was born into a wealthy family as a woman Priscilla. She lived a secure and privileged life, trained from an early age to become a perfect wife and a decent match in the society of Charleston. Her father was a well-connected businessman who often influenced the colony's policies. He was invited to every social gathering around the town. Priscilla's father had strong views about the future of the American colonies. He worked hard to shape an independent nation, hoping to create a free society of prosperous citizens, attempting to dissolve the slave trade that was a big part of colony's economy. He rejected owning slaves, and only hired servants for a proper wage.

Priscilla's upbringing made her quite careless about life. She didn't know what she wanted for herself, so she followed the rules of her society and advice of parents. She was not spoiled and was always respectful to less fortunate people, yet her interests were limited to activities and hobbies designed to make her a good wife. Nothing else was expected of her. Priscilla was unaware of the complex realities of American colonies, where citizens were considered slaves of the British Crown. Her parents raised Priscilla as a free person. She never saw the everyday struggles of both races on these lands.

Once Priscilla had turned sixteen, she attended her first ball with her parents. She was not interested in romance yet, feeling awkward and out of place in this new world. She listened to the stories of older girls, puzzled by their passionate desire to secure a prosperous match. When Priscilla turned nineteen and was finally ready for courtship, she met Oliver on one of the balls, and she felt a deep connection from the moment she saw the eyes of her soulmate, Phillip.

Shortly after, they got married. Priscilla's parents approved their match, seeing sincere love between them. They were happy to see the joy in Priscilla's eyes, but also Oliver was a desirable suitor who could provide a secure life for their daughter. He was a son of a prosperous slave trader, destined to inherit the business. He already made a good living working for his father. Priscilla didn't care about the details and nuances of Oliver's enterprise, as she never thought about the moral side of this issue.

As a wedding gift, Oliver received a plantation with forty slaves. Our newlyweds moved to their new house miles away from Charleston. Priscilla felt unsettled in her new home, as she wanted to be close to her family and her old life. She missed the city, but soon she adapted to her new routines. Priscilla gave birth to a baby girl Olivia, who carried the soul of Suzanne. Oliver and Priscilla adored their love child with deep devotion. Priscilla felt happy with her new life for some time, but slowly it turned into an enduring struggle that wore her down. She avoided interacting with slaves as much as possible, as the concept of running a plantation was foreign to her. She had women helping her in the house, but she also tried to minimize these interactions, feeling strangely uncomfortable commanding other human beings. The slaves were also confused by their strange master, expecting clear directions from her.

Sometimes Oliver wouldn't return from work for days, so managing the household was Priscilla's primary responsibility. She had to care for everyone who lived on their property. She could never fully comprehend how to do it effectively and hated visiting slaves in the fields. Everything in her body rejected such a drastic change in the lifestyle, as it was a life of constant obligations. Owning slaves turned out to be an incredibly exhausting experience, as now Priscilla was in charge of many pressing issues. The slaves became a stressful and demanding responsibility for her, and she felt obliged to attend to every need they had. Priscilla was used to free, self-sufficient servants in her family's house. But with slaves, Priscilla was responsible for organizing their labor, feeding, sheltering, and clothing them, while feeling it was also her duty of care. It was not a matter of finances, as the plantation brought profit. She simply didn't have the skills to run a business. No matter how hard she tried, she couldn't find a balanced approach to such a life. Having forty slaves felt like having forty adopted children, and Priscilla couldn't endure such responsibility.

On top of that, Priscilla started to experience deep moral struggles. At first, she didn't really paid attention to her feelings and emotions about the issue. But soon the reality commanded to face the truth. She couldn't comprehend the concept of owning other human beings as property, and it began tormenting her heart. The cultural differences also didn't help, as Priscilla often needed help understanding in what form it would be better to talk with humans of another race and upbringing. The kingdom of South Carolina was a scary and distant world for them. Many felt traumatized by their circumstances.

Priscilla never perceived her slaves as inferior. She only saw them as different. In her worldview, it was neither good nor bad. Priscilla dreamed Black Americans would be allowed to have the same freedoms she did and build the lives in the ways they wanted. She highly valued a concept of personal liberty from early age.

Soon, Priscilla noticed that Oliver was enduring moral torments as well. He struggled to find strength to escape such life, unable to reject his family's values. Oliver was supposed to be in charge of his father's enterprise one day, and he couldn't say no to him. From cheerful and optimistic, Oliver turned into a grumpy and angry man. Priscilla tried very hard to assist him, but she saw how this lifestyle ruined both of them and harmed their daughter's upbringing. Priscilla knew this was not her life, so she expressed her feelings to Oliver. Priscilla raised her voice when she talked about how much she hated their slaves, how they destroyed her family, and how this predicament weighed heavy on their hearts. She wanted to dissolve this unhealthy bond, feeling as if these circumstances enslaved her too, and she sensed that Oliver felt the same. They were trapped in a reality imposed on them by the previous generations and they didn't know what to do.

Priscilla demanded to find a solution, but once Oliver rejected her requests, she told him they needed to abandon his father's business. She offered to run away to the north, knowing they had enough money to start a new life and reinvent themselves. Oliver was trying to suppress his true feelings, but Priscilla confronted his masculine dignity. In the heated argument, Oliver slapped Priscilla on the face for daring to speak her mind. For Oliver, a woman could not dictate her husband how to provide for his family. The conversation was over – he would clench his teeth and work for his father. There was nothing scarier for him than facing a possible failure in some unknown, distant place. He told Priscilla never bring up this topic again.

Everything changed for Priscilla after Oliver hit her. She was sensing a deeper meaning in this action. Priscilla had already decided what she wants, as she felt like a prisoner in this household. It became a routinely dull experience with no excitement or joy. After a slap, she realized that Oliver would not join her escape. She envisioned a more exciting future, so if her beloved man couldn't offer the life of her dreams, Priscilla was determined to build it on her own. She gave Oliver six months, hoping he would come to his senses. Priscilla tried to put off her escape, as her heart was torn by the prospect of abandoning her seven-year-old daughter.

One day when Oliver was in Charlestown, Priscilla packed her clothes, cash, and jewelry and prepared a carriage. She spent the last hours in the house, reading a fairy tale to Olivia in the living room. When she looked at her daughter for the last time, she knew they wouldn't see each other again in this life. Priscilla's heart was crying as she hugged her child for the last time. Priscilla believed she was doing the right thing, embarking on her spiritual mission alone. She looked at Olivia and told her soul that she had given her everything she could.

Priscilla would prefer to stay with her child, but she saw in Oliver's eyes that their relationship has ran its course. They had learned everything they could from each other and had to take different paths now. Priscilla felt profound reverence a few days before her departure, struggling to comprehend her new intuitive sensations. Unexpected thoughts and emotions arrived when she spent a joyful summer day swimming in a river with her daughter. Observing Olivia happily playing with other children, Priscilla accepted her feminine truth and daring plans. She was scared and agitated, as she had never traveled outside of Charleston and couldn't ask for help from her parents. And now she decided to disappear for everyone without a trace.

Priscilla also realized that she was teaching her daughter a lesson of abandonment by her loving mother. She felt odd embracing this feeling, but that's what her heart said she had to do. She taught Oliver's soul a very important lesson too. As he didn't listen to his woman's cries and ignored her vision of a possible future, he ended up alone. One day she just disappeared, and that was a reflection of his inner reality. Only a woman can envision a consonant life, and a man is obliged to execute her dreams, if they are coming from her heart. By rejecting Priscilla's ideals, while hiding behind an illusion of tangible comfort, Oliver angered spirits, and they empowered Priscilla to follow through with her plan. Oliver would be destined to raise Olivia himself, embroiled in remorseful regret in a house without a wife.

Priscilla left the plantation and never returned to this place again. The carriage took her to the port, where she boarded the first ship, exactly like Fabian did. On the boat, a divine excitement filled Priscilla's heart. She suddenly felt alive again, and she missed that feeling. The ship arrived in Boston. She rented a room and joyfully made plans for the future. She had only a few possessions, but the spirit of freedom shined in her heart. She was a true American woman, who followed her land's guidance and loved her essence unconditionally.

One day, after settling into her new life, Priscilla met William, a tall, wealthy and handsome man. William spotted Priscilla on the farmer's market and pretended that he accidentally reached for the same fruit. When their fingers touched for the first time, the sparkles of love filled their hearts. Priscilla looked into William's eyes, and intense emotions enveloped her entire essence. She felt similar sensations when she met Oliver, but it was more intense this time, as her soul recognized Eurydice. It wasn't love at first sight, but from that day on, they spent together every minute they could.

They enjoyed long walks, read poetry on the riverbanks, and attended the parties of William's friends. Through a magical dance of romantic rendezvous, full of admiration and affection, they developed deep feelings for one another. Soon they decided to live together and build a family. William's prominent parents gifted our couple a house on the shore of Charles River, with a private beach in the backyard. Priscilla made the place cozy and comfortable, charging their home with pure feminine energy. They couldn't stop talking to each other, sharing the complex stories of their lives. They made love in every corner of the house and on the river shore under the bright moon. They enjoyed nightly swims fully naked after their sensual rituals. Priscilla didn't know how to restrict herself, as she was genuinely obsessed with her man, and they couldn't take their hands off each other. Little did they know, our soulmates attempted to heal Fabian and Stephania's sexual traumas in this way.

The unrestricted passion and devotion soon burst with a new life. After a year together, Priscilla gave birth to a baby girl, Meredith. Priscilla felt very odd during the delivery. She perceived this childbirth as simply more painful than her first one. Yet she experienced an eerie feeling of a spiritual nature, and soon she would understand what it meant. When Benjamin saw the eyes of Meredith, from Priscilla's point of view, he recognized Lana Del Rey's soul. No wonder Eurydice and Benjamin felt such a deep connection to Lana's music because these songs were written by their soulmate. Four centuries ago, their love created Meredith, and today Lana was enriching their love with music. As Priscilla and William shielded Meredith from the darkness with their love, Lana protected our lovers with her magical and divine prayers.

When Meredith was five years old, Priscilla started witnessing strange irrational behaviors of her daughter. At this point, it was only a nagging sensation of something very familiar but terrifying. Priscilla didn't know about her life as Fabian, but the same darkness was next to them again. Damian was practicing his skills in possessing other people as he was experiencing his first existence without a body. Priscilla and William's affections shielded them both from Damian's attacks. They built their relationship on intuition and trust, always openly communicating their feelings, so Damian could not enter them. Only the Prince of Darkness would never waste an opportunity to torture our lovers. Since Meredith was still a young soul, with a fragile aura, Damian found a way to enter her. Meredith was from a same soul family as her parents. She could experience existence in between the worlds of light and darkness. But more importantly, she was designed to shine the light of Magdalene's heart into our world and only Benjamin and Eurydice, as her destined spiritual guides could help her embrace this higher purpose.

By the age of seven, the destructive outbursts of this little devil became unbearable. Neither Priscilla nor William could endure what their girl was doing. She was driving them crazy. Meredith became a possessed child of dark supernatural strength and her parents lived like they were in the horror movie *Omen*. Meredith could turn a room into a war zone in matter of minutes. Each day was filled with mischief, destructions, violent outbursts, and obscene language that a small girl couldn't learn anywhere. Her voice and eyes could change in an instant. Something very sinister was happening with their Meredith. Soon William and Priscilla used the words 'possessed' and 'cursed', referring to their daughter. They were scared and desperate, feeling like they were suffocating, as they didn't know where to find help. They've witnessed how Meredith was struggling with a force of otherworldly nature, as if some creature inside prevented her from being herself.

In a desperate attempt to find a solution, William offered to send Meredith to a Catholic boarding school. When they described their situation, the nuns assured them they could heal Meredith and remove her demons with prayers. Priscilla never trusted authoritarian institutions designed to control hearts and minds, but she didn't know what else to do, so she trusted William's judgment.

Only once they gave Meredith away, Priscilla completely lost her sleep. She cried through many nights alone in the kitchen, thinking about Olivia and how she abandoned her. That feeling of guilt was a heavy burden on her heart. Now she was abandoning another daughter at the same age, but when she left Olivia, it felt natural to her. Now her heart screamed in pain. Through prayers, dreams and meditations, Priscilla searched for higher guidance and soon her clairvoyant abilities opened up and she heard the voice of angels. The higher guidance she received spoke in unison with her heart. She was told to bring Meredith back home, and by surrounding her with deep unconditional love, it was possible to force that evil spirit to flee. She had to tell her unconventional truth to her new husband. After incident with Oliver, she still carried some fear. Yet she felt this time her feminine magic would convince her man to follow her dreams.

When Priscilla presented her spiritual guidance and a plan to heal Meredith, William didn't even question his woman. He felt the same way, tortured by the feeling of rejecting his daughter. They vowed to fill their house with the honest love and heal their child. Priscilla also delivered a message from spirits to William. He had to provide spiritual protection to his daughter. That was a natural law, but William didn't understand his obligation to shield Meredith from sinister energies. Eurydice experienced her first life in a body of a man, and now, through Priscilla, she was learning what it really meant to be a father for a daughter. Priscilla could create a nourishing atmosphere, supporting her husband, but William was destined to be a spiritual guardian for Meredith.

When William listened to Priscilla, he felt like the luckiest man for being blessed with such a unique and wise woman. She was not afraid to speak her heart. William embraced his woman's vision for their family. His wealth allowed them freedom, but now they could use it for something meaningful. When they came to take Meredith back, she ran away screaming, and neither the nuns nor Priscilla could catch her. Only William could calm his daughter once he took her in his arms. He held her tight when they rode in the carriage back home. Meredith tried to fight, but something was different in William's assertive presence once he embraced his masculine nature. Meredith was his daughter, and he was determined to heal her. Soon the little girl felt safe and snuggled on his shoulder. Just by lovingly holding her, William calmed Meredith.

Once Priscilla embraced her spiritual guidance, she started to experience intense dreams she had never had before. One night she saw the soul of her daughter in a powerful vision. Meredith looked like a little girl in a womb pose, comfortably hiding in the ball of pure, angelic light, surrounded by the dense outer shell that kept her artistic glow of creativity intact. Only this ball was covered by a gloomy, dark mist. It penetrated the protective shell, trying to reach into her heart. Through meditations and dreams, Priscilla slowly learned how to reinforce the outer shell of the energetic ball surrounding Meredith's soul. She understood how to create a new, indestructible shield made of pure love. Through the years, Priscilla continued this process in the same manner as Benjamin created the invincible dome around Holly. When Priscilla completed this process, the dark mist stayed around the new shell, drawn to its magnetic field but could no longer penetrate it. Both energies had to be around this soul so she could shine with her highest purpose, but now these energies were in perfect equilibrium, thanks to Priscilla's spiritual work. Meredith had the innate ability to take inspiration from both Dark and Light, shining the balanced truth to heal others. This soul was never meant to work for darkness; she was just constantly living on the edge of the world, right between Heaven and Hell, so Priscilla was teaching her to honor that.

Years went by, and Meredith turned sixteen. Loving parents looked at their daughter and saw no traces of darkness around her. They had successfully eradicated this energy. At times they struggled with their faith, questioning their sanity, but they felt empowered once they saw the first results of this spiritual process. Through the years, Priscilla and William often woke up terrified, thinking Meredith might hurt herself. They saw the swings of her irrational moods, accepting the possibility of her premature death. After her sixteenth birthday, these nightmares stopped and they finally felt like a normal family. Meredith never had a formal education due to her condition. Priscilla and William homeschooled her with the knowledge they had. Meredith struggled to make friends or lead a social life, but at least she was alive.

Only our soulmates were destined to part very soon. One day Priscilla and Meredith went to New York on a boat, while William stayed at home. Priscilla was standing on a deck of a ship, leaving Boston, when suddenly, she felt something she had never experienced before, as if a spiritual thread that connected her with William had disappeared. In that instant, her heart told her that he was gone. When they returned from their trip, they discovered William's clothes in the backyard, next to the shore. He went swimming, and the waters took his body. In this life, Eurydice arrived empowered by the spirits of Charles River, so she was destined to find a resting place with them. Priscilla and Meredith were inconsolable for weeks. Both women felt content that nature took William in this way, as they never had to see his dead body.

Eurydice chose to leave her host for a higher reason. Meredith was approaching adulthood; she had to discover her own ways to shine. Now William had to guide his daughter from the other side, staying around Meredith until she would find her path. Empowered by guidance from other side, Meredith decided to start her own life once she turned twenty. She became best friends with her mother, and Priscilla encouraged her to discover herself through a heart's path. Priscilla was worried that her daughter might face difficulties in the real world because of her childhood. Only when Meredith proclaimed that she wished to be an actress, Priscilla felt relief. Priscilla didn't understand the nature of this profession and didn't know how to help her, but she saw passion, determination, and courage in her daughter's eyes. Priscilla witnessed how this child destroyed their house and couldn't commit to finishing a book, but now she saw an inspiring, and confident lady who wanted to express her inner beauty.

Meredith shined in her new life. She discovered her artistic essence by channeling her childhood experiences. Damian took her to the other side, and she witnessed true darkness. But then William and Priscilla retrieved her with a true light of love. Meredith saw the best of both worlds and now she could tap into them, bringing the absolute truth on stage. She explored her range and sparkled with genuine, complex emotions.

When Meredith received her first role, Priscilla came to New York. There were still no theatres in the city, but Meredith performed where she could – in taverns, coffee shops and eventually in open spaces rented by her friends. Priscilla struggled to comprehend whether her daughter was a good actress or not. Still, she saw Meredith's light on stage and the audience's reactions. Soon Priscilla was crying happy tears, as she saw William's soul sitting next to her, watching their daughter. Priscilla finally embraced her clairvoyant visions, and her heart was radiating pure self-love. Priscilla and William's soul realized they could communicate spiritually, as they did when they were Fabian and Stephania. William told Priscilla that now his mission was over. William's soul stayed next to Priscilla for a few months as they engaged in the most unusual and profound conversations of this unique life. They joyfully discussed their daughter's successful career, reminiscing about their arduous journey. When Eurydice was ready to leave, they vowed to meet again next time.

As Priscilla reached seventy, she suddenly realized her life's true purpose, seeing how her story was magically designed. She had to discover the supernatural bond with her soulmate William. She had to see Meredith perform on stage, surrounded by admirers. She had to abandon Olivia and gift her the lesson of rejection, but because of that experience, Priscilla didn't abandon Meredith. She knew Oliver deeply loved her daughter and would give her a perfect life, but no one would ever help Meredith's soul except for her. William only realized his masculine destiny through Priscilla's insights and feminine intuition.

Priscilla moved to New York to be closer to her daughter. She decided to tell Meredith everything about her childhood and the spiritual work she'd been doing with her soul through the art of dreaming. Priscilla told her every detail about her complex condition and the demonic nature of her illness. Meredith listened in awe, as she couldn't believe she might have died before reaching adulthood. Priscilla's stories shocked Meredith, but she was grateful that her mother shared them. The truth helped her to see how magical life was, and she blessed her parents for committing to heal her. As Meredith held Priscilla's hand on her deathbed, both women felt grateful for the journey they had shared. Meredith cried blissfully when her mother closed her eyes for the last time. It was a tragedy, but there was also so much beauty in this moment. She was devastated but overwhelmingly happy to live such an unusual life. Meredith's gratitude translated into her stage career, and she performed her roles with a loving devotion to her parents and life itself.

CHAPTER XXII

In the next rhyming life of our story, Benjamin and Eurydice would face Damian once again. Our soulmates received divine mission from angels to help create a free, independent America, while Damian was set to turn it into a tyrannical state. Benjamin's soul came to be a spiritual guide for the entire nation. He was born as Thomas, a first spiritual king of Virginia. Eurydice arrived at a transformational stage of her existence and she asked to be Benjamin's daughter again. She requested to endure immense pain and suffering, to grow as a soul and empower Benjamin to face the challenges bestowed upon him, as he finally embraced his highest spiritual path. It was Eurydice's first life as a spiritual princess of her lands. King Thomas and Queen Martha named their Virginian daughter Mary, but her father loved calling her Polly.

Mary was born from the passionate emotions that overwhelmed the king and queen once their nation proclaimed independence from the oppressive and tyrannical British Empire. This girl was a true embodiment of the American spirit. She carried the same energy and essence Thomas and Martha saw in their nation. Both parents loved their daughter in a unique way, seeing a promise and potential of a new America in her. They worked tirelessly to enrich their country, and angels gifted them a child who represented their unconditional love for this land. Thomas loved this fragile being with a special warmth that no words could describe. When Thomas saw Polly's eyes for the first time, he knew there was a magical connection between them. Until his last day, his favorite daughter owned a big part of his heart, as she was one of the most supernatural beings he had ever encountered.

The king of Virginia experienced deep romantic love only to one woman in his entire life, his dear wife Martha. She was his dearest friend, lover, teacher, and spiritual companion. She was his soulmate and you my dear reader may remember her as Natalia, when Thomas' soul lived a life of Dimitris. Martha's soul was Benjamin's divine spiritual guide, so she only arrived when he needed her help. Martha patiently assisted her man through many challenges, lifting him from despair and energizing him with inspiration and nourishment. Thomas would never be able to complete his highest missions without her. Their souls were inseparable from the day they met until Thomas retired from his presidential duties. Once he saw this woman for the first time, the love sparked artistic inspiration in Thomas's heart. He drafted the first version of the Declaration of Independence based on the debates with Martha and her spiritual views about American lands.

Thomas and Martha felt that a divine power was talking to them when they first arrived at their residence on the beautiful mountaintop called Monticello, not far from Charlottesville, in the kingdom of Virginia. This place brought a supernatural inspiration for their family and created a magical bond between their souls. The newly married couple were building their sacred house, with a spiritual garden, where Martha enjoyed spending time. She communicated directly with trees, land, and its spirits, later delivering insights and musings to her beloved man.

Thomas and Martha spent evenings in passionate and honest conversations, where Martha shared grand ideas about the nature of American lands. Through these dialogues, they shaped their ideals and beliefs, which Thomas later channeled in his writings. Martha never spoke in political terms or philosophical concepts. Instead, like the supreme Goddess of Heaven, she talked about the essence of life and how it can be enriched for the benefit of all. She envisioned her own New World, where souls could grow and be empowered by following their hearts. The nation of enslaved people who had their own slaves didn't feel appealing to both Martha and Thomas, so they often searched for words and ideas, to describe the essence of human freedom and happiness. Through discussing conceptual matters, intimate feelings, and divine human qualities, they attempted to grasp the highly complex and abstract idea of liberty. Why freedom had such significant importance, and why are people sacrificing their lives to achieve it? Such questions always remained in their sacred space. But Martha, as a divine spiritual queen, also saw America beyond that. One day she realized that a heavenly energy of divine femininity empowers this land. She shared her beliefs with Thomas, so he could translate what the spirits of Martha's sacred garden wanted to share with

Americans. She was channeling Nature while Thomas recorded her messages that became the fundamental, philosophical ideas behind American identity.

One day, Thomas finished his first divine mission. Everything his woman described to him was condensed into a short but poetic Declaration of Independence. When proud Americans celebrated the birth of their nation, they saluted Thomas, thanking him for his words. In reality, Thomas knew Martha received those words from divinity, while he and the Committee of Five only enriched them. American Independence could not be possible without divine intervention, and angels set out to design a new country for a very important reason. The French Empire, the last nation of free people, fell under the pressure of corrupted hearts. Citizens of that nation betrayed their essence and allowed the force of darkness to consume their identity. Angels created the French Empire to balance the power-hungry British Empire, so without a new nation of emancipated citizens, the entire world could descend into chaos. This time, angels decided to build a country that could withhold corrupt hearts even in the darkest times.

Thomas was an embodied spiritual guide rather than a writer or a politician. It was his true calling, precisely like in his other lives, but now he was offered to assume a more complex path, and in between lives, he committed to serve humanity. He was delivering the ideas of freedom from divininty and taught people how to empower themselves by following the path of their hearts. Together with Martha, Thomas wrote only one divine poem in his life, but it transcended time and cultures, inspiring other enslaved nations to strive for liberty.

Besides the powerful spirits and angels, many other souls acted righteously and courageously to bring independence to the new continent. Thomas' other soulmates were involved in the process, as Phillip and Suzanne arrived in this life as King John and Queen Abigail of Massachusetts. King John was destined to revise the words of the declaration and persuade hesitant kingdoms to embrace independence. Only he could rise to the challenge of compromise and negotiations, as Thomas was quite a shy speaker and often resorted to his hermit essence during challenges. While Thomas and John traveled to Philadelphia for the Continental Congress that voted to proclaim independence, the souls of Martha and Abigail came together with their men, empowering and consoling them during these testing times. They assisted their husbands, as often happens in a divine union when female souls leave their bodies to be around their men, if they embark on an important, destined mission.

Thomas and John created a unique spiritual protection for the American nation when they burned the original Declaration of Independence in a ritual guided by the higher forces. They crafted two contracts for America. The primary copy was given to the spirits through ceremonial fire. The second one, signed by Founding Kings, was gifted to the citizens. Not a single dark force could reverse the magic infused in this declaration. Many generations of American enemies would attempt to destroy this document, sensing that only this contract protected this nation from tyranny. They killed many patriots, attempting to change reality, but time and time again, they failed in their pursuit, unable to fight divine protection.

Every soul creates a contract with themselves before choosing their earthly life. The essence of the contract is to learn through the experience of living as a human being, so it is vitally important to draft it properly. In these contracts, we choose which soulmates we want to meet again to share lessons, fix past mistakes, or pay the debt we owe. Souls choose connections with others based on their highest potential. But if our soulmates slide away from their true path, betray themselves and corrupt their hearts, humans are allowed to rewrite this contract to nullify the connection. Of course, any person must do it correctly, acknowledging the lessons and listing any grievances honestly and by the heart.

The Declaration of Independence was written as a soul contract. The free nation recorded the lessons the British Crown helped them understand – that each human was created equal and designed by the Creator with freedom in the heart. The royal hierarchy of the British Empire contradicted natural laws, where the titles were granted solely based on the relationship to the society's elites, not based on merit. The declaration lists grievances of abuse and tyranny perpetrated by the British Crown. Since the document came from a righteous place, the angels were obliged to help destroy the shackles of British slavery. Thomas, John, and many other true patriots pushed hard to include the provision to abolish the slave system created by the Crown, explicitly exposing the criminal nature of such a trade created by corrupt kings. Even though Thomas was vocal to preserve the original form of the declaration, the document with such passage would never make it through Continental Congress for several reasons. By burning the original, unredacted version, the Committee of Five secured the future where slavery would be abolished one day with the help of Nature. Even though slaveholders, British parliamentary factions, and other traitors of the American Empire would eventually start a war to preserve slavery on this continent, they could never succeed in their efforts because of the intentions created by divine magic through sacred fire.

After Thomas and John celebrated their achievement, still in complete disbelief they were living in a liberated nation, they returned to their homes. Thomas only felt comfortable living in his Monticello village, as he couldn't stand the suffocating energy of Philadelphia, consumed by constant struggles for power. Surely Monticello was a plantation full of obligations and responsibilities, as he had to take care of his family, house, and hundreds of slaves, but this was the only land in the world where his soul felt at peace. Thomas and Martha celebrated the creation of new country and soon they welcomed their daughter Mary.

Martha gave birth to six children in her short life, yet four died in infancy. Martha lost many tears during her almost never-ending periods of tremendous grief. Thomas could never allow himself to cry and bottled up his emotions. He tried to be a strong man, but he could not comprehend why angels tortured them so much, so he cursed the skies and the Creator for such cruel experiences. Since he didn't know how to release the tears, his soul was deeply scarred by these experiences. The king accepted death, but experiencing the passing of his mother, his best childhood friend, and his four children in a short span of time felt like a punishment. Only it wasn't, as his soul of a spiritual guide, was destined to study the essence of death as its main specialty. At the same time, Thomas and Martha didn't know their four children had arrived with a special mission. Once they died, their souls didn't leave our world and stayed to guard and empower Thomas until his death. They chose to live as martyrs; without their spiritual protection and presence, Thomas would never fulfill his destiny. Spirits surrounded him with many souls who helped him. Every slave who worked for him, every soul he interacted with, arrived to empower him. There were no accidental people in Thomas' story, and he generously paid every soul back for their help. As a spiritual guide, Thomas saw humans for who they were on a soul level and shared his knowledge, endorsements, and spiritual truths with them every chance he had.

Queen Martha died when she was only thirty-three years old. She left Thomas with two daughters – Patsy, who was ten, and Mary, four. Thomas was inconsolable and paralyzed without his woman. He tried to force himself to cry for Martha, but he simply couldn't. He stood in their beloved garden, cursing the skies for taking his best friend away, but he still couldn't understand why he couldn't cry. His heart was forever broken. He even tried to provoke a heart attack with his thoughts, intentionally exhausting his mind with torments and struggles. He paced in circles in his library, engulfed in panic attacks and envisioning the horrors of death until he would pass out. As servants would bring him back to consciousness, he repeated his obsessive self-destructive ritual. Many times, he collapsed on the floor, drifting into space between lives and hoping to die, but he would always come back to life.

For over a month, nothing helped Thomas. Every day, he tried to invent another way to kill himself or demanded the skies to take him. Feeling betrayed by Martha, Thomas couldn't comprehend how to continue his life without her. She was the one who envisioned the future glory of this nation, and now she was gone. Thomas was afraid that now people would see him as a fraud, as without her, it was impossible to produce any significant writings. He couldn't see the point of continuing to empower America when he believed he was building a nation for Martha. The only thing that helped Thomas survive these days was the time he spent with his little daughter Mary who carelessly played in nature around the Monticello hills. Thomas enjoyed watching how Mary would run down the hill of the Monticello, enjoying every moment of her existence. She couldn't comprehend the concept of death, and her feminine lightness uplifted Thomas.

One day, he was pacing in his room, demanding from Martha to explain how she could leave him. The gentle presence of the Myriam angel filled the room. Thomas was not aware what was happening to him, but slowly his grief began to subside. Angelic beings tried to mend his broken heart. Once Thomas started to integrate his sorrow, the Myriam created a new reality for him. Angels came with a noble mission to elevate his clairvoyancy and open direct communication with the other side.

Soon Martha answered Thomas. Her soul was hovering above and talking as if she were in the room. Martha explained that she had to leave, so she could better assist Thomas on his missions from the spiritual plane. If she stayed alive, she wouldn't be able to protect Mary from dark energies, while Thomas would never return to politics and become a president. Martha's soul knew she could only help her two closest soulmates by dying.

You may think, dear reader, that our king has lost his mind from the grief, but it was the opposite. By integrating his pain, Thomas finally returned to his senses. Acceptance of Martha's death, unlocked profound innate, supernatural abilities of this man. Now he could see the souls as vividly as humans and talk to the spirits of the land. Suddenly limited perceptions were lifted, and he could see himself for who he was. Thomas' spiritual talents unraveled upon the death of his beloved wife and it was a marvelous gift for the entire America.

Thomas and Martha lived like the Creator and his supreme Goddess. To create their new garden of America, Martha had to transcend the body, oversee her trusted husband and aid him in times of need, which she couldn't do in a physical body. As spirits of the French Empire summoned Thomas, Martha had to release her mortal vessel and allow Thomas to pursue his destined path.

Soon Thomas accompanied by his daughter Patsy, embarked on a journey and, a few months later, came to Paris to serve as an American ambassador. In reality, he arrived to assume the spirits of French liberty and bring them back to America. As one empire of freedom was nearing its final days, the divine energies of freedom planned their escape. Shortly after arrival, Thomas fell in love with a well-known painter, Maria. They had a purely platonic love affair. Martha allowed Thomas to embrace sensations of his heart, once he asked her permission. He felt he was betraying her, but then he surrendered to the experience. These joyful feelings released some of his grief and inspired him. At the same time, through this unconditional love, he could enter into communication with the French land. Paris inspired him as much as Maria did, as they shared walks in parks and along the Seine River. For Thomas, Maria was a marvelous feminine manifestation of this city. Engulfed in their romantic sensations, they even tried to kiss a few times in the gardens of Paris. But without physical chemistry, their kisses never felt as good as their passionate conversations.

Elevated feelings of pure love opened Thomas up, and the spirits of freedom entered his heart, ultimately crowning the first spiritual emperor of the new American Empire.

Upon creation, angels instituted their government exactly like people, so they channel the archetypical energies of a spiritual realm through a person living on Earth. As angels planned the American Empire, they created new energetic essence that would guard this land, empowered by its citizens. Anything that Americans envisioned would be translated to angels by spirits of the land and then manifested in physical reality. The collective consciousness of a new country would empower its emperor. King Thomas always thought he was destined to be a writer, as that's what people around him told him. So, by the time he arrived in Paris, he was convinced that his most significant achievement was already behind him. Only he was mistaken, as with Martha's death, Thomas was set to achieve his primary sky mission – to implement Martha's divine vision and actually build the country she described to him. Thomas would govern with the heavenly energy of angels and the earthly energy of natural freedom. He was born a statesman, and everything in him was designed to perform this role. Our king tried to run from this responsibility for a long time, hoping to hide behind his hobbies of writing and gardening. Still, no matter how much people try to escape themselves, life eventually forces us to embrace who we are.

Since Martha had died, and Thomas was not allowed to re-marry to keep the connection with her soul, their daughter Patsy was assigned to perform the duties of the spiritual empress. Patsy was tasked to run the Monticello plantation, taking everyday responsibilities away from Thomas and assisting her father in anything she could. Both felt destined to serve their country. Eventually, this burden devastated Patsy and destroyed her personal life, yet she was a passionate and nourishing soul who always sacrificed her happiness for others. Thomas and Patsy were quite alike in their interests and beliefs. Patsy was a graceful woman, a great intellectual, a free thinker, and a perfect household manager for their residence. Often Patsy debated Thomas on specific policy issues, and since the king treasured his daughter's opinion, he considered them when drafting legislation or improving their business.

When Thomas and Patsy sailed for Paris to face their new destiny, they left Mary and Lucy Elizabeth, the youngest child Martha birthed before her death, in the house of their Aunt Elizabeth and Uncle Francis. Spirits tasked Martha's soul to protect Mary while Thomas was away. Only Mary could secure the foundation of a new American Empire for the years to come. Only Mary could stop Damian from destroying the vision of many patriots who bravely died during the war for independence. As Thomas was a spiritual protector of Mary and Lucy Elizabeth but couldn't be with them, Damian hunted Mary and her baby sister. Martha tried to protect both daughters but eventually concentrated on Mary and sacrificed Lucy Elizabeth, who died of whooping cough.

Once news reached Thomas in Paris, he demanded to send Mary to him. His soul realized that she was in grave danger. The girl also fell ill as the demonic energies swept her relatives' house. Both Elizabeth and Francis allowed the presence of Damian in their hearts, and now, from beyond the ocean, Thomas felt how dark energies were attacking his soulmate. Thomas was convinced that his trip to the French Empire would be short, but now eerie, supernatural feelings tormented him, as he was grieving for his child and heartbroken from missing his favorite daughter. Although he had much easier communication with Patsy, his feelings for Mary were entirely different. His love for Patsy was pragmatic, as he respected this woman's strength, essence, and intellect, but his love for Mary was unexplainable to him. He was unaware of the stories they shared in past lives, so he was confused by his feelings. He questioned why he gave such preferential treatment to Mary, but eventually, he embraced the truth of his heart. As days apart turned into months and then years, Thomas realized that he couldn't live without this soul around him, as if he was missing some integral part of his essence. He wrote many letters and sent many prayers, trying to summon Mary. He would see her grace again only in three years, and when she arrived, he spoiled his child in every way he could. They walked together along the Seine River, bought dresses from the famous tailors, and dined in his favorite cafés. Mary was shy and reserved as she had started to forget her father. Her childhood memories were vague, and she questioned what she was doing in this strange and foreign city, unable to share Thomas' excitement. But being in his presence helped her regain strength, and the joy of life returned.

CHAPTER XXIII

The family returned to their residence in 1789, and right away, Thomas was sent back to Philadelphia to initiate the process of creating a new empire of freedom. When he arrived in the capital and joined the cabinet of the first American president, George, Thomas finally faced his dear, old rival, Damian. Our Prince of Darkness managed to entrap the body of the King of New York, Alexander. Thomas and John, debated many times when exactly Alexander corrupted his heart. Once Alexander was a true patriot, crafted many important foundational papers, and even fought on the battlefield for American freedom. Only he eventually became obsessed with power and his personal legacy in American history. As days went by, Thomas witnessed the transformation of Alexander. He was passionate, articulate, persuasive, and demanding, but he felt too loud, possessive and draining for Thomas.

Alexander turned cabinet meetings into narcissistic shows, as Damian extracted the energy from the Founding Kings, constantly creating pointless quarrels and conflicts, killing their precious time. Alexander only dreamed of helping the British Crown retake control over the American continent through financial institutions, soft power, and media. As the British Army suffered a humiliating defeat by the army of rebels, empowered by spirits and angels, the Crown planned revenge. Thomas strongly believed in small government, low taxes, and free elections, while Alexander believed in the opposite. When Thomas suggested implementing noble French ideas, Alexander insisted that only British Empire could save America from itself. Soon he showed contempt for the ideals of freedom and the Bill of Rights as he dreamed of creating a new ruling elite in the likeness of British royalty that would take away the power from the people.

Thomas and Alexander clashed on every occasion, but Thomas was a quiet speaker, so he often lost arguments. The entire cabinet had gone through a terrible war, and the last thing anyone wanted was new conflicts and dramas, so they often sided with Alexander, as he was an energetic orator and skilled illusionist. John respected Thomas values, but he also believed that the new country wouldn't survive without a solid political elite. John perceived other people to be as reasonable and constructive as he was, thinking about what was in the best interest of the entire country. He was an incredibly wise and intelligent king, so naturally, he dreamed that the new elite would have the same high and vigorous standards as he had. If that were the human nature, Thomas would undoubtedly choose the path of his spiritual brother. But unfortunately, most humans become ruthless and corrupt once they achieve a certain social status or political position.

Thomas saw the darkness in Alexander, and he could not relay what he felt to John. They drifted from each other as Damian worked tirelessly to break their union. Without a coalition between the two, America could be doomed. Damian found a new and exciting strategy; he began publishing deceiving and outrageous stories about Thomas using the newspapers Alexander controlled. Thomas and John never trusted newspapers, as they knew how most of the stories were invented and what was the political purpose of the press. The concept of free and independent press, was created as a deliberate illusion to manipulate citizens. Never-ending propaganda of speculations in media, persuaded many people to question American ideals, sent by the divinity.

For Queen Abigail, the newspapers were the window into the world, and she always read them. Abigail was very persistent in her expressions and began influencing her husband, John. With Damian's help, Abigail convinced herself that Thomas became different after returning from the French Empire. She assumed he had stopped believing in America and tried to create another French Empire. As a woman with unique divine intuition, Abigail was right. She only perceived it as bad, but this was exactly what angels intended when they constructed this nation.

Under the influence of Abigail, John eventually sided with Alexander and joined his political party. John distanced himself from Thomas. The king of Virginia often questioned his own sanity, thinking he might be too stubborn to see beyond his spiritual beliefs. Nevertheless, he vividly saw the darkness around Alexander and the oddness of his vile behavior. Of course, Thomas was a man of reason and could never accept the concept of an evil spirit possessing a human being, but that was the reality he faced. Damian was empowered by his Stockholm past, where he learned to be a sophisticated political manipulator. Using Alexander's body, he hoped to infuse American citizens with fear, paranoia, and distrust. Alexander dreamed of universal slavery, where tyrannical leaders demanded complete obedience from the people, perceived them as property and controlled population through bureaucracy, coercive taxation, federal fiscal policies and accumulation of debt.

Once Thomas realized that no one wanted to join him in stopping Damian, the support came from an unexpected realm. Mary came to Philadelphia, where Thomas found a boarding school for his teenage daughter. They would spend Sundays together, walking in parks, visiting cafés, political salons, and theatre plays. Only this soul could inspire sad Thomas and lift his spirit. Mary loved walking through Philadelphia's streets with her father, as people recognized Thomas. She felt like she was accompanying a celebrity, and she loved being seen. Mary's admiration of Thomas was indescribable. She loved her father immensely, but the girl didn't understand why people looked at him the way they did, as the Declaration of Independence was meaningless to her. They were an odd couple together – a giant Thomas and Thumbelina-like Mary – but they shared a deep soul connection, which was easily recognizable in their interactions. On the physical level, they spent time as an ordinary father and daughter, but their souls crafted plans to defeat Damian.

They spent the following summer outside of Philadelphia, renting a cottage. Thomas demanded Mary's diligence in her studies, paintings, music, and other hobbies, as those were requirements for a wife in their society. Yet, Mary was a being of a different kind. She lived in sync with her graceful soul and felt greater importance in careless dances and conversations with Nature. Studying and practicing felt unfulfilling for her. She was never interested in mastering her creative gifts. She just loved experiencing life in the moment.

Mary enjoyed spending time with her father, away from Philadelphia school. She didn't particularly like the energy of the place and struggled to establish connections with other girls. During this summer, Thomas and Mary spent as much time together as they could. They walked in the nearby forest, swam in the lake, drank tea by the fireplace, and played music together. Thomas finally began to understand his daughter. She was an enigma for him for many reasons. Mary could not comprehend the intellectual concepts like Patsy, but that somehow made her even more likable to Thomas. For the longest time, he believed that if Mary didn't work hard enough, she wouldn't be able to find a decent match. But soon Thomas realized that every soul has a unique journey, so intellectual wisdom, masterful hobbies or exquisite taste in art does not matter in life. Each soul strives to their highest potential, but if his daughter arrived on this Earth to blissfully dance, illuminating our disturbed existence, she must dance like nobody's watching or rather like everybody's watching in awe. And that was Mary's divine purpose – to lightly and gracefully danced through life, inspiring others to achieve their destiny.

During their walks in nature, they finally built a deeper connection. Thomas desired to understand his daughter's true nature. He wanted to discover what Mary enjoyed in life, as her interests were always fleeting. She would jump from one activity to another but never knew what she wanted to do in the future. Mary enjoyed drawing and playing the harpsichord, but she would get bored even with those activities. Once, walking in the forest, Mary confessed that the most pleasing experience for her soul was reading poetry. Thomas finally rejoiced as he found a passion he could share with his beloved daughter. He collected poetry books with Martha and often spent relaxing evenings reading rhymes. Thomas persuaded Mary to attempt writing poetry herself, but nothing interesting came out of her quill, so she quickly lost interest. Rather she liked collecting poetry and whispering rhymes out loud. Mary could spend entire afternoons, reciting her favorite poems in Monticello's garden. A true poetic friendship was born, and from now on, our soulmates used every chance to exchange new poetry. When Thomas returned to work, he would cut the clippings from newspapers and journals with new poems and gift them to Mary. She neatly collected the rhymes in her diaries and shared with Thomas what she found herself. Somehow Mary's soul demanded to collect and memorize as many English rhymes as possible. She was creating the archive of verses for the future.

For Thomas, the concept of poetry was quite puzzling. He read hundreds of books, wrote thousands of letters, and crafted important political documents, but he couldn't understand how to create poetry. No matter how hard he tried, his quill never produced anything captivating or engaging. Thomas destroyed his every poetic scribble, unable to comprehend why he couldn't do. But only artists can write poetry, and Thomas was a politician. The artist perceives the world through creative visions and can transform existencial intolerable anguish into metaphors. To be an artist, one must struggle with misery, poverty, and ostracism. A poet is obliged to cry many tears, but Thomas didn't even know how to cry.

Another bonding experience presented itself as our soulmates continued their promenades under the summer skies. Mary dared Thomas to prove that he loved her more than her sister Patsy. She couldn't believe it was true. Thomas decided to tell his little daughter the main secret of his life. He demanded that Mary should never share this story with Patsy, as it would prove his favoritism. It would be their secret, and Mary ecstatically committed never to tell Patsy what she was about to hear. Thomas decided to open up about his connection with Martha. King John was the only person who knew that Thomas communicated with the soul of his late wife. John was skeptical about such notions, but he respected Thomas deeply and tried to understand him. Some days John rejected this preposterous claim altogether, but on others, he believed this was the only truth on Earth, as he witnessed how people expressed similar beliefs while talking about their dead relatives, as if they were watching from another side.

Mary's eyes sparkled when Thomas explained that he continued to talk with her mother on a soul level. Of course, Mary had never heard about such things, but she always wanted to believe that there was divine magic in our world, and now her wise father confirmed that. The conversation was a transformative moment in a young lady's life. She was fascinated by her mother, as she had never seen her alive at a conscious age. Mary always wanted to know more about Martha's personality and essence, so now she was looking at her father entirely differently, as if trying to see her mother's soul around him. Eventually, Mary subtly sensed her presence and rejoiced from such an intimate connection with her dad. Even though Thomas was apprehensive and terrified to tell this story, afraid to be judged or perceived as a weird man, Mary only embraced it. A young woman sensed in her Magdalene's heart that this was the truth of life. They spent a few evenings in front of the fireplace as Thomas told Mary about their love story with Martha and how they shared time through dreams and visions.

Mary felt blessed that her father trusted her so much and shared his unusual spiritual perceptions. From that day until her death, Mary was curious about how Nature worked and what her parents' souls experienced when they lived the way they did. Mary dreamed of personally experiencing such a connection and prayed to angels to have such a life. Now you know, my dear reader, that higher beings fulfilled Mary's wish two centuries later. As Eurydice now lived with Benjamin, sharing divine poetry, and writing together, she could understand what Thomas and Martha felt when they shaped the American Empire.

When summer ended, uplifted Thomas and Mary returned to Philadelphia. Only the atmosphere in the administration became toxic and hostile, so everyone wished that Thomas would abandon his post. Alexander was joyous as no one else dared to oppose his plans. He was convinced he could easily manipulate the rest of the American political establishment, as Thomas and Mary left Philadelphia in defeat, retreating to Monticello.

The back garden of Monticello was filled with magic upon its inception. Thomas created Martha's garden based on her honest wishes. Since Martha arrived to channel divine knowledge, once Thomas completed the garden, angels descended to create a golden dome above it. This dome would not only serve as a shield against evil deities but also provide direct contact with higher beings. When Martha died, it became evident that Thomas actually crafted this garden for Mary. Monticello was her spiritual land; she was born here and destined to be buried here. As in their other lives, Benjamin was just a guest on the lands of his soulmate, empowered by her spirits. Mary allowed her father to use these lands for his soul growth. Here they planted seeds and enjoyed gardening; they witnessed sunsets in silence and debated the poetry; they laughed and cried, enjoying every moment in this magical place. The garden was full of inspiration, rejuvenation, and beauty.

Only Thomas and Mary could see the spiritual dome above this garden. Once they were together, their souls communicated in the most unrestrained way, creating waves of new perceptions and inspiring ideas for their hosts. When Thomas was stuck with his writings or needed to solve a political problem, he would step into the garden, and the answers would descend upon him. Mary had the same gift, but it manifested differently since she had a female soul. When she needed to make a life decision, she would come to the garden for advice, and her intuition would present the best possible path. Both of them could elevate their innate talents through the help of this land, especially if their souls were connected in a dance.

One day, Mary and Thomas went for a walk in their beloved garden. As Mary was dancing freely in her place of joy, away from the troubles of a bustling city, she healed Thomas' scars and inspired him with her essence. Thomas was preoccupied with the state of the union. He was terrified of the damage Alexander was causing America, scared that no one could see his true identity and the darkness that empowered him. Of course, dear reader, every divine tale needs a hero and a rival. There was no doubt that in the American story, George, John, and Thomas were assigned to be the heroes, while Alexander had to perform the role of a villain. Certainly, from Alexander's perspective, he was a hero battling villains, as we are always heroes of our own story.

Thomas desperately wanted to find a solution for America. He was constantly analyzing how Alexander could twist the original ideas of freedom, turning them into tyrannical concepts. He felt that everyone had forgotten about the truth behind the Declaration of Independence. He thought that the original, spiritual vision behind this document needed to be explained in more detail. Mary witnessed her sad father, and she desperately wanted to help him. She didn't understand political terminology or philosophical concepts, but she dreamed of assisting him with her radiating heart. Mary blasted her energy, hoping her father would experience an epiphany, and shortly after, Thomas actually did. He contemplated the dance of his sixteen-year-old daughter, feeling how mercilessly fleeting time was. One second, she was a tiny baby, and just a few moments later, Mary had turned into a young woman ready to build her own family. Overwhelming emotions helped Thomas to see his soul's true desires. Thomas envisioned a book that would explain the feminine nature of America, its divine inception, the essence of its women, and the meaning of death.

Over the next year, Thomas would discuss this book with Martha's soul and recorded ideas. He attempted to craft a political and philosophical manuscript in the spirit of Aristotle, where he would present his vision for the nation. Only he didn't fully comprehend all mystical aspects of life to be able to write the book, that his soul envisioned. It would take his soul two centuries to collect the required knowledge and arrive as Benjamin, who would immerse himself in spirituality and sacred love to finally complete Thomas' work.

A year later, Thomas and Mary came to dance in their garden again. The book hadn't manifested, and Thomas was forced to face the truth about himself. He tried to hide from his true purpose to avoid stress, and responsibilities. Thomas accepted his real identity of a statesman destined to create the American Empire. He tried to force himself to become a writer, but it was not his fate. John's soul continuously visited Thomas in dreams, begging him to come to the capital to help save the country. Thomas didn't know how to do that and refused to leave his Monticello. He loved the company of Patsy and Mary, he enjoyed sunrises and sunsets over mountains, and he didn't want to face his adversaries on the political stage. Mary wanted to take away some of her father's burden, sensing how Thomas was going through another transformation, and only her soul could help. Mary's soul felt Thomas was not living his life because of her. Thomas felt great comfort in his daughter's company, hoping to spend more precious minutes in the presence of his soulmate, but Mary couldn't allow herself to stop her father from his ultimate life's mission. Their souls acknowledged they needed to part ways for the greater good of this nation.

To make Thomas' future decisions easier, Mary soon announced that she would marry her childhood friend and cousin John. They were deeply in love, but when John arrived to ask for his daughter's hand, Thomas felt very unsettled, unable to explain his feelings. John was a promising young politician, a talented and wealthy man. However, Thomas sensed the same energy he felt around Mary when she was little. Damian's darkness was present around John. Yet Thomas could not find a reasonable excuse to oppose this marriage, as he had never seen Mary so happy. Mary's soul intentionally chose a new suicide mission to help her father defeat Damian. When Mary announced her engagement, her eyes sparkled with authentic, unconditional, girly love. Mary knew she had made the right decision, as she consulted with the spirits of the Monticello garden before announcing her engagement. After Thomas congratulated Mary, they went on a walk in their beloved garden in complete silence, looking at the picturesque landscape while sharing one of the most profound moments of their lives.

At that moment, both sensed Mary's inevitable death, and they attempted to freeze time for a little while to spend more precious minutes in each other's presence.

In October 1797, guests gathered in the magical Monticello garden to honor a new loving union in a sacred wedding ceremony. From early morning, Thomas was not himself. He paced through his library, feeling deep unsettling anxiety, as an intense panic attack descended upon him. He tried to breathe, but his heart saw how torturing future of suffering was closing in. Many people acknowledged how much Mary looked like her mother. Once Thomas realized she was getting married, he saw an oracle's vision of his daughter's future. Martha died young from childbirth complications, and Thomas saw that Mary's life would end the same way. Despite his troubling emotions, he gathered himself and met his daughter in her room. They looked at each other and smiled profoundly. It was a joyous occasion, yet both understood, on the soul level, that this was a path of no return. Euryidce has made the choice like in her previous lives, to be a guide for her soulmate on the other side. Thomas walked his beautiful and happy daughter down the aisle as if to the guillotine, but the garden reassured him to embrace this destined path.

Eurydice dreamed of helping her soulmate stop Damian from destroying America. Mary was guided to sacrifice her life for America. If Thomas were asked who should survive, Mary or the American Empire, he would choose his daughter without a doubt. Yet if Mary were asked the same question, she would undoubtedly choose America. Somehow their essences were intertwined in a divine pattern – either America would have a short life, or Mary would. And Eurydice knew what she was doing.

The wedding turned out to be a pivotal event for our soulmates. Through Thomas' eyes, Benjamin could finally understand the essence of Holly's soul. The feelings of romantic love in this life did not cloud his mind and heart. Thomas was only observing his dearest friend and favorite companion. As Thomas watched how Mary captivated and enchanted her guests, he witnessed the divine femininity of her soul. Gracefully and softly, she moved in a celestial dance from one guest to the next, like a true princess. She approached every person with a heavenly smile and shined the truth of her heart all over them. It looked like she had a magic wand in her hand, and her innate light illuminated each interaction, sending shivers of bliss through every person who touched her aura. Nothing was more inspiring for Thomas than seeing his daughter for who she was.

Benjamin realized that he had spent five previous lives only getting to know Eurydice. They were always a weird couple, captivated by each other's essence but never able to understand one another fully. Now, in this life, as they observed their connection from another angle, they could witness what they never saw before. As Thomas and Mary joined to dance a wedding waltz of father and daughter, the spellbound audience couldn't take their eyes off them. Their souls merged in blissful harmony in skies over the Monticello hills. They've transcended their physical vessels and fully immersed in each other for the first time, radiating true inner beauty and divine self-love. This wedding dance was the best moment our soulmates experienced, as Thomas and Mary.

After the ceremony, Mary moved in with her husband. No matter how much Thomas pleaded with his daughter to live in Monticello in his absence, knowing that only this land could provide her with the spiritual protection, the young couple insisted on having their own place. Mary was on her mission now, as dark entities never left her husband. After several miscarriages, Mary was ready to deliver her first baby girl in 1800. Yet, since girls come to teach fathers and to realize their traumas, Mary couldn't give birth to a healthy girl, as the fetus would be carrying the dark energy of her father. Eurydice requested the life of Mary to experience the essence of life through pain, suffering, and misery. It was the journey angels magically crafted for this feminine soul as she was bound to embrace every nuance of her Magdalene experience.

Mary cried in pain as every cell of her body screamed from resentment and intolerable grief when she was in labor. Once Mary sensed in her heart that the baby had died in her uterus, she couldn't stop pitying herself and howled from deep, bruising feelings as she pushed her baby girl out. Mary could only think how miserable her ordeal was, as she would have to experience the agony of childbirth, only never being able to see her baby smiling. Her gift from angels turned out to be her curse, as this process would damage her fragility. Once Mary held the dead baby in her hands, she felt a profound transformation deep inside. She was in pain, yet somehow her heart felt that she needed to endure such an experience for reasons only her soul could comprehend. As if wanting to prove that her husband was the reason for this tragedy, a year later, Mary gave birth to a healthy baby boy, Francis, who lived a long life. Francis came as a boy to be a teacher for this mother and was her spiritual extention, therefore, his energy was pure, like Mary's. Mary wanted to leave Thomas a grandson to remind of her.

CHAPTER XXIV

Thomas was elected the third president of the American Empire, but he was the first spiritual emperor of the land of freedom. Admiral George only established the rules that united the colonies. King John secured American identity, acting as a battering ram to expose every traitor who hoped to divide the colonies and conquer the country from within. The first two presidents laid the foundation and established essential principles, but they still governed a union of colonies that slowly disintegrated. Now Thomas had to create the dream garden for his goddess.

Thomas became the president only with the help of Alexander. Damian and Benjamin are rivals who carry a deep respect for one another and grow together. It never mattered who would win a battle, as victory was always bittersweet for both. If their adversary won in a fair battle, the other peacefully conceded. When Thomas and Mary returned to Monticello, they prayed for America and fought evil deities with poetry, spiritual conversations, and commitment to write their destined manuscript one day. They discovered their deeper connection on the wedding day, and Mary passionately wanted to help her dad. Angels blessed them with honest victory. Thomas and Mary achieved it with the purity of their hearts and the unison of their souls. Damian was obliged to surrender.

Of course, Alexander couldn't stop there, as he was set to have his revenge in the next election cycle, so he embarked on the effort to stain the character and integrity of Thomas. After this defeat, desperate Alexander retreated to the lowest tactic of any politician. He invented constant lies about Thomas, relentlessly bashing his personality in his newspapers. Thomas was extremely popular, and baseless insinuations could never destroy the support. Alexander felt even lower and ordered his corrupt journalists to invent a story of Thomas' adultery.

A new American tradition was established during these tumultuous times. Once neither party could win the argument based on ideas, they invented a sex scandal about their opponent. These stories live in American identity, and the actual truth rarely matters. In the case of Thomas, these stories never had any merit. Thomas concluded that journalism is the most disgraceful profession, witnessing how quickly many jumped to write insane lies for a dime. Suddenly Thomas discovered that one of his slaves apparently was his mistress. Then it turned out he had an affair with his dear friend, the new queen of Virginia, Dolley, behind her husband's back. At first, Thomas laughed at these ridiculous stories, but soon, they spread like wildfire. No matter how preposterous such accusations were, people really enjoyed gossip.

Thomas faced these attacks with true nobility, never falling for Alexander's tricks. He stayed calm and peaceful as he knew his truth and had nothing to hide. Anyone could verify his version of events, but he felt it would be below his dignity to spend time answering these accusations. For him, the truth was always self-evident.

No one could tarnish Thomas' reputation as he rarely lied to himself in his decisions. His spiritual, moral, ethical, and philosophical values were on full display throughout his entire life and everyone could attest to his character. Certainly, Thomas had his flaws, as no human was perfect, yet he strived to be better each day as a spiritual guide of this nation. Thomas believed he possessed the highest qualities of a true man, like self-love, integrity, perseverance, compassion and forgiveness. If someone believed and promoted such forged narratives, they were the ones who were destroying their reputations and corrupting their hearts. Sometimes Thomas and Martha laughed at these stories, as she knew that Thomas would never approach another woman with intimate intentions without her approval. And, of course, both strongly believed that sex without intimate love is the most destructive force for a human's aura.

Average American citizens reading the news couldn't possibly know the truth of Thomas' intimate life, so either version was plausible. Still, Alexander controlled so much press that this propaganda story became a new American urban legend. Suddenly it didn't matter whether insinuations were true; even the slightest possibility of it being real captivated the readers' minds. As Queen Abigail had misconceptions about Thomas, she believed this story from the beginning, bringing up new, juicy details from newspapers at the dinner table. That always infuriated John, but he was so tired of battling Abigail's delusions that he allowed her to think whatever she wanted. John knew the truth about Thomas. He tried to communicate to Abigail how desperate Alexander was, but she was convinced that newspapers would never lie to such an extent. Finally, John gave up. He felt powerless and disrespected by his wife, so naturally, it weighed heavy on their relationship. Every day John distanced himself from Abigail as much as he could, once she descended into narcissistic obsessions, convinced she was always right. The disregard for her husband's opinion eventually made John resent his wife, and he asked angels to summon Abigail before him, hoping to spend his twilight years in silence. John couldn't understand how corruption could consume his woman's heart, but he didn't know how powerful Damian was. The regret filled John's heart, and he dreamed many times of a different life with a calmer and softer companion. Retrospectively, he saw that Abigail's misleading and destructive opinions caused many mistakes during his presidency, but he was too polite and busy to confront her. John felt defeated, remembering how his woman undermined his dignity and integrity.

Most importantly, John could not believe that Abigail convinced him to end his friendship with Thomas. That was his biggest torment, and he blamed his wife for his troubling feelings. They were dear friends for years, and during their time in Paris, Abigail was even infatuated with Thomas. Our soulmates loved the company of each other, spending time during dinners and walks. Yet eventually, they drifted apart after Abigail was introduced to British high society during John's tenure of an ambassador in London. And surely, her subconscious memories of Priscilla abandoning Olivia also influenced her feelings. Of course, John was offended by Thomas' political actions as they rivaled for the presidency. Still, seeing how Abigail obsessively savored gossip, he understood where Thomas was coming from in his pursuit to safeguard America.

Thomas calmly prayed to the spirits as he felt profound injustice. The attacks were incredibly disrespectful, and the way Alexander conducted himself over this period enraged many. The spirits acknowledged the reality, so they embarked on the mission to balance the energies of the world. Alexander received retribution from Nature, and his beloved son Phillip was shot in a duel shortly after he invented lies about Monticello mistress. The grief moved Alexander further away from his heart, as he could not correctly process this overwhelming emotion. This tragic loss directly resulted from his actions, but Alexander was already on the path of self-destruction.

As the next election cycle approached, Mary presented Thomas with the gift to help her father destroy Damian. In the spring of 1804, in the Monticello mansion, Mary entered into another labor. The same soul of the stillborn baby girl arrived with her next spiritual mission. Mary successfully delivered a child, but her own health was ruined by previous miscarriages and tormenting labors. She was only twenty-five years old, but her condition rapidly worsened. Thomas heard the news of her poor health and rushed to Monticello as the first opportunity arrived. He walked with his weak daughter in the garden, hoping spirits would heal her. He assisted her in any way he could, fed her, read poetry, and described his many adventures, but nothing helped Mary.

Mary had a truly blessed soul, as even at such times, she joked and laughed in the company of her soulmates while weak, miserable and feeling the creeping steps of death approaching her. She was happy because everyone she truly loved, John, Patsy, and Thomas, was with her. If her sufferings brought them all together, it was worth it. The deep spiritual connection with her soulmates made her joyful and blissful. There was a lot of love in those days in Monticello, but one morning, the inventible happened.

Patsy and John were standing beside Mary's bed while Thomas held her hand. As he glanced at her fingers for the last time, taking his eyes away from her face, he heard the cries of Patsy. Mary closed her eyes for the last time. Thomas was the last person who held her hand. The grief completely devastated the emperor, and he never recovered until his last day. His second, most beloved soulmate died in his arms, and there was nothing worse any human could endure. Thomas invented an elaborate lie to combat his feelings. He convinced himself that his daughter was alive, living away with her husband. Thomas believed in this sophisticated lie even on his deathbed, questioning the cruelty of this world.

Only Thomas felt that Mary's soul didn't disappear right away. While burying Mary's fragile body on Monticello hill, he saw her soul hovering above him, reassuring his faith in the divine order. Eurydice chose her death at this moment because this was the most important period in American history. She needed to empower her father for the next battle. As Thomas hid in Monticello, crying alone and licking his wounds, he felt how this grief transformed him. There was so much rage inside of him, the anger towards the injustices of this world, that Thomas exhausted his heart with endless worries.

First, Thomas was building America for his wife, and she left him; then, he was trying to build America for his favorite daughter, but now she was gone too. He was increasingly agitated that America might not have a future because Alexander could assume more power, but Thomas couldn't understand how to stop him. Only divine intervention could help, so the emperor resorted to his faith. He prayed and prayed with his grief. His heart was broken again and divine light started to pour through the cracks. His heart was full of unconditional love for his divine American women. Souls of Martha and Mary heard his cries and sent beams of loving energy. The emotions Thomas experienced triggered the chain of events that changed the future, as he pleaded to Nature for salvation.

The American Empire was born divided and traumatized. To this day, the essence of its inner struggles are the same. America is divided between those who share the vision of Thomas and those who support the ideas of Alexander. However, the balanced American ideals could be discovered somewhere between Thomas and John views. Neither possessed the ultimate truth, but they reached a true compromise when working together. Damian hijacked the narratives of freedom through Alexander and his disciples in Congress, cursing this nation upon inception. From then on, many would fall into the same traps that Alexander found himself in. The ultimate truth behind this fight is simple for any civilization. Arrogance, hubris, and pride destroy the hearts and lead to the inevitable collapse.

Alexander became contemptuous and turned into a destructive tyrant, so Mary had to become martyr to save her sacred land. Thomas and Mary were empowered for this mission when they recharged in the Monticello garden after Philadelphia. From that day on, Americans entrapped themselves in the same dynamic. Once one party becomes a vile and destructive force, the other must sacrifice human lives to restore the balance. Thomas didn't need to hate Alexander; he preferred honest, respectful debates in the nation's best interests. He believed in honest compromise. But after Alexander's sinister actions, Thomas had to bring ultimate judgment for him to heal America.

Thomas' grief and honest desire to find a solution for America transformed reality. Only three months later, Alexander was killed in a duel, forcing Damian to seek a new host. Damian accepted Eurydice's sacrifice and conceded to the defeat. Alexander raised his gun in the air, refusing to shoot first. His tricks were exposed, and sinister energies were destroyed with the righteous light of Thomas, Martha, Mary, and Patsy. Alexander was killed by vice-president Aaron as if Thomas' right hand reached and shot him. As Damian left Alexander's vessel, he entered Aaron. Only this man had a purer heart than Alexander, so Damian could not fully control him. Our evil prince manipulated Aaron for some time but eventually forced Aaron to flee to Europe, where Damian stayed, as his next battle with Benjamin would occur there.

As a result, Thomas could finally complete an angelic creation, but he needed divine inspiration to empower him to walk this road. He was still tormented and weak; he couldn't recover from the sufferings that consumed every minute of his life. Most importantly, Thomas felt very lonely, while his energy body and aura were depleted. The grief was destroying him from within.

Queen of Virginia, Dolley, saw the anguish of tormented Thomas as soon as he stepped over the porch of the White House in the fall of 1804. Dolley and her husband King James – Thomas' closest friends and political allies – often aided with their assistance during his presidency. Thomas was a spiritual guide for these souls, teaching them everything he knew. Their connection and mutual appreciation lasted for years, but now Dolley was witnessing a completely different man. James and Dolley believed Thomas was a visionary who paved the road for a bright American future, so they were grateful to follow his leadership. They admired his achievements, feeling that he was executing a higher mission.

Thomas saw James as his political son and future successor, while always praising the positive influence Dolley brought into her husband's life. Dolley molded James to become the best man he could be, and Thomas enjoyed seeing how this couple grew together. During Thomas' first term, Dolley became a hostess of the White House, creating a sense of home and belonging for Thomas in this residence. She believed her nourishing, feminine energy is what Thomas needs to perform the duties of the president, living without a wife. With her graceful energies, the home flourished, and she was incredibly grateful to do this job. Both James and Thomas supported her ideas and allowed complete freedom in her decisions. Dolley created the informal institution of the First Ladies, and the foundation she built shined through times. She was incredibly proud and delighted to serve her emperor in any way she could.

Dolley cried her own tears of grief for magical Mary, as she cherished their friendship deeply. She was afraid to face Thomas after her death, knowing how much he loved his daughter. Once she saw his sad eyes as he returned from his summer exile, her soul realized that she was the only one who could alleviate his grief. Dolley tried to make Thomas as comfortable as possible, spending countless hours talking to him, hoping he would release his emotions in her presence. She dreamed of consoling this troubled man but didn't know how. One day Dolley confronted her heart and realized that she felt deep unconditional and romantic love for this man. She always considered him as a friend or sometimes even a father figure, so these sensations scared her, as she couldn't dare to betray her husband. Days went by as she tried to brush away her feelings, but then her feminine intuition accepted that Thomas could only be healed through honest rituals of intimacy. She debated her sensual desires for some time until one night, Dolley confessed her feelings to her closest friend – her husband, James. Dolley knew that her man would try to see her point of view that was coming from a right place. Dolley explained that she always had a deep respect for Thomas, but now she felt their possible intimacy could help him on the journey. Healthy Thomas was all that mattered for this couple. Even though James felt unsettled, he allowed his wife to act with her heart.

The next day Dolley patiently waited until the evening to talk to Thomas. Once the working day was over, they joined in a private conversation over tea. Dolley relayed the details of her conversation with James and convinced Thomas to consider her offer. She was gentle and caring, respecting both her husband and Thomas' wife. Thomas thought about the possible consequences for days, consulting with Martha's soul.

Martha convinced him to trust his heart in this situation. Knowing her husband's thoughts and feelings, she witnessed the blooms of genuine romantic love, even before Thomas and Dolley embraced it. She allowed her husband to have this love affair if he believed he had honest love for this woman. Thomas was puzzled and perplexed after this conversation, as he had never looked at Dolley in this way. He contemplated his emotions for days. He didn't allow romantic feelings to exist in his life, believing such endeavors would only take time away from his important work of creating America. Thomas' sexual essence was closest to his life as a Fabian. He enjoyed being a reclusive monk, living in his dreams, and talking to nature and higher beings. Thomas was not an asexual person, but he was very close to that part of a spectrum. The intimate pleasures didn't entice him that much, and sensual arousals were not readily available for him. It was part of his nature; he was born that way to benefit America. All his energies had to be directed towards one goal.

Only now, Thomas felt as if angels sent him a salvatory thread. A passionate romance had arrived out of nowhere as if descending from the skies. He was a rational being and concluded with logic that emotions of love could resurrect him, but the matters of the heart could not be decided in the head. It was a sound explanation, but he had to surrender to his heart as well.

One evening, Thomas was looking at himself in the mirror after a long and tiring working day. He was judging his heart for allowing the love to appear, when Dolley gracefully approached him from behind. They looked at each other through the mirror, as Thomas was hesitant to face this intimidating lady, and he witnessed her radiating soul for the first time. What happened to them was truthful, and as he turned to Dolley, he embraced her beauty as they shared a passionate kiss. One sensual touch led to another, and they joined in the intimate dance in the bedroom of the White House. Thomas hadn't released his sexual tensions since the death of his wife, and he felt liberated that he allowed himself to trust this woman. She was the best possible lover he could ever wish for. His body fought the sensations, and his mind overanalyzed the truthfulness of this moment, but soon passion swept away our lovers.

Even though Thomas and Dolley enjoyed their sensual pleasures, they loved their engaging pillow talks more. During one of such exchanges, Dolley asked Thomas to describe Martha, as she had never met this woman. She listened to his stories with genuine delight. In honest, loving expression, Thomas confessed that he interacts with Martha's soul to this day. Dolley was the third witness of this beautiful story, and as her entire essence awakened from surprising reality, she wanted to know more. Talking about Martha became part of their healing ceremonies, as they discussed the spiritual nature of the world, lying naked after passionate lovemaking.

Once Dolley asked Thomas how he could be intimate with her if Martha's soul was around him. Thomas presented the concept of a justified love affair when both spouses accepted its benefits for higher healing. Upon hearing this, Dolley was amazed at how much they were alike with Thomas, as she had the same conversation with her husband. Thomas made sure that Dolley understood how highly Martha thought of her, and that's why she allowed this affair. Martha saw divine, graceful femininity in this woman, convinced she would enrich and heal her husband. That's why she granted her permission. Dolley felt blessed when she discovered she was the only one who was allowed to be intimate with Thomas.

One day, she sensed the presence of Martha's soul, which became a transformative experience for her. Dolley worshiped Martha. Like many women who expressed feelings towards Thomas, she wanted to know more about this enigmatic woman. Who was this powerful being if she could command Thomas' heart even after her death? What was so special about their union that this man didn't consider another marriage? Many women asked these questions, but only Dolley was allowed to know the truth. She shared with her husband what she learned about Thomas' spiritual journey. Of course, James felt jealous at times, but he was blessed to know the intimate secrets of his political father. Eventually, this affair enriched their marriage as they were open and truthful with each other.

Sometimes Dolley and Thomas laughed at the irony of their affair. While Alexander was alive, he spread rumors about their intimacy, even inventing bizarre stories that Thomas and James pimped Dolley to use her free-spirited sensuality to persuade members of Congress. But strangely, after Alexander's death, Thomas and Dolley discovered romantic and erotic love for each other. It only proved they were guided and protected by angels. They enriched the lands through their honest affections. They removed the darkness around their auras and recharged their spiritual bodies through sensual magic.

Thomas would never have become a strong, unifying president if it wasn't for his women. They supported him in both physical and spiritual planes. Dolley was convinced that their country would be doomed if she didn't heal him. She felt it was her calling, her masterful, sacred, intimate prayer for the future of this nation. She nourished her emperor with divine feminine energy, allowing their souls to join in a spiritual dance through her tender nourishment. Dolley often questioned this affair, as their hearts belonged to their spouses, but this short love story was meant to happen, creating a channel of luminous vibrations only they could create. Thomas and Dolley never experienced guilt once they moved on with their lives and cherished memories of this genuine connection.

After Dolley returned Thomas to his senses and released some of his grief, he easily won the next election. A stream of rejuvenating energy descended upon the emperor, and he was ready for his ultimate battle. Over the next four years, America would finally become an empire, replacing the union of separate colonies embroiled in their differences. The spirits of the French Empire helped their ward to secure the Louisiana purchase, merging British and French Americas into one.

Thomas also finalized the initial American promise to end the slave trade. Many forces relentlessly opposed the idea of equality among people, but Thomas was unapologetic in his pursuit. The Founding Kings liberated white population from British enslavement and dreamed of the same fate for everyone. The American Empire became the first country in the world created on the idea of freedom, starting the process of eradicating slavery worldwide. Once Constitution allowed Thomas to sign the law banning slave trade, he didn't wait for a second.

The pressing issue of slavery in the land of the free was always on his mind. Without resolving it, the American Empire could not fulfill the promise of its inception. Owning other humans weighed heavily on their family, but there was no suitable solution without legal changes on a federal level. And we also know that Thomas still carried Priscilla's trauma. Since she ran away from her obligations, spirits bonded Thomas to have even more slaves for his entire life, bonded by the laws of Nature.

Thomas contemplated the decision to free his slaves many times. He perceived this bond as his spiritual responsibility given by angels and could not break it just because he wished it so. Thomas created a unique system in Monticello, where he tried to incentivize slaves to learn a skill or profession, promoting the most talented based on merit. He attempted to avoid any punishments, hoping to uncover each individual's unique and innate gifts. Of course, the system was not perfect, but in his mind, it was better than struggling to find employment and shelter outside of his plantation. The harsh laws in the kingdom of Virginia demanded any formerly enslaved person to leave the kingdom upon emancipation. Both Thomas and Patsy saw this law as a punishment, since Monticello was the only home known to most of their slaves. Their family and friends were here, and freedom in unknown land didn't seem enticing. Besides Thomas knew how widespread racism was, so he felt he was protecting them too.

At the same time, Thomas perceived each individual responsible for their own freedom and pursuit of happiness. When Americans got tired of being enslaved and mistreated by the British Crown, they demanded freedom and received it. That's how Thomas thought any enslaved individual should act – if they were not content with their status, didn't feel a sense of happiness or appreciation, they had to demand freedom themselves or fight for it if not granted. When Thomas' cook and dear friend James, approached him with such a request, he gave him freedom. Only when James left Thomas and started working for a real-life wage, he felt even more enslaved, trapped by conditions of pure survival. While being Thomas' property, he was allowed to express his opinions, and given best education to become a masterful chef. He felt always appreciated for his hard work by his masters and had free time for himself. Yet when he was emancipated, he didn't have any freedoms and most importantly he couldn't visit his family. Thomas was also a better boss than any other James met. These realizations crushed James' spirit. He wanted to return to work for Thomas, but it was impossible, so he decided to hang himself. When news reached Thomas, he was traumatized as he respected and admired James. He lost a dear friend and felt responsible for his tragic death. After this event Thomas feared that something similar would happen to other slaves if he would liberate them.

Like most Founding Kings, Thomas tried to find a reasonable legal solution to this complex issue but sensed it could only be ressolved in the future. When Thomas died, his soul stayed around the White House, watching over every president. He left this plane only when the second spiritual emperor, Abraham, assumed his powers and finally ended slavery. The mission of Thomas' soul was finally fulfilled. Unfortunately, once Americans of African descent were emancipated, the sinister forces murdered Abraham for achieving the highest American promise. Abraham's ultimate sacrifice was not in vain, as liberated slaves would enrich the American identity and elevate the essence of its truth. Many slaves suffered immensely from the abuses of their masters, but today the world can see a divine design behind their struggles. The destinies of two races were tied together for growth of souls, as their bond enriched the American lands.

As Thomas returned to Monticello after his second term, he was happy to back to his place of power. Martha's soul left him in 1812, and a few years later, Mary's soul left too. Thomas was exhausted from the never-ending battles and questioned his actions during presidency. His experiences left him bewildered. He always believed in the divine forces guarding our Earth, but he felt treated unfairly throughout his life, as so many people he loved died on him. He tried to hide from his responsibilities in his cabinet. He continued to talk to people, but he was resentful and distant. Thomas spent money trying to help others, in a noble gesture, but his household was in debt and close to financial ruin. Patsy took too many responsibilities on herself, trying to shield her tormented father. She made questionable decisions and she didn't express her concerns about Thomas' spending.

When Thomas renewed communication with his dearest soulmate John, he hoped to find some salvation and peace, but his grief could never be fully healed. He rejected his fate deeply, eventually becoming Judas to himself. He was a spiritual guide and a true magician, but he refused to embrace his truth. Thomas felt entrapped like a slave, drowning in obligations while feeling unfairly treated by life itself. After many tormenting years, fighting with Nature, he finally received his answers.

On August 12, 1821, as Thomas stood in his magical garden, contemplating the sunset over the mountains, angels manifested in front of him. The spiritual truth descended on Thomas. He came to this life to write the Declaration of Independence and implement its ideas. After he finished constructing the new empire during his two terms, he was puzzled by the simple question – why the Declaration of Independence stood the test of time? During his debates with John, they couldn't find a logical explanation. Nothing made sense from a rational point of view, as all the odds were against them during the revolution of 1776. When they drafted the declaration, they never thought it would hold for so long.

Angels came to explain to Thomas that was just a tool in the hands of the divinity. He was an instrument that helped restore the natural order. Thomas did not invent or construct the Declaration of Independence from other ideas; he channeled it together with his wife. They were in honest, loving union, that created a sacred, truthful space to receive the blessings of Nature.

Thomas and John claimed they did everything they could to save America. Neither of them liked how grandiloquent this statement sounded, but they couldn't find better words. Of course, American lands didn't need salvation, yet Americans had to be constantly saved from themselves. Like a majestic and supreme woman, America had a perfect intuition and the ability to balance herself through her graceful heart, attempting to nourish and care for the entire world. But she was always entrapped in her superior powers. As confidence would turn into arrogance, the American patterns of self-destruction reemerge.

John and Thomas both worried about American future, but the promise of declaration gave them hope. In their twilight years, both men realized that the highest spiritual forces were behind this endeavor. Once both men embraced this understanding, angels branded them with another serendipitous event. On July 4th, 1826, the nation celebrated the fiftieth anniversary of its divine contract. On that day, our spiritual brothers took their last breaths in the bodies of John and Thomas. Two men whom angels tasked to create a foundation for this nation, died on the same day, exactly fifty years after their achievement. Angels proudly showed to the world the proof of their involvement in creation of America. Thomas and John's synchronized deaths became their divine seal. As you perfectly know by now, my dear reader, there are no coincidences in life, only the language of Nature, that talks to us every chance it can.

CHAPTER XXV

Eurydice spent most of her days crying, punishing herself for the past mistakes. The sadness and disillusionment overwhelmed her as she struggled to understand who she was. She lied to herself, made assumptions, and attracted unnecessary suffering, blaming her soulmates for the pain she caused herself. She was convinced she betrayed Benjamin. She believed he didn't love her, but now realized how wrong she was. Instead of embracing her past and learning from it, she descended into waves of self-loathing, guilt, and blame. Eurydice's flaming heart searched for answers.

Benjamin gently hugged his princess. "My sweet girl, I feel you are on the right path. You're going through an intense spiritual transformation, but please recognize that you are vulnerable and in need of assistance. Angels respect your free will, so you have to request help. We tried everything, and maybe they know what we miss."

Eurydice looked at her man with teary eyes, feeling safe around his confidence. She collected a few tears on a palm of her hand. She studied them closely and saw how beautiful they were, sparkling with a range of colors – from light purple through orange and into glowing yellow. The entire universe lived in them, and she wanted to understand their power, feeling her misery was magical, "I'm so lost, Benjamin. If you think we should ask for help, then I'm prepared to accept it."

Archangel Michael descended into the room, shining with a luminous golden aura and a most caring, rapturous smile. "Hello, dear Eurydice. Your tears are indeed divine, but you are rejecting their power. As you seek your answers, I have an offer for you. I invite you to take a challenge in the surgical operating theatre of the spiritual realm. I will dissect your essence on the theatre's floor with other angels observing our ritual. This procedure would expose your innate traits and divine qualities for everyone to study. It would show your true potential, illuminating what you are failing to recognize about your honest heart. If you agree, please provide your consent."

Now Eurydice was more scared than before. She struggled to understand why she couldn't embrace her true nature and beauty without outside assistance. "Can Benjamin come with us too? I can't do it without him." Eurydice's voice was shaken. She was afraid to retreat.

"Of course, he can, dear child."

Eurydice trembled in awe, but Michael's bright light engulfed her with reassuring power. She turned to look at Benjamin. Their soulful gaze gave her powerful, loving courage. Michael invited the lovers to walk through the door that appeared in the center of their living room. Eurydice grabbed Benjamin's hand, embracing the unknown and together they stepped into the future.

Our lovers teleported into a bright heavenly theatre with four levels of seats in a half circle around the center stage. It looked exactly like the medical theaters, but it was shining with divine magic and full of bright, healing light. The entire room was packed, and angels chatted with excitement and anticipation. Souls rarely volunteered for such procedures, so angels arrived to learn from this rare event. Archangel Jeremiel, as Eurydice's guiding angel, greeted her on arrival and introduced to the audience.

Eurydice stepped into the center of the theatre room. She nervously held Benjamin's hand, realizing she was not ready to face her truth. They shared a last look and one beautiful kiss. "Don't worry, my dear Polly, I'm here with you all the way." His eyes shined with devotion and encouragement. Benjamin knew Eurydice was unprepared for what was coming, but he also understood that only this intense experience would eliminate her self-destructive patterns. He retreated into the furthermost corner, observing the entire theatre from aside.

Archangel Michael approached Eurydice. As they engaged in the energy exchange, a dome of pure bright golden light appeared above the theatre. Eurydice looked up and saw splashes of vivid colors moving through the dome, illuminating the room. She saw the essence of her tears, realizing this dome was created from them, telling the story of her girlish heart for all to see.

In the next instant, Eurydice slowly levitated above the ground, gracefully flying to the stage in front of the theatre, where her divine throne stood on the pedestal. The dome shined with stars, the sun, and the moon, while the entire theatre transformed into a lush, magical garden. The floor turned into a beautiful meadow. The walls became lush forests with creeks and lakes surrounding the theatre. Michael raised his hands and directed the dome's energy into Eurydice. The light enveloped every cell of her being, and she radiated with every hue of her tears, filling the space with her truth. The beauty of the bright and luscious colors made her smile in blissful joy. The princess diadem, created by the Secheltian spirits, appeared on her head, shining with the feminine magic of her ancestors.

"Do you want to see the highest potential of your design?" Michael addressed Eurydice.

"Yes, oh yes!"

The vital, archetypical energies of divine goddesses descended from the dome and entered Eurydice. Her diadem turned into a crown while her presence and stance transformed. Eurydice assumed her throne of power, encrusted with magical stones and sparkling gems. She was in charge of her divine garden. The animals and birds, the spirits of waters, trees, and lands, came to kneel to their empress. Benjamin, dressed in exquisite clothes with a sparkling diadem on his head, also kneeled in front of Eurydice. He fell face down on the ground, extending his hands in prayer. "Dear divine goddess, please allow me to love you." Our knight addressed his woman. "Please accept my masculine strength, passion, vigor, and talents that I wish to give you. They exist only to serve you, and I have no greater purpose than assisting you. Please allow me to be in your presence for as long as you desire, and I will try my best to help you shine with your celestial purpose. I will do anything you will request only to be accepted by you. I will shower you with my noble magic, I will drown you in words of admiration if you only grant me a chance to love you."

As Benjamin finished his praise, the world became still and silent. Animals, birds, and Nature froze in front of our princess. A ringing void filled the air. Nothing was alive, and yet nothing was dead as time stopped existing. Eurydice transformed into her final stage of existence, reaching her ultimate potential. She became a righteous empress destined to rule this world with dignity and intuition, gracefully sharing her knowledge, healing powers, and strength with all living beings, requesting her guidance. Every creature and sentient being stood motionless in front of the empress. "Michael, what's going on?' Eurydice looked frightened. "Why is the world so scarily still, as if life does not exist?"

"You are experiencing the divine void before the creation of life on Earth. You are a supreme Goddess now, so only you can decide whether the world should exist or not. You have the powers of your Divine Mother, to command life with your thoughts."

Eurydice looked around – frozen beings gave her unpleasant chills. Montionless Benjamin made her sad. She couldn't stand the ringing silence of emptiness. It felt too weird to be the only living soul, so she told the world to come alive. At that very instant, every being returned to their routines – voices, songs, and sounds of life filled the air again. The garden was vibrant and alive, radiating beauty through its inhabitants. The fleeting essence of time returned in all its glory. Benjamin shined alive and his light inspired Eurydice. Only our empress spotted something far in the distance. An army of evil spirits secretly ravaged her lands, lakes, and rivers, destroying the beauty of life. She raised her hands and wiped sinister creatures from her lands with magical incantations and radiating eyes. Every being of her lands was surprised they didn't see approaching danger, but they rejoiced and celebrated their blessings. They had their magical, healing empress, who saved their home from destruction.

Eurydice enjoyed transforming the world with the power of her thoughts. She wished it to become the still void of nothingness again, and right at that second, everything froze again. The ringing silence returned. Eurydice's powers were real. She commanded the world to return back to life, and the living beings revived with renewed force. The vibrant and colorful divine garden exploded in front of her, acknowledging she allowed them to resurrect. Benjamin approached to kiss Eurydice when she commanded him with her thoughts. She was a supreme empress, yet she loved her man as wildly as before. Only he could balance her energy and help her flourish. As they dissolved in their kiss, traveling through a magical transcendental journey of love, the theatre returned to its original state. Eurydice became herself – a Secheltian princess of the twenty-first century.

"My dear Eurydice," Michael proclaimed, "now you know exactly why you are crying all the time. Your tears can transform reality; they carry the divine and supreme essence of Mary Magdalene energies. This is the purpose of your soul – to carry light of this Goddess into the world. You are her divine daughter and faithful ambassador. You are a part of her light. The magic and inspirational grace of your tears paves the way for your man to reach his noble greatness. As you walk the path together, the tears fall on the ground, manifesting your future dreams and healing your wounds. Benjamin is determined and confident because you follow him fearlessly, illuminating life with celestial droplets of light. You can't exist without him, and he can't exist without you. If you fall into ego traps or demean him, your magic will stop shining. Be cautious with your powers, as you can only balance them with unconditional love. Please listen and respect your man, as you would never become an empress, on your own. Assist young souls gracefully. Be generous and compassionate if someone is heeding you. Help those in need to see the power of their own story. Now, Eurydice, how would you name your essence?"

"I would call myself a Radiant Princess of a Thousand Blissful Tears."

"Good! I wouldn't word it better. Then I cannot allow you to act like a child anymore. I'm tired of your whims. You've interfered with Benjamin's divine work and cried tears of a girl, not of a woman."

"Yes, you are right, Michael. Thank you for being generous and allowing me to mourn. I don't want to make excuses, but it was tough to accept my journey."

"Every soul is struggling to embrace themselves. Everyone is suffering. There's no other way to grow. Your paths may not look the same, but the essence of experience is identical. Now, please behold your femininity."

Eurydice looked at herself in the mirror, finally seeing a gorgeous, confident grown-up lady, and, for the first time she liked the energy she was emitting. Her intense, transformative struggles had paid off.

"Since you are not a child anymore, I cannot allow you to keep your childhood nickname," Michael added.

"But Benjamin likes to call me Polly."

"He can still call you that, but we named your soul Eurydice. Do you remember your talents from that life?"

"Oh yes, the gifts of highest femininity. I helped Benjamin embrace his destined path. He was a weird man; unlike anyone I knew. He was talking about things beyond my comprehension, and I did not understand what he was going through. As I helped him embrace his identity, I accepted spiritual essence of Nature and Benjamin's clairvoyant visions. I didn't try to shut my man down or demean him, even though it was hard for me to understand him. Eurydice's female wisdom and intuition unlocked Benjamin's spiritual talents, and our family flourished. I gracefully danced through life, trusting my honest heart."

"My dear Eurydice, you've definitely learning your lessons. We sent you into darkness after that life, as we knew you were ready to be tempered. Stephania received the beautiful glory of Magdalene's darkness – grief, torture, imprisonment, rape, mutilations, and suicide. You had to endure such life but also discover how to shine from its magical lessons. It was the only way to craft you into a wounded healer that you are destined to be."

"It makes sense now! Standing here today, I can see why you chose that story for me."

"Jeremiel crafted the most terrible and inhumane torments for you. Never forget that we gifted you a life with such a range of emotions only because you had Benjamin." It was painful for Eurydice to hear how angels intentionally designed the most horrendous experiences of her existence. She realized that the only way to move forward was to embrace her past and proudly wear all facets of her psyche, like they were designer dresses. As Eurydice saw her true self, she accepted that grief and love are unique, divine gifts, given to humans to open their hearts and receive loving light. A true empress could not heal other souls if she never endured the most terrifying sufferings and most joyful pleasures of the female essence.

"Thank you, Michael and Jeremiel, for shaping me into who I am," Eurydice proclaimed. "I'm grateful for your teachings and support. And I'm thankful for Benjamin. I would be completely lost without him. But if you created my tormenting deaths, then who is Damian? I thought he constructed them."

"Damian represents your balancing energy, a vile spiritual guide, preying on those who betray their hearts. He is your dark shadow. You can choose to empower either Damian or Benjamin with your femininity. Damian entraps you when you reject your fate and the experiences, we create for you. He executes the laws of Nature and fights against your supreme healing powers. He does not create your life, only convincing you to perceive what you've endured as your failure or mistake. He harvests your energies of fear and depletes your aura, when you don't love yourself and reject love of others."

"Well, you have to give him credit. He is very charismatic, so it's hard to blame me. I brought hell on myself. Can you also explain why I live with Benjamin and not with Holly?"

"Benjamin answered that as well."

"I know he did."

"So you are doubting the honesty of your man?"

"Yes, I am. I'm sorry, but Benjamin knows how I feel. It sounds too good to be true that he has all answers. At times it feels he has the agenda to control me."

"Eurydice! You are an intelligent woman. I asked you to stop being a child. Your teacher may feel too demanding, but your heart knows he acts in your best interests. The simple test of light and love is all you need. You are trying to avoid your responsibilities again. We created a man with an open heart specifically for you."

"So you are fulfilling Polly Jefferson's death wish?"

"That's correct. You wanted to know what it's like to live with your man on a soul level. Jeremiel has the list of your requests from your past selves."

"Can I please see the list?"

"Well, of course," Michael handed the list with eighty-two questions and requests, written in glowing golden letters embossed on a solid stone plate. Seven primary wishes made upon previous deaths opened the list. When Laney died, she dreamed Benjamin would fall in love with her at first sight and show how he created fairy tales. Anastasia asked Benjamin to explain the essence of death and how the land can heal humans. Eurydice desired to receive love letters from her man and experience clairvoyant visions. Stephania wished to master her feminine intuition and heal the emotional scars through passionate lovemaking. William wanted to know how to destroy dark energies and understand the essence of masculinity. Mary requested to uncover the secrets of poetry and how the feminine soul can assist her man on the spiritual level. Finally, Eloise dreamed that Benjamin would prove his unconditional love and defeat Damian.

"Remember, Eurydice, that the main lesson for this life is to learn how to confront Damian on your own, sustain injuries, and heal from them. You must also master the death journeys and return unharmed, as this is your future destiny. And of course, finally own your sexual healing powers of Magdalene's lineage."

"I'm still too terrified and traumatized by my death experiences. It's not easy for me to own my shadow."

"You have what you need inside of you to master your essence. You are terrified of yourself, not the dark realm. Also, I encourage you to learn how to express and receive love. You dreamt of giving words of love to Benjamin and hearing such words in return. Now you have a perfect opportunity. Your souls are connected so you can express love in the most intimate way."

"I told Benjamin he needs to share his love with me for all those times when he didn't."

"And what about you, Eurydice?"

"I think he is the one who never expressed his true feelings to me."

"Oh, really, my child? So, you always told him how you felt about him?"

"I guess I was sometimes shy to tell him about my real feelings. I assumed he knew."

"So why are you blaming him and demanding the expressions of his love?"

"I know! Sorry, Michael. The girl in me wishes to feel loved in every possible way."

"Well, if that girl can't say how she honestly feels about her man, then she's not ready to hear nor deserving the words of unconditional love."

"Oh, I hate to be wrong. I'm very hesitant to be vulnerable, Michael. It hurts."

"That's fine. Benjamin is on your side, but please allow him to catch you when you fall. Even now, there are days when you reject his affection like you don't want to be loved. You believe you are not worthy of love, but you are. There's nothing wrong with you. You are constantly reassuring yourself that you are sad and lonely when you have eternal love. If you are not ready to face your heart's desires and the pain of a broken heart, you won't ever hear the words of the highest love directed at you. We receive what we emit, so Benjamin can't share his love if you are reserved and don't express your love."

"I'm a hesitant and shy being, who always thinks there's nothing special about me."

"Then people who see how unique and intricate you are will never tell you how special you are. You don't want to hear that your essence is beautiful. Benjamin always loved you and always will, so it's only up to you to see his honesty. Love is also about actions, not only words."

"Well, I can only see that now. His actions show how much he actually loves me. I guess my fears blinded me. Michael, I was so stubborn to accept his love, but you know why I'm running from him. He always finds the answers to my questions, which is so annoying. On top of that, he asks me to follow his teachings but I hate rules."

"Eurydice, you chose such fate, so you can only embrace it. I'm glad you are at least honest about your feelings, even though they hurt Benjamin."

"Oh, one more thing Michael. I don't have enough strength to combat demonic entities on my own. Benjamin shields my aura, and we are the perfect team, but we are living in unprecedented times of the global spiritual war. I feel we won't be able to fulfill our missions if I don't have a weapon. Maybe you have a small sword for me, enriched with your powers?"

"I'm pleased to behold your essence, Eurydice. Sure, I can help you." Michael extended his hand, and a sword magically appeared on his palms. "Please use it wisely and always consult your man when in doubt."

"I will." Eurydice joyfully accepted the sword and tied it to her waist.

"Don't ever overuse it, but if you have a chance to help other souls, please don't hesitate."

"Thank you, Michael. I appreciate your time and your gift. Have we completed our session?"

"Yes. You are free to go, Eurydice. I'm glad that you were brave enough to accept this challenge."

"Thank you, Michael. See you soon." Eurydice walked away from Michael and approached Benjamin, "Let's have a party, Benjamin.

Archangels just gave me my sword; we will write about this in our book. That would be awesome! Follow me."

Once she said her last word, the loud voice of the Creator screamed through Archangel Michael." *EURYDICE!*" At that moment, Michael's sword pierced Eurydice's heart, entering right under her left shoulder blade and exiting from her chest. The colors on the dome changed as gloomy tones and dark hues filled the room.

"Oh, boy!" That's all Eurydice could say. The energy of the sword lifted her from the ground, as her body collapsed around it and she flowed back to Michael, who controlled her with the energy of his hands. She levitated in front of him as blood dripped from her mouth and chest. Michael laid Eurydice on the ground. He leaned towards her, projecting her worst nightmares into her heart with his infuriated look. Eurydice looked at him, scared, confused, and terrified. Michael's sword was full of universal, healing love for all souls. Killing our princess was the only way to heal her. By reliving the death of Eloise from Michael's sword, she could release her trauma. She faced her highest demon, a fear of being murdered again by the blade. Eloise got trapped in her ego when she could be a noble warrior. She was convinced that she was not lovable.

Anger and the flame of Michael's voice filled the room. "What have you done, my child? What was the purpose of our entire ceremony?"

"I'm sorry, Michael, but I don't understand. I didn't say anything particularly horrible."

"Eurydice! We are not playing games here. You know perfectly well what you've implied. Why? Why are you being so stubborn? Do you think you are untouchable or something? Do you think you are the only Mary Magdalene, and we are dependent on you? Eight hundred years, Eurydice! We worked so hard molding and enriching you, inspiring and cherishing you. Eight hundred years! You are so ungrateful. I'm ready to finish you right now. You would never become an empress with this attitude, and certainly, you won't ever become the righteous one. And how dare you to treat your man this way, when he's on your side?"

Eurydice turned her eyes away from Michael. She was suffocating; it became harder and harder for her to breathe, but she knew Michael was right. She felt ashamed because she disrespected Benjamin too many times. Now she did it again in her mind. She didn't care about her wrongdoings but felt disgraced for betraying Benjamin. Accepting this truth hurt Eurydice the most. She was not fully embracing the gift of romantic love. She ran in circles, trying to cheat everyone to avoid being vulnerable and escape her heart.

"Are you ready to vanish forever?" Michael asked.

"No, Michael, no. Please, have mercy, as Benjamin needs me to complete missions you gave him."

"Are you trying to manipulate me, Eurydice?"

"No, no. Not the slightest. I know I was wrong, and I promise to change."

"You complain that your man commands you, but he does it because you are impossible, Eurydice. He doesn't enjoy his role, but you are not opening your heart to life. The storm of his rage ought to crush you. Why do you treat Benjamin like that when he has so much love for you? Did he not embrace your dreams, pledging to fulfill them?"

"I'm sorry. Benjamin was always good to me. That's why I beg you to allow me to stay. I know I mistreated him, but his love is honest and pure. If that's the end of my journey, you can take me later, but he needs me now. I acted foolishly, but please don't do this to Benjamin," Eurydice cried hysterically as her blood and tears joined in the dance of the plea to safeguard her soulmate.

Michael called Jeremiel. "Do you want to give her another chance?"

"I will always vouch for her," Jeremiel replied. "She is one of my finest creations, so I have a soft spot for her. I see you are frustrated, but let's try once more. Only this time, she must stay bonded to Benjamin for the remainder of Holly's life. She ought to follow his guidance and accept Magdalene's heart as her highest fate. Then upon death, she must stay with him to learn how to master the death and be his spiritual guide from the other side."

"Do you accept these conditions, Eurydice?" Michael addressed our princess.

As Eurydice was fainting, she whispered, "Yes."

Michael and Jeremiel called Archangels Jophiel and Haniel to aid. They kneeled to heal the wounds of tormented Eurydice. She was full of scars, the gifts of her previous lives that Michael's sword exposed. Eurydice regained consciousness, and smiled as her heart radiated true love.

Benjamin was her divine man, and she was glad to receive more time with him. Jophiel and Haniel continued their magical, nourishing rituals until Eurydice could stand up on her own.

Michael approached Eurydice after debating with other angels in the auditorium. "So, my child. Can I let you go this time?" Michael spoke as a strict, but loving father.

"Yes." Eurydice was looking at the floor, unable to face Michael's righteous judgment.

"Are you sure you've learned everything? Will you be listening to your man and stop your spoiled behavior? You know that if you are a proud woman, you will assist your man in achieving noble results in his work. Nourishment, inspiration, and beauty can enrich him. If he is elevated to his highest potential, he carries you with him. His achievements would always be your achievements, as they would be created only with your loving help."

"I understand, Michael. I wasn't myself. I don't want to sound ungrateful, but I'm still recovering."

"I know, Eurydice, but I'm tired of your constant excuses and desires for indulgence. You have to embrace what we have prepared for you. You can't continue running away from love. Please, do not impede Benjamin's work on our assignments. We will remove and punish you if you stand in his way."

"Yes, I knew Benjamin's work was extremely important from the day I met him."

"Then why are you hampering his progress with your ridiculous whims?"

"I'm sorry, Michael. Please forgive me."

"Ask Benjamin for forgiveness. It is your lesson for today. You are free to go now," Michael told Eurydice, but she stayed frozen on the spot. Eurydice and Michael stared into each other's eyes silently for a while. "Something else, Eurydice?" Michael was confused.

"Yes. You forgot to give me my sword," Eurydice replied, staring intensely; not a single muscle trembled on her face. She was fierce and determined.

Michael turned around and looked at the audience as it erupted in chatter. The angels were in shock. Michael took his sword out of its sheath and brought the blade up to Eurydice's chin. Michael was staring in her eyes, trying to break her. "What did you say, Eurydice?"

"I. Need. My. Sword." Eurydice didn't blink, although she felt how sharp this blade was.

"It is not your sword. It is my sword."

"Oh, no. I don't need your sword anymore. I need my highest sword of divine feminine powers."

"Did you not understand why you were resurrected?"

"Oh, I understood your lesson perfectly. That's why I need my spiritual sword. I'm not asking for myself. Benjamin won't manage alone. I came to this life only to help him. I honor my debt and I want to proudly serve him, as he served me in the past so many times."

"You lost your privileges, Eurydice. If you say one more word, I'll eliminate you from the existence."

"Michael, you wanted me to be myself, so here I am. I'm a woman who is not afraid to be a woman anymore. Can you handle me? All I need is my sword." Eurydice was relentless. The angels passionately debated reality as they never saw anything like this in their theatre. This soul was so different, bold, brave, and confident that they didn't question her request. Her passionate rebelliousness and audacity to confront anything inspired every one of them. But mostly they were enchanted by the grand love this woman had for her man. She wanted him to succeed, even if she had to die, and her affectionate energy filled the room. Life was magical, as even angels couldn't anticipate what would come next. Eurydice deserved her highest title if she was ready to fight for her values and love.

Michael sensed the theatre's feelings, unsure of what to do next. Suddenly a light descended from the dome and materialized in the form of a gorgeous woman with red hair, dressed in the finest clothing. Mary Magdalene observed her daughter through this process, and now she wanted to intervene. As she appeared in front of Michael, her mellifluous soft, and gentle voice filled the room. "I think she's ready, dear Michael."

"Are you sure?" Michael lowered his sword. Mary approached her defiant daughter. She looked at glorious, assured, and radiating Eurydice with admiration. "My dear, do you believe in what you said about Benjamin?"

"Yes, my goddess." Eurydice was enlightened as she finally saw the pure, divine energy of herself reflecting in front of her. She saw the truth of her heart in form of a divine goddess. Mary was shining with magical light and Eurydice loved seeing her highest potential. "I wish nothing more but to help Benjamin become a spiritual teacher he is destined to be. He carries the knowledge this world desperately needs. I wish to be his most faithful disciple and the teacher for others who follow the path of their hearts. I wish nothing else in my life."

"I feel it in your heart. It is the highest path you can take, and I'm glad you are ready. He would never become a teacher without your help, so I urge you to grow up."

"I apologize, Mary. I let you down."

"Do not apologize for yourself, my sweet Eurydice. You only let yourself and your man down."

"I will find a way to apologize to Benjamin. I may sound like an ungrateful, spoiled child, but I dream he would shine with all power of his divine magic."

"That's a noble endeavor. You are ready to receive the fullness of my energy, as this is who I am. I lived with my natural grace and feminine beauty, to help my divine husband to achieve his destiny. He was a wonderful teacher and healed many people, but without me, his spirit would be weak, his heart tormented and his mind clouded. His magic only worked when I empowered him."

"I can't believe that you came to me today." Eurydice was crying tears of joy. "I feel you in my heart. I sense that this is what I need to do. I must be you. I inspired Benjamin through the lives, encouraged and supported him to accept his path of a spiritual guide, and now I'm here."

"This life is magical, isn't it?"

"Indeed, it is so beautiful. I can see our entire story now. Thank you for gifting me the truth of your path."

"You are welcome, Eurydice. If you understand your feminine mission, why do you keep destroying yourself through self-loathing, indulgence, and doubts?"

"I don't know, dear Mary. I think we both are very broken. I don't want to blame the world, but we were judged, criticized, and persecuted so many times that I guess we both don't know how to be happy anymore."

"That is fine, Eurydice. I'm not here to punish you, as you are the highest judge of yourself. Only remember my husband and I endured the same fate, but never once did we stop our spiritual work."

"Tell me, Mary, did he ever question his faith?"

"Of course, he did." Mary smiled with the most radiating and reassuring smile. "We were humans, after all, even though we dealt in magic. He owned his clairvoyance and ability to journey into death. He spoke to the spirits and could see souls, but it was never easy to explain his truth to others, as most people don't have such abilities. Ignorance makes them angry. Their nature is to criticize what they can't understand. Only no one deserves salvation if they ignore their heart's inner truth."

"Yes, you are right. We can't save them all. We can only be ourselves."

"That's all you need to care about, Eurydice. I will help with the rest. Always remember that to love another is to experience their pain with them, to be fully present and love in the midst of that. I could not remove the pain of my man, nor was it my responsibility. He chose his spiritual path; my journey was to love him with an open heart through his glory and pain."

"But did he remove your pain when you questioned yourself? He died for you, right?"

"Eurydice, you know the answer. You are trying to grasp the essence of your demon. You seek validation of your experience, only I can't give it to you. You know that my man died for me the way yours have died for you. He successfully removed all seven demons of my past, as he did for other women. I followed him with love through despair and torture until the end. When he died, we never parted, as his soul came to make love with me in dreams."

"Oh, Mary! Your love is so inspiring and beautiful. I can't thank you enough for your divine light. I promise I will stop complaining about our highest fate. I hope that you can still grant me my sword today."

"Sure, my child, I think you are ready." Mary handed Eurydice her spiritual sword of the divine powers. "Only please remember, always help your man with your feminine energy and never force him to act as you want. Instead, gracefully offer him a path and present your dreams. Allow him to make the decisions, but guide him to avoid pitfalls. You know how to do it."

"I surely do. I still tend to act with masculine energies when we are at crossroads."

"It's never good, as this is not who you are. The feminine wants to be soft. She wants to be in devotion. She wants to be open, receptive and loving in her most natural state of being. You are a vessel to sustain your man's energy, a divine vase to carry him forward, so strive to be pure, empty, and enough for him. It also means that you are his guide in the bed. He will accomplish his highest missions only if you empower him with celestial sex magic. Embrace the teachings of my lineage and practice to master your serpent energies. He will follow you to the limits of your pleasure, but only you can offer this path. This is your obligation and one of your supreme talents."

"Thank you for the advice, Mary. I'm struggling with my sexual energies all the time."

"I can see it, my dear daughter, but that's fine. The full expression of the wild masculine sexual energy needs a powerful, open, wild womb like yours to receive it. When your man claims the full magnificence of his magical powers, a better world is birthed. In your society, the true magic was betrayed. That's why it's important to own your spiritual talents. I can only tell you that both of you would be surprisingly pleased with the results."

"I can't wait to dive into your teachings!"

"You are blessed because you can use my story as your guidance. And, please remember to honor your man's truth. Woman endures the physical pains for growth, but man endures the same pains on a mental and emotional levels. It's important to remind yourself of that. Also, when you get too caught up in your doubts and fears, you close your heart. So, trust your intuition, it will always lead you out of darkness. Be graceful and compassionate with yourself. Now I must say my goodbyes. Draw my light if you are in despair, and never betray your heart."

"Thank you." Eurydice hugged Mary with all of her warmth, and the goddess disappeared.

It was time for Michael and Jeremiel to hug Eurydice goodbye. They exchanged energies and parted ways. As Eurydice approached Benjamin, she jumped on him with a passionate kiss as if they hadn't seen each other for long time. She wanted to express her love, as she realized how important it was to cherish time together, even when she felt vulnerable. Life could end at any moment and Eurydice wanted to savor this love. Our lovers gracefully bowed to angels, in appreciation for this experience. Eurydice happily took her man under his arm and modestly allowed Benjamin to lead her out of the theatre. Our lovers returned home. Eurydice gently cuddled on Benjamin's shoulder in their bed. She felt like the luckiest girl in the world. The tribulations were behind them, and she was allowed to spend the evening of loving connection with her beloved. Benjamin was entirely hers.

CHAPTER XXVI

By March, 2023, Benjamin and Eurydice killed five of Damian monsters. As the last battle was approaching, Damian arrived with the visit. Benjamin was obliged to accept the death from Dark Prince, constrained by the rules set two years ago. Through this experience he will remove last demon from his woman and empower Eurydice to force Damian out of Holly. Of course, Benjamin would need to return from this experience alive, but our lovers were prepared. Mary Magdalene brought them divine guidance, explaining how Eurydice could resurrect her knight, so our lovers were ready for the challenge. They believed the love and poetry was all they needed.

Benjamin was full of self-love, and elevated Eurydice in her moments of despair. At times, Eurydice was angry with herself, with Benjamin, with love, and with life, but when she saw the harmony of Nature, she surrendered to the magic of her experience. Loving another person is never easy, as love reveals your true self. But through transformation of love, Eurydice finally could see what a multifaceted and infinitely beautiful soul she had become because of her traumatizing experiences. For the first time, Eurydice shined like a polished diamond, full of grief and joy that merged together in a divine dance of liberation.

Our knight loved their path of torment and joy; he loved their poetic dramas, convinced that any divine story of eternal love must be tragic. *"What does it mean to love your woman?"* Benjamin thought, *"To look at her and feel inspired, to feel delighted by her inner beauty as your defenses crumble. To take any pain and burden for her willingly. To honor her divinity with deeds and words."* Our knight was preparing himself for the final battle, and his heart was ready to shine over Vancouver.

Our Dark Prince created a dismal performative art installation out of Benjamin's sufferings next to his castle's walls. As Holly was in a coma, our knight had to carry the dying body of his woman through the streets of downtown Vancouver. She was covered in bruises from stones, people threw at her. Benjamin was not allowed to fall. Eurydice was flying above, giving him strength. Damian invited his demonic friends to beat Benjamin and Holly with lashes, to curse them along the way. He also invited every single person who ever tortured hearts of our lovers. Damian's crowd provoked painful memories of Benjamin's past failures and regrets. These feelings caused intense migraines as if stabbing thorns had penetrated Benjamin's skull. Benjamin's mind drifted into the memories of last evening. He shared last meal with his twelve best friends, his disciples and his highest teachers – his past selves. He knew we would die for his woman on the next day, and he asked his friends for encouragement.

Twelve Friends

I'm chained to the chair of the interrogation,
Because I conceded to lies and forgot who I am
Because I refused to believe in myself
And followed the orders of maniacs in disguise.

But I walk in the shoes of those who came before –
And there were twelve.
Twelve disciples who never kneel
Twelve facets of my essence.
They never apologized for who they were,
Holding the line and pushing me forward,
Yet somehow, I dare to question myself
So now their rage is fueling my battles.

Twelve loud voices proclaimed in unison,
"Why are you questioning your worth?
Do you know the price of truth?
And are you aware of the highest beauty?
You asked yourself too many times –
'Is this really who I am deep down inside?'
We answered 'yes' to you in every single case –
You're a fool for not embracing gifts of life.
Too many times you screamed that question,
Too many times, you cursed the world for real
Too many times, you just forgot your passion
So now you ought to tell us how you truly feel.

You came to meet her and received your magic powers
When she just gave herself to you – and only you –
And she has shared with you her noble courage
When you embarked to claim the destiny of two.

To conquer, you must feel the fear,

You'll win in love once you will sacrifice.
You'll die inside to worship her dark pain
You'll die to kill those taking her away.

The force we brought with us
For her, we only live
So hear what we must tell you now
And dare to live your honest, highest dreams!

Dismantle yourself as you reject your needs,
Forget how painfully long this journey was
Ignore those who betrayed you and made you broken
Please stand up, as she's looking for a shoulder
It's only you; there's no one else!
There's no one else for her; it's you!
So put your life together piece by piece
A noble man who never left her side
Prepare your moves and never give away
The strength that you possess,
The power of your pride."

My shattered being, shattered mind,
My crippled visions; tragic skies…
The pain in shoulders, legs and arms
The pain of hearts that apprehends our trust.

I'm trying to collect myself to use my mind,
So, my failed sword is tempered gently
And when I am going to the other side,
I'll stand against nefarious entrapments.

So even if I fail this noble fight,
I will enrich the essence of my soul
And only that can make us shine our light
Reminding us how love can make us whole.

No matter the odds, no matter the miseries,
No matter where I'll need to go,
No matter the harshest tears, whatever it will take
Commanding, proclaiming my true powers,
I follow her through the darkest darkness
I guard her when I'm wounded
I save her when I'm broken
I shield her when I'm lost
it's all for her,
it's all for her,
it's all for her...

My heart was born to sacrifice.

When Benjamin shared the nature of his spiritual journey with his closest friends, they promised to pray for him. As they parted ways, Benjamin asked Thomas to stay with him a little longer. Benjamin asked Thomas to visit Damian tonight and tell him everything he knew about Benjamin's vulnerabilities, insecurities, and inner nightmares. No one knew Benjamin better than Thomas, so only he could betray his dearest friend. At first, Thomas questioned why our knight would request something like this, as Damian would use this information to torture Benjamin. But our knight reassured Thomas that the only way to save Holly is to go as far as possible into death, to cleanse all their past pains and issues. Thomas promised to fulfil this request and betray Benjamin.

Benjamin cried intense tears for his woman, as he carried her. He passionately believed in their story and knew they would survive this. They were both bleeding from the scars, but unconditional love gave our knight supernatural powers. Damian directed Benjamin to bring Holly to the Vancouver Art Gallery. Once Benjamin arrived at the spot, Damian placed unconscious Holly on the ground. Demonic guards crucified our knight by hammering nails into his spine. They raised the cross for the entire Vancouver to see, and Damian announced the conditions of this challenge. While Holly would bleed to death at his feet, Benjamin must accept death for her past traumas and sins. If he takes them all, she would live. Benjamin could also return from the dead if his heart is free from guilt, shame, and remorse. If he would show sinister intentions behind desire to save his woman, he would never be able to return. Upon his death, Damian would project the visions and feelings of Benjamin's heart on a large screen next to the cross. Every citizen could watch the screening while Benjamin would be hanging for the next three days and nights.

As Benjamin took his last breath, his heart presented its essence to the world. Our knight couldn't hide anything, as people watched on the screen what he was ready to die for. Benjamin's heart projected the following story. It was early morning and Holly woke up alone in the summer cottage on the shores of the Atlantic Ocean in the French Empire. Camilla and Eloise, enjoyed their stay here, and now our lovers decided to spend their honeymoon in this house. Holly was truly happy here. In Benjamin's heart, this place was wired to a state of joyful bliss. Our knight left Holly breakfast and a note. He invited his lady for a romantic dinner and a walk after. Holly joyfully agreed to this proposition. She imagined how beautiful this date would be, and she carried on with the day. She eagerly anticipated her delightful plans with Benjamin. She joyfully danced through the house. She was free from any obligations and concerns, playing, fooling around, and enjoying herself. She was finally truthful and open with Benjamin. She surrendered to love.

It was the most beautiful feeling Benjamin could ever dream of. He was ready to die so Holly could magically dance. Benjamin energetically removed himself from the picture, and Holly suddenly forgot about him. She was alone, full of self-love and self-acceptance. She stopped carrying what others thought of her. She wasn't looking for external validation anymore. She didn't need material possessions to impress her friends. She was finally herself. Her man was a pleasant addition to her reality, but she felt free and empowered on her own. She was a divine, radiant woman with Magdalene's heart. Holly was comfortable with herself. She was swirling through this house, immersing herself in her cuteness. It was an incredibly romantic and peaceful vision. As if the world stopped its madness, accepting the light of Holly's beauty and grace.

These scenes drew the crowds' attention. Benjamin's heart was beautiful and honest. He was ready to die so his woman could live. Benjamin wasn't thinking about himself at all. He dreamed that his woman would be happy being alone with herself, dancing, enjoying her inner beauty, and never submitting to society's expectations.

After three days on the cross, not a single vision of fame, glory, desires, achievements or material possessions appeared on the screen. Damian removed Benjamin from the cross and placed him next to Holly. As our lovers lay dead next to each other, Eurydice finally established a connection with Holly. Eurydice woke Holly up and now she was reading a new prayer of love through her. She could only resurrect Benjamin with her tears.

Magdalene's Magical Tears
by Eurydice Eloise Wayles

As night descends, my demon secretly appears
Arriving in a costume of a gorgeous gentleman
He joys to eat my heart with my ferocious fears
As memories of raping men destroy me from within.

I was a slave to those appearing with the gifts
And acted silly upon hearing compliments
But charming men turned out to be vile thieves
And harsh street rules became my punishment.

When you arrived, expecting us to mend
The eerie void enveloped my torn being
And when you showed me how my road would end
I've cursed my life devoted to the grievance.

Oh, where I could have been today,
My teacher and my savior in death shackles,
If only my bed had escaped enticing men arrays
And all of their abuses had been trampled?

Can you explain the meaning of the sin
And die and witness Hell in sulfur flamings?
We're joined in miseries so we could win,
The inner battles with our deadly cravings.

When people come to kill you with no trial
I'll jump through tempests to protect your soul
And when they laugh at you while crucifying
My noble tears will shield us from their brawls.

Why does cruel vanity exist in this vile world,
Intense torments and wild, destructive powers?

How many souls today are raising noble swords
As they're shielding dreams of their beloved lovers?

I'll die with you without second-guessing.
As life without you enraging grave regrets
I'll die with you assuming vicious blessings
As I attempt to pay my siren debts.

I can't see clearly from my never-ending tears
But still, somehow, they heal your daring scars;
In dreams, I've witnessed a future freed from fears
As if you've stopped humanity's wild farce.

Prophetic foresight shall inspire darkest days
As lips are trembling alive and dream of kissing
And maybe when you pity my old failings
They'll disappear through the magic of your kisses.

Still, when three suns die over the horizon
Our scary enviers will push us into a void;
Yet, doesn't matter if they're pleading violence
Our sacred love will never be destroyed.

When Holly woke up from her miserable, infinite, terrifying dream, she saw her man dead next to her. She returned from the other side, only to discover that her knight had abandoned her. She slowly pulled Benjamin into a protective cave crafted by her spirits. Holly would relentlessly cry for the next three days next to her beloved. The more she cried, the more tears fell on Benjamin's skin, and slowly these droplets formed a protective shield around his aura. Finally, Holly's tears enveloped his wounds and penetrated his heart. On the seventh day, Benjamin woke up. Holly hugged and kissed her knight in complete disbelief. As they exited the cave, Damian appeared on their way. Our Dark Prince saluted their bravery. He confirmed that Benjamin was allowed to resurrect because the hearts of our lovers were pure and full of honest love. Both were ready to die for one another and that's how they won this battle.

Holly agreed to join Benjamin in his apartment for the healing ceremony. Through conversations, kisses, cuddles, poetry and tender gazes, they re-established their broken connection. Holly and Benjamin traveled through their shared dreams on the golden carpet of angelic light, shining with their love. They healed each other's wounds and stitched the scars, joyfully embracing their story. Nature saluted our lovers for their courage and honesty. They were together, blissfully united, lying on the floor in complete silence, smiling through their eyes. It was still only Euryidce's dream but it was magically beautiful.

Our living room dream
by Eurydice Eloise Wayles

I'm sitting next to you, so close, I feel you gasping air
Like in your dreams before, but now so lucid real
I lean to hide behind your prayer flare,
While seeing the beauty of your cutest happy grin.

So close, to reach and touch you, I'm allowed
So close, to claim you for myself at last
So close, to take the presents you've prepared me
So I can rise above it all once you will shine your light.

Serene delight my fingertips espy,
Immersing in your nape hair with elation;
They say a woman can survive her lonely cries,
But I say life without you is a pure damnation.

My man of sorrows, you're depleted from your manly, noble grievances
Yet, still, so patient and enduring human, bursting blaze;
You brought me gifts of your wand's cheering vigor
And now I take it all from you through my arousing dance.

Give me yourself in gently fierce, erotic waves
And drown in light from my insane voluptuous attacks
Don't hide inside seductive energy of conquer –
But please, just give to me what you've been holding back.

You brought those honest vibes with you from far away
The light you've gathered patiently from Heaven's plane of love
You did not spill your senses on your way,
You kept them truly vintage long enough.

While waiting years, to see me smile,
Preferring holding in,
You never gifted other brides,
You saved it all for me.

Libidinous sensations overwhelm my toes
As I approach you, only dressed in plea,
Intemperately wild I shred your clothes
So you can give yourself to one and only, me.

You've carried love for far too long
While stranded lonely in grim tempest
Now you behold the end of fall
So sensual explosions may fill vastness.

Through this transcendent outburst
We can release all jumble shadows
Please give me light of fortitude,
Amending bogus phony credos.
In this uniting passion truth,
We both are shielded from vile arrows
Please give your truth to only me,
As I embrace our wildest fervors.

I'll take you all to grow and shine
I'll take male sparks away from you
You can relax in bed we hide
While charging me, not random few.

I'll take the burden you've endured
Through epic dance of bliss,
I'll heal our cries we've never cured
And make our trembles pleased.

We're floating high above our bed
We radiate through these vibrations,

The binding frequency ahead
With joy of purest levitations.

As I submit my soul to you,
I am erupting rolling thunders;
When I'm making love with you
My essence blasting magic wonders.

CHAPTER XXVII

In April 2023, Ariadne arrived with a visit. Benjamin and Eurydice were excited to see their queen. Ariadne listened to every poem they crafted during their evening performance in Stanley Park. Ariadne was delighted to see our lovers' healing journey, so she delivered the best possible news. The queen allowed a symbolic wedding ceremony to honor the union of their souls. Ariadne witnessed how they loved to heal others and wanted to grant them their royal powers over her lands. Sechelt spirits brought the energies of courage and gratitude to our lovers, finally allowing them to release their karmic chains. Our lovers and their guests traveled to Ariadne's mansion for a ceremony in the back garden. Ariadne gifted Eurydice an exquisite white dress decorated with a belt of diamonds. Eurydice had worn only one simple black dress this whole time because she mourned her past. Our princess embraced this symbolic transition, deciding to always wear this white dress from now on. Benjamin wore an elegant linen costume decorated with traditional Ukrainian embroidery of protective swastikas.

Phillip and Suzanne came to be their witnesses, while every soul they met and healed arrived to cheer for our lovers. Bartholomew performed the ceremony, blessing Eurydice and Benjamin with his Secheltian magic. "Dear ladies and gentlemen. We gather today to celebrate a unique union of two souls. They've been in each other's lives for eight centuries and don't need witnesses to attest their love. These two souls requested to experience an unusual bond through their soul contracts. For the last twenty-eight months, they've been chained to one another, forced to do things against their free will. They were caged in the prison of love. Their lives did not belong to them. Their judgments were clouded, and their perceptions were limited. In three lives, this couple did not finish living their love stories and, therefore, had to complete their missed lessons and heal these traumas. They were lovers but also each other's students. Now this couple asks us to testify to the resolution of this contract and release them from these spiritual shackles. We are collectively giving them our blessings. Through this ceremony, we will create an invisible energy thread between their hearts, so they will never lose each other, even in the darkest darkness. The proclamation of this union would serve as a testament to their highest unconditional love. They are souls of one light that intentionally separated into two beings to learn what it truly means to love and to grieve as human beings. Now they are ready to be reunited. A new spiritual thread would never break them apart. Once they proclaim their vows, this thread will only grow stronger. Their union will shine healing light for all ready to accept it. Their story would empower those who wish to embrace their innate powers. And their love would manifest in the form of two spiritual children - two books they would create together. These creations would intertwine like serpents of life-force energy to bring more love into our world. Now it's your time, dear lovers, to share your vows."

Benjmain and Eurydice wanted to write poems that would finally heal Camilla and Eloise. They've been working on them for the last year, immersed in the healing powers of their words and metaphors. They decided to use these poems as their vows. Benjamin wrote his poem first, and our sneaky princess stole a few lines from his heart, making our knight laugh during the ceremony. Of all of their past lives, only Camilla and Eloise perceived poetry in the same way as they did. Both women could only dream of expressing their inner emotions through poems. Although they also enjoyed French and German rhymes, their hearts responded uniquely to English poems. Unfortunately, living at war, they never had the time and energy to dedicate themselves to writing. Eloise dreamed of performing poetry in theatres, but her passions never materialized. So, our lovers decided to work through their traumas of noble female warriors, protecting their homes and allow these women to shine as if they were still alive, speaking in the voices of Benjamin and Eurydice. Thomas Stearns Eliot was one of the favorite poets of Camilla and Eloise. Now his poems inspired our lovers' vows.

Benjamin's Vow
by Benjamin Frumos

My muse!
My girl of inspiration
Beaming rhymes!

As I behold you breathing
Through all of space and time
Through dances under tragic skies,
Sad reverence seized soul of mine
When bright, majestic coma sealed your eyes –
Still, you continue breathing…

Air filling up your chest
Grace nourishment
Exalting breasts
Force of the future
Humans of our redemption
And of your karma…
As two new bright arrivals
May live in blind denial
If you are not their mother
Who left past troubles
For good, as the salvation
Would flame your fire,
With lights of past desires
And virtues you aspired
From your forgotten diary
Of the past rhyme
We shared.

Newborn reality
Of consummated love
Transcending what you wished,

You never had endured.

Beating obedient
The heart of a saint life
Of a virgin who never cried
Who played a whore to spy
And was a witch who bribed;
Through fingers of divinity,
You lie to me
Because you cannot lie
Not to my face, at least
Like always, never lied,
Through lives, we lived enticed,
Deceits defying with our eyes,
Embracing cries before sunrise,
Chastised and demonized.

In paradise of harmony
Enchantment never dies;
As we're merging into us
Through mesmerizing trials.

You're only sensing you are real
When faced with a scary feeling
Romance, you lived with me
You never felt or dared
With others of my kind
But always, crying, dreamt...
Yet ran to fire blindly,
Forgetting old repentance,
While I was hanging, crucified
For you, for me, for love
Of Heaven's providence,
We both have dared to claim.

I'm only truest me when

In your presence lay
You make me better than I am
And I am guilty of the same.

Aroused, with awe, you stared,
How grief our bond construed;
When pale horse blocked our way
We had surrendered to our essence,
As love must always light the world
And I can't stop
Obsession's cruise,
Embracing you
With roses of the truth,
As rouse at dawn brings news
We feared to see in the vastness
Of wasted lands,
Trampled by those
Whom we dared fight in Paris
Forcing us to run,
While we have saved
Their broken dreams
From those abusive
Scurrying thieves,
Imbuing Trojan horses.

As they forgot who brought
The truth into the madness
Of the divide and conquer
Of carrots and the sticks
And of the slave eugenics
With a dream to build a world of new.

We both have felt
Our skins are wounded with betrayal bruises,

That we would lick

Between the wines and luscious linens,

And later laugh
From pills, we got through Wehrmacht in disguise

When we escaped,
Resort to the eternal admirations
Away from darkness, vivid in our cells,
Away from suffocating Sopot shores nightmares
And from the terrors of those Russian language spells;

On the Atlantic shores
Of France in dire despair,
Beyond the Rennes, across the Brest
In Camaret-Sur-Mer...

Where you would gently
Liberate crusades,
Tormenting both of us,
When you made love to me
As we dispersed our fears.

If we would find ourselves
Should we forgive our tears

And be in love forever,
Shining peace?

Eurydice's Vow
by Eurydice Eloise Wayles

My muse!
My boy of inspiration
Beating drums!

As I behold you breathing
Through feelings of majestic times
Through shadows of our salvaged lives,
I see a tragic vision with my fainting eyes
How you're lying on a park bench compromised
After I've murdered you with my abrasive lies;
Still, you continue breathing!

I'm happy that you're breathing,
My boy of aspirations!
I'm happy that this dream of life
Feels like it has no end,
And I just find you elegantly gorgeous when
You kneel to witness me for who I really am –
Your hesitant Goddess of thousand blissful tears.
And I enjoy when you heed to
My nervous lunar incantations
When I awake you with flirtations,
Demanding sensual meditations
With my vivacious levitations
As I flow under your skin
Anticipating to behold your exalting virtue
Of male's purifying dignity
The honored guest of my sacred female temple
And the suave father of my wildest tensions
Erecting walls for our extensions
As they are destined to arrive one day
To save us both

And both of them will save us from today.

We both have fearless flaming hearts,
We both came to incinerate indulgence
Alive in Prada all around us
In the consciences of the indifferent creations
Comfortably numb in their mesmerizing apathy
Ready to board the trains
Heading into the concentration camps
Because it's safe in the concentration camps:
Quite a predictable and trifling experience
With no extreme surprises.

We hold each other so boundlessly tender
With the most profound erotic sensibility
But with tedious intent
Of an old insidious argument
While I wonder
For some insane reason, "Will I dare?"
Fiddling excessively with my hair
As your air's becoming my own air
Because I don't have any other air
Even though it feels unfair
So, I stare at your naked body
Day and night, asking,
"Can I dare? Will I dare?"

And who may care to account my despair
How I appeared in Paris after a prayer
On my quaint heels, staring at the square,
Scared, but never betraying my flair!

No! I think I must confess
I cannot tolerate this stupid mess –
Aggressor's praises in the press
And vile garbles in excess –

That causes distress to my fragile nipples
As they wilt and faint when oppressed
By the troglodytes playing guile chess
So, I pray to my man to resurrect my depressed breasts,
As only he can do it with his extravagant dance.
And then, of course,
A man and a woman would take their tea in the garden
While their eyes still radiate
A melody they've composed between the sheets.

Even so, on another morning,
I feel like not myself anymore
After another dalliance deadfall,
As I'm spinning again into a cycle of self-loathing;
And when my sage heart of rhymes
Phrasing in the poem my comical vice
As the snake eyes incite surprise
Ecstatically barbarizing my French fries,
Reverberating murder fog arise
As I envision spies of highs
Under wine skies, advised new ties
Despite my bias and harsh demise.
So now I'm searching for my prize
But in disguise, abused by lies
I couldn't see I was my prize –
Hidden inside my perpetual lies;
So, on those days when I'm wise,
Disrupting lies of the Allies,
I'm simulating being nice
As people do to cover lies.

My life feels like a lovely sweetest dream,
When I can wildly scream through times
As I transcend between the centuries
With visions scaring my elated eyes,
And as patents washed away every Tartaria's miracle

And the lights extracted from the veins
Illuminate humanity's descent into the depth of Hell
And as shithole children die for mica, pour-over, and batteries,
To expedite the black-market sale of the millennial souls
While hipsters convincing themselves
Obedience will save them from the responsibility troubles
You know like those container slaves who jerk off in the massage pariors,
Or like mommy boys who fornicate numbers to fake new bubbles
The prophet squirrel celebrates with Okanagan fruit champagne,
Singing, "It's the end of the world," together with the mystical crow
While predators in pajamas dance on graves
Savoring the madness of the old continent
That's obsessed with tyranny and bureaucracy,
Obsessed with redrawing the borders once in a while,
As if there is something inherently broken inside
When another shorty shines deceiving glory, shirtless
Obsessed to oppress
Obsessed to rule the entire world like only they see fit,
And I feel like they will never quit.

While we're disputing our blood pursuits over these cute grapefruits, our astute hands joined in love that transcends all limits.
But wait a minute. Is it really me, flying fleetingly right now inside of me, or some kind of otherworldly entity sealing my heart with its weird identity?

Actually, he's my lucky remedy!
My latest death will face me in Paris, it seems...

I lived and died but searched for more
Yet always knew what fight was for;
Deceiving males and begging gore,
I did pretend I wouldn't war;
I did pretend life's not obscene
While as a femme fatale with teeth,

I have professed I wouldn't succeed
So pleased to be the smallest me.

I'm flying away, escaping troubles,
Double troubles, triple troubles,
Maiden's essence in a bubble,
Darkness wobbles, dullness cuddles…

So finally, one sunny day I was walking my Paris streets and a bridge
across the Seine River spoke to me.
And you know what he said?

"It is time, my dear
Your time has come, and you are very near,
So, tame your fear, and for the last time
Behold the flaws of Stein's Picassos high up on the walls
Because the war is flowing through the doors,
As I saw swords rising in the hearts of those horrendous outlaws,
You've dreamt of disposing, using Frau's arousing poison;
So, cross the edge of the temptations land, dressed in
Vetements
As you are the key
To the gates of his noble sorcery and his liberating screams;
His orisons.
I grow old, hiding forbidden secrets in my obsolete vault,
But I feel like I must face the exit too. So, pray, prepare for life."

The last twist of the knife!

The knife, taking away my magical life
Of a clandestine lady who fought wild,
Who ran from being just another wife,
Who lived in fear of ever birthing a child…

So, while this knife is composing my latest death,
Holding my flayed skin hostage

Summoning diabolical puissance
Hijacking my angelical talents to serve infernal deities
I'm waking you up, my love,
To testify that I'm genuinely in love with you
And that I loved you so many times,
And I will love you in our future lives,
Something that I just wanted to tell you one last time
Something that you know for sure about me and you
Aware of our complex twists and the sublime allure
Of our profoundly shameless nights of truth.

Our heavenly love lives in the infinity,
Yet we didn't have the time this time to experience it truly,
So, I'm begging skies to grant us another chance for pure romance,
Hoping you won't ever forget your coy, whimsical admirer,

My friend, my love, my muse.

I'm not confused.
But, yes, I was abused
By my distorted views,
But not by your refuses
Although I have accused your bruises
When I've enthused amusements,
Infusing my pervasive ruses
Demanding you would soothe me…

And I'm truly sorry,
My divinely sacred muse.

Once Bartholomew proclaimed the blessings of spirits for this union of souls, Eurydice and Benjamin assumed the magical powers of the spirits. Eurydice officially became the Secheltian princess, receiving the royal diadem of her grandmother. It was not only a sophisticated piece of jewelry, but had magical powers. Eurydice could take the sparks from it and spread them in the air, helping souls to find their purpose. Eurydice received new healing abilities, oracle clairvoyance, and the privilege to knight any soul of her lands with their sword of spiritual empowerment. Benjamin received his diadem made of alive flowers, as he could only perform the duties of the prince, never becoming one. Nevertheless, it gave him new magical talents. From now on, our lovers worked in perfect union – Benjamin received the ability to discover the spiritual swords for female souls in need, while Eurydice would perform the initiation rites of accolade.

After the ceremony, Eurydice unlocked the powers of her diadem in a beautiful ritual. She closed her eyes and took Benjamin's hand, asking spirits to help them use their magic wisely and never harm anyone. When she opened her eyes, she sensed how sparkling pieces of energy from diadem rolled through her body. Our princess looked at her palms, and the glittering particles emerged from the skin. Eurydice blew over these magical grains, sending them to every guest in attendance. Every soul that our lovers healed had unique and beautiful inner powers, so Eurydice's magical sparks of spiritual blessings helped them shine brighter with their light. Phillip and Suzanne also received their sparks. Suzanne started to trust Phillip again but she only committed to receive spiritual help from her man. Phillip and Becky spent a year living together, but Becky became a narcissistic abuser, still perceiving Phillip as inferior to her. She has never surrendered to their love, and constantly attacking him for the past. No matter how much Phillip tried to ask for forgiveness, Becky's heart was closed off from love. Eventually Phillip moved out and concentrated on helping Suzanne spiritually.

When guests left after reception, Ariadne invited Benjamin and Eurydice for a ceremonial tea in the parlor.

"I would like to thank you, my Queen, for helping with my permanent status. I can't express how much it means to me to be on these blessed lands with Eurydice." Benjamin acknowledged Ariadne's help.

"Benjamin, you know we didn't do anything special. I cannot really help you on your journey. It is your path, and if you would not work as hard as you did, you would never receive it, even with my assistance."

"And yet you still removed demonic blocks from my path, so I will always be thankful."

"I think I'm the one who should be thanking you. Without your spiritual struggles, we would probably stay in oblivion about the state of corruption in Ottawa and the levels of fear in the hearts of our citizens. You showed me your experience, honestly presenting your grievances in a constructive way, and we acted accordingly for highest good of everyone. The punishments have to be equally administered as blessings. I didn't know how many truly evil people live in my kingdom. You also agreed to lead our soldiers on many occasions, which says a lot about your character and integrity. I'm genuinely impressed with the two of you. I still can't believe how Eurydice masterfully summoned you. Observing how intricate your eternal love is, how you grew together and how both of you enjoy healing others is very inspiring."

"Your daughter is pretty special. I would walk to the edge of the world for her."

"Well, you already did. You came to Vancouver and you traveled in Hell, just for her. Your love shines over our lands, and I wish you a joyful union. I can't wait to see what the two of you will do next."

"Thank you, my Queen. I hope our writing endeavors will be successful, and somehow these manuscripts will help us defeat Damian."

"Yes, I see why he dreams of breaking your union. You are an unstoppable force together."

"Yes we are. But all I can ask is to aid Eurydice with nourishing and empowering energies. She's scared of the future, thinking she's not ready to face him."

"I'll help with what I can. Now we should celebrate."

Ariadne praised the connection of our lovers throughout the evening. She still couldn't believe she was one lucky spirit who witnessed such a magical love story unfolding on her lands. The queen expressed her admiration of Eurydice's spiritual growth and how her daughter was no longer shy about claiming her powers. In Benjamin's presence, she apologized that she stopped believing in Eurydice. "I can't thank you enough, my dear children, for how much I learned from you," Ariadne said. "Your love brought so much joy into my life, and I feel inspired again. Somehow you two can only be tempered through painful experiences, but it's magical to witness."

Ariadne cheered for the future happiness of our lovers and presented a special gift for Eurydice. The eyes of our princess sparkled with exciting anticipation. Eurydice received confirmation that her mother forgave her and accepted her rebellious nature. She wanted to be seen not only by her lover, but by her relatives as well. She mostly praised herself, for not giving up when she was forced to face her darkness and for not rejecting Benjamin's help. She fought his love relentlessly after her experiences in Underworld. She was tested many times, but now she was looking back at herself with pride and joy, as through accepting his love, she discovered the path of her heart.

Ariadne created a secret garden just for Eurydice and now she gifted it to her. Holding hands Eurydice and Benjamin eagerly entered into this magical garden. The queen had planted special trees that bloomed with glittering neon words. Eurydice grabbed a basket at the entrance and joyfully danced through this majestical place, picking the words from the branches for her next poem. The new wave of inspiration descended upon our poetess. She connected with Eloise. Together they crafted one last healing poem and performed it for Benjamin.

Любовь Научит Меня Жить
Еридиси Элоиз Уэйлс

Моя высокомерность оправдана
Пока не пересечена черта
И вот тогда
Я снова чёрта приглашу...

Я снова призываю смерть
Но ты подхватишь вновь меня
В последний разрушительный момент
И полыхающим дыханием огня
Очистишь мой безумный бред
В котором я все тороплюсь
Трагически погибнуть смело
Ведь я так ненавижу жить...

Ты мне прошепчешь
Все яркие слова любви
Что ты не в силах удержать
И вдруг воспряну я...

Я есть
И значит я есть свет
Что льётся сказочно с небес
И заполняет страстью нашу хтонь
И это был твой праведный завет
Но нет —

Love Will Teach Me How To Live
by Eurydice Eloise Wayles

My arrogance is vindicated
Until the line is crossed at revels
So, I'm anticipating

I must invite my devil back again ...

I call to summon death again
But you will pick me up
Right at my last destructive moment
And with a blazing breath of fire
You'll cleanse my crazy nonsense
As I am so passionately trying
To die so tragically again
Because I really hate to live...

You'll whisper brightly
Your tender words of love
That you can't keep inside
And suddenly, I glow again...

I live;
Therefore, I do emit the light
That's pouring fabulously from Heaven
And passion fills the chthonic world
And that was your celestial behest
And yet –
Себя не видела во тьме
Сама себя я предала
И душу полную любви
Все время я отречь хотела...

Сбежать от жизни чтобы соблюсти
Традиции надломанных иллюзий
Сбежать и оттолкнуть
Весь свет что так не мил
И вновь забыть тебя
Всю боль что я надумала ты шлёшь
Хотя ты только шепчешь
Правду сердца твоего...

*Я верила что я живу
В полнейшей пустоте
Что не нужна я никому
И что несу я в этот мир
Лишь женскую поверхностную красоту
И ничего волшебного
Внутри меня не существует*

Что я нелепая ошибка бытия...

*Но рассмотрев себя
Твоими лучезарными глазами
Что так заманчиво переливаются
Божественными красками души
Я поняла что я есть я
I couldn't see myself in darkness
When I betrayed my heart
When I betrayed your soul of love
I kept denying every time.*

*I ran away from life, complying
With traditions of insane illusions
I run and push away
Entire world that wasn't ever nice to me
I'm trying to forget about you again,
Forget the pain I falsely claimed you caused
While you were only tried to whisper
The loving truth of your amazing heart...*

*I've trapped myself believing that I live
In dark and empty vastness
And no one needs me here
That I can only bring into this world
A superficial female beauty
And nothing magical
Exists inside of me*

That I'm an absurd miscarriage of existence...

But once I could behold myself
Through your illuminating eyes
That shimmer so seductively
With bright and magic colors of your soul
I realized that I am me
И правда только в этом
Раз я живу то я творю
И я рисую новую реальность
Лишь своим легким женским бытием
Своим лишь мне доступным
Божественно-духовным танцем
Магически кружась во тьме войны...

Раз я пришла – меня здесь ждут
И не хватает бренной жизни моего
Столь трепетно-безумного
И нежно-девичьего сердца...

Я просто есть
И все замрут
Завидев суть
Что я создам

Приняв твою любовь.

This is the only truth that matters
If I'm alive, then I create
And I can paint a new reality for me
Just with my delicate existence,
With my
Divinely spiritual dance
As I swirl in the darkness of the war.

Since I was born – I am wanted here
This mortal life's in dire need of my
Uniquely reverently-crazy
And tender girlish heart ...

I just exist
And people freeze
Beholding essence
I'll create

Once I'll accept your love.

Benjamin wholeheartedly cried as he stood on his knees before his princess in the central meadow of the garden. Besides French, Eloise dreamt of writing poems in Russian and English, and now she delivered her last one in both languages. Through Eurydice, Eloise asked Camilla for final forgiveness. Only Benjamin never needed an apology from Eurydice. He loved his soulmate for who she was. His Magdalene woman fell into the demonic traps, but that only made their tragic love more beautiful. Still on his knees, Benjamin held Eurydice's waist and wept like never before. Eurydice never actually rejected him. Our lovers realized that only dearest soulmates could cause the most pain to one other, but they are also the ones who bring the most joy. Our princess Eurydice also kneeled with her noble grace, to cry together with Benjamin.

Once their tears ran out, full of love and devotion, our lovers engaged in silent gazing meditation. They talked without words and couldn't stop smiling. After they exchanged their energies and emotionally allowed their partner to enter their inner space, they waltzed into Eurydice's bedroom. Many books disappeared from the room after their last visit. It felt spacious and cozy, as our lovers danced through the room, cleansing the space in preparations for their intimate ritual.

Benjamin's wedding gift waited for Eurydice on the table. The princess gently unwrapped the box, discovering a book inside. It had the most exquisite binding she had ever seen, plated in gold and encrusted with precious stones. Archangel Jeremiel helped Benjamin to craft it in the Temple Library. The cover had no title, just moving images presenting the story in few vivid scenes. Once Eurydice opened the cover, the magical hologram hovered over the first page with the phrase in Russian, 'rukopisi ne goryat'. She was holding Mikhail Bulgakov's *The Master and Margarita*. The phrase 'manuscripts don't burn' sounded poetic and beautiful, but Eurydice didn't dare to ask Benjamin about its meaning. When Eurydice turned the first page, she was disappointed. Instead of fine paper and clearly printed letters, the book was printed on the ancient dox matrix printer and bonded with a clinch.

"Benjamin, why would you gift me such an ugly book on our beautiful day?"

"Because this is a magical copy. Back in Soviet Empire this book was banned. Hungry for knowledge, people secretly copied foreign vinyl records to x-ray sheets and printed forbidden books on scarce office printers. It was dangerous, as you could get in jail for this. But more and more people read, and soon the Tyranny of the Soviet Empire crumbled. Art transformed reality. My father made this copy of the book, when he was a student. If you look closely, you can see another layer of meanings."

Eurydice glanced through the pages and saw how different words levitated above the pages, capturing the personal perceptions of Sergemir, Benjamin, and Phillip.

"Thank you, Benjamin," Eurydice said. "Now I can see the value of this gift."

"This copy tells you a powerful message. Be aware, dear Polly, of those who ban books, because it means they are in panic and hide their corruption."

"It means that our words of love can also transform the world." Eurydice joyfully hugged her knight. "But you won't mind if I just watch the story of this book in your memory?" Eurydice dived into Benjamin's imagination. She enjoyed reading, but she wanted to observe this story through cinematic images Benjamin created in his imagination. Our princess wanted to enrich the meanings of the text with the visions of her beloved. Once Eurydice saw his memories, she exclaimed, "This book is exactly like our story, Benjamin! Souls of two lovers are flying at night full of tragic love. This Woland creature is like Damian's brother. And I like how Nature talks to the characters through serendipity too."

They settled down on Eurydice's bed, trying to digest their emotions. Our lovers couldn't believe that only yesterday, they accidentally found each other in total darkness, and now they were fully empowered. They silently looked into each other's eyes, afraid to destroy the magic of this moment. Eurydice gently reached for her knight and softly kissed him, immersing herself in his tenderness. Then she pulled away. "I still don't fully understand why 'manuscripts don't burn.' Yes, the story is alive, but Benjamin, the manuscripts can be burned, as they are printed on paper."

"Yes, Eurydice, you are right. The fire can turn any book into ashes and destroy every copy."

"Then I don't understand this phrase."

"Oh, Eurydice. I'm so happy being with you. You amuse me with your cuteness."

"Why? Are you going to answer my question or not?"

"Acknowledge, my princess, how much you've grown. Please behold the beauty of this moment."

"I'm not following, Benjamin."

"For the first time, you are not reaching to undress me after a kiss but asking a spiritual question. It has never happened before. You are becoming Eurydice."

"I am, aren't I? I do feel different. I can kiss you and still talk about philosophical concepts. It feels natural. So do you have the answer or not?"

"Well, the short answer is no. Do you remember our journey to visit my sky spirits? We traveled through many planes of information. Some are closer to the skies and others to the lands, but all these planes contain shared knowledge of our collective consciousness. The writer does not 'create' the world with their imagination. Any art is available in other realms, and artists are born to deliver these stories to humans. When Bulgakov wrote *The Master and Margarita*, he was sick and lost his vision, so he could only dictate his book to his wife. His soul existed between two worlds, - connected to a higher plane and attached to the broken vessel to deliver this divine story. People create stories together, and they belong to everyone. They exist because we share our thoughts, dreams, and visions. Writers only channel them back to us."

"So, it means that all books exist all the time?"

"Well, pretty much. It means that even if you burn every copy of a certain book, it can be channeled again. The personal voice of the author would be different. Yet a new writer would preserve the book's essence, - the fables, parables, and lessons."

"I see. Then we should be very cautious of those who try to burn the books. From your words, I can say that they are fighting Nature itself. Only I'm not scared of them. I will shine with my light and I won't stop, even if they try to persecute me. I'm so in love with you, my knight!"

"And I'm so in love with you, my dear princess."

They embraced each other with passionate kisses, and soon, they were immersed in their intimate dance. Our lovers finally felt safe under the sheets. The new challenges were ahead of them, but they didn't care what was in the future. They forgot their troubles and engaged in the most sensual experience of their lives. Eurydice didn't need to be terrified anymore; Benjamin didn't need to worry about finances or being deported. They were two souls making love in the divine, spiritual house, after becoming spiritual protectors of their lands. They felt every possible feeling a man and a woman could share, channeling and exchanging their sensations on energy and emotional levels. Their passionate dance paved the road to their future, and they were looking forward to what life had prepared for them.

CHAPTER XXVIII

In July 2023, our soulmates were guided to perform their final ceremony. They created sacred, magical bonfire on the shore of Burrard Inlet to present their final decisions to the land. Eurydice gathered her army of female warriors in Stanley Park. Our lovers healed and empowered many female souls over the past two years and they came to support our princess, as an army of light warriors.

Eurydice started drumming and through the process of recapitulation she released the emotional wounds Benjamin endured from Holly. They had to cleanse the past to start a new life. Now Eurydice made her final decision, and she invited Damian to join this ceremony. Our Dark Prince saluted Eurydice for embracing the path of Magdalene's heart, and with a magical ritual, he released Holly from imprisonment. He retreated and agreed to surrender. In this life, Eurydice won the battle by facing her fears and trusting her heart. Yet now, she needed to clearly state her intentions in front of witnesses before Damian would allow her to return to Holly. Eurydice invited Mary Magdalene to assist in this ceremony. Benjamin and Eurydice sat around the fire while Phillip and Suzanne came to act as witnesses.

Phillip was invited to state his decisions as well. He decided to move to a remote Mexican village, where he could continue his spiritual education. He wanted to dive deeper in the dreaming practices of ancient cultures and explore every facet of his essence. With the help of the sacred fire, he released all emotional attachments with Becky. He moved on from this toxic relationship and with renewed hope, invited future into his life. He promised to assist Suzanne for as long as she needs, but he wanted to open himself up to the possibility of new love, that would be equally embraced by both partners. Phillip believed he deserves to be love unconditionally.

Now it was time for Eurydice to present her truth. "Benjamin, I made my final decision. I thank you for everything you brought into my life. I feel liberated and empowered. That's all thanks to you, my dear man, and I'm a lucky girl that I had a privilege to be your student. I'm making my decision today with my Magdalene's heart and in the presence of witnesses for the highest and best of all involved. My dear Benjamin, I decided to guide Holly to death and not bring her back."

"Why, Polly?"

"Well, Benjamin, it's only my decision, correct?"

"Of course, dear Polly, only a soul can decide when to die. But I thought we had our dreams."

"Benjamin, do you remember that from the beginning, all I dreamed was for you to be happy? I told you that if you heal me, I would bring Holly so you could be happy."

"But I thought that would make you happy too."

"Do you remember how I said I'm completely happy with us interacting only on a soul level? Back then you said that it's most likely because Damian captured her. But now I see that I chose Holly's a life, to be lost, so I could find you. All I actually wanted is to live with you as a soul."

"So are you just going to abandon her? She is a sweet, and fragile girl, even though she rejected her heart."

"And Polly, was also such a girl. But now I know that I chose that life to suffer, to be misunderstood, and to feel out of place. I chose that life to die in pain, even though she was a wonderful person. Polly had that life to help you. And I feel the same is happening now. Damian left Holly, but Washington is still entrapped in his darkness. Maybe it's just my divine destiny – to sacrifice myself when darkness descends on America. I know how to do it already. Polly died to heal America and maybe Holly has the same fate. Maybe there's no other way to restore the original, divine promise of America."

"That kind of makes sense."

"I won the battle with Damian and he surrendered. I can return to Holly, only I will guide her to death because that's what I need for my growth. You know I actually enjoy dying. I just refused to accept that. I made so much noise about my traumas, but I feel like I was just seeking attention. You see, this is the only way I can truly empower you in this life - by assisting you from the other side."

"It doesn't make sense, Polly! I need you here, I love Holly and want us to be together. I'll be lost without you."

"Okay, Benjamin, let's do a test. Can you open Holly's Twitter page, look at her pictures and tell me if you still love her? After two and a half years with Damian, she has changed and you don't even know her anymore."

Benjamin opened up Holly's Twitter. He scrolled through her latest photos, and profound shock enveloped his whole body. "Polly, you are right. I don't feel anything to this woman anymore. Her aura is completely different. I was clinging to her image in my head."

"You see! Because you love me, not her. Camilla requested to love Eloise's next embodiment, but once we healed our traumas, the love ended."

"Yes. Together we learned that real love does not appear from the inside. It always descends on us from the Heavens for a higher reason."

"Exactly! Now your mission of loving Holly is complete. You loved her to heal our shared wounds and now that love has fulfilled its purpose."

"I still love you, so what does it mean for us?"

"I think we were too confused by our past love stories that ended abruptly. But now the fog has cleared, and we can see our truth. I feel like we are spiritual siblings who came to heal the world. Like we are twins, born on the same day, only I'm a few minutes younger. We've never been a brother and sister before, but we need to experience that kind of love and connection too."

"You know Polly, that's what I feel too. Our story is so weird. I'm confused and perplexed from my emotions."

"It's because we lived our past love stories, chained to each other so we could write our books. Once we solved our mysteries, it feels more natural to call you brother."

"It feels natural to call you sister."

"You see! Brother and sister can teach each other so much too. Yes, we still need to heal our grief of Thomas and Polly. But we will do that by writing your American book. After that, I'll guide Holly to light, and then I'll be helping you from the other side."

"It is so sad, dear Polly."

"It's not Benjamin. It's divinely beautiful."

"But I want Holly to continue living, to experience the fullness of life."

"Benjamin, don't fool yourself. You know that I'm a special being. Holly lived a full life."

"What do you mean?"

"You see, life is a burst of energy. Life can be brief but bright or it can slowly burn. Only the amount of energy would be the same. What other people experience in three years, Holly experiences in one. So, if she would live for twenty-seven years, it actually means she lived till eighty-one. And that's a full life! It's just a condensed version of it. I arrive to illuminate the world, and to sparkle with my dances. So, it's okay that Holly would never experience life like others because she is not like others. She is a cherry blossom girl. This is how it should be, Benjamin."

"But will you bring her to me? I wish to spend some time in her presence. I wish to see her for the last time, to have closure. I don't want any romance, after what she did to my heart. And yet just maybe a day, or even an hour in her company would be enough for me. Or maybe I could hold her hand before she dies."

"But Benjamin, we are trying to heal you too. Burying me was always the most traumatizing experience for you. You could never recover from seeing my dead body. So maybe not burying her would be actually the most healing experience for you in this life?"

"Maybe you are right. Oh, this is so complicated. Here's what I'm offering. You can decide what would be the best for me once you return to her. If you would think that I don't need to see her ever again for my highest healing, then I trust you, my dear soulmate. Maybe you can just guide her to read this book? I just wish her to know that she was loved unconditionally in this life too. I loved her for her soul, for her heart, for who she is deep inside."

"I will try to do that, Benjamin."

"Polly, are you sure you will have a safe journey through death? I thought you needed me next to Holly."

"Benjamin, we've been on dozens of death journeys together. I think I know every single trap, fear, and illusion. You've taught me everything I should know."

"I'm scared of letting you go alone. Maybe we should do our last death journey right now, just to make sure?"

Eurydice agreed and settled comfortably on the shore, laying on her back with her feet in the water. She drifted into the death plane, while Benjamin held her hand. She entered her death as Holly and traveled through the world of darkness. Nothing intimated or scared her. She easily navigated every challenge and safely guided Holly to reunite with pure, heavenly light. Then she had to create a list with lessons from this life. Yet once she started writing, an intense but beautiful vision consumed her imagination. She needed to return to assist Benjamin from the other side and now she knew how to achieve that.

Eurydice exited the trance and happily smiled. "My dear friend! Yes, I needed to discover one last answer. I saw you with another woman. You were making love, and you were both so happy that you found each other. You couldn't believe how beautiful your romantic story is. She would be the love of your life. You will love her like you never loved anybody else, more than you loved Holly."

"I don't believe you. Why are you making this up? It really hurts hearing this from you."

"Benjamin, you've done so much for me and other souls. You deserve to be happy, and you should be happy. You deserve to love and be loved. I will not leave you until I find that woman for you."

"My Polly, I don't want another woman."

"And yet, my dear knight, this is not what life has prepared for us. You looked so happy with her!"

"I don't know. I don't want that."

"Mary, can you please tell this man to calm down and accept the new love that will appear on his path?"

"Benjamin, you are a wonderful man, and I know how much you love Eurydice. But she is right. A new woman, would appear on your path soon. You've been guided to meet her all of this time. You succeeded in cleansing your karma and paying off your debts. You helped Eurydice to embrace her truth. Now you will be rewarded with divine love." Mary gracefully replied.

"Mary, you've been tricking me all this time. I don't believe your guidance anymore. I don't need another woman. If Holly would leave this Earth, please just give me my house in Sechelt, and I will live there forever alone. I can't be with a woman. Every woman in my life, betrayed my trust. They lied and manipulated me. They don't know what they want, and I can't I understand them."

Eurydice, Mary, Suzanne, and every female soul in presence burst into laughter. Our knight was lying to himself, and his women came to gently envelop him in their nourishing energies. He helped them only because he understood them. He saw their highest potential when they couldn't. He saw their highest dreams and desires. He saw the essences of their souls. He was just scared to face what life has prepared for him in the future.

"This woman would be good for you. You will know that she is the one when she will appear." Mary softly encouraged her apprentice.

"Benjamin, please allow me to find this woman for you. Please, pretty please! Just think about it. I can see clearly that you are destined to be transformed into a king one day. I see your highest potential. And even though I love you, I am just a princess in this life. But a king would never shine without a queen next to him."

"I'm not sure what you are talking about. I'm just a knight. There's nothing else in me."

"Adjust your crown, my dear man. Eurydice is right." Mary replied with support and admiration.

"Okay, what kind of king I will be?" Benjamin was irritated by this conversation.

"You will be a king of sexual healing and death journeys." Mary answered.

"Wow! That's so awesome! Yes, I can clearly see it now." Eurydice started to dance around her knight. She could see the true powers of her soulmate, before he could.

"I'm so confused." Benjamin shyly tried to hide.

"Mary, this man is so funny. We are offering him the queen of his dreams, but he is fighting us." Eurydice burst into laughter, and Mary giggled together with her. "Benjamin, if this life exists to fulfill Polly's death wish, then I'm living like Martha. And Martha needed to die so Thomas could be transformed into an emperor. She had to guide him to his destiny from the other side. Now I need to die, so you can assume your role of a spiritual king. I will guide you, so you wouldn't fall into the traps of ego."

"Well, if that's the case, I don't need a woman. I just need my house with a garden in Sechelt. I'll be a hermit like Thomas, and you will dictate new books for me."

"Only Thomas was not a sexual healer, but you are. I can assure you that you won't ever become yourself without loving your queen." Mary patiently explained.

"Well, maybe I can try to open up to a woman again. But I'm not sure I can. Maybe if you would send me a woman you think I need, then I promise, I will try." Benjamin started to let his guard down.

"You have to describe what kind of woman you wish to be wtih," Mary answered.

"What? This is too much. Just give me a woman you think I need for my missions." Benjamin angrily replied.

"This is not how it works, my dear beloved. You need to willingly invite the possibility of a new love in your heart. And you have to imagine how you want to feel next to the woman of your dreams. Once you will describe her, then I'll help Eurydice to find her." Mary was openly enjoying the conflicting perplexities of this troubled man.

"Well, I guess first of all, I need to love her with such love that would help me forget Holly and heal the remnants of my grief. I need to love her more than I loved Holly, otherwise it won't be fair to her. I wish this woman would understand who I really am, just by touching me. I want her to sense the essence of my heart, without me telling her, who I am. That's how I will understand that she is my destined woman. I want to desire her like I never desired anyone in my life, with intense sexual sparks between us. And yet I want to take things slow, to guide us through intimate Magdalene practices. I want to be vulnerable next to her and trust her. I wish we would always talk openly about our feelings. I wish she could inspire me with her beauty and grace. I dream to find a life partner and share dreams with her. She should also know how to talk to the trees and be curious about magic. I dream to explore the laws of Nature with her. I wish I would feel like a man next to her and she would feel safe, when I would hold her. And, of course, she would have a soul with Magdalene's heart. Oh, forget it! It's impossible to find such a woman. I will be alone forever. If such a woman exists, she is not in Vancouver. I can feel it." Benjamin closed his heart again.

"That's it! Thank you, Benjamin!" Eurydice ecstatically jumped. "You are right. She is not in Vancouver. Because she is on Vancouver Island!"

"How do you know?" Benjamin was confused.

"Benjamin, you trained me to trust my Magdalene's heart, and this is what it says. I saw how she looked, and now you told me where I can find her. I will guide you to meet her. Just give me some time." Eurydice joyfully danced around fire, happy to live her story.

"Okay, whatever. I still don't know if that's a good idea. But if you want to try, I can agree for one meeting with her. If I won't feel an emotional connection, I will retreat into my hermit existence."

"Then it's a deal, my dear teacher. I have only unconditional love for you, and I promise I will serve you well. I can feel her right now, as she carries the same Magdalene's heart in her soul. Our story is so fantastically magical!" Eurydice was completely happy at this moment.

"Polly, it seems like true, unconditional love means letting go of your beloved, as then you are not seeking to possess. It was always so hard to let you go, but now I see the highest lesson you came to teach me. I need to let Holly go. This is how I will express my highest love for you."

"I think you are right. We are living the lessons of divine love. How to let your beloved go. Sending you to another woman is as painful for me as for you to allow me to die. It seems like this is the main lesson of love we came to learn in this life. I believe you can pursue your happiness by following your queen, and I can pursue mine by dying. Seeing you happy with your woman was so inspiring." Eurydice looked at Benjamin, and both finally surrendered to life. Eurydice was ready to make a choice for the highest benefit of all involved. Benjamin felt ecstatic from the grandness of life. He accepted he might not see Holly ever again and he finally understood how to let her go.

This journey brought so many overwhelming lessons for our soulmates. But now both were at peace. Panic attacks, anxiety, frustration and expectations disappeared. Benjamin and Eurydice accepted everything that life had prepared for them. And even though their romantic love has come to an end, they were both happy. Their eyes said it all. Their souls were in harmony. Like two serpents of golden light, they flew up in the skies, intertwined and entangled in the magical dance above the waters. They danced and exchanged their energies like they always did. Nothing was more beautiful than a new empowering light they were emitting. And, of course, they also knew they would meet in the next life to live another weird and crazy story, unlike anything they had lived before, because eternal love between these two souls would never end.

EPILOGUE

My dear reader, this is how my healing journey ended. I summoned Benjamin to help me, and he kindly agreed to train me in his ministry for lost and stranded souls. I fell in love with my teacher, so I could finally fall in love with myself. I accepted my highest truth when this man enveloped me in his love. Even though our romance didn't last long enough, it was incredibly powerful and transformative experience. We lived our love story based on sacred intimacy and we elevated each other to new heights. We welcomed this love, and life showered us with blessings. We savored every minute of this love and dared to follow each other despite all odds. Our love shined with true magic and healing powers.

In all of my existence I never dreamed that I could actually become a writer. It took me centuries to arrive to this point. I was always shy and reserved. I was always full of pity for myself. I carried the baggage of my traumas for far too long, despising and hating who I am. I was a woman who pretended to be a girl. I avoided my responsibilities and always blamed others for my problems. I refused to face myself and own my story. I suppressed myself many times, afraid to be seen for who I am. I enjoyed being a victim and loved immersing in my past miseries. I was full of self-pity, seeking attention and hoping others would feel sorry for me. When I finally integrated my shadow and healed my deepest scars, I discovered that I am a wounded healer, and carry a unique light. I embraced my essence and now I dare to be bold, different, and follow my dreams. I don't care if someone will judge my truth or my choices. I live my life the way it should be lived. Each one of us was created to shine with supernatural talents only available to us. Each one of us is a magical being.

As I discovered how I can serve divinity and fulfil my purpose, I saw how this life is full of everyday wonders and miracles. I discovered truth only because I was in a committed relationship, and my man was always there for me. No matter how painful it was, he was next to me, protecting and comforting me. He held a sacred space for my tears and encouraged me to express myself through art. He created a safe container in our apartment, where I could spend time rediscovering myself and exploring true desires of my heart. He gifted me the time to reflect on my past, so I could finally embody my truth. He fought our battles with outside world, while I cared and nourished him after. Next to him I could finally surrender my weapons and look within, without any distractions. He was holding a protective dome of noble masculinity around me, so I could finally see how much beauty I have in me.

Yes, everything in this life ends, and all we can do is learn how to let go, especially when we are truly in love. We can fully express the light of our hearts when we know how to let go. Then we shine brighter because we embrace the life for what it is. We are not holding on to benefit our ego, as true love can never hurt. The grief opens us to receive more love. We are letting go of a person, but we should never let go of our love. We don't own another, but we own our heart full of love. It stays with us and make us more beautiful, even if our loved one is not with us anymore. Honest unconditional love never fades away. It always shines with luminous glory, benefiting us every day. If love is pure, then we are forever together with our beloved, as such love will always transcend death.

I wish you to experience true love, dear reader. I wish that you won't ever ran away from it. I wish you would just allow it to envelop you. Life if pointless if you never loved. Don't be afraid to feel the pain of a broken heart, as this is how a light of self-love gets in. This world becomes a better place if we share the words of love, even if we won't hear loving words in return.

Today I'm radiating self-love and self-acceptance, because I dared to love. I know what I bring into this world and I see my worth. My tears are my glory and my art is my purpose. Through love I discovered who I am. I love enriching this world with the light of my heart. And my heart if full of love for you, my dear reader. Thank you for being on this magical journey with me. I hope you've experienced magic in your life too. I hope you will dare to love and dare to follow your dreams, like I did. I hope your light will shine for all to see.

Forever yours,
Eurydice Eloise Wayles.

Printed in the USA
CPSIA information can be obtained
at www.ICGtesting.com
JSHW082115141123
52027JS00002B/12